# THE WINE-DARK SEA OF GRASS

# OTHER WORK

## POETRY

*Rainflowers, 1969*

*I Have Lost My Heart Again. I Pray I Will Not*
*Lose My Head, Amen. 1974*

*The Grandmother Tree, 1978*

*Seven Ways of Looking at Watercress Farm, 1990*

## HISTORY

*Provo, A Story of People in Motion, 1974*

## NOVELS

*The Earthkeepers, 1979*

*Good-bye, Hello, 1984*

*The Earthkeepers Trilogy: Thorns of the Sun, 1992,*
*Shadows of Angels, 1993, Royal House, 1994*

*Statehood, 1995*

*Christmas at the M&M, 1999*

*The Holly Christmas, 2000*

## MUSICAL THEATRE

*The Nutcracker, The Musical, 1996*

*Midsummer Night's Dream, The Musical, 1998*

# THE
# WINE-DARK
## SEA OF
# GRASS

by
Marilyn McMeen Brown

Salt Press at Cedar Fort, Inc.
Springville, Utah

ISBN:   1-55517-529-5
v.2

Published by Salt Press

Distributed by:
925 North Main, Springville, UT  84663 • 801/489-4084

CFI Distribution • CFI Books • Council Press • Bonneville Books

Typeset by Virginia Reeder
Cover design by Adam Ford
Cover design © 2000 by Lyle Mortimer

Printed in the United States of America

For Maxine Adams Miller

# ACKNOWLEDGMENTS

Most of my thanks must go to Juanita Brooks for her excellent work in her history: *The Mountain Meadows Massacre*, and recently Anna Jean Backus for *Mountain Meadows Witness*. Because my research spanned a twenty-year period, much has happened since I wrote that first manuscript, entitled *Stones of Blood*.

For this version of the manuscript, *The Wine-Dark Sea of Grass*, I have many people to thank. First, my sister-in-law Leslie Hansen Brown, who read the manuscript years ago, and mentioned she'd like to see it in print. And then very important, my generous and helpful publishers who made that printing possible: Lyle Mortimer, Lee Nelson, and their dedicated Cedar Fort staff—Adam Ford, Virginia Reeder, Erik Busath, Cindy Bunce, Margaret Stone and Tammy Daybell.

My friends and university teachers who have supported my work over the years deserve special mention: Douglas and Donlu Thayer, Richard Cracroft, Bruce Jorgensen, Marden Clark, Eugene England, Valerie Holladay, Lavina Anderson, Veda Tebbs Hale, Elaine McKay, Peggy Bohn, Francois Camoin, Carol Houck Smith, and many more. Much gratitude is also due to the Association for Mormon Letters and its magazine *Irreantum* for striving to create a climate for quality Mormon literature.

I am also very grateful to those who came forward after the first printing to add insight, especially ninety-seven-year-old gunsmith Alva Matheson of Cedar City, who owns not only the pistol Joseph Smith had in Carthage Jail, but an entire collection of guns the Mormons used in the massacre. His son Leon invited me to his home where Alva was kind enough to tell me in his own words what he heard as a boy when John Higbee related his stories as they sat on the steps of the old mill.

Many thanks must also go to a Lee descendent, Liz Pew, for reminding me to mention that during the era of BYU President Rex lee, John Lee was fully reinstated in the church, and that when the monument on the hill overlooking the meadow was dedicated, the families of the Lees and the Fanchers came together to make amends for the tragedies on both sides. It is only in this climate of healing that the stories repeated here may in some small way serve to cleanse us.

To my "adopted mother," author Maxine Adams Miller—always a cherished fan and inspiration—I have dedicated this book for her ninetieth birthday, December 31, on the eve of the millennium, 2000. And to my husband and family for their continued tolerance, I give my love.

# FOREWORD

Twenty years ago, after *The Earthkeepers* was published, I completed a manuscript about the Mountain Meadows Massacre. This is that story, *Stones of Blood*, revisited and—inadvertently echoing some classic references—renamed *The Wine-Dark Sea of Grass*.

I have been to see the monument that overlooks the grassy meadow scooped out of the hills, a meadow that resembles a small empty sea. At the bottom of the sea is the dark secret of our history that has always threatened to drown us as a people in its horror. I, along with Juanita Brooks, Lee Nelson, and many others, have been fascinated with how the events of the Mountain Meadows Massacre could ever have happened.

One of the reasons this manuscript was abandoned for so long was that I found so much more about John Lee than I could use in this story. I felt that the Lee family would find so much missing, and so much wrong. However, taking a risk, I decided to go ahead with this book, and possibly write another novel about John Lee. I came to admire the man. Several times I visited his grave on the east edge of the grassy Panguitch cemetery, finding myself impressed by the open space and the loneliness. There is a fence there now. It seems not so lonely after all. Many more people have died in Panguitch and have joined John Lee's resting place on the smooth green sward close to the little town surrounded by the astonishingly beautiful and empty hills.

This is only one version of the Mountain Meadows Massacre. Some have suggested cutting, or beginning in the middle, but to preserve the whole I kept what I wrote twenty years ago. Because it is the stuff of legend, it is, of course, a novel. I believe that if we are to empathize with our ancestors, to understand how they lived and loved, we must dig deeply into our own imaginations as we retell their tales. The major incidents, however, are reconstructed as accurately as I could make them.

Because it has become the fashion to let the reader know which events are based on fact, I have given a chapter-by-chapter account of the research at the end. Because a novel purports to accomplish a design other than academic, it is not a complete list, nor is it meant to be. I ask the reader to discover a truth here that defies record or verification. As Don Quixote states in *Man of LaMancha*: "Facts are the enemies of truth." Because for this story we are faced with the dilemma that facts are almost impossible to come by, this is an adventure of spirit. And I hope those who accept the challenge to read it will try to understand this method of dealing with the past.

This is a story about a land teeming with secrets and life. It is a place about which few know or care. And yet the reverberation of history cannot help but increase in meaning as years pass. There is a story here that amplifies the message which Hannah gives us at last in her closing paragraphs, a message that all of the world would do well to heed: "*We have asked for forgiveness, that we can all be together in God's love.*"


M.B.

# PROLOGUE

Because I never wanted to put my feet on the very spot where John Frederick died, I didn't think I'd ever go down into the basement on those stairs again. But it wasn't really the stairs that took him. It was a sneeze. I was standing at the sink cutting the tops out of the radishes when I heard it. It was very loud. He sneezed and it blew him off the steps.

After they put him in the ground, I kept having dreams for a long time. I could hear him breathing in and out right next to me on the pillow.

That day Johnnie died, he was on his way down into the basement to find his father's papers. Penrod Green had been sitting with him at the parade a few weeks before, and just happened to take up a tormenting thread of conversation. "Not you nor nobody else knows nothing about that massacre," Penrod Green told him. "Nobody told us nothing, so all we know was what we heard about John Lee."

"It wasn't true, what they said about John Lee," my Johnnie told him. And when he got back from the parade he stomped around the front room a long time, saying the story ought to be told with "nothing fancy like Charles Dickens or William Wadsworth," but told, nevertheless.

"Wordsworth," I corrected him.

"Well, at any rate, it ought to be told just the way it happened," he said.

I never thought I'd go down and bring all those papers upstairs, but when I heard the breathing on the pillow next to my head, I decided that maybe Johnnie was trying to tell me something—that he was anxious to finish his unfinished business.

I didn't touch those boxes of papers that first summer. It was hard work to weed the strawberries. He had been an ambitious gardener, and he had put in both corn and cucumbers that spring. I couldn't keep up with all of it. I let the beans drop off the poles. I let a lot of the apricots fall in the grass. I put up some peaches, but Florence wasn't any help. I was overwhelmed. Sometimes with tears.

If there was anything I didn't want to do it was to go down there and get those boxes, but when I heard Pa breathing, I couldn't stop thinking about it. So, even though it was October by the time I got to those stairs, I walked down with the intention of bringing those boxes up and setting them on the dining room table.

There were other boxes of papers there, too, behind the sugar bags. Jacob had written on some papers. And Elizabeth kept a diary. John Lee himself wrote a diary and another record some crooks published after his death to make an anti-Mormon statement. We didn't pay any attention to that since John Lee was rightfully hurting those last years, being ignored by Brigham Young and all. When we talked to him just before he died, he whispered in a low voice, "I love the Church more than you will ever know." He had tears in his eyes. "It still means everything to me. I hope someday you'll know what really happened to us all."

The minute I got downstairs and started carting up those boxes and crates, and then pulling out little notebooks and scraps of this and that, I was astonished at what I found. Especially some things Jacob and Elizabeth told about that I never knew. Diary entries just leaped out at me like big birds flapping huge whooping wings. I took the pieces of paper, smoothed them out and weighted them down with Johnnie's polished paperweight carved out of that old horn that came off that big ewe we had in Panguitch. Then I separated them into piles and marked them by name. I devoured every word. Then later when I began to write it down, I made the most surprising discovery of all—that it was my story as much as theirs.

So here's the story as complete as I could reconstruct it. Sometimes I had to guess how John, Jacob, and Elizabeth felt. I'm sure it's not absolutely exact. But I did the best I could. No one may ever see these pages I've written. And even if they find this manuscript in some old crusty envelope with spider webs in it, they may not want to read it. But it is mighty close to the truth, if they're at all interested in it.

I do not hear breathing on my pillow anymore.

*Hannah Dunham Lorry Lee, 1927*

# I

*Kanarraville, Utah, Thursday, July 16, 1857, Jacob*

He was not in a hurry. Following the cow south along the newly dug canal on the eastern edge of the valley, Jacob shaded his eyes from the bright sun sinking into the shadows. Always at dusk the sun seemed to make music before it slid behind the black mountains in the west, and he was listening to the music. He thought he heard rhythms in the distance as though the earth were shifting. Or perhaps all he heard was the rhythm of the cow's feet against the rocks and sage, and the singing of the willow switch he used against her legs.

In the distance, beyond the brush, into the east mountains, he could see smoke from the house rising into the twilight. His mother would be there, and Elizabeth too, her apron starched and smelling like rose water. And tonight, if things went as his mother said they might, his father would be home.

The first shot was a far-away crack from deeper in the valley, as though it could have come from rifle practice at Jensens' barn. But the next shot skidded into the brush, closer to the new canal. It frightened the dog.

Was it Indians? Or was it the advancement of the United States Army? Always, the isolated settlers in the southern corridor expected both. Especially the U.S. Army. Not long ago the Mormons had learned that more than eight hundred troops were on their way west to quell the Mormon rebellion. No one knew when they would arrive. But eight hundred armed men could certainly finish in a hurry Governor Boggs' order to exterminate the Mormon people.

Another shot sounded, this time closer. Jacob ducked. He heard the whistle of the bullet in the brush, and a muffled thud. Suddenly, the old cow leaned to the side, its head a patch of blood. Crying like a calf, it swayed on its forelegs, caught itself, swayed again, and finally buckled to the ground.

"Lil! No! Lil!" Jacob winced as he watched the animal lean and fall.

On his belly now, Jacob hissed at the dog, who cocked his ears and stood, nose up, alert. Close by—perhaps only a hundred yards away—a murmur of voices rumbled behind him.

"Hush, Tag," Jacob breathed. The dog growled. There was another shot. Terror flooded through him. "Get down, Tag," Jacob whispered, springing for the dog. He felt something like an insect graze his ear. "Down," he said, choking. Backing up, he scrambled into the canal. The earth swelled around him, smelling new and fresh. His father had been digging here only a few days ago. He spread himself along the edge of the ditch, still gripping the dog in his arms. Tag lay quiet now, panting softly while the voices in the distance drew closer.

"It's a lump of a cow."

"I thought I saw a kid behind it."

Jacob froze.

"He run off."

"Sorry to do this to the old Mormons," one voice mocked softly.

"They got it comin'."

"Funny I should be in the middle of Mormon country, and I ain't killed no Mormons yet."

There was a terrible pause.

"And you won't if they kill you first."

While the men approached Lil, it seemed Jacob could hear every word, as though they stood over his head.

"I though about that. Heard that one Mormon come down here. Lives close by."

There was another pause as the gunmen stood at Lil's side.

"Was you in that line?"

"Had a turn at his nine-year-old daughter?" The words stabbed Jacob's ears. "Yeah, I was hot on the skillet with the brother of that Fancher. They was seven of us. Give me a hand."

A sharp sound, not a rifle, split the air. A hack hack scarred the quiet of the valley. His heart in his throat, Jacob dared to raise his head. The two men were cutting into Lil now, chopping away at her hide with an ax.

"Good thing the U.S. Army's comin'. They'll make dog meat of the Mormons."

Jacob stared at the two bent figures, not fifty feet away. As he pulled himself forward, half sitting to peer over the mound of newly dug dirt, the heel of his hand struck a warm wet spot on the ground. It was his own blood. For the first time he felt the pain.

"The U.S. Army won't take no guff from the Mormons."

"They'll kill every one of them blood-suckin' polygamists."

"They deserve it. Soon as they shot Boggs I knew my life mission."

"It's an old cow. But there's a lot of meat here. We're going to need the wagon."

Feeling weak, Jacob ducked again and held himself against the edge of the ditch. For a brief moment he imagined that the ground, warmed by the afternoon sun, was his bed. He wanted to turn and pull the dirt over him like a blanket. But the sound of the men's voices kept him alert.

"I'll guard the beef if you'll fetch the wagon," one man said.

"Got to unload. Might take an hour or two," the other answered.

Jacob closed his eyes against the pain in his head and turned his face to the ground. His left arm still circled Tag's warm body. The dog growled softly against him.

"Shhh," Jacob whispered, burying his head in the animal's neck. Tag growled again and stirred against Jacob's grip. Jacob knew he couldn't hold the animal quiet now. "Go," he told Tag, pointing to the house. "Go home!"

The dog, scrambling to catch his footing, sprang forward. Jacob's head swam with the pain.

"Who . . . who goes there!" Another shot rang against the twilight sky. There was another thud, and a terrifying yelp.

"A dog! Harker, you just shot a mangy cur."

Jacob dared not breathe. He thought his heart would rip from his chest. He heard the man who had been chosen to fetch the wagon tramping away from them across the bleak countryside. He felt the quiet, the death-still emptiness of the darkening blue hills.

He forced himself to his elbows and began to crawl slowly, breathlessly for at least ten yards. Then, more rapidly, he dragged his knees across the black ground, annoyed by the blood in his eyes, the stinging pain in his scalp. Then he began to run. At first he ran, bent over in the ditch, then climbed up out of the earth and struck out across the field. He ran like an Indian, soft on the balls of his feet. And he never made a sound until, gasping, he tore open the door and flew into the house.

His mother stood at the kitchen basin. Her hair was almost white in the brilliant light from the oil lamp she held in her hand.

"Oh my soul, Jacob!" She looked at him, and her round dark eyes widened. "He's hurt!"

Jacob fell to a chair. She set the lamp down and came to him, her hands trembling as she used her apron to wipe the blood away from his eyes.

"I know they done this," she said quietly between her teeth. "I know they done this." And then behind the hanging blanket that separated the rooms, Jacob heard his father move.

"We knew there was going to be war. First it'll be with them stray settlers coming through from Missouri, the ones that raped and pillaged, and then murdered Brother Pratt in Arkansas. And then it'll be the U.S. Army. I told you we'd all have to put a stop to it, sooner or later, and now already it should 'a been sooner."

Through the blur in his eyes, Jacob saw his father dressed to go outdoors, the rifle slung over his shoulder, his hat in his hand. He came into the kitchen long enough to see the blood in Jacob's hair. His eyes glittered deep in his gnarled face.

"And they shot . . ." Jacob breathed in heavily with the pain beating in his head. "They killed Lil. The gunmen are out there now . . . one of 'em at least. Half a mile down the canal. They killed Lil . . ." He choked. "And Tag. And almost me."

J.B.'s eyes flamed. "Eh . . . what? Lil?" Not Lil. The grasshoppers, the drought, the crop failure, and now Lil.

"Lil!" Suky Lorry's hands dropped from Jacob's face to her lap. "Lil, dead." She said it as though it could not be—her face unmoving, as though by repeating words the truth would go away.

"Yes, it's true," Jacob whispered. "And they bragged—in Missouri they raped somebody that lives around here."

Suky tightened her hands into fists.

"Where'd you say they were, son?" his father asked, as he drew on his gloves and reached for the door.

Elizabeth had come down from the loft so quietly that Jacob hadn't heard her. Starched and white, she stood and waited as he expected she would. She placed her slender hand on a chair and watched.

"A half a mile." Jacob pointed toward the canal.

Suddenly his mother walked between his father and the door. Her face was set. "You won't go out there, J.B."

Suky had seen two of her nephews massacred at Haun's Mill. Standing behind a door and watching through a knothole, she saw the mobber raise the rifle on her two young nephews in the mill. "Nits make lice," one man had said. She had watched her nephews' brains spatter the hay. She remembered everything clearly. She feared Commander Johnston's army coming west to exterminate the Mormons that got away. Jeremiah Butler Lorry, though he remembered, did not let the past cheat the present. He was often stern with his wife Suky as well as his two childless wives, whom he had finally left in Salt Lake City to fend for themselves. It was the present that demanded one's best efforts, he often said. He had followed the Prophet's advice never to let a woman's emotions deter his will. He lowered his voice as he spoke to her. "Of course I'm going. Step aside, Suky."

"Please, no, J.B.," she said, her face blank with fear.

It was then that they heard someone in the woodpile, a loud clatter in the darkening yard. Jacob saw Elizabeth's hand tremble slightly on the chair. Suky flew to J.B. and clutched his right arm. "There's a killer out there!" she gasped.

J.B. threw her from his side and rushed for the back door. Elizabeth lifted her hands from the chair, and Jacob stepped quickly to her side. He pulled her down behind the table as J.B. flung open the door.

"Who goes there?" he called into the gathering dusk.

A dark figure stood beside the woodpile, a silhouette, a shapeless form plucking wood into his arms. "I need some of your woodpile to build a fire."

"Who are you?" J.B. called out.

"Passerby," the dark silhouette said. Now the white of his face was partially visible in the light from the house.

"Where you passin' by?" J.B. asked.

Jacob recognized the cap, the plaid wool coat. "That's him," he breathed. "That's him, Pa."

Suky pulled on the arm of J.B.'s coat. "Jacob says that's him! He killed Lil and our dog. And tried to kill Jacob." Her whisper died in the wind. If J.B. heard her, he did not say.

"Passin' through to California."

"You wouldn't happen to be from Missouri?"

There was an empty silence. And then from the white face in the dark, "Now what'd be the reason ye'd ask that?"

"Usually it's the Missouris that don't ask for things but just take 'em. There's been innocent people raped and killed. You must know, coming on ahead of the U.S. Army." There was a heavy silence. "You're not the U.S. Army, maybe? You knew they want us dead? The U.S. Government canceled our mail contract. They think we're in rebellion." No one spoke for a moment. The figure by the wood pile seemed paralyzed. Jacob continued. "We're not. But they hate us because we have our own government." He paused as though testing the visitor's savvy. But there was nothing in the man's face. "If your part of the country is comin' to shut down the 'Mormon Rebellion,' let me tell you there ain't no rebellion. But even Brigham Young says we ain't standing by to get wiped out, either."

The figure at the woodpile was silent. Then with unusual calm, and without a word, he turned and continued loading up the Lorrys' wood.

Suky pulled on J.B.'s coat. "He's a killer."

"You know anything about somebody that shot our boy and his dog, and then our cow?"

There was more empty silence while the man continued to help himself to the wood. Suky's eyes blazed. Jacob feared for her, her hands tight claws, her knuckles white. "Don't let him get away," Suky cried in a forced whisper.

A grin played across the man's face as he set down the wood.

"I asked you a bunch of questions and I didn't get no answers," J.B. said.

Suky backed up against the cupboards. She reached toward a crate and pulled aside the small curtain. Jacob did not see what she took from it. Then she slowly moved to the open door.

"Don't see as how I owe you no answers, old man," the visitor snarled. "If you're one of them Danites ransacked Missouri you have a debt to pay longer'n your ass's ears. I don't feel like waitin' for Johnston's army. And I'll just collect here." The man twirled his rifle in his fingers like a walking stick, then raised it into position.

"It's him!" Suky screamed. "Shoot, J.B. Or I will. Shoot. He's raising that gun!"

The man was calm. He grinned at J.B., whose old "Youger" stood uncocked and out of position under his arm.

Suky stood behind J.B. Without warning, she raised the Colt revolver. Slowly, she sighted toward the stranger. Her hands shaking, she pulled the trigger. J.B. turned back toward her, stunned. Jacob saw the blood in the pale face of the man as he slid to the cold grass, the rifle falling out of his hand.

Only the sound of wind in the tops of the pines whistled through the valley now. In the quiet, Elizabeth was the first to move to the yard. She knelt beside the body and reached for the man's head with her long white hands.

J.B. moved noiselessly, his boots whispering on the stoop. "Well, if the other one is anywhere about, we better hustle now," he said in a thin voice. "Jacob, help me get him to the canal. We'll bury him in the place we dug near where I was to route it tomorrow."

A shudder of cold rippled through Jacob. He watched Elizabeth release the lifeless head and rock back on her heels. Her hair, glowing in the light of the house, burned gold. Even in this terrible moment, he wanted to go to Elizabeth, bury his face in her skirt, and cry. In the silence, the sight of Elizabeth bending over the body gripped him so forcefully that he could barely move his legs to obey his father's request.

"Jacob, give me a hand." J.B.'s voice seemed far away.

"Hurry." Suky's whisper hurt his ears.

As he stepped through the door and into the yard, Jacob's shadow loomed across Elizabeth and J.B. bending over the body of the man lying on the ground. When Elizabeth stood, Jacob thought he could smell the rose water in her apron. He was conscious of her hands.

"Get him gone," Suky said between her teeth. But her voice cracked as she said it, as though she were unsure.

J.B. quickly spread out the tarp and rolled the body into it. He tied the rope under the man's armpits and beckoned Jacob to fetch the mule from the barn. As Jacob walked, he consciously sorted out concrete objects that would save his reality. "This is the ground," he thought to himself, "There is the barn." The darkness of the barn clawed at him. As he drew the mule from the stall, he was afraid to turn his back.

J.B. tied the rope to the singletree and gave the knot a jerk. When Foresight, their mule, moved forward slightly, the body, wrapped in canvas, moved over a few inches of ground.

"He's dead," Suky said, staring. She pressed her hands together tightly in front of her as though by pushing against herself she would keep from breaking apart. Still, Elizabeth had not said a word. When the mule moved the body across the yard, Jacob watched the girl in the light from the moon. Her neck was bent and she leaned forward as though toward something only she could understand. But he knew how he felt about her. And it was not how he had felt when she had first come to live with them. He had been thirteen. At fourteen she was something of an older sister, though she was not a sister, not even a cousin by blood, but an orphan girl distantly related by marriage, who had needed a home.

Two years had passed. Jacob and Elizabeth had become friends. But it had been three weeks since that friendship had become something more—at least for him. It had been an accident. He had seen her as he should not have seen her—in the candlelight flickering from her small bedroom window under the eaves in the loft of the house J.B. had built of pine. By mere chance, Jacob had been in the barn on the ladder, climbing up to fetch hay. And he had looked back at the house. The moment he had let his eyes rest on her in the light through the window, the moment he saw her white shoulders and the brown curls fall on her slim neck—that moment had changed him forever. He had not looked away. In wonder and amazement he had been sucked up into confusion. He had climbed the ladder twice more since then, to find the answer. No one knew that he stood on the ladder in the barn.

"Jacob, help your father," Suky's voice came from the dark.

Moving into the distance, leading the mule, Jacob's father seemed but a small figure in the black night and the deep valley that rose in jagged hills against the western sky. Behind J.B., the mule carried the body of the man who only moments ago had been alive.

"Don't breathe a word of it, you hear," Suky was saying to Elizabeth as they followed J.B. to the canal. "Never say you saw nothing. We'll clean up the cow, the dog. Everything. And don't never say you saw nothing."

Though he strained his ears to reach backward toward the light, Jacob did not hear what Elizabeth replied.

After J.B. dug the body into the dirt beside the canal, they hooked the travois to the mule and tied Lil's feet, letting the mule pull her onto the tarp on the travois. Keeping her blood inside the wrap, they hauled her into the shed behind the woodpile. J.B. roughed up the marks the travois made, dug up dirt to cover the bloody spot on the ground, and scattered it with stones. They accomplished all the tasks within two hours. No discordant voices or sounds from the wagon wheels betrayed their movements. The other man had not returned. J.B. walked ahead of Jacob into the dimly lit house. Elizabeth had gone to the loft to sleep.

Only Suky stayed in the yellow light. "He is dead," she said evenly, still staring as though transfixed. She sat beside the table reading her scriptures, her face gray as ashes. "Don't breathe a word of it to nobody."

J.B. came to her and pinched out the candle. "Come to bed." He took her arm.

Jacob listened, deathly still, as though he could hear the second man advance over the ground in the distant hills.

"Nobody breathe a word of it, hear," Suky said. Then in the darkness she turned into the hollow of J.B.'s arm. Her voice was now muffled, filled with fear in the silence of the small house. "J.B., I killed a man." Suddenly there was a wracking sob. "I killed a man."

J.B.'s voice sounded almost monotone. "Calm yourself," was all he said.

Jacob crowded into his cot by the fire and heard the emptiness as though it were filled with the whir of the earth in his ears.

## 2

*Friday, July 17, 1857, Elizabeth*

Elizabeth Worley woke to the light streaming through her loft window. She lay still on her bed, not breathing, but listening to the sounds in the barnyard. Suky was throwing grain to the hens. It must be late. Jacob and J.B. must already have gone into the fields. She had been startled awake by the same dream she had dreamed many times before—of the large black box rocking on the wagon until it tipped into the muddy river and spilled her father's body to the mercy of the stream.

She could remember when it had not been a dream. Suky Lorry had placed a palm against Elizabeth's cheek, turning her face into her bodice so that Elizabeth, age thirteen, would not see the high priests chase the box down the river, only to find it smashed on the rocks downstream. But Elizabeth could not stop shaking. She had held to Suky Lorry's roughened hands. Jacob had been sitting in the back of the wagon. But J.B. had stayed beside her, and had pressed her thin shoulders so hard she thought he would fold her like the covers of a book. "Hush, child. We'll take you with us," he had said.

Before he had become ill, her papa had said, "Go with the Lorrys," and so she had gone. Suky was the sister of Elizabeth's stepmother. When the stepmother died of typhoid on the plains, Suky had been prepared to take care of the Worley children. Then Elizabeth's father had died near the last crossing of the Platte River. Elizabeth had never dreamed the Lorrys would take her so far away—so far south of the Great Salt Lake, further south even than Cedar City. She had never dreamed the Lorrys would bring her to the bleak hills of the Kolob country, near red stones rising under the burning blue sky.

"Hush, child. Hush. We'll care for you." The thick sound of J.B.'s tongue had frightened her, and the pressure of his arm. "Do not be afraid," he had whispered, drawing her so close that she could not breathe without smelling the strong odor of his skin and coarse dark hair.

This morning she felt a vague, empty fear. She knew it was because of all that had happened in the night. They had stayed at the canal until J.B. had tamped down the last shovelful of dirt over the body of the dead man—until Suky had cut Lil into pieces and carried the chunks into the cellar, and gone back out into the yard to dig the blood into the earth and stamp on it with her shoes—then brush over it with a broom and walk over it again.

This morning, as she looked through the loft window, Elizabeth could see two men riding toward the house slowly, like beetles, black and distant against the hills in the south. Beyond them lay Harmony, the last outpost. Who were these men? She felt afraid. Nothing would be the same, now, in this place where her stepmother's relations had chosen to take her.

"They will protect you," Papa had wheezed through his congested lungs before breathing his last breath. But how could there be protection in a time of war? The army from the United States of America, ordered to come west, was threatening to exterminate the Mormons from the face of the earth. "Promise me you will go with them," he had said. She had promised, and she never made promises lightly, but she'd thought her father's words a lie. Aunt Suky had been good to her. She couldn't complain. J.B. was gruff, but a decent man. And Jacob had been a good friend. But she now felt an ominous dread that the death of the stranger would change everything.

One of the men in the distance rode in a jagged pattern as though he were looking on either side of the road for something. The horse stopped often to paw the ground as he meandered up beside the canal. The other man, impatient, rode toward the house. From her small room under the roof, Elizabeth heard Suky enter the house below her, shut the door quickly, and struggle to fasten the latch.

"Who is it?" Elizabeth peered from the loft.

Suky's face looked white in the smoky light. "Oh, may heaven help me," Suky breathed hard. "Elizabeth, help me."

"Wait for me." Elizabeth pulled on her dress, ran her fingers through her light brown hair, scrambled down the ladder into the room. "Who is it?"

"It's John D. Lee!"

John Lee! The most prominent man in Harmony, who, as Indian agent, often acted as sheriff, judge, and mayor all in one. He had been a close friend of the Prophet Joseph Smith. Elizabeth's friend Rebecca Jensen had confided to her while they were walking home from Church one day, "When he was on his mission in Tennessee, Brother Lee healed my grandfather. He told Grandpa to get up from his bed and walk, and that's what Grandpa did. Brother Lee went on five missions. I have always admired him more than any other man in the Church except the Prophet."

Elizabeth wondered why Lee was coming and how much he knew. She wondered if he was clairvoyant or if the angels had told him.

"It's him with another man," Suky said. "Looks like somebody not from these parts."

As Elizabeth reached Suky, her stepmother's pale hands slipped from the latch as she lurched backwards.

"Lie down, Suky. You're not well," Elizabeth said. "Go up into the loft. I'll take care of it. Lie down. Please forget about it. Everything will be fine."

Elizabeth helped Suky climb the ladder into the loft. At the top of the ladder, Suky fell into the straw bedding and drew the blue chintz quilt over her head.

Shaking, Elizabeth peered out of the front window of the loft. Brother John Lee—yes, it was Brother Lee. He was riding toward the house alone, but not entirely alone. Behind him, at some distance, was a stranger. This man behind Lee was snaking over the road like a scout, as though he were looking for something. He rode in and out of the canal. Then he began to follow the old creek bed into the hills.

Elizabeth could still hear Suky's sobbing in the loft and hoped Brother Lee would not come into the house. She took a pan of grain and slipped quietly out of the door. Shaking almost uncontrollably, she tossed a handful of grain to the scattering hens.

Brother Lee was an imposing man with transparent blue eyes. The coarse blond thatch of his hair resembled a haystack beneath the stark black of his hat. He was somewhat stocky, muscular, with strong legs. Elizabeth had known John Lee only as a local authority who gave inspiring speeches at the pulpit, both in Cedar City and at the meeting house in Harmony. She had known only what Rebecca had told her: Brother Lee, who had been an orphan raised by a black nurse, had become one of Brigham Young's most loyal soldiers for Christ. When the Missourians began their raids against the Mormons, he had been there to defend his friends. He had been present at the death of one Missourian, whose demise had prompted the others to exaggerate to the U.S. government that the Mormons had committed fifty murders. He had faced the retaliating Missouri mob when they took many Mormons captive, killing six. The Missourians had been ready to blow out his brains at one time. It was only because of a miracle he still lived. His non-Mormon neighbor had been in his barn forking hay when he happened to see the unspeakable act of seven men. Later, when it was quiet, the neighbor had been the one to cut the cords away from the fence post and set the child free. It was the neighbor who had come to the rescue of John Lee. "Spare him as a citizen. He's all right," the man had shouted.

But Lee had been scarred forever. Later he witnessed the Missouri gunshot that plowed into David Patten's bowels. Lee watched the much-loved commander suffer for several days in agonizing pain before he died. "How the mighty are fallen!" John Lee had cried out.

Rebecca had said she would not mind marrying into the family of such a man. He called himself a son of Brigham Young. Admired by everyone, he was wealthy, a prominent leader in the area, a man with many wives and many impressive children. As Lee rode toward Elizabeth, she caught a clear, strong glance from his blue eyes. She looked away.

"Miss Lorry?"

"Hello, Brother Lee. I'm . . ."

While she hesitated, he spoke up. "Oh yes! I believe I remember. You're not a Lorry, are you? You're Sister Suky's niece. Isn't that it?" He climbed out of his saddle, landing heavily on the ground.

"It's Worley," Elizabeth offered.

"Yes. Worley." As he moved closer to her, she backed away. "Was it Elizabeth?"

"Yes," Elizabeth said, surprised he had remembered.

"I don't often forget the name of a pretty girl," he said, smiling.

Elizabeth tried to smile back, but fear had tightened her face.

"Are the Lorrys here?"

"Only Suky and me, and Suky's sick. Is there something I can do for you?"

"Are you women alone?"

When she did not respond, he finally turned to look toward the man still on his horse, who was now approaching them from the road. "Do you know anything about the folks on their way through here yesterday?" John Lee must have been able to see her fear—a fear she could not hide. "This . . . gentleman came to me this morning. He said his friend disappeared. Perhaps he was taken by Indians." He paused. "Jensens heard a shot last night up against the hill."

Elizabeth felt the beat of her heart shake her body. Last night she had promised not to breathe a word of it to anyone. But John Lee was staring at her as though he could read every thought in her head.

"He is a traveler in these parts. From Missouri." Lee barely smiled, his face bright. "You know about that?"

Elizabeth's heart continued to pound. She found herself wanting to tell him everything. But she dare not. And for some reason, she felt it was not necessary, for she could feel that this man read every trace of evidence in the intensity of her expression. "I . . . we, that is . . . my aunt is so sick. Please . . . I can't . . ." She was stammering.

John Lee's eyes did not waver. He raised his hand quickly to halt her speech. He glanced back at the traveler behind him. He spoke boldly enough that the man could hear his words. "If it was close to this vicinity where he disappeared, there's nothing to show for it, not even a drop of blood on a blade of grass."

Slowly, the man prodded his horse up the hill. Lee's eyes wandered again to Elizabeth's face. He stared at her, his voice strong as he turned to the man. "All that's here is a sick woman in the house. Look if you want to look." When he turned again to Elizabeth, she saw a look she could not recognize—close to amusement, an almost visible sparkle in the pale blue eyes.

When the man arrived in the yard, Elizabeth froze. "My aunt is sick," she said softly. "She is in the upstairs bedroom." The horseman from Missouri was large and dark-eyed, the flesh on his face the color of gnarled pine.

"Two women here alone," John Lee said, his eyes still very bright.

"My aunt's husband and son are in the field," Elizabeth managed in a voice that sounded not her own, but forced, distant.

"You see any Indians here last night?" the man from Missouri asked. His voice sounded scratchy in his throat.

"No." Elizabeth shook her head, grateful she could speak honestly. She gripped the pan of grain against her waist.

"Nobody who looked like Indians, even?" he asked again.

"No."

"If they ain't Indians—" the stranger still mounted on the horse tightened his mouth. "Then Frank Henry cheated me. When I went to get the wagon, he left on me." He spit the words through hard lips.

"You see anybody that looked like Indians coming through here any time the last while?" Brother Lee asked Elizabeth in a very level voice.

"No, there haven't been Indians here for some time." She paused as if remembering. "Well, I did see some Indian children passing through here last week."

"No," Lee said. "No." He continued to keep his eyes on hers, his voice ringing with a perception she sensed with awe. "Not the children." He turned to the visitor. "The Lorrys have been here since I been at Harmony," he explained.

"Indians don't come here much anymore, knowing we won't stand for it." He climbed into the saddle, controlling his horse. "No. If there was Indians after your friend, they were further east in those hills. Or, like you say, your friend thought to leave you and he's gone back to Cedar . . ." He paused. "I'll follow you north that way a while, and we'll pass the Hamilton Fort. If there was Indians there last night, they could have taken him, scalped him, laid him in the creek to die."

The man from Missouri looked out across the valley toward the western rim of hills far away. The morning sun washed the tips of the mountains in gold. "I would have swore that he was close by this here ranch. With the dead cow. I went back to fetch the wagon. He ain't here now." Suky had swept the canal and yard with a broom, walking on it afterward, leaving no clues.

From his position on the horse, John Lee stared at Elizabeth for what seemed like a long time, the glint of his eyes like steel. "Thank you, Sister Worley," he said. Although the words were well-mannered, she felt a grin behind his tone. "I will see you in church on Sunday."

She said nothing, but nodded slightly.

"Good-bye now. Take care."

She waved, but she could not make "good-bye" come to her lips. She wanted to say, "Brother Lee, if only you would stay. My stepmother has given up. I fear my stepfather, never certain what he will do. Please, if you can, I wish you would stay." But she said nothing. She watched silently as Lee and the Missourian rode northward toward Cedar City, their horses swaying on the road. When she turned back to the house, Suky was waiting for her in the doorway.

"What did you say?" Suky's gaunt cheeks betrayed a weariness Elizabeth had never seen before. She leaned on unsteady legs, holding tightly to the doorjamb with one thin hand.

"Suky, everything's going to be all right," Elizabeth said, although she did not believe it herself. "I told him you were sick. He passed us by."

# 3
## *Elizabeth*

Elizabeth knew that J.B. was supposed to drill with the militia at the Jensens' in the evening, but on the night of Friday, July 17, 1857, when he came in from the fields, he decided he ought to stay home with Suky to calm her tears. He tried to settle in bed early, but Suky kept him awake with her crying.

Long after Elizabeth climbed into her bed in the loft, she could hear the low murmur of J.B.'s voice comforting his wife, his voice humming in the heat. Elizabeth strained to understand, but the words were not clear. She began to feel the weariness in her eyes drag her toward an uneasy sleep. She lay, half-conscious of a memory, or a dream. The rain was blowing dark leaves across the graves on the bleak Iowa countryside. Her father's head was bent in his hands. Her little brother was moving quickly across the wet ground. He had returned to the wagon dangling a snake from the branch of a willow.

"No!" her father shouted. "No! Put it down I say."

"May I keep it, Father?"

"No!" her father shouted. "No! It's poison!" Elizabeth had heard that fear in his voice only once before when her mother died on the trail. "Let go!" He gripped the boy's wrists and shook them until the branch with the snake flew up. When it came down, it landed on little Robert's bare feet and bit him with lightning speed on the toe. Poisoned, the little boy had languished in the wagon until they had reached Nebraska, where he died. Elizabeth would never forget the gray face of her dead brother as they set him in the ground. Without wood to build a box, they had covered him with clumps of cold grass.

Jolted from her sleep, Elizabeth felt the loft rocking. She thought someone stood behind the curtain in the loft door.

"Elizabeth." The voice was not a dream, because if it had been in a dream, she could wake from it. "Elizabeth, I need you, girl." It was the voice of J.B. Her heart pounded so hard it shook her. But she kept her eyes closed.

"Elizabeth, I need you," J.B. whispered.

Through a blink, she saw his rough fingers pull aside the curtain in the moonlight, revealing his white face. He looked worn, as though he needed more solace than he could find in all of this world. Though her dreams seemed to hang over her still, they were fast dropping into an even darker reality.

"Elizabeth, move over, my girl."

She could not believe what she was hearing.

"I need you." J.B. was choking with something like far-away tears that he could not let fall. He crept across the coverlet and into the bed beside her. Keeping her eyes closed, she stiffened. She could feel his breath on her cheek.

"Let me in," he demanded in a coarse whisper. He pushed her with awkward gentleness toward the loft window, his large hands tugging at the bedding as he crawled slowly beneath the quilts, moving his feet and legs close to hers. "Let me in," he said again.

With her heart knocking at her ribs, she lay still. His hands circled her body and cradled her.

"I need you, Elizabeth." Then he whispered almost inaudibly, "Suky is not herself."

She did not move a muscle. An unusual light began to flicker behind her eyelids. The earth seemed like a tilting planet.

"Please let me be with you. Marry me."

She could not breathe for fear. This was not what she had dreamed.

"Are you awake?" he whispered. "I think you can hear me."

But Elizabeth could not move. He pawed at her until she could feel his body fully against hers. She tightened, but she did not dare speak.

"It's all right, my darling. There is nothing to worry about. We'll wait until we can make vows." He held her as though reining in his passion with iron control. "But it must be soon," he whispered into her ear. "I need you, Elizabeth." His words drew on her ear a long draught as though he would inhale her. "Suky needs you. She needs to know that you will stay." He paused again. "She is . . . too frail to bear up under . . . all of it." Elizabeth heard a deep sob in his throat. "Please, Elizabeth. We need . . ."

Her mind reeled. She held to the bed as though clinging to a sinking boat, remembering the interrupted dream vividly—the snake. Then she saw John Lee's face in the blue sky and heard the monotone of J.B.'s comforting words into Suky's ears.

J.B. still clung to her. She could not move but lay terrified under the circling rhythm of his hands. "Sleep," he said again in her ear. "Sleep, my darling."

She felt her senses dropping away with the motion of his hands. Before she could protest his touch, he moved away from her, caressing her one last time. "Good night, my darling," he said. She lay shaking for what seemed to be hours until she fell into a dreamless sleep. When she awoke, it was a bright morning. And J.B. was gone.

### 4

*Saturday, July 18, 1857, Jacob*

Jacob believed he lay awake all night. On Friday he could hear J.B. and Suky murmuring softly to each other in the large bed. Though he could not hear their words, he heard his mother sobbing and his father's quiet "Shhh." Later, in his dreams, he imagined that his father loomed over him in his cot in the lean-to, whispering to him that his mother had died and Elizabeth had taken her place. Terrified, he shook his head, forcing himself awake.

From the window of the attached back shed where he slept, he could see the dawn. Yesterday Brother Jensen had offered them the milk from one of his cows if they would fetch it. J.B. had told them Jacob would be there early. There was no more Lil to milk, and no more Tag. The hurt that had stayed with him all day yesterday settled on him again. Getting out of bed, he tried to shake off sleep. He had not really had enough for two days.

He dressed quickly and left the house. Not far from Jensen's he could see Percy, a dark speck in the early light. He was walking out into the field with his rifle. Percy had been invited to substitute in the militia. He had probably attended drill last night when J.B. didn't go.

Jacob envied Percy, who was two years older and whose father had allowed him to drill with the men. J.B. had never allowed Jacob to discuss the militia. Jacob watched Percy's long legs spring across the grass away from the barn. He watched while Percy raised the rifle, sighted, shot. He shot again and again. Jacob would like to have carried J.B.'s rifle instead of the milk bucket. He would like to have been the one who killed the Missourian who had shot Tag. The hard pain pressed on his chest. As Percy drew closer, he waved.

"I come after milk again," Jacob called.

Percy nodded, and then beckoned for Jacob to come to the barn. The painted target against the pinewood walls was chewed up from a hundred accurate hits.

"I guess you went to drill last night . . ." Jacob began.

Percy's eyes brightened. He nodded and drew the gun to his shoulder again. The shot echoed around the valley, the sound hanging on the air as it volleyed from rim to rim.

"Bull's-eye!" Jacob shouted.

Percy grinned. "You want to try to beat that?" He thrust the gun into Jacob's hands. Jacob cradled it as though it were a rod of gold.

"You sure have a nice-lookin' gun, Percy."

"It's a prime-kept Kentucky. My pa don't mess around with poor equipment when it comes to war. Both the Indians and U.S. Army better watch out."

Jacob lifted the smooth firearm to his shoulder, felt its weight like lead against his bones.

"Just aim careful. Allow a little bit of an arc," Percy explained.

Jacob felt the warmth of Percy's grip still on the handle. He loaded it, breathed in, and aimed. He pulled the trigger. The explosion pushed the gun back against his shoulder. The wound on his head under his cap began to throb. The bullet hit off to the side of the target to the left of the barn.

Jacob had never shot a rifle before. Once he had aimed J.B.'s Colt at a rabbit, but before the bullet left the chamber, J.B. had sneaked up on him, gone crazy, and taken the firearm out of his son's hands. Jacob had been only ten. For years J.B. had been wrought up about guns. "We had too much gunning in Missouri. No son of mine is going to shoot a gun." He had been worse than ever the past few days since the accident in the yard.

Percy reloaded. "Not so tight," he said. "Hold it looser. For best control, you guide it, but let it go."

Jacob loaded it and pulled the trigger again. This time he hit the bottom rim of the outside blue circle. A strange joy crowded up into the top of his head.

"That's better," Percy said. "Aim higher."

On the third try, the bullet cracked another chip of paint near the bull's-eye.

"Lucky one!" Percy shouted. "Or else you got a good eye! A little training and you'd be good!"

Though the throb of his wound spread from ear to ear, he was in some miraculous way moving through the pain, putting it away, perhaps to deal with it at some later moment. What he felt now was a strange ecstasy, a companionship with the gun that lay in his arms. It had become a much-savored extension of his flesh. He had shot only three times. Yet, comfortable with the feel of it now, he found himself reluctant to let go.

Percy took it from his hands like he would take a baby. Jacob felt an emptiness when the rifle was gone.

All the way into the barn and while he was milking the Jensen cow, Jacob began to think of different ways he might approach his father to ask him for permission to drill. He knew J.B. would not want to hear that he had been shooting this morning, so Jacob would not tell him.

Later, when he came into the house, Elizabeth and his parents were already at breakfast, talking in quiet voices about something. From what little he heard, it sounded like J.B. wanted to take Elizabeth to Salt Lake City during the first part of August. But when Jacob appeared with the milk, there was a lull in the conversation. Suky hurried to pour milk over her gruel.

In the quiet, Jacob ventured to speak. "Percy Jensen went to drill last night."

Suky paused, bringing the spoon to her mouth. She stared at the table; her hand trembled with the spoon midair. J.B. stared at Jacob from beneath his bushy brows, a question in his eyes.

"I was wondering if . . . He's only sixteen. I'm almost fifteen. I was wondering if you wouldn't let me go next week? They say they need men . . ."

"Men," Suky said, putting down the spoon.

J.B. smiled. The silence hurt Jacob more than a "no" would have hurt him. The silence left his mother's one-word verdict still hovering in the air.

Jacob grew angry in the silence. But he knew he dare not argue because it would only make things worse. "It wouldn't hurt to go, to be learning something," he said, holding the anger from his voice.

Suky stared at him. "This isn't a child's game. The president of the United States canceled our mail contract because a jealous Mormon-hater convinced him the Mormons is mixing religion with the state. So the U.S. Army's coming to exterminate Mormons and install a governor. We want to save our lives."

J.B. wiped his mustache with his handkerchief. "She's right, son. It's not for boys."

Jacob bristled. "Percy is only sixteen."

"Let the Jensens worry about Percy," Suky said evenly, her eyes half closed as though she could not breathe.

"Your mother needs you," J.B. said.

Now Jacob's voice lost its calm. "Nothing's changed!" Feeling the tension rise in his voice, he tried to pull himself together. "I just want to learn something. That's all." His hands tightened around his spoon until Elizabeth placed her white hand over his. The gesture was simple, but it calmed him. She could somehow soften the devastation of his father's blows.

Suky held the napkin to her mouth. She looked as though she would cry.

"I'm still here, Mother," Jacob was able to say.

"It isn't enough that J.B. goes and gets himself killed, and Elizabeth goes off and marries someday . . . and you . . . my only child . . ." The uncertainty seemed too much for Suky. She lowered her face into her napkin and held her breath so that she wouldn't cry.

"Nobody's going to leave you." Elizabeth held Suky's arm. "Please, Aunt Suky."

Jacob saw a strange look in his father's eyes. The man put his napkin down and began to rise from the table. "Elizabeth won't disappoint us, will you, Elizabeth?"

Jacob did not understand why Suky held so fiercely to Elizabeth's hand or why his father said *Elizabeth won't disappoint us, will you, Elizabeth?* Sobbing, Suky cried out, "Oh, my darling. You know I want you to stay. You know I want you to stay."

J.B. stood over Jacob on his way out the door. "And Jacob, my boy." He glared at his son while he pulled on his gloves. "On Friday evenings—during military drill—you will stay right where you are."

## 5
### Sunday, July 19, 1857, Elizabeth

Sunday morning the first thing Elizabeth saw was the red sky. She saw the mist in the trees, almost liquid in the hills, and the sunlight on the far mountains. She opened her eyes to the rose-colored light that filtered through the glass in her loft window.

It was Sunday. She would face Rebecca today. Rebecca. How would she do that? It would not be easy to hold back all of the Lorry secrets. Rebecca had always been welcome to know everything. Elizabeth feared there was no possible way she could keep from telling Rebecca about the man who lay buried beneath the dirt near the canal. And now there was something else that burned even more heavily inside of her. J.B.'s intentions. This morning he had said nothing as the family prepared for church. If no one spoke, if no one talked, perhaps the heaviness in her stomach would subside.

In the wagon, Elizabeth half closed her eyes to shut out the hot light. The countryside blurred beyond her as they moved westward into the valley toward the road that passed through Jensens' ranch. The Jensens were in the yard climbing into their own rig. They would say nothing of the past two days. The Lorry secrets were not written upon their faces. Perhaps Elizabeth could concentrate on holding them inside. There was Rebecca. She was smiling. She waved as the Lorry wagon drew by.

Elizabeth sat numb as they turned the mule northward on the road to Cedar City. The flat valley rose to a narrow ridge of mountains. The city lay behind the mountains nestled in a hollow.

Elizabeth might have looked back and waved at Rebecca, but she did not. She was not sure how she could hide what had happened. Even a misplaced wave would have given Rebecca a clue that something lay heavy in her heart. Rebecca would be able to read through her hello.

When they stopped at the bowery in Cedar City, Elizabeth did not get down. She waited for a moment, searching the crowd. In the distance near to the pulpit stood John Lee. In a moment J.B. came to her and held out his hand.

"Are you coming, Elizabeth?" he said.

"Yes," she answered and leaned on his arm as she stepped out of the wagon.

"Your collar needs a tuck in back," he murmured. And then he touched her. She could feel the caress of his fingers as he touched the back of her neck.

"Today I can take care of our . . . matter with the authorities," he said. He meant their marriage. Elizabeth stared at Suky because she wanted to know if Suky was aware of what was going on. The older woman did not flinch. Instead, she smiled slightly.

"You will be fine, Elizabeth," J.B. said.

She nodded. Not in agreement, but in submission. Submission to Suky's eyes and the pressure of J.B.'s hand on her arm. She felt relief only when he finally let her go as he turned to meet some brethren at the bowery. Today was the stake meeting. Because today's meeting included many different wards throughout the area, both the inside and outside of the small church house were filled with hundreds of members. They spilled into the bowery outside of the small church building. They sat on rough benches, chairs, and even blankets on the ground where their families gathered around them. When Elizabeth turned, she saw Rebecca getting down from the Jensen wagon.

"Elizabeth!" Rebecca cried, waving, running, almost stumbling toward her. "Elizabeth!" she called again.

Motionless, Elizabeth smiled, preparing herself for the encounter with her friend. J.B. was still close to her. And he was alert to her in a way she feared. Though he was talking to others, pretending to hear them, he was still watchful. "Speak to no one," he had said.

"Lizzy!" Rebecca cried and threw her arms around Elizabeth's neck.

Elizabeth welcomed Rebecca's warm cheek. She returned the squeeze as she would be expected to do. Then, in spite of her fears, she laughed.

"How are you?" Rebecca smiled.

"You look excited," Elizabeth said.

"Oh?" Rebecca returned with a mysterious grin.

Elizabeth wondered if Rebecca knew somehow. But when she looked in her friend's eyes, she realized she had not heard one word.

"I have a secret," Rebecca whispered.

Elizabeth began to breathe more easily when she realized her friend had a secret of her own. She glanced at J.B. He was gazing at her with intense narrow eyes of warning. She held Rebecca's hands and began listening as though her life depended upon it.

"John D. Lee," Rebecca whispered.

The sound of the name charged through Elizabeth's head. John D. Lee. She and Rebecca had talked about John D. Lee many times. But something had obviously happened to Rebecca since their last time together.

J.B. was standing close enough to hear Rebecca whisper the name. He pretended to turn away. But Elizabeth knew he was still very much present.

"John D. Lee!" Elizabeth said loudly enough so that J.B. could hear. He visibly relaxed as he talked with the other men. He turned his back to her.

"Yes! John D. Lee!" Rebecca said. "I have asked him if I could marry him!"

Elizabeth caught her breath. She became conscious of the smooth skin on her friend's cheek and neck. She felt the brightness of the girl's hair.

"You have asked him if you could marry him?" Elizabeth repeated.

"He came to see my father," Rebecca continued. "He asked Father to cut some fence lumber for him. I reminded him about my grandfather who was healed by him in Tennessee. And I told him I admired him more than I have ever admired any man." She paused.

Elizabeth wanted to ask, "What did he say?" But she didn't need to ask it.

"He said I was young." Rebecca offered.

J.B. turned his head toward them, and Rebecca took Elizabeth's hands and tried to pull her friend with her.

"And then what?" Elizabeth hung on her words now.

"He told me that if I still felt the same way when he was ready to marry again, he would take me up to Salt Lake City to be sealed to him." She grasped Elizabeth's hands between her own. "Oh, Elizabeth!"

Elizabeth withdrew her hands from inside of her friend's grasp and pressed them over Rebecca's. "Are you sure, Rebecca?" she asked.

"I'm sure. Oh yes, I am sure." Rebecca's eyes darted to the front of the bowery to catch sight of John Lee. Her cheeks were flushed. The man stood with his back to them, the golden thatch of his hair like ripe wheat in the sun. "He's here. He's here now," Rebecca whispered.

Elizabeth nodded. "I see him," she answered. "I saw him as soon as I came." She glanced at J.B.'s dark face. He seemed to have heard everything Rebecca had been saying.

At that moment, on the platform where the pulpit stood, John Lee turned, and, unexpectedly, Elizabeth saw his expressionless face. She felt the same blush come to her cheeks that she had felt when he had come to the house and executed his strange justice. Stunned, she could feel J.B.'s presence close by.

"God speaks through him," Rebecca said. She did not try to keep her words from J.B. or Suky. "I know this is right. I knew I must go to him because I saw his face in a dream." She finally lowered her voice, but only because Elizabeth was so quiet. "Elizabeth, someday you will know what is right. It will come to you like a great light in your heart."

When J.B. walked to her, she shuddered when he took hold of her arm. She did not acknowledge him. "You are brave, Rebecca," she whispered. "How wonderful for you." She paused a moment, feeling the power of J.B.'s grip. "He is a great man. I am so happy for you." But she wasn't happy. She was confused. The specter of J.B.'s heavy body in her bed terrified her. Now he was gripping her elbow. More words fought to form in her mouth, but she could not force them to come.

J.B. was pressing her forward into the bowery now and she was compelled to move.

"Elizabeth! What about you!" Rebecca tried to keep up.

Elizabeth did not answer her. She was surprised at how easy it seemed at this moment to hold back from her friend. She hadn't believed she could do it.

The conference began like other conferences: announcements, prayer, song. But it became different when George Albert Smith stood at the pulpit. Alert, Elizabeth sat still, aware that J.B. was gripping his hands together with a tension unfamiliar to her. Suky continued to bring a handkerchief to her lips and knot it conspicuously when she held it in her lap. Jacob leaned forward, hanging on the apostle's every word.

"They were determined to wipe out Mormonism then, and I believe they are determined to do so now, but their excuse is different. The snug sum of twenty-five hundred men is ordered out now to put down Mormonism, but in Missouri Governor Boggs ordered out seventeen thousand men to exterminate us. They burned three hundred and sixteen houses, killed a few men, ravished a few women and plundered and stole, and arrested our leaders. And they thought they had wiped out Mormonism. But just as they got it wiped out they found it was bigger than before."

When he paused, only the sound of women's fans rippled through the air.

"What excuse have they for their course now? They will tell you it is the sin of polygamy! What was their excuse in Missouri, before the doctrine of polygamy was taught the Saints? It was something else. The truth is, polygamy is not the cause of their hatred to us. They hate and fear us because of our unity; because of our obedience to the holy priesthood; we are damned Mormons, anyhow, and must be killed . . . They say the Mormons must be used up, there is too much unity. If they are not stopped they will grow too big."

Only a cough here and there broke the silence.

"They intend to hang about three hundred of the most obnoxious Mormons; Brigham to be hung anyhow—no trial necessary for him or the principal leaders—and then go through a form of trial for the rest. They are sending out officers, the governor, judges, jury, and troops. They expect that one half the women will leave their husbands and cut their throats, and that one half of the men will join them. They hope thus to split us in two and have an easy victory over Mormonism and make an end to it."

There was a murmur as he had noted that not even the participation of five hundred Mormon men in the country's "Mormon Battalion" seemed to have softened the hearts of the citizens of the United States. "Evidently they still think of us as rebels trying to establish our own government combining church and state. And they are sending their army to quell what they think of as the Mormon rebellion. We must be ready. Unless you want to be driven again, made to tramp the white hot desert where not a leaf can grow in the sand. Brothers and Sisters—" He grew solemn now, "—there is a desert surrounding us. A desert. And if you had a difficult time during this past two years with the grasshoppers and drought . . . the abyss is out there . . ." His words brought silence. "This is the last outpost," he was saying. "Let us not allow the Missouri Wildcats or the United States Army to drive us from Deseret, our last home."

During the break for lunch, while the women prepared the bread and cheese from their baskets and poured the milk warmed by the sun, the men chatted freely about arms, ammunition, drills. Elizabeth noticed that J.B. left for a short time before lunch. When he returned to eat, Elizabeth thought she felt his eyes on her, though she did not raise her own to verify it. She sat with Rebecca and the Lorrys and the Jensens, helping the Jensen children to butter their bread, making sure they hadn't spilled on their Sunday clothes. J.B. chatted with Brother George Jensen while Suky remained quiet, eating and staring through the shady bowery toward the pulpit.

John D. Lee had disappeared into the church building with President Smith and the other brethren for an interim meeting. Though J.B. was still near,

Elizabeth was able to whisper with Rebecca about the war, about Rebecca's plans. They became quiet again when Nancy Eggers and Priscilla Hunt joined them to talk about lace for their petticoats, how to curl their hair, or what the boys had done on the Fourth of July.

In the afternoon there was more talk about the passing settlers, the U.S. Army, and the Church members' responsibility toward both. Isaac Haight emphasized the growing policy of embargo. "You all know we've suffered the grasshoppers and drought these last two years. Our supplies are so limited, the brethren in Salt Lake City are asking us to sell nothing. Nothing." The insistence in President Haight's voice struck a note of fear in everyone. "We've been asked not to do so much as trade a loaf of bread with the outsiders coming through these southerly cities. Some are bent on making their way to this area to chase us into the desert to die. But if they cannot eat, if they have no supplies, it will weaken them enough that they will not be able to overcome us."

J.B. reached for Suky's hand.

The next speaker was William H. Dame. "I know our God will stand beside us to revenge the spilled blood of our Prophet," he exclaimed. "If they shall come here to destroy us again, we will be held up by some power that, I promise you, even you will not understand."

Seated between J.B. and Suky, Elizabeth listened to the speeches with alarm. When George Albert Smith rose again to give the last address, there was a hush in the congregation.

"Brothers and sisters," he began, "I want you to listen carefully to what I tell you." He paused. "It has been almost ten years since we came here. Are you saying 'All is well in Zion, all is well?'" He waited. Everyone was quiet. "Well, let me tell you, all is not well. We are facing a pincers movement like the claws of a crab. As I speak there are letters being written by greedy enemies to the president of the United States to prejudice him against us—to dishonor the mail contract—to allow the army to destroy us. Also, there are rumors that a group from California is coming from the West." There was deadly silence. "Now you tell me. What will happen here if we have to face armies from both east and west, while we are facing hostile Indians at the same time?"

No one in the audience moved. He paused, waiting, letting them absorb his words. He spoke of how anxiously they were making preparations. "We should be grateful to Brothers Jacob Hamblin and John D. Lee for securing our peace with the Indians. They have walked into the jaws of death to make friends with these natives. They have sacrificed their time and talents—even their material goods—to appease the Indians. We must honor and support these men. If they shall ask anything of you, please respond with willing hearts. Give honor and support to Jacob Hamblin and John D. Lee."

*Rebecca had asked John Lee to marry her!* The very thought of it stunned Elizabeth.

"And now we'll ask Brother Lee to offer the benediction," President Smith said, turning to sit down.

Through the closing hymn, Elizabeth's head swam with a strange fear. She believed Brother Lee had seen her eyes on him earlier. She looked over at J.B. Before John Lee bowed his head, she could see J.B. trace the gaze of the man at the pulpit to Elizabeth's face. His eyes narrowed before he closed them in prayer.

"Our eternal Father, our God," Lee's voice resonated like the rumble of thunder. "We pray humbly for thy mercy, our God. Deliver us from the presence of our enemies."

# 6
## *Jacob*

While Jacob also listened to the speeches and the prayers, he sometimes stole a glance at Elizabeth's face. Her eyes did not stray from the pulpit. He thought it strange that she sat between J.B. and Suky in the afternoon session. After the closing hymn, he watched J.B. move to the front of the bowery to speak to John Lee.

He waited for a moment before he followed J.B., who was standing in a line waiting to shake John Lee's hand. Jacob waited, too, with Suky and Elizabeth, though Elizabeth was sharing something with Rebecca that he could not hear.

He watched J.B. as he spoke with Brother Lee. Brother Lee's eyes scanned the audience until they rested on Suky, Elizabeth, and Rebecca as they stood talking. Lee nodded as he spoke to J.B., though he did not smile.

On the way home in the cart, J.B. seemed more serious than usual. At one point, Jacob considered mentioning the militia, but the air felt so heavy with heat, and his father seemed so preoccupied, he was unable to speak about anything. Suky, and Elizabeth, too, were silent.

When they finally came to the house, J.B. handed the reins to Jacob. "Will you drive Foresight into the barn?" he said.

"Yes." Jacob's scalp seemed tight. Of course he would drive the mule and wagon into the barn.

"Walk with me a while, Elizabeth," J.B. said. He stepped down from the wagon and reached for Elizabeth's hand. Jacob watched her face, searching for a clue that would tell him what was happening in her heart. She seemed as empty of feeling as he had ever seen her. But she reached out her hand and leaned on J.B. to step out of the wagon while Suky followed and headed for the door of the house. Jacob's heart leaped up into his throat. He believed he knew what was going to happen.

*Something is off kilter. The sun? There had never been a sun so hot nor a sky so blue. All that happens in life can change in an instant, in the flicker of an eye. There are moments you will never forget. As a child, you looked up to the sideboard without seeing the loaf of bread or the glass of flowers. Finally, tall enough to see the vase, you found that it was empty. "They are sisters, Jacob. Esther and Vera. They are here because they had no place else to go," Suky said. "And your father was asked to give them a home."*

*He was eight years old, and he stood with his eyes level to the sideboard, and he had wondered how long it had been since his mother put flowers there.*

J.B. took Elizabeth's hand and walked her to the canal. "Stop!" Jacob felt like shouting. But he was numb. His heart plummeted as he watched Elizabeth and his father walk away.

<br>

### 7
#### *Elizabeth*

When J.B. took Elizabeth's elbow, her footstep quickened, as though by walking faster, she could keep a step ahead of his touch. But he pulled her back to walk with him. She focused on the light of the hot afternoon growing almost orange in the west.

They neared the heap of earth where the canal turned. At the corner, the earth appeared to loom toward them, mountainous, freshly dug. Elizabeth could not avoid the thought that somewhere, below the mountain of earth in the corner, lay the body of the murdered man. She paled. But J.B. did not stop there. He took Elizabeth's elbow firmly and guided her down the path at the side of the canal.

"The other morning in the loft . . ." he began. "I couldn't say anything for certain until I got permission."

Elizabeth let him take her hand, but the feel of his rough skin against her fingers unnerved her. She walked forward along the canal, as though if she kept moving she would escape what he might say.

But his words came at last. "I asked John D. Lee and Isaac Haight if we could . . ." He paused for a moment. "Marry." The sun hit the hills and seemed to reflect toward them with a lethal heat.

Elizabeth's throat felt swollen and she could not speak.

"Suky isn't well, as you know." He seemed uneasy, though this would be his fourth marriage. He had the two wives without children who had wanted to stay in Salt Lake City; he had only visited them briefly during the last two years.

Elizabeth tried to quiet her fears, recount her obligations to the Lorry family. J.B. was a better-than-average man she told herself. He was a steady worker, an honest man. But her talk dissolved into thin air. She felt nothing at the moment except panic.

He stopped in a clump of juniper that separated them from the house and the barn. He waited for a moment, seeming unusually patient while Elizabeth stared at the ridge of blackening hills in the west. The sun burned with an oblique light into the sage and the brush. She thought of the journey she had taken two years ago. "Go with them. Let them help you find peace, Elizabeth," her father had said on his death bed. And so she had obeyed her father.

Elizabeth had always felt J.B.'s strength, saw that he wielded an insistent authority in his household. If the supper was late, the bedding dirty, or the house cluttered, a few stern sentences had always brought quick action. If he was loved, it was out of respect—or tolerance.

"Elizabeth," J.B. began again. "When I leave for Salt Lake City in a few days, I will take you with me."

No, Elizabeth said in her heart. But it carried no force. She dared not open her mouth. She winced when he put his hands on her waist. Though she felt annoyed, she closed her eyes and prayed for a kind of strength she had never needed before—the kind of strength one must have to make the best out of any situation. She breathed inward. She noted that it was not unpleasant to sense the weight of his hands on her waist. What was happening to her now might have happened to Rebecca if John Lee had touched her. Was this what Rebecca had meant when she said, "It will be shown to you"? Elizabeth felt no sudden light. Instead, she could only imagine John Lee's narrow look and hear her friend's sigh.

When J.B. turned her face to him with his rough fingers, she felt power-less. His furrowed head seemed large, rough, his eyes deep set under the thick brows, his eyes pinched by deep crow's feet. She was aware of the request by the brethren to the men that they should avoid arousing emotions inappropriate to proper courtship and a solid marriage. Yet, she believed that J.B. had been trying in subtle ways to win her heart for the last two years. He had been masterful in that quest, though the feeling he had inspired in her was most akin to fear.

"You'll be a good woman for us," he said, assuming that her silence was acceptance. "This is good for our family. You're a good woman, Elizabeth." When he drew her close and lifted her chin with his large hand, she kept her eyes fastened to his Sunday vest.

"Look at me, Elizabeth," he whispered. "Look at me, girl."

Slowly she raised her dark lashes.

"Can you change from being a daughter to my wife?" When she did not answer, he supplied the answer. "I believe you can love me."

Whether it was simply his power or her need to be agreeable, she could not tell, but she found that every tense muscle in her body began to relax in his embrace. He held her gently. He was still her father. Yet she was no longer a child.

"Let me love you, Elizabeth. Let me take you with me." Though she had resisted him, she felt a warmth stirring somewhere. He stroked her hair, and pulled her close. "You will love me." He was smiling now. She felt his body shaking. He took her head from his shoulder and pressed his lips in her hair, on her forehead. "You're so lovely," he said. Then he released her, and, taking her hand in his, led her back toward the house. In all of these moments, in the bright afternoon light still orange in the bleak hills, she had not said a single word.

### 8

*Tuesday, July 28, 1857, Elizabeth*

*We are here at Salt Lake City in the hotel. He was patient with me, asking for nothing. Now we are married by the authorities in the endowment house. As a wedding gift, he gave me this writing book—an old diary. He had written on only one page. We ate pork and biscuits in the dining room. At 6:30 p.m. he said he was going to visit Vera and Esther, his other wives. He wanted to know if I would come along, but I said no.*

*As I am writing now at the desk by the window, some soldiers have come down the street to the hotel. Through the window I can see them come in below. They are noisy. I hope the lock holds on the door.*

Elizabeth closed the book and felt the cool pages on her fingers. Through the dark mirrors of windows above the street, she saw the lights below, the torches carried by the men who led the procession, the flashes of gold on the brass bits of the horses, the rivets in the carriages. The crowd below was a flurry of color and activity. She blew out the oil lamp in the room.

*They could have seen me in the lamplight. Now that I am in the dark, they are visible—soldiers and families traveling through Deseret.*

For the next two hours, Elizabeth sat at the window watching the crowd in the torchlight of the street, using the faint glow from the moon to write in the book about her new life. However, her sentences soon became cramped in the dark, and she thought she heard the heavy sound of boots on the floor of the hotel lobby below. She feared that if any of them had seen her stare from the dusky glass, they might have guessed she was alone. Although the door was locked, she felt uneasy. She did not move from the large chair, but drew the afghan close and sat staring into the blackness, wishing now that she'd been willing to go with J.B., who had begged her to come along.

*Now it seems that most of the people on the street are coming into this hotel. I can feel them like thunder on the floors.*

When the large chimes in the lobby rang ten times, her eyelids felt as heavy as lead. She realized she had been staring into the street for more than two hours. Quietly, in the blackness of the room, she removed the afghan, then her dress and her stays. She did not bother to find her nightdress in the dark. With the camisole loose around her waist, she breathed in and out several times and slipped into the large bed next to the flowered paper on the wall.

She lay for only a moment staring up into the ceiling, listening to her own regular breathing, when she heard heavy footfall outside her door. Boots. Perhaps soldiers. She held her breath. Someone rattled the knob on the door.

There had been no light in the room for two hours. A sick wave of fear washed over her. Someone was trying the door. She clung to the wall beside her, lying dead still. Then she heard the sound of metal in the lock. Whoever it was had a key.

The lurch of her heart seemed to drown out the sound of the door. She wondered how many men would come in and what she would do when they found her. She held her breath. A low voice said something that sounded like, "Training is what they need." A glow passed over her eyes. Someone had lit an oil lamp.

"Shhh. She's asleep." It was the voice of J.B. "Take that bedding over there by the window."

It might have been a relief to hear that one of the voices was the familiar voice of J.B. But in all of the maelstrom of the last weeks, she could not put any of the pieces together. Why did she still feel terror?

There must have been only two people. She dared not open her eyes. Soon there were no more voices, only the sounds of boots and coats thrown to the floor. Finally there was a gruff whisper, "You'll do us good if we have to prepare to fight any of them tough Missouri cowboys. I never seen such big men."

"They ain't children or cowards."

"I understand the Missourians was hired to take care of the livestock." The unmistakable voice of J.B. "The larger train is following."

"Thanks for putting me up tonight. I appreciate it. I hope I didn't interrupt nothing."

"Naw. Plenty of time for that." A chuckle, low, under his breath.

Trembling, Elizabeth felt the bed rock away from her, a great weight pulling it down, the body of J.B. fumbling near her. She could smell the dank clumps of his hair.

"Good night, Patrick."

"Good night," from the far end of the room.

For a moment there was quiet, and soon heavy breathing. The man, Patrick, had fallen asleep.

But J.B. had begun to roll closer to her. "Elizabeth," he whispered.

She did not answer, but pretended to be in deep slumber.

"I'll make it up to you. I promise, girl." She wished her heart would stop pounding. He lay his sweaty hand on her camisole. She didn't move. Then his breath seared her neck. *Oh please don't let him try to wake me*, she prayed. She waited, barely breathing, listening to the heavy snoring of the visitor across the room. Soon J.B. began to inhale noisily, and she knew he had fallen into deep slumber.

She could not sleep, however, She lay as still as she had ever lain in her life, her heart still pounding. In a moment, listening to the two men snoring, she let go of her own tense breath and tried to calm herself. The blood was hot in her face. How she longed to be in Kanarraville, in the loft again. Alone.

## 9
### *Friday, August 3, 1857, Jacob*

Jacob knew his father and Elizabeth would be arriving in Kanarraville today because one of the Lee boys brought news from Scoville on his way home with a load of lumber. Suky had been out in the yard with the chickens when she saw the heavy wagon lumber past. She had run to the gate and called him back. Jacob followed her.

"You seen my husband J.B. Lorry and my stepdaughter Elizabeth?"

"I reckon I did. They was spending a day in Scoville making up an order of munitions, but they should be through here sometime."

Jacob had hated to see Elizabeth go with his father, but no matter how angry he felt about some of his father's decisions, he wanted to see both of them again. And the prospect of fighting in the coming war became the hope that absorbed him more and more every day. Percy had told him that war was so imminent that Brigham Young had called for all the Indian Chiefs in the area to go up to Salt Lake City to smoke the peace pipe with him.

"We can't fight both the Indians and the U.S. Army at the same time," Percy told Jacob. "Both my father and me was asked to help Mr. Hamblin take Kanosh and a few of the other chiefs around here into Salt Lake City."

Jacob felt sick. He was angry that his father wasn't back from Salt Lake City so that he and his father might go with them.

"Somebody up north reported J.B. was bringing a commander from California with him," Percy said.

"Sounds like a war, not a wedding," Suky mumbled almost inaudibly. But Jacob heard her.

"At least he'll be back in time," Jacob said tentatively. "Maybe he'll offer to go with Brother Jensen and the Indians before it's too late."

"You aren't going," Suky said immediately.

"Percy Jensen is going."

"I doubt it."

"He is, Ma. I know it."

"You know nothing of the kind." The muscles of her face tightened. She went into the house before Jacob had a chance to comment further. She brought her knitting out on the stoop while her beans were boiling in the kettle over the fire. After a while, when Jacob got restless, he took his hoe out to the road and hoed toward Cedar, not fooling anyone, least of all Suky. She would know that he wanted to talk to his father about going with the Indians. But she was tired of contending with all of them.

Jacob finally saw the wagon at about four o'clock, a black mark in the road crawling slowly in front of a veil of dust. "They're here," he shouted, though no one heard him in the empty field. Finally he dropped the hoe and ran, not thinking how he would feel seeing Elizabeth, now his father's wife. There were three of them in the wagon. J.B. and the commander from California sat in front. Elizabeth, behind, lowered her eyes under a large sun hat, a new lawn bonnet trimmed with blue lace. She was beautiful. And quiet. He ran to her, excited. She smiled and waved.

"Elizabeth!" he called. "Elizabeth!"

The commander was a large handsome fellow with great brown eyes framed by dark waves of hair similar to his father's, though J.B. had begun to grow a little gray. The commander was also much larger than J.B. He must have stood six foot three and weighed two hundred pounds. He had been sent down by Colonel Conover and Brigham Young to help Colonel Dame in Parowan, J.B. said. What the militia needed was a man like Moore to shape them up. Moore was not a Mormon, but he was a good military man who believed in protecting the rights of the people who had made their homes in the West.

Jacob felt a chill of excitement, though he dare not breathe his own desires to his father so soon. At the supper table he burst with questions about what kinds of action Moore had seen. At one point J.B. said, "When it comes to war, I thought all an interested man had to do was grab his gun and defend himself. But Sergeant Moore says that isn't so."

"Rhythm is important in defense. The rhythm of drill."

Jacob sat on the edge of his chair.

"Following instructions to the letter can make the difference between life and death in a battle. It's skills that need to be taught, learned. Even you could learn to use a rifle as well as any man." He nodded toward Jacob. "And you ought to. It's the duty of everybody in a time of war."

Jacob glanced toward J.B., tense with hope.

"Any young man can learn," Moore said again.

J.B. chewed thoughtfully on a chunk of beef as he looked at Jacob. "Any young man can die, too," he said under his breath. But he said it so that Moore could hear it, then added, "He's older than he looks. He's barely fifteen."

Jacob's heart seemed to stop. For a moment there was silence. Suky handed a dish to Elizabeth to pass around the table.

"Will you have more stew, Mr. Moore?"

"Yes, I believe I will," Moore said. "I can't tell you how delightful this is! My first home-cooked meal in . . . well, a long time."

"Do you have a family, Mr. Moore?" Suky asked.

"Well . . ." Moore seemed slightly taken back. He glanced downward at his food. "I had a wife in California." He paused and chewed. "There was a lot of men and very few women. Someone else came along . . ." He did not continue. And no one pursued it.

"But I could learn, Pa," Jacob dared to return the subject to the war.

"If you'd like, I can work with Jacob some in private time. Make sure he knows how to do what he has to do," said Moore. Jacob's heart began to race. J.B. began picking a string of beef out of a tight space between his teeth. Jacob knew better than to push his father at times like this. He waited.

"I know how to use the rifle good," Jacob finally said, feigning nonchalance, his heart beating in his breast. "And look who you've got from here. Not more'n oh, maybe a couple dozen big men you could say shoot well from a distance . . . or at least any better 'n me. There's Murdock, and Jensen, Deany, President Haight, and of course the people from Parowan under Colonel Dame."

J.B. had stopped chewing and held a napkin to his mouth.

"I don't want to sound pessimistic, Mr. Lorry, but I'd sure be surprised if we didn't need every man your boy's size and over for the kind of war we're expected to fight here. And I'd be happy to help you train him."

J.B.'s face looked drawn. Jacob watched him carefully. Out of the corner of his eyes, he also watched both Elizabeth and Suky grow pale. Both of them stopped eating.

"You remember, Lorry?" Moore continued. "We run into that bunch of rabble rousers on horseback in the hotel that night in Salt Lake City—the hired cattlemen for the big party behind?"

Suky began to shake her head slowly. "He's still a boy," she murmured so quietly that Jacob wasn't sure he heard her. "He wants to grow up too fast. He's still a boy."

## 10

### Elizabeth

Elizabeth had watched Captain Patrick Moore sitting tall in the wagon. She had noticed the curve of his back. She had watched him lay out the bedding not too far from the cart both nights they had spent on the road. She had watched him while J.B. stood with her near the tent.

"This is not how we'll start out this marriage," he had said in a quiet speech to her. "I'll make it up to you, girl."

She had shaken her head no.

"What do you mean?"

"I don't mind," she said quickly to avoid his anger. "It's all right. I just don't mind. That's all."

"Brigham Young assigned me to host him. It wouldn't be polite not to take him with us."

"I don't mind. Really."

She had seen Jacob on the road as soon as the cart drew over the hill at Cedar City, and clearly when they drew around Hamilton's old fort. Her adopted brother Jacob stood with his hoe in his hand, looking small.

No one at the house that evening said anything about the marriage. Suky had greeted them all with narrow, searching eyes. In Moore's presence the majority of the conversation was about the war. All evening at the table they talked about equipment, drill, and how much preparation would be necessary to teach Jacob how to use a gun.

After she washed the dishes in the old bucket, Elizabeth crept quietly up the ladder to the loft and into her straw bed. She held the quilt to her cheeks and did not move for a long time, even to dress. She knew everything was different now. Finally, as the dusk deepened into blackness, and the ridge of mountains outside her loft window faded into the star-studded sky, she lit her candle and let down her hair. Though she dressed for bed as she had always done, she was aware of the texture of every piece of cloth she touched, as though that awareness would keep her grounded somehow.

Overhearing the faint rumble of talk, she believed they were still discussing Patrick Moore's war experiences. When she looked down the stairwell into the main room, she could see his hands spreading in broad gestures as J.B. questioned him. Stretching to look, she saw the bedding by the fireplace where Patrick Moore was to lie. She thought about Patrick Moore, about the tight muscles of his large back. "We're in an unusual situation," J.B. had told her. "I'll make it up to you, gal." Patrick Moore had come between them, and she had welcomed his intrusion. She rolled back into the straw. She would be asleep in a few moments.

For a time, while she continued to hear the murmur of the voices below her, her mind drifted into the vapor of half-conscious slumber. She saw the jagged hills in her dreams. They seemed to crowd toward her as though she were being shut in by the sharp corners of a great dark box that folded out the stars, blackened the sky. She saw the face of her father. He was holding her little brother in his arms. The boy who had been killed by the snake was crying out in pitiful gasps when a blurred figure in a flowing black cape fell over him. Was that the face of John Lee? Her father lay the boy on the damp ground and bent over him, sobbing into his hair.

She heard a sound on the loft ladder. She opened her eyes to search for the moon in the sky. How long had she slept? She did not know. Her heart pounded against her ribs. It was J.B. He had climbed the ladder and entered her room on light feet. Her heart pounded as he let himself down to the bed. His weight crushed the straw, his huge head loomed over her as he tore away the quilts. She gasped, suffocating in the raw power of his breath.

"Elizabeth," he whispered. "Elizabeth. I told you I'd come."

He touched her cheek and leaned over her to kiss both of her eyes, his hot body close to hers. He began pressing his hands against her waist, gently. She held her breath as he pulled her close. "I told you I'd make it up to you, girl," he whispered, his breath sucking out the air she breathed. She gasped. "Calm yourself, Elizabeth," and he pressed her, pawed at her, tore at her, until she was pressed against him—her tears hot on her cheeks. There was so much pain.


## II
### Tuesday, August 4, 1857, Elizabeth

Morning came in a hot wave over the hill. Elizabeth felt the light on her hair before she opened her eyes. The loft was empty. J.B. was not beside her now. Then she heard the voices in the yard.

She woke feeling raw, ill at ease. She would like to have forgotten what had happened in the night. But the shock of its sharp pinch still clung, aching through her whole body. As she sat up in bed she continued to hear voices out on the road. Then she was sure she heard correctly. It was J.B.

When she sat up to the loft window, she could see the men in the road on horseback. Startled, she strained to see. One of them was Jacob Hamblin, the scout whose influence among the Indians had saved them all countless difficulties. She would have recognized him anywhere—the man with the deerskin shirt.

With Hamblin was Patrick Moore, talking with his expressive hands. In front of them stood J.B. The cart was hooked up to Foresight, their mule, and looked ready to go. She stared, her eyes fixed, not knowing what could be happening. Then below her, she heard the door in the house crack open.

"God bless you, boy." Suky's voice.

"Good-bye, Mother."

Elizabeth hurried to the ladder and peered down from the loft. Jacob looked up at her from where he stood, still inside the door. He was dressed in his boots, the rifle on his back. He looked surprisingly old, but his eyes were dancing with fire. "Jacob! Where are you going?"

Jacob looked at Elizabeth with a look she had never seen before. Though he was silent, the pensive way his eyes scanned her seemed to say, "Elizabeth, look at me now."

"Let me tell her, Jacob. You run on," Suky said.

But Jacob would not let this moment pass. "George Jensen come down this morning with a fever," he said.

Elizabeth was puzzled. Suky entered with an explanation. "George and Percy were supposed to go with Jacob Hamblin to gather the Indian chiefs—take them up to Brigham Young." She added, "But George Jensen come down with a fever."

Elizabeth understood now. She stared at Jacob. He looked inches taller than she remembered. She climbed down the ladder slowly. "And so you are going," she breathed lightly to Jacob.

"J.B. and me," Jacob said, his eyes still on fire.

Elizabeth looked at Suky, who whispered, "And they're taking the wagon and the mule."

"We'll take the grain to buy some ammunition. And I'll bring the ammunition back in the wagon," Jacob said.

Suky shrugged her shoulders. "Patrick Moore's going to stay with us while they're gone. I told them we'd be okay without the menfolk. We don't have five little ones like the Jensens do."

Elizabeth didn't answer. She looked at Jacob and saw his pride. He was going with the men to do a man's job. He looked suddenly shy.

"Well, good-bye," he said uneasily. He added the words: "Aunt Elizabeth." His tongue was slow to speak her new title as his father's wife.

Elizabeth smiled, feeling old and wise. Finally she climbed down the last few steps of the ladder, rushed to him, and put her arms around his neck. His shoulders felt so narrow; his face was downy with his new beard. She kissed him on the cheek. When she drew back his eyes were misty, almost with a hidden anger, though she could not tell.

"Good-bye, Jacob," she whispered. "Take care."

## 12
### *Jacob*

Traveling the road in the August sun, relieved only by the shadowy mountains looming on either side of them, Jacob was unable to calm the thrashing of his heart. Hurrying, he had responded to the preparation of the wagon and mule with impressive speed. Because he had known where everything was in the darkness, he was ready before Hamblin or his father had grown impatient.

Sergeant Moore stood for a few moments with them by the wagon, talking with them about their journey. They would stop and pick up as many of the chiefs as they could successfully talk into going to Brigham Young. On their way to take the Indians to Salt Lake City, they would stop and leave the grain in Scipio to pay for a load of arms. On their way back they would pick up the guns and ammunition and take them to Cedar City. The trick would be to haul the goods without letting the Missourians, or the Indians, know.

"We'll have to hide the guns under hay and cover them with a tarp," J.B. said.

Good luck to you," Moore had said, saluting, clicking his heels.

When Jacob returned to the house to say good-bye to Suky one more time, he knew the main reason he had returned was to see Elizabeth. As she climbed down from the loft, she was not fully awake. Her disheveled brown hair framed her white face. Jacob stood in the door—tried to keep his heart from bumping.

"Where are you going?" she had said—as if it mattered to her.

*Does it matter to you, Elizabeth, what happens to me?* he thought. But for a moment he did not say anything. He stood in the door, conscious of the sun on his back, his deerskin shirt, and the boots.

"Good-bye, Aunt Elizabeth," he finally said. And then she had come to him with that faint vaporous freshness of rose water and wrapped her arms about his neck. "Good-bye, Jacob," she whispered to him until every part of his body throbbed. "Good-bye. Take care." She had kissed his cheek. He would never forget it.

When he released her, he felt dizzy in the morning light, and cold where her warmth had so briefly burned. Good-bye, Elizabeth, he had said over and over to himself as Foresight stepped out on the road to Cedar City. The rhythmic clop-clop of the mule's hooves accompanied the beat of his heart jerking inside of his chest. Good-bye, Elizabeth. The leather of the rifle sling cut into his shoulder. Jacob felt the bite of the rifle's steel. He thought of Percy at home with his father George, who was ill. He could not believe his good fortune—that he had been invited to make this pilgrimage to see Brigham Young.

## 13
### Jacob

It was not the usual scorching August day. Some clouds rolled up from the west looking a little black along the edges.

"Could be a midsummer storm," J.B. predicted. The air was heavy. Jacob was sweating more than he had during the entire journey. His hair was plastered down under J.B.'s hat. Even the Indians seemed uncomfortable, often shifting on the bare backs of their ponies.

They picked up Ow-Wan-Op at Kanosh. In the wake of the news that the Missouri Wildcats—the cattlemen to the big train—were not far away, Jacob felt some safety when the old gray-headed chief in broken English said, "If Mericats come here, we kill them before they kill you." Jacob would never forget the dark faces that surrounded them—the few young braves with stern, knit brows. He had never liked Indians, but in that moment of Ow-Wan-Op's pledge of alliance, he felt a surge of admiration and gratitude.

"You come and tell that to Brigham Young," Agent Hamblin said warmly. Old Ow-Wan-Op had joined them without a moment's hesitation. Some of the others had been more difficult to lure away. Hamblin stopped long enough to chat and smoke with them, making it seem like a social event, not a summons for military action. Jacob and J.B. often waited for several hours seated on the hot cart before the Indians were ready to go.

It was only a few days into the journey that, as they crossed the meadow and rounded a bend, Hamblin first caught sight of the Missouri cowboys. A couple of men on horseback advanced rapidly, stirring the dust. When the travelers caught sight of Hamblin, the mounted Indians alongside, and the wagon carrying J.B. and Jacob, they hung back momentarily.

"How up!" one of the men called as he neared. He raised his hand in greeting and waved. "How!" But he did not stop. Instead, he increased his speed. As he drew close, he let out a strange curdling cry. The man who followed the first rider slowed considerably and nodded as he passed them, peering at the Indians curiously from beneath his bushy brows.

"A couple of outsiders, all right," J.B. murmured, gathering this information from his sharp observations of the saddle, style of bit and bridle, hat and a pair of silver spurs.

Only moments later, the same two men returned, passing them from behind in another thick cloud of hot dust.

"Those men are scouts," Hamblin observed.

"Pshaw," J.B. gasped, fanning with his hand. "They kick up enough dust to bury an army. What are they trying to prove?"

"Har!" Jacob could hear the first man growl to his horse. As Hamblin's party reached the crest of the hill, they could see the rest of the Missouri travelers on the horizon now, a group of six or more lumbering wagons drawn by bedraggled oxen along the middle of the road. They looked like scattered toys, small, harmless in the distance, the sheep and cattle swarming about them like beetles and flies.

"That must be them Missouri Wildcats, all right," said J.B. "Though I can't recognize none of them. It was dark when I saw them in the streets of Salt Lake City. I guess I heard they was followed by a huge train." Hamblin kept an even pace as they pressed forward in the narrow road.

"Yyy-up!" the man on his horse could be heard to yell. "Yyy-up!" And soon the settlers, whipping their animals, struggled forward in grim silence, never moving a single wagon aside for Hamblin and the Indians. Hamblin indicated to J.B. that he should draw the cart off the road while the Missourians passed.

"They are a rough-looking bunch," J.B. said under his breath to Jacob. Jacob stared as the wagons lumbered by. There were only two or three pale women in brown dresses. The rest seemed to be bearded, sun-hardened men.

"That's it, Mormons! Stand aside for Missouri!" one of the men cursed, baring his white teeth and tossing his grizzly head until Jacob could see the black hair on his neck. His throaty laugh filled the air as though he were echoing thunder. J.B. snapped the whip so close to the wagon that Foresight jumped.

Jacob, who sat on the wagon and held the reins, tightened them now. "Easy, girl," he cried.

"The dregs of Missouri," J.B. murmured under his breath. "The Wildcats."

It took nearly an hour for the company to pass. Stirring the dust up into clouds, Missourian after Missourian trampled past, scorn written in each face. With the last wagon, Jacob sensed that everyone in the Mormon party began to breathe more easily again. They might have continued their travels in a pleasant way if they had not seen the boy on the other side of the bend.

About half a mile away, a young boy stood at the edge of the road beating the sage with a stick, dirty tears streaking down his cheeks. Brother Hamblin saw that it was his cousin's son, Serjay Seymour. When he stopped his horse and dismounted, the boy broke into fresh tears.

"They gone and killed my calf," he cried to Hamblin in gulps. "I was walkin' with my calf and they was shootin' around and shot it in the leg. Then somebody hollers to put it out of its misery and they blasted out its brains."

Jacob felt the taste of bile come up into his throat.

Facing the twelve-year-old boy, Hamblin laid a hand on his shoulder. "Why don't you come back to Scipio with us, Serjay? It's going to rain."

The boy stared at the Indians, then at Jacob and J.B. He did not say anything else. When he returned his eyes to his uncle again, there were more tears.

Hamblin scooped the boy into his arms and lifted him to the back of the saddle. "Hold on tight around my waist," he said. The boy leaned his cheek against Hamblin's shirt as the party started up again. They had traveled only a few feet when, in the grass by the side of the road, they saw the bloody body of the boy's calf.

# 14
## *Jacob*

As they drove through Scipio, Jacob could feel the eyes of the townspeople staring at them out of the windows. The children in the front yards ran behind the horses, whispering to each other about the Indians, pointing and shouting questions at Serjay.

The trek through town, an embarrassing parade, took forever. At last Hamblin stopped at a house on the north side of town, a clapboard two-story white-washed home standing in a wide empty field.

"I'm so glad you got here safely," Hamblin's cousin greeted them. Althea Seymour was a horse-faced woman with a thick waist and large worn hands. She was happy to see them, she said over and over again, and she led them into the front room and insisted—boots, dust and all—that they sit for a time to talk. When the Indians dismounted, however, she looked at them warily and pointed them toward the barn.

This house was one of the few Jacob Lorry had ever seen with a polished wood floor. He felt self-conscious as he followed J.B. and Hamblin into the cool room. The thin white curtains at the window allowed only a shadowy sunlight to play over the few small scattered rugs, the overstuffed sofa and chairs, the white walls. At the two doorways, the eyes of voyeurs began to appear. A few of the Seymour children were bold enough to wander into the room and sit down. One of them was a girl about Jacob's age, her face almost hidden by dazzling black curls.

While the visitors sat and waited for a cool drink to come, Jacob grew uncomfortable when he realized the girl was staring at him. She sat in the deep sofa next to Brother Hamblin. Serjay sat on the floor. Jacob heard the others call the girl Maggie, sometimes Margaret. Her hair was her best feature. She was not ugly, but not pretty, either, he thought. Not like Elizabeth. The sudden thought of Elizabeth wounded him, but he put it away.

Margaret seemed a combination of paradoxes. He knew she was young, but she looked older than her years. Though her limbs were slender, her waist seemed thick. He thought she looked rather out of proportion. If he had been better acquainted with women's conditions, he might have guessed why. Her hands were large like her mother's, but much less worn-looking, without a blemish.

Jacob knew Margaret was eyeing him. But if he glanced her way when her mother left the room, she would quickly cast her eyes on her Uncle Jacob Hamblin and his friends. When her mother called her, she ignored the voice from the kitchen the first two times. Her rudeness was none of Jacob's business; still, it stuck in his craw. Finally, on the third call, she rose heavily off the sofa and disappeared into the other room. When she brought cookies to Jacob, she smiled at him, though she never said a word.

He took a cookie while he was trying to pay attention to what the men were saying now. But he had lost part of the conversation.

"Well, if Proctor goes with your boy to take the ammunition to Cedar, you might as well let Margaret travel with you at least as far as Sadie's in Fillmore," Mrs. Seymour was saying as she entered the room carrying a tray that held empty teacups and saucers on a scallop of doilies. Her face seemed suddenly expressionless, almost gray. She looked like an old woman too worn to speak of war, of guns.

Jacob wondered what he had missed. They had been making plans, and he had been paying attention to the irritating girl. Though he had only vaguely heard

Mrs. Seymour's words to J.B. and Brother Hamblin, he could more than feel the tension in the dark room, the edgy voice that stayed high and thin in the woman's throat. But the words began to come more clearly to him as he realized what was happening, though he could not believe it.

"Yes, of course. And I'll go with Brother Hamblin and the chiefs," J.B. said, not noticing the glaze in Jacob's eyes.

"What?" Jacob dared to ask, waking from his reverie.

"I'm going on into Salt Lake City with Hamblin and the Indians," J.B. said. "You and Proctor here will take the wagon back to Cedar City with the guns under the hay. That will save time." Not waiting for Jacob to respond, he turned back to Mrs. Seymour, who seemed anxious to finish the arrangements.

"That would be fine," Mrs. Seymour allowed. "And Margaret can ride back with you two at least as far as Fillmore," she said in an unnaturally high-pitched voice.

Jacob couldn't believe what he was hearing. With hardly a blink, J.B. was leaving Jacob to fend practically for himself. Of course, Margaret and her older brother, Proctor Seymour, would be there. But they would be traveling with all of those guns! All kinds of images closed in on Jacob. Hamblin and his father were sending him back with Proctor and the ammunition alone. And a girl.

"That's all right with you, boy, ain't it?" J.B. asked Jacob, already knowing the answer.

"Sure," Jacob said, shaking, but not betraying his surprise.

"Then we'll do it that way," Hamblin said.

"And Proctor would like to see if he can find his girl in either Beaver or Parowan, marry her, and take her to Cedar, or Penter." Mrs. Seymour was addressing Hamblin now. "If you have some extra space down there, could you set him up in a farm near to you?"

J.B. smiled now. "You've got a girl in Beaver, Proctor?"

"Someplace down there. Beaver or Parowan." The mother spoke for her son.

Jacob examined Proctor now, a big boy with a prominent nose. He was so dark he looked half foreign, like an Arab or a Jew. So he was going down to find his girl? They decided he would ride his mare, his most valuable possession, which would also make it possible for him to haul a saddle-pack to carry the rest of his belongings.

Althea held her hands in her lap, anxiously pulling on her fingers. "We wanted a family wedding for Proctor, but it will do if he just marries Emma at

Uncle Edward's in Cedar. It will be good of you to help me get this boy settled down," she said in her nervous high-pitched voice. "And Maggie . . ." She paused now, unable to go on.

"Yes, of course," Jacob Hamblin said finally, nodding. "Of course . . ."

By that time, Margaret had come back into the room with the Brigham tea. As she spooned the sugar into the teacups, there was a heavy silence for a long time. That night Jacob slept on a pallet out by the porch. He had slept well on the ground before, but tonight he lay awake under the stars.

**15**

*Saturday, August 8, 1857, Jacob*

Jacob, feeling exhausted by morning, heard the wheels of the wagon bringing the arms. Looking up from his bed on the ground he could see an old farmer sitting high on his wagon seat, lumbering down the road to the Seymour house.

"Halloo!" the farmer waved to them.

Jacob scrambled to his feet, light-headed, sure this was the farmer who carried the guns. He couldn't remember when he had felt so alive. He keenly felt his father's trust—the grave responsibility of transporting these arms to Cedar City. He felt drawn to the ammunition as though it were more precious than gold. When he saw his father approach the wagon, he slowed his pace just so that his father would not guess how anxious he was to look.

Some of the guns in the load were new. As the men sifted through the rifles, they let the names slip across their tongues like silk rope—music to Jacob's ears. Jacob memorized the names. He wanted so badly to hold one of the rifles in his hands. It seemed he could taste the gun powder on his tongue.

While he fastened his eyes on the guns, he was only vaguely aware that J.B. was fetching Foresight from the barn. When they began to clear out the wagon to make room for the new cargo, J.B. emptied the wagon box of a pair of stirrups, an extra pair of boots, and a pair of chaps. He would put these items on top of the guns and under the hay, he said. There could be no guessing by strangers if they should come and lift the tarp. They would see the boots and the stirrups, but they must never see the guns.

"Well, now you got guns available to the citizens of Cedar City," the old farmer said. "To get the job done," he emphasized. *The job?* Jacob thought to himself. *The Job.*

Chewing on a straw, the old man continued to bend their ears. "I tell you, comin' down here, right in front of me the whole time was that hired party—them Missouri Wildcats. They've gone on down the road by now. But right behind me the whole time was the ones that hired them—that huge train from Arkansas going to catch up with them—the Fancher party. They been asking for supplies." The old farmer scratched his head beneath his cap. "And of course, instructions are we're not to sell them nothing now. And now they've put up their big camp just out of town."

Hamblin's face clouded with concern. "You're lucky nothing's happened yet, brother," he said.

"I'm lucky. But my horse ain't so lucky," the farmer said. He was still holding his hat, his fingers still working against his scalp. "She died this morning."

"Your horse died?"

The old man's eyes narrowed now, as though he did not want to dwell on the subject. "She took a drink out of a bad spring. I think they poisoned it. Put poison in the spring."

Poison in the spring? Jacob watched Hamblin's eyes focus on the farmer for what seemed like an eternity. "You don't think . . ." he began.

The old farmer was not sure. So he shrugged his shoulders. "Yes, I do think that's what it was."

Finally, when they packed hay over the guns and gun powder, and tied the tarp securely over it all, the wagon was ready to go. Jacob watched the new guns disappear under the hay, the stirrups, and the tarp. He would never have let his father know how much of a lump lay in his stomach now.

Althea Seymour stuffed packets of food in a bag for Margaret and Proctor. She had even added some sandwiches for Jacob. She accompanied her gifts with a natural motherly concern. "Now, I hope it don't rain," she clucked, making last-minute adjustments to Margaret's bag and her hat strings. It had been threatening to rain since yesterday, though not a drop had fallen. "Be good now, Margaret. Remember what I told you about Aunt Sadie not feeling well. Be a help to her."

Margaret nodded dutifully and bounced up into the cart beside Jacob, not seeming in the least bit shy. He was struck by a strong—and not unpleasant—perfume.

J.B., holding the bridle of a borrowed horse, stood with Hamblin and the Indians on the other side of the drive. "Good luck, boy," J.B. called. "In case of trouble, you've got guns. Which you shouldn't be afraid to use."

Jacob nodded, hardly believing what he and Proctor had been charged to do. He wasn't sure he was hearing right. It seemed his father had changed overnight. He was not sure what he would do if the opportunity to use the guns should arise. But if it came, he knew he would not fail to take it.

There were kisses and shouts between Margaret and Mrs. Seymour and finally the little children, especially Serjay, who looked sullen because he could not go with his big brother Proctor to their Uncle Hamblin's ranch.

"Good-bye! Good-bye!" Mrs. Seymour shouted, waving so vigorously that her large bosom bounced up and down.

As the wagon moved out, Jacob noticed that Proctor, mounting his big horse, kicked it in the belly. He saw Mr. Seymour stare after his son, but the older man said nothing.

Jacob knew J.B. wasn't much for good-byes, but this one seemed to loom much larger than any they had ever said before. As he waved, Jacob watched his father's party head in the direction of Salt Lake City with the Indians.

Soon the distance broadened between them. The Indians on their horses had fallen behind J.B. in a somber line.

## 16

### *Jacob*

Because Proctor rode separately on his mare, Jacob found himself on the seat of the wagon, alone with the girl. He was not sure whether he felt shy because he was attracted or dismayed. At first she did not talk. Jacob was not sure why. She answered any questions he asked her with simple answers.

"Doesn't your brother know exactly where his girlfriend lives?"

"No," she said, and lapsed into silence.

"Why is that?" Jacob felt forced to ask.

"She left here and didn't write."

"Oh." Jacob did not try to say anything else. They continued in quiet, making good progress on the Sabbath day. It was August 9. Proctor rode ahead of them, occasionally moving away from the road, trekking into surrounding washes and farms. He reached Fort Buttermilk long before they did, and they found him waiting at a spring, squatting on the ground skinning a dead cow. Remembering Serjay's dead little calf, Jacob wondered if the settlers had killed this full grown cow. But after looking at it for a moment, he could see that it had not died from gun wounds, but some sickness. It was swollen into a balloon-shaped mass, with its legs bulging from the bloat like huge misshapen hayforks.

"Somebody's left this carcass to rot, and its hide is still good as new," Proctor exclaimed, peeling the thick skin away from the flesh with his knife.

"Oh, no, Proctor!" Margaret drew back and gasped. "Leave it alone! It belongs to somebody!"

"There are two of them," Proctor said, nodding his head to a clump of sage on the other side. Another hideous swollen animal lay behind a clump of brush as though to hide the embarrassment of its death.

"It still isn't yours, and none of your business!" Margaret continued to cry out, tightening her pink fingers into fists, bringing her fists to her cheeks.

Proctor drew a good section of the hide off the animal without a blush of shame. When it began to rain, he held the palm of his hand flat to determine how much was falling.

"At least I got this much before the storm," he said, rolling it and tying it to the back of his mare's saddle.

Margaret unsnapped her umbrella and whipped it over her head. "You shouldn't have done it, Proctor." She reminded Jacob of his mother, Suky.

Now the rain began to fall in steady drops over the spring.

"You see, just in time," Proctor said, leaping to his horse and staring up into the sky. He was hit by large drops and began to rub them out of his eyes.

When the rain began to pour, Margaret moved her umbrella to cover Jacob. That was nice of her, he thought. But soon not only the umbrella, but the girl under it moved also, sitting so close to him on the cart that a shock went up the back of his spine. And yet, it was a pleasant feeling. She was soft, still smelling of perfume. Very close, now, she began clinging to his elbow with her free hand. Jacob felt alarmed.

In a few moments, drenched with rain, Proctor came to ride his mare closer to the cart. As the rain fell on his face, he began rubbing his eyes with his fingers.

"My dumb eyes is swelling shut with this rain. I can't see a thing," Proctor said at last.

Jacob saw that Proctor's face was beginning to swell. And there was no relief from the rain.

"I can't see a thing," Proctor complained again. "Lorry, I'm going to ride on as fast as I can into Fillmore. My face is swol' up and I can't see a thing."

There was no question that something was seriously wrong.

"Oh my," Margaret was wailing in between little gasps. "Ride fast, Proctor.

Get to Aunt Sadie's. We must make it, even in the rain." She grabbed Jacob's entire arm at that moment, and buried her face into his shoulder, still holding the umbrella above them. Raising her knees, she knotted herself up. "Oh, I hate this rain."

Jacob could not sort out his thoughts as he watched Proctor's horse ride off through the distance. He felt a shade of panic. And, soon, as the distance widened between them, he began to feel a full-fledged fear.

Though he rode with Margaret in silence for another mile, the girl was soon gripping him like a cat held over water. All they heard in the silence was the tap tap of water on the cart's tarp behind them, the wheels, and the soft clop clop of the mule. Soon Jacob heard a sniffling sound and the sound of harsh breathing. And though at first he could not know for sure, he soon realized that Margaret was crying, her hands still gripping his arm.

His mouth clamped shut. He did not know what to do with a girl in tears. His immediate decision was to do nothing. Without a word he continued toward Fillmore in the rain. But soon, when the sobs began to shake the curls against his shoulder, he believed he ought to make some attempt to say something.

"We're almost there," he tried.

She burst into sobs. "Oh, I am so miserable." Immediately he wished he could recall his words, for they had only increased her dismay.

"We'll be there soon," he found himself trying again.

"No we won't. Fillmore's still four or five miles away."

"We'll stop here, then."

Her hand tightened on his arm. "No, you will not," she blurted with renewed vigor, the tears falling on her cheeks and draining from her pointed chin down to his shirt, her hands, and the umbrella handle below.

Jacob did not know why he touched her hand, except that it seemed the natural thing to do. He placed his left hand over hers and stroked it as gently as though she were a kitten. At once the sobs seemed to subside. At last one of her hands came up to her cheek and brushed her tears away.

"That's better," he said, as though he were her father and encouraging her to be brave.

But he may have been too convincing, for she began asking difficult questions. "Do you believe in God?" She turned her face toward his now, a face framed by the shiny dark hair and the gray rain.

Jacob paused, taken off guard. He had never questioned the existence of God. God had brought them to this place. Everyone he knew worshipped God with no questions. "Well, yes," he stammered. "Don't you believe in God?"

"No, not anymore. He brought us to the state of Deseret. Brigham Young said, 'Give us ten years.' Well, the ten years are up and the army is still coming. And the Missourians. Do you know what they did?" Now she whispered. Jacob had to strain to hear her. "One of 'em done it to me. And I'll kill him if I see him again."

The shock rippled through Jacob like the shot of a gun. Of course he knew the Missourians were capable of such an act. He had heard of it—often. He dare not ask the details. At a loss for words, he could not speak. "You mean . . . ?"

"Yes, he done this to me," she said. "That's what this is." She lay her hand on her belly. "Please take me to Fillmore," she said quietly now. "No matter how much it rains."

When the mule drove into Fillmore, Margaret was asleep on Jacob's arm. Though he lifted her gently, she awoke with a cry.

"It's dark," she said, frightened.

"And you've been asleep," he whispered.

"Oh, Jacob," she said softly, pressing her hands against his arm again. "Don't leave me. Stay with us at Fillmore. I'm afraid."

Jacob's heart leaped again. He couldn't do that. "Your brother's here. Your aunt's family is here," he said.

"But the Arkansas settlers are close by. And there's lots of them," she shuddered. "I'm afraid."

"It'll be all right," Jacob patted her hand. "Now show me where your Aunt Sadie lives."

But Margaret was no help, for she buried her face against his shoulder and closed her eyes. Finally it was Jacob who caught sight of Proctor's horse still saddled, drooping in the rain, standing down a side street in front of a modest, freshly shingled pine home. He turned and drove to the fence, slipping Foresight's rein through the wooden slats.

When he stopped, Margaret finally raised her eyes. "This is it! This is it!" she nodded. She picked up her needlepoint bag and wasted no time in stepping off the wagon down to the road. Before she turned up the path, she waited for Jacob to come around. When he reached her, she stood in front of him, not allowing him to pass. The gaze in her dark eyes was a hungry one. She was not pretty, he thought, but he admitted there was charm in her mouth.

"Jacob . . . it is so hard to say." She still held the umbrella in her arm.

"Let's get out of the rain," he said.

But she shook her head and dropped her bundle and the umbrella to the ground. Flinging her arms about his neck, she pulled his face to hers. She held his head and reached for his mouth, bringing her lips to his lips.

Jacob was stunned. When he caught her by the wrists to draw her away, she managed to pull his hands down. At first her lips were cutting to him, and then softer, and finally almost warm. He found that he was responding, stroking her hair with his hands.

When she drew away, he saw an impish gaze in her eyes. "There. That is how I say thank you for all you have done for me," she said.

When she pulled away, Jacob missed her warmth, and for a brief moment almost wished she would kiss him again.

"Will you kiss me again?" she asked.

He did not have a choice, he thought. She pulled his head between her hands and tugged at his mouth with her lips, warming his chin. "Thank you, Jacob," she said.

Startled at his own response, Jacob tasted her kiss again while they stood together in the driving rain, until he grew conscious that someone must have been watching them through the window. When he finally had enough nerve to look that way, he saw not one, but two faces withdraw from the glass. He backed away from Margaret, feeling embarrassed.

The fact that someone was watching did not bother Margaret at all. She pulled away from his embrace, laughing silently to herself. Then suddenly, without a further word, she bent to retrieve the bag and the umbrella. Cradling them close in her arms, she turned and hurried toward the door.

On their way into the one-story house, they found Margaret's Aunt Sadie and Uncle George waiting. No one said a word about what had happened out by the wagon. The elderly couple hugged Margaret and shook Jacob's hand.

Jacob noticed the furnishings of the house—a worn French sofa in gold brocade, a large cane rocker near the black stove. Close to the high ceiling, a plate rail held a row of porcelain figurines.

Yes, Proctor was here. He was sleeping in the back room, Sadie told Margaret. He had arrived only a few hours ago, very ill. There was certainly some question as to whether or not the condition of his eyes would keep him from going on with Jacob into Beaver or Parowan to find his bride-to-be.

"More cattle was found dead up to the spring," Uncle George Halliday was saying. "We think it was the Missouri Wildcats that put poison in it." Uncle George had a deep voice, a rasp that sounded as though it came from somewhere in his throat rather than his mouth. "When they poisoned the spring, someone said some Indians was killed. The Fancher party coming along just behind them Wildcats was also poisoning the spring when the Saints wouldn't give them no supplies. They are a few miles behind you, waiting out the rain at the meadow now. I know because my hired boy just come from there."

Jacob heard a desperate tone in Uncle George Halliday's words.

"President Smith come through here a few days ago and praised us up and down for getting our troops ready for war. The first word the brethren give to fight, we're ready. We are ready to surprise them all if necessary."

Jacob felt so weary he could not work up much emotion at this point—not even fear. His main concern was that he must get some rest so that he and Proctor could travel as far as they could the next day. Every bone in his body felt sore and he barely got through the meal of fried potatoes and squash before his limbs drooped, almost paralyzed.

No one suggested rest. Margaret's Aunt Sadie, a rough-hewn mountain woman, seemed not to notice that Jacob was tired. She did not fuss over Proctor, though she dutifully honored his hoarse throaty calls from the back bedroom when he clamored out for a drink of water. Finally, Jacob felt that he had to ask where he could lie down. He felt half dead, and his legs were about to buckle under him. Reluctantly, Sadie took him to the back bedroom where Proctor lay, and pointed out to him the other half of Proctor's double bed. When he looked at the only sleeping space they could give him, he felt a little sick. Proctor lay on the far pillow, a mound of flesh with a face as swollen as a gray mushroom.

"I don't have no other place for you to sleep, Mr. Lorry. Proctor's eyes is just swollen up with some kind of poison. It won't be catching, and anyways, he's sleeping and he won't wake up for the night. I'm sure of it."

Because he had not slept the night before, Jacob went out like a light. Nothing—not Proctor's big bones or his raspy wheeze, or the eternal tap of the rain on the roof—could keep Jacob awake. In moments he was in a leaden sleep too deep to admit even dreams.

## 17

### Saturday, August 29, 1857, Jacob

When Jacob first woke and listened for sounds, he heard nothing. Even the din of the rain had stopped entirely. A gray light filtered through the window. At first, he had to orient himself, to move through the events of yesterday so he could analyze what lay ahead of him. For a long moment he studied the flowered paper on the ceiling in the back room. Already, the rain had marked it with water tracks.

His next thought was that Proctor needed to wake up. Though the bed was supposed to fit two people, it seemed very small. Jacob could barely get out of the mound of soft bedding without jarring the huge body next to him. He felt the weight of Proctor's bones, the heavy dark head on the pillow. He hated to wake him. But he knew Proctor was a slow mover. And he would especially be slow if the swelling had not yet gone all the way down.

"Proctor," he whispered. He touched the swollen arm lying on the coverlet. The arm felt cold. He pressed it more firmly. It felt like meat kept for a few days in an underground cellar.

A sharp taste of bile stung in Jacob's throat. He could not hear Proctor's breathing. "Proctor!" he said again, with more urgency, and he began to shake the boy. "Proctor." There was nothing. Jacob sat up in the bed, terrified. He pulled the wooden head toward him. The gray flesh was swollen like a chair cushion, puffed beyond recognition around the nose and the mouth. Blood had poured from his eyes and dried in a shriveled crust. "Proctor! Oh! Have mercy!" Jacob breathed. Proctor was dead.

Swallowing hard, Jacob moved swiftly out of the bed and pulled on his pants and shoes. His heart beating hard, and his mind working, he dashed into the middle of the house. Sadie, sleepy-eyed, was heating the frying pan over the stove in the kitchen. She looked up, her hair in disarray.

"Did you and Proctor get any rest, Jacob?"

Jacob took hold of himself. "Yes. I was tired," he said uneasily. He told himself he must tell her what had happened, but for some reason, the moment seemed to pass. In her lethargy, she turned toward the frying pan away from him, and for a moment she did not ask any more questions.

"Help yourself to them two eggs. The skillet warn't hot enough. Proctor's probably still sleeping. He was so sick he needs it. We won't bother him yet, poor boy." Then she turned to Jacob again. "You going to wait out the weekend until he's better, Mr. Lorry?"

"Uh . . ." he began. He could not be sure what possessed him, except that he was dizzy. And he knew he wanted to get out of there. "I've decided I ought to be going on alone."

"You can't wait for Proctor to get well?" she squinted at Jacob.

When she put the eggs before him on a plate, he was not sure he could eat them. But he tried. The food dropped like cold lead into his stomach. He gulped the milk.

"I'd never go on alone if I was you with all that ammunition. There's both Indians and Missourians on the road."

"I just can't stay," Jacob rasped.

She stared at him now, then twisted her mouth into a faint smile, a glint in her eyes. "Don't have nothin' to do with my niece Margaret, does it?" The smile became a grin. "I saw you kissing her by the wagon."

Jacob felt cold. He could not deny that Margaret's presence here had helped him make the decision. He knew she was in the loft at this very moment, hopefully sound asleep. "I just can't stay. They need the ammunition in Cedar City. I got to get down there." He stood up and grabbed his sack of belongings. Sadie followed him to the door.

"She's sweet on you. There's no question about that, young man," she beamed, waving the hotcake spatula. "She'll be disappointed you left without saying good-bye."

"It's best," Jacob assured her. "Tell her good-bye for me."

Quickly, he fed Foresight and hooked her up to the wagon. He checked the rifles and the ammunition to see if it was still dry under the straw. All was still in good condition. While the tarp was off the load, he took a moment to linger over the guns, running his hands along the smooth barrels, wondering, if the time came, whether or not he would be able to load the stock and spring the trigger? The metal felt like silk under his hand. He pulled more of the straw and hay over the firearms, stashed his bag, and took time to tie down the tarp.

Every moment he worked, he felt the house was alive with eyes from the windows where Margaret, Sadie, or George might be watching. He could not help but picture in his mind that moment when Sadie would go into the bedroom and find that her nephew was dead. He wondered what she would do. Would she scream? Or would she treat it with the same nonchalance she had treated everything else? He shuddered and urged the mule to go.

The morning seemed stagnant. In the dead quiet, Foresight made good time until almost noon. It was then that he saw them—the main party, the huge Fancher train—moving down the road ahead of him with a vast herd of cattle and sheep, and nearly a dozen wagons. Feeling his hair stand on his neck like wire, he whisked the mule forward. He planned to skirt the company—he hoped without mishap. But "out of the frying pan into the fire" was an old cliche J.B. had always used. Jacob hoped it wasn't always true.

He slowed the mule as he saw the huge train filling the road for half a mile. There was no way he could skirt it. And there was no turning back. He slowed, but kept his animal steadily moving forward. Finally, at one point, he stopped the cart and just waited, watching the train crawl like a giant lizard down the draw. At his back he still felt Margaret's breath. Before him moved an impregnable hostile army. With his heart pounding hard, he sat on the cart in plain sight, feeling dangerously exposed. Finally, when the last party in the train spotted him, his scalp froze. He held his breath. The man was on foot. Seeing Jacob, he walked back to him.

"What are you selling, brother?"

Words stuck in Jacob's throat. His voice sounded weak. "I'm not selling nothing."

"What is it you got in your wagon?"

Now he felt raw panic. He was silent. He felt his stomach churn, empty now of the half fried eggs he had eaten this morning.

"If you got any grain, we'll buy some. None of your Mormon friends around here wants to sell us nothing."

Jacob's tongue felt swollen. As difficult as it might be for the travelers, Jacob knew the Mormon people would be obedient to the authorities who had asked them not to sell supplies to the wagon trains. He was silent.

"You got grain?"

Jacob shook his head.

"What you got, then?" Now the man came to the load and tugged at the tarp, though Jacob had re-secured it. All the traveler could lift was a flap, and he saw the straw.

"It's just a load of hay," Jacob said, feeling his throat tighten. For a moment he prayed, but only in his mind, "Dear God, please . . ."

The man was not a tall man. He was stocky, well built. He was not as rough a traveler as some Jacob had seen. Though he was not shaven, his beard looked neat, as though it had been combed. His hair, reddish brown, lay at a modest length against the collar of his open shirt. And he carried the whip as though he were a gentleman who knew exactly how to use it. He placed the flap of the tarp back against the hay.

"Where you headed?"

Jacob's mouth was dry. "Parowan. Cedar City."

"You're goin' our way, then?"

Jacob nodded, trying to smile. He shook the reins at Foresight.

"We wasn't going this far south," the man said, "but it's so late we don't want to get caught in the snow like that Donner party done. You heard of the Donner party?"

Jacob sat still, nodding slightly. He had heard a little about them. They had been caught in a snowstorm in the Sierras and hundreds of them had died. In their hunger they had begun to eat each other. A wave of terror rippled through him.

"You one of them Mormons?"

By now Jacob had urged the mule forward behind the man's wagon at the end of the train.

"Yes, I am," Jacob said, still frightened.

"Oh well." The man paused, lowering his eyes to the dirt he was kicking up with his feet. Finally he raised his head. "You got any influence with them? Could you talk them into anything? They're swarming the place, but you can't find no whiskey nor a plug o' tobacco, let alone food. We got money, but nobody will sell us nothing. The last few days we been forced to eat our own cattle. We got quite a few, but they ain't gonna last us all the way to the Pacific Ocean."

Jacob thought it looked as though they had enough cattle, but he wasn't going to argue with them.

"You're just a kid, ain't ya?"

Jacob felt his skin crawl as the mule drew closer to the train. He felt the huge presence of the Arkansas company on the landscape as though it were a hungry giant searching for its prey. The man on foot had fallen into a rhythmic stride beside Foresight. He talked to Jacob as though he were not a stranger anymore.

"Say, you know anything about these Indians around here?"

"There is Kanosh Indians on the creek. We just stopped there on our way up."

"You friendly with the Indians?"

Jacob shrugged his shoulders. "Try to be." He didn't know much about the Indians, but he had seen the Kanosh camp when Hamblin picked up their chief.

The man beside him searched his eyes and curled the whip into his hands out of habit. "We don't know exactly where we stand with the Indians," he said.

Jacob did not speak. His strategy was silence, and all he could do was pray that it was working.

"They must be getting along pretty good with you Mormons?"

Of course the stranger wanted something. But Jacob would play dumb.

Finally, to keep the conversation going, the man asked something he expected that Jacob would know. "You got any family?"

Jacob nodded. "In Kanarraville."

"Never heard of it."

"There is a lot of towns from here to Santa Clara."

"All Mormon towns, I guess." The man played with the whip in his hands and surveyed the moving wagons before him. "We are going as fast as we can. I'll be glad to get out o' this Mormon country." His voice seemed far away.

They moved in silence after that. From the man's wagon ahead of them, Jacob saw two tow heads occasionally poking through the back canvas: a boy and a smaller girl. When the wagon turned on a curve, Jacob could see a woman on the wooden seat, holding the leather reins. She wore a blue and white bonnet. From her chin to her lap she was swollen with child.

*The child riding inside of that body at this moment would be born any day,* Jacob thought, *a child of Deseret.*

"Robert!" the woman called. "What are you doing?"

The man walking beside Jacob looked at him briefly. "I've got to go now. My wife . . . I need to keep close," he said. And then he added: "You won't find our party favorable to Mormons. But if you want to travel with, us I suppose it's all right. And if you want to think about it . . . If you'd ask your Mormon friends if they would sell us some of their grain, I'd pay you for it."

Jacob nodded. As he watched the man walk forward, he slowed the mule. From a distance he watched the party progress at a snail's speed. It looked as though the entire countryside was moving. He let his eyes close slightly until there was a blur.

They are going in the same direction I am going. Nothing has happened. Step by step I am covering the road to home . . .

He thought to himself, if he traveled with the Fancher train, there might be some protection. He would not count on it, but he thought it might be his good fortune to travel with them if he kept a good distance behind.

When they stopped just before dusk, he stopped not far from them. Tonight there was no rain, but an almost crisp stillness in the air—an atmosphere sharpened by yesterday's storm.

Even before he unrolled his blankets on the ground, he saw the sight that both he and the settlers feared. Indians. At first he saw only the tops of heads appearing above the gentle slope of the far hill, bobbing like the movement of leaves. But then he saw that they were full heads with bodies and that they were coming his way. He could soon see their faces in the dusk. He watched them rise fully mounted over the curve of the hill toward the sheep.

Jacob had never been able to distinguish one tribe from another. Even though he had just taken the journey with J.B. and Jacob Hamblin to pick up the chiefs, he could not have told anyone which Indians were which—which were friendly, which were dangerous. Indians had always been just Indians, and he had learned to be wary of every one. He froze as he watched the horses advance toward the tents beside the spring.

Now he could see that the Fancher party had spotted the visitors. The men stood grouped close to the wagons as though to protect the women and children. The Indians were not visibly armed.

One man who looked like a leader—perhaps Mr. Fancher himself—moved forward away from the circle of wagons. Jacob could see that several men at the back wagons were fumbling in their gear to get out their guns. If they knew what Jacob carried, they would be on him like a swarm of bees. He must be absolutely quiet without making one sound that would betray his presence. Parking apart from the wagons behind a large clump of brush, he lay on the ground and strained to hear what they were saying.

Jacob did not know which Indian tribe had also encountered incidents of poisoning at the springs. He had also heard a rumor that one of the Indian tribes-women had been raped by an earlier train. He watched the Indians, not daring to breathe. But the visitors did not seem hostile. They were conducting themselves in a rather pedestrian manner, giving no indication that they were out for revenge. Although they did not seem angry, Jacob saw that soon they began to make firm gestures, indicating that they were expecting to trade on their terms. In their own language, they asked for blankets, guns, a few sacks of flour, an animal or two.

From his position on the ground, Jacob could hear almost every word exchanged in the trading. As it progressed, the settlers gave the Indians beads, jars, and rope. Some of the settlers tried to get away with what seemed less than fair, and Jacob cringed. Finally, he heard one of the Indians stamp his foot. In a moment the native became very loud and angry as he made it known he did not like the way things were going.

Jacob wanted to shout to the Fancher train that it would be worth giving up all they had to keep the Indians in a friendly, peaceful mood. But he thought they must surely know that by now. If he had dared to do it, he might have climbed away from the brush and shouted to them "Do it their way!" He would have told them to be extra cautious, for he knew more than they knew—that the Indians had already been warned by Jacob Hamblin that the "Mericats" had come for war.

Jacob held his breath. In the trading circle he could see that the Indians had offered one of the settlers some bows and arrows for a saddle. But the transaction became heated when it was clear that the white man wanted to see the arrows before he would consider the trade. When he reached out his hand to inspect the arrows, the Indian must have misunderstood his gesture. Drawing back, the mistrusting Indian bristled. Some sign language was exchanged and there were harsh words spoken on both sides.

When the settler reached out for the arrows a second time, he cried, "I have a right to inspect what I buy!" The Indian, now livid with anger, gripped the shaft of one of the arrows and jabbed the point of it into the white man's breast.

One of the Fancher party drew a pistol. It was done so quickly that it was hard to identify who it was. Without hesitation, the immigrant shot the Indian through the head. The sudden crack of the explosion rang in the dusk. Both parties stiffened with fear. Seeing the men behind the wagons with their loaded rifles, the unarmed Indians backed away.

Jacob felt his own heart pound swiftly as he watched the white man yank the arrow from his deerskin vest and crack it over his knee. The dead Indian fell into the arms of his friends, who, dragging him away, warily eyed the large number of settlers standing ready at their guns.

Jacob's breath came hard and his head reeled. He crawled into his bedding not far away to wait for night to come. Lying on his back, he studied the empty sky. They shouldn't have done that, he thought. That was what the Indians had expected them to do.

He waited without making a sound until he saw the stars. The sky through the brush above him was clear and far away, as though it were lying at the black end of a tunnel. The usual sounds of night seemed exaggerated. the sound of the crickets in the grass washed by yesterday's rain, the tapping of small animal feet somewhere in the dust, the scratch of their burrowing into the ground. He tried to melt into quiet, yet he needed to breathe. He was aware of the sounds of camp, of fearful voices as the settlers discussed the consequences of the Indian's death. Some were confident all would be well.

*How many other times have they violated this land—stretched out so far. With one more breath of tension, it breaks, it breaks, it breaks. In this land it is so easy to break . . .*

It seemed that he stayed awake in the quiet for hours, unable to sleep, until finally the sounds of the camp, the movement of tiny animals in the brush, and the music of the crickets faded away.

## 18

### Elizabeth

At first it was only lethargy—an uneasy listlessness which overcame her. But soon there was soreness in her breasts, until finally the nausea came. Elizabeth was sure now that she guarded a special secret: she was going to have a baby. Her feelings were mixed. She was glad that Suky would now have the child in the house that she had wanted. But Elizabeth would not breathe of it to Suky. Not yet. But she wanted to tell someone.

It had been some time since J.B. and Jacob had gone, but she had not seen Rebecca for a while. Though she was without the mule, she decided to set off to try to make it to Jensens' on foot through the gathering clouds and a few showers of rain.

"I think I'm going to have a baby," she whispered to Rebecca.

"Oh, Elizabeth!" Rebecca clutched her arms. "You are? And J.B. doesn't know it yet!"

They talked through the afternoon, bent together in the attic window, foreheads touching, their fingers entwined. They talked for what seemed like hours before Percy Jensen raced upstairs and told them to come to supper. On their way down the stairs they could hear a visitor chatting to someone below. Elizabeth recognized the voice immediately—John D. Lee.

"She's now a young married lady," Mrs. Jensen was saying.

John Lee looked at Elizabeth again. His blue eyes registered surprise. "Is that right?" he said.

"Yes, she is," Rebecca said, interrupting. "She's only been married a few weeks." Elizabeth felt a stab of pain. "To her own stepfather, J.B. Lorry," Rebecca went on, babbling like a child.

"Is that right?" John Lee looked at Elizabeth. His eyes narrowed. "Ah, yes . . . you are . . . he's . . . yes." He seemed to be working out the information in his mind. "J.B. went with Hamblin to take the Indians to Brigham Young." Elizabeth wondered if he had remembered that Sunday conference when he had stood by Isaac B. Haight and given J.B. Lorry permission to marry the young orphan girl who lived in his home. "I'm happy for you, Elizabeth, that you have found the answer to your heart."

Elizabeth wanted to share the truth, "It has nothing to do with my heart!" But she kept still. She did manage to blurt out, "I married him because of my stepmother." But it came out in a lame stammer.

"Percy, get the butter out of the crock," Sister Jensen ordered, and after Percy answered her, there were other interruptions in the conversation.

Lee had pieced it together now. "Is your stepmother still sick?" he asked.

Elizabeth felt a barb of fear. Now she wondered if he had remembered too much. She still feared the Lorrys' secret about the man buried in their canal. What did he know? Rebecca, sitting at Elizabeth's side, was beaming, staring at the man now seated at their table. Elizabeth felt her friend Rebecca was still a child, too young to be suited for a man like John D. Lee.

"Suky's better," Elizabeth said, controlling her voice.

"Good," John Lee said. He spoke with measured words. "I know it has not been easy for your family." The words might have been said to anyone who lived in the valley now. But Elizabeth felt the weight of the statement and longed to begin at the beginning and tell him everything she knew. He seemed like a safe harbor where she could rest and be understood. His voice crowded out the other voices in the room. His eyes were brighter than the eyes of the others. When he laughed, it was a full-throated, deep laugh with an element of reverence as well. She watched him carefully now, afraid that he could see into her heart.

"Elizabeth, you are a remarkable young woman," John Lee suddenly began, and he leaned toward her over the table. "I will tell you what I have seen in you. I can discern your spirit, and I feel that God has destined you for a life which is even greater than you have dreamed."

Elizabeth felt her heart clamoring in her chest. The others in the room faded into the background. She felt alone with this man. Yet she was aware of what was going on about her. As the children began to chatter, Mrs. Jensen disappeared into the pantry and brought out the crock of butter she had asked Percy to empty. Percy was finishing up and begging his father to be excused. Reginald was helping the little boys to wipe the milk from their chins.

"I hope you are not offended if I tell you I believe I have known you— from before."

Elizabeth's breath caught at his words.

"From before this life." He laughed gently. "It is a strange memory. And I don't know what it means."

Now Elizabeth felt as though she were floating in a strange light. Perhaps it was the sunset. It had begun to blaze red in the west. For a long time no one in the room seemed to be listening. Not even Rebecca's voice broke the spell. Finally the children left with Percy to milk the cows.

"We don't have much space, Brother Lee, but you're welcome to stay the night if you have a mind," Sister Jensen finally broke the silence.

"Oh, no," John Lee responded. "Thank you for your kindness. No, I have some clothing from the federal agency I must distribute to the Indians."

"By the way, how are you doing with the Indians?" George Jensen asked. He had been totally quiet during most of the meal. Now he was dipping the last of his cornbread in the corn and flour gravy and getting ready to finish up and go. With the Indians of critical concern to all of them, he would not let the opportunity pass to learn what he could from the resident Indian Agent.

"I meant to talk to you about it, George," John D. Lee said, also rising with the permission of his host. "I've been instructed to make even better friends with the Indians, to guarantee they'll become our allies if there should be war. Now you had mentioned to me an extra cache of tanned cowhide, enough to make leather breeches. Maybe even two dozen pair." He turned to Elizabeth and Rebecca. "Sister Lorry, Sister Jensen, it was nice to visit with you."

Elizabeth smiled faintly as Lee followed George Jensen into the backyard. The red sunset cast its light in their faces so that she could see only the silhouettes of the two men, John Lee with his arm on George Jensen's shoulder.

"Thank you, Sister Jensen. Thank you for supper."

When she turned to Rebecca, Elizabeth saw an expectant smile as her friend looked after John D. Lee. Rebecca whispered, "He is the most wonderful, spiritual man I have ever known."

Elizabeth didn't answer her. She had caught something that had been floating in the room. Some heat of a powerful kind. But she would not bring words to the matter. Finally she said, "I really ought to go. Suky is alone."

"It's all right, Elizabeth. It's all right." Rebecca reached to embrace her friend. The words seemed to float over them, never making contact with reality. But Rebecca was trying. "You will be happy, Elizabeth. You will make the best of it. I love you so."

Rebecca's breath felt like the warm flame of a candle in Elizabeth's ear. "You see," Rebecca continued, "you are a miracle. For my future husband sees that. He knew you even before you were born." Still, Elizabeth could not speak. "Do you believe there is something wonderful that is going to happen to all of us?

I do. I know that God is there, that he loves us and he is watching over us. And that you are as special as John D. Lee says you are."

Rebecca paused, waiting for Elizabeth to say something, but there was a strange crowding in Elizabeth's throat, and still she could not speak.

"Do you want to know a secret?" Rebecca asked.

Not really, Rebecca, Elizabeth wanted to say, but she stayed silent.

"I was wishing that before you got married that you and I could both go with John Lee."

So, this was something Rebecca had dreamed—a friendship that would have been sealed in a family forever.

"But you will be happy. That I know," Rebecca said.

Elizabeth let her friend's liquid voice flow through her as though it were a warmth that could flush out the cold. "Oh, Rebecca, I pray so." She clung to her friend who all of a sudden seemed ages wise.

"Elizabeth, we will stay together as friends always!" Rebecca whispered. "I love you so!"

## 19
### Jacob

It was not something he heard, but something he felt, some presence in the brush. Yet it was not until the third day of traveling behind the Arkansas party that he was sure someone was following them. On that day he saw that a party of Indians had been following the train at a distance of almost a mile. They seemed to be waiting for something. They did not stampede. They were not advancing rapidly. They simply followed the Fancher party for several days.

Jacob did not sleep much for the following two nights, just knowing the Indians were there. He could feel them if not actually hear them, sense them if not see them. He knew they would be aware of every move he made, of every stop and turn of the party ahead of him.

As they neared Beaver, Foresight developed a slight limp on her right front foot. That night Jacob decided he would get started before dawn the next morning so that he might pass the huge train and get into Beaver early to scout for another mule. But as stealthily as he walked beside the Fancher camp, one of the men raised up out of his sleep and pointed a rifle toward him.

"Who goes there?" the immigrant snarled. "Friend or foe?"

"Friend," Jacob called back.

"Better not a red man," the gunman growled. And still in a stupor of sleep he lay back down on his pillow. "No red man, or no Mormon, neither." Jacob quieted Foresight and widened his circle around the sleeping camp. As he passed them by, he felt such relief that he thought he was in danger of breaking into laughter.

Weary, without sleep, he came to a farmhouse just outside of Beaver by eight o'clock that morning and asked the way to the bishop's house. The man of the house was currying his horse in his yard.

"Halloo!" Jacob called, glad to see a Utah inhabitant at last.

The man greeted Jacob with warmth. "You didn't come here alone, did you, son?"

"Well, not exactly," Jacob stammered.

"Because the Indians are out all along here."

Jacob stared. So everyone knew.

"And that traveler train ain't far down the road with 'em. They say that the Indians that was poisoned in the springs is waitin' to pounce on them immigrants with a fury."

By the time Jacob reached the bishop's house, Foresight was exhausted.

"Bishop Anderson is in the town square," the bishop's wife smiled at him. "Surely, you best leave your mule here. I've got a boy that'd be glad to bind up that leg for you," the woman added.

Jacob thanked her and went down to the center of town. The bishop was in the square. A half dozen other men and a few Indians on horses had gathered around him. Jacob did not rush into the group, but listened from a distance to what they were saying.

"Well, we don't want to fight," the sandy-haired Bishop Anderson said in both English and sign language to the natives. "Of course, they ought to make amends if they killed your cattle by poisoning the spring."

First on one foot and then the other, trying to look inconspicuous, Jacob stood on the edge of the group in the town square.

"There they are!" someone finally shouted. When Jacob followed the man's pointing arm, he could barely see the Arkansas train now, like small blades of grass rising over the far hill.

"Well, we'll have a talk with them," the bishop said. "They can't be poisoning any more springs."

Jacob watched, breathless, while the first of the Arkansas party rode toward them.

"Halloo!" one of the Arkansas leaders greeted them.

"Hello! What can we do for you?" the bishop said in a voice Jacob thought was more friendly than the immigrants deserved.

Drawing close, the travelers stared at the Indians in the square with a puckered face. "Some Indians is following us," he said to Bishop Anderson.

The bishop drew up his full height, and stood very still in front of the Indians and townspeople. "From what I heard, you been causing them troubles," the bishop dared to say in a stronger voice. "I heard maybe you poisoned the waters up to the springs."

For a moment the immigrant stared at the bishop. When he turned his head, he saw the faces of the Indians and townspeople surrounding them. There were serious questions in their eyes. "Well, you heard wrong. We ain't caused nobody any harm. We saw some mugwort growing in the spring. But we got our cows out pronto. We done nothing wrong." He paused. But he didn't look at any faces this time. "You folks must know how to get along with the Indians. Well, we might need help to get through this country." His eyes seemed fixed and heavy. "You Mormons in this town, too?" He said the words as though they were acid on his tongue.

"That's right. We Mormons have to get along with the Indians twelve months out of every year."

The immigrant pondered the bishop's words. "Then you know how to do it all right. Will you help us?"

"You don't need any help if you conduct yourselves proper. You can't kill an Indian and not expect to pay for it," the bishop said evenly. "If there's wrongs done, you'll have to answer for them."

Two or three other Missourians had now joined the first group. The speaker turned his head to take in the situation, looking over the Indians, the townsmen, and Jacob himself. "We ain't done nobody any harm," he repeated. When he turned to the men who had joined them from behind, he spit first. Then he growled, "Them Mormons won't lift a finger to help us against the Indians, their friends." He spit the last words like buckshot. "Well, we don't need any help from them Indian-lovin' Mormons!" the man sneered. He waved to a group of wagons waiting at the edge of the town.

In the distance, the driver at the first wagon flourished his whip. "Har! Brigham! You crazy ox!" The animal jerked forward. "What's the matter, Brigham?" he continued to shout. "A little gout got ya?" Then he tossed his head back and broke into a loud peal of laughter that could be heard in town.

All afternoon Jacob watched the Fancher train crawl through the Beaver streets at a snail's pace. No one mentioned a word more about the poisoned springs. On sad-looking ponies, the Indians watched long-faced from their positions along the crests of the hills. They kept vigil while the party set up camp just outside of Beaver for the night.

"If I was you, I'd get your ammunition to Parowan just as fast as I could," Bishop Anderson told Jacob that night as Jacob checked Foresight's leg. "If you leave before dawn, you can pass up the Missourians. And if I was you, I'd keep well ahead of them. The Indians won't hurt you."

Jacob thought it would be wise to take the bishop's advice. Announcing he would leave at the crack of dawn, he slept on the ground outside the Anderson home by the wagon. Sister Anderson gave him a packet of bread and cheese to take in the morning. So concerned was he about keeping close watch on his cargo, that he didn't sleep very well. All night long he thought he heard gunshot in the hills. At one time he thought he heard someone running on the road. With his heart pounding, he climbed out of his blanket and went to the wagon. As he stood beside it listening, he slipped one of his hands under the tarp and touched one of the smooth barrels lying cool under the straw. It was a formidable moment—the first time he had actually thought he might pull one of the firearms out of the hay and use it. He wasn't even sure he knew how to load these particular rifles. But just touching them was enough to pump blood into his head.

Luckily, after a few moments, the road again grew quiet. The moonlight skimmed the ground with a gray sheen like water on the beaten grass. Drawing his blanket around his shoulders once again, he lowered himself uneasily to the ground.

Finally, at dawn, he was wakened by horses in the road. A scout whipped up to the bishop's house with a breathless message. Barely awake, Jacob heard what he said to the sleepy bishop who cracked open the door. "They was hunting rabbit in the hills and killed an Indian."

"Just what we needed," the bishop said sarcastically.

"The Indians is still camped out on the other side of that north hill."

"God help us. I'll wager with a little help from us, the train'll leave this morning. I'm almost tempted to give them the supplies we was told not to give them—just so they'll go."

"Oh, you mustn't do that!" the scout responded.

Jacob was awake enough to hear everything the men said. Soon the bishop went back into the house to dress, and the scout turned on his horse to go.

## 20

### *September 1, 1857, Jacob*

Though he heard the bishop's conversation with the scout, Jacob fell asleep again. For the second time he woke, this time to the sound of hooves on the gravel. While he lay on the ground in his bedding, he saw two men on horseback carrying rifles past the corral. He wondered if the bishop saw them and had chosen not to stop them. The men rode into the barn and carried out two bags of grain as though they had a right to them. Jacob thought he recognized the man whose breast had been punctured by the Indian arrow outside of Fillmore. The top of a large bandage was visible under his shirt, and he wore the same blue bandanna tied around his neck. Jacob hunkered down in his blanket.

As soon as the men were gone, Jacob got up off the ground so quickly his head spun. The day grew brighter with every moment as he packed his bedding under the tarp. He puzzled over whether or not he should knock on the bishop's door to say good-bye, but he finally decided against it. Some of the men had talked of sending a partner with him. But he felt he could travel more quickly alone. It was time to leave Beaver.

He pressed Foresight as rapidly as he could, though she still favored her leg. He was ready to get away from the Fancher train as fast as he dared.

He knew something now. The immigrants had not hesitated to steal from the bishop's barn. He felt angry. The train would take advantage where they could. Someday, he vowed deeply, someday—if there were ever an opportunity for all of them to obtain justice—they would.

Hurrying as quickly as he could along the road, he finally reached Paragonah by noon. With the sun so hot in the sky, the mule became overheated and spent. She continued to favor her leg, and Jacob worried about her. On the outskirts of the town was the blacksmith shop. The sign leaned to one side. It said "Keep your horses shod." He drove in.

The blacksmith worked in a small adobe shed built into the side of a large old log home with lace curtains and boxes of bright geraniums. When Jacob peered into the dark smithy, a large fleshy man with a dome-shaped head turned toward him. He was standing so close to the heat that his face ran with sweat. His mouth was round, and his lips moist, as though he had just enjoyed a morsel of food. He was a bit impatient with Jacob's sense of hurry.

"I don't do miracles here." The blacksmith had a slightly affected speech. "You running away from somebody? You heard anything about that big train that's coming?"

"I been in Beaver," he answered. "They're behind me camping in Beaver."

"Well, I don't want nothing to do with them," the blacksmith said. "From what I hear they're the same ones that raped some children and killed Parley P. Pratt. And also the Prophet Joseph. A fellow from Buttermilk said they poisoned their springs and killed the cattle. Stole flour too. The fellows in Buttermilk were sorry they hadn't shot them on the spot."

Jacob nodded, not wanting to stop long in Paragonah. Parowan was now only a few miles away. He urged the mule forward and pointed at her shoe. "Could you maybe see if she needs a nail or something?"

But just as Jacob spoke, Foresight's leg buckled and she began to lower herself to the ground.

"Har! Har!" Jacob cracked the whip again and urged Foresight to stand, though she lifted her right rear foot up and would not step down on it.

The blacksmith cradled the animal's leg between his knees. "Your mule has an infection, young man."

**21**

*September 1, 1857, Jacob*

For fifty cents the blacksmith, a Brother Deany, would house Jacob in the shed added onto the back of the house, get his daughter to put clean sheets on the bed, and serve a couple of meals.

Jacob accepted at once, but was a bit less than enthusiastic when he saw the blacksmith's daughter. A tall, heavy girl with sunburned cheeks, she surprised him by making frank remarks. When she came to prepare the bed, she practically flipped the sheets into his face. She was as ample as her father, with large, soft arms milky white beneath the wide open gingham sleeves. Her moist lips reminded him of her father's mouth, and when she opened them into a hungry smile, he knew he would be glad to go tomorrow.

When the bed was finally put together, she told him she would be back with "some other necessary things," and as Jacob watched her trying to negotiate the doorway, he was startled by her size. One of the "necessary things" turned out to be her cousin. Birdlike, the wispy girl wore an apron so white it blinded his eyes. When she held the porcelain pitcher, she smiled at him. Jacob caught his breath. She reminded him of Elizabeth. Her hands were the same long white hands, her wrists as narrow as spring willows.

"You need a big pot or a little pot?" the blacksmith's daughter, Greta, broke the spell. She was carrying an empty basin.

When Jacob hesitated, unsure, she broke into a long crude laugh, glancing at her cousin and back to Jacob again.

"Don't you use no commode in the middle of the night?" she laughed.

Jacob suddenly remembered seeing such a chamber pot once in somebody's house in Salt Lake City. But he had never thought he would use one for himself.

"I'll leave it anyway so you'll have one in the middle of the night." The coarse girl repeated her loud laugh and led her cousin by the elbow out of the room. When he finally stood in the small room alone, Jacob breathed a sigh of relief.

That night of September 1 in Paragonah he had a strange dream. He thought he was lying in a small box shaped like a coffin. Suddenly, as he looked up, he saw the faces of twenty or thirty Indians peering down at him from over the edge. The red men began to chant. And Jacob felt the coffin moving upward, upward on the air, as though it were borne by wings.

As he had suspected might be the case, he did not sleep in Paragonah, either. By now a lack of sleep had begun to produce a gnawing tension in his muscles and bones. He felt as though he had been awake every moment of the long night, although he knew he must have dozed.

By now he was so anxious to get to Parowan to unload the guns, he decided he would ask the blacksmith if he could borrow one of his mules for a few days. He promised he would come back as soon as he could to fetch Foresight, who by that time should be able to walk without too much pain.

In the morning he was irritated to be wakened by the coarse, red-faced blacksmith's daughter, who told him she was waking him for an early start so that he might get ahead of the "Missouris." She herself, she said, was careful not to get in the way of the Missouri Wildcats, because they would "stop at nothing, including my womanhood." She said it as though she had thought about it several times.

"Men in general is pretty much no good," she rattled on. "Even Emmy, my cousin, is here in Paragonah to escape a fellow from Scipio who insists on chasing her clean to Beaver."

A fellow from Scipio? Jacob hadn't been listening to Greta's chatter until now. She was whipping open the deerskin blind at the window and pushing aside the curtains, urging him to hurry or his breakfast would be cold. The girl Emmy was carrying a towel and wash basin into the room.

"What was his name?" Jacob asked.

The pretty girl looked at him, then. "He isn't known around here. Proctor Seymour. Why? Do you know him?"

Jacob felt cold, unwilling to answer the question. He did not speak for a moment, which allowed the red-faced girl to continue her talk.

"Emmy don't want to marry Proctor Seymour. She wants to marry John D. Lee."

After Jacob nodded thank you and followed the girls to the door, he closed the curtains to his room. While he washed his face in the cold water and dried himself with the towel, he felt shaken. Why? He wasn't sure he understood why he felt so out of sorts. He was not sure what it was that irritated him so about the blacksmith's daughter, or the fact that the beautiful girl Emmy had run from Proctor to marry John Lee. He thought it was because the story reminded him of Elizabeth's marriage to J.B. Jacob thought he had put it aside. But now it gnawed at him. All he wanted was to get home—to get the guns and ammunition to their destination, to fight his way free of the girls in Deany's house and avoid the threat of the traveling settlers and Indians not far behind.

At the breakfast table he nearly inhaled the hot cereal.

"My, you're in a hurry," Mrs. Deany said.

He left as many coins as he thought would cover expenses and hurried to the blacksmith, who was working in the yard. Yes, Mr. Deany said, he would be happy to lend him his mule if he would bring her right back. "Matter of fact, it will give your animal a few more days to heal." Jacob paid him the last few coins J.B. had left him and struck off down the road without saying good-bye.

## 22
### September 2, 1857, Jacob

Parowan was only a few miles away. Yet he counted almost every revolution of each wheel on the cart. He multiplied in his mind the borrowed mule's every step, imagining her progress long before the progress was made. A rangy multi-colored animal who answered to the name of Flossy, she was annoyingly slow. Jacob fastened his eyes on landmarks and tried to hold his breath until the cart passed each one.

Three, four, five miles away from the blacksmith's, he felt relieved to be that much further away from the Fancher train, away from Proctor's body, away from the Deany girl and her cousin who stirred up memories of anger, or fear. Now he began to feel some relief, because the journey was almost done.

No one could have been more surprised than he that the cart drew into Parowan still containing the load of ammunition. But there was no time to congratulate himself. People in the town must have been notified by a scout of his arrival. Standing out in the road with a troop of men was Colonel Dame.

The colonel greeted Jacob with a long vigorous handshake. He said he had never been so glad to see anybody in his life. He asked Jacob several questions. Jacob told him what had happened to Foresight, his mule, and told him that he would have to return. Brother Dame wanted to know exactly where the immigrant train was.

"They're behind me. About ten miles. Almost to Paragonah. I wanted to get here before there was trouble."

"How did you keep 'em from searching the load or tearing you apart?"

"I stayed away from them," Jacob answered.

"Well, you did well, son," Dame smiled. "And you'll do well to keep that distance, still." He walked around the cart, lifted the tarp, and thrust a hand into the straw. "A good, strong rifle," he said with pleasure. He lifted the gun into his hands. "A beauty."

As he pulled at the other firearms in the hay, the other men came to help him lift them out. Jacob watched every rifle move through several pairs of hands.

Dame nodded and handled each gun carefully. After he had looked at several of the weapons, he nodded, satisfied. Jacob's throat hurt.

"Did you have a chance to try any of these, son?"

"No, sir." Jacob replied. "I never took them out."

"They told you not to?"

"Yes, sir."

For another long moment, Dame looked at the long sleek machines gleaming with copper, brass and silver. "Do you have any interest in arms?"

"Yes, sir." Jacob wasn't sure what the man was thinking, but he felt his blood racing.

"Too bad you have to take that mule back to Paragonah, or you could stay for tomorrow's drill."

Jacob caught his breath in his throat. He wondered why words wouldn't come out of his mouth. He was so glad when Colonel Dame followed his sentence with an invitation. "Unless you want to stay tonight. You're welcome to do that. We need more men."

"Yes, sir. I will, sir." Jacob tried not to show too much enthusiasm.

"Now we got some couple hundred rifles and several hundred pounds of gun powder," Dame said. Jacob watched him as he slicked the barrels with a chamois, handed one to each of the brethren, who one by one carried them into the house. When all of the arms had been removed, Dame invited Jacob to come into the parlor with the others. Standing at the door, he could see the sleek firearms lying on the carpet. "To say nothing of nearly one hundred muskets, two dozen swords, and a few Colt revolvers. And nineteen units of fairly good-trained men," he added.

Finally, after he had finished unpacking the weapons, the colonel strolled into the house, sat in one of his parlor chairs and asked the others to sit down. Jacob, still standing in the doorway of the sitting room, was surprised to see Dame beckon to him with his long work-roughened fingers. "I guess the rest of you know who we have to thank for getting these arms here," he said. Jacob's head spun. The others were nodding and approving. "He'll be drilling with us in the morning before he goes back to Paragonah to get his mule. Isn't that right, Brother Lorry?"

Jacob's heart bumped against his ribs. *Brother Lorry!*

While the men in the room continued to talk, he studied them. Two of them were neighbors of Colonel Dame's. Jacob knew them from the meeting house in Cedar City, only a few short miles away. One was the tall lanky six-and-a-half foot man, David Lewis. Rangy, he seemed nervous, inspecting each fire arm, clenching his hands. Jacob knew he was one of those who had escaped the massacre at Haun's Mill.

"Well, I'm anxious to see who these Missouri and Arkansas settlers are," Lewis said uneasily in a low voice. "If they're the same ones who opened fire at the mill, as far as I'm concerned, they're dead men."

The other man was Laban Morrill, an even bigger man than Lewis. He nodded at Lewis's statement. "It has to be that way," he said with his booming bass voice.

Colonel Dame's eyes narrowed at his words. "There is no way they can chase us out of this territory this time. Because, God willing, we will not let them." His knuckles looked white when he flexed his fingers. He had put down one of the rifles, clenched one hand in a tight fist, and pounded it into the other. "They won't destroy us, either. First we'll destroy them." *We'll destroy them.* When

Jacob heard the words, he felt the blood rush to his face. He thought he might burst with some exclamation, though he held himself back. If only his father could see him now! He would never have dreamed . . .

That night, in Mrs. Dame's small loft room under the hot attic roof, he did not seem to remember his father's face, let alone his father's warning only a few weeks ago—that he was too young to drill. He vaguely remembered the face of Percy Jensen when he lifted the gun to his shoulder or jostled with the other men. He thought about Percy, who wasn't there, and he smiled to himself. He laughed silently in the hot attic. In his exuberance, he wanted to hit the bed with his fist against Mrs. Dame's straw ticking. Then, in a few moments, he could not believe that he had wanted to laugh at all, and he rolled over in the straw, pulled the sheet down, and stared at the dark wood beams under the Dame roof, trembling.

## 23
### September 3, 1857, Jacob

In the morning, still trying to sleep in Dame's stifling attic, Jacob heard a horseman come to the front door. He could hear the small knock, and the creaking of Dame's springs as he left his bed. The floorboards creaked below him. The man was slow; Jacob could hear every step on the stairs. Finally, when the door was opened, Jacob could hear the scout murmuring softly, and Colonel Dame answering him with a blatant holler. When Jacob peered out of the small attic window, he saw the rider gallop away, his right hand looping the ends of his reins in the air.

Jacob got up immediately, put his boots on, and went down to intercept the colonel on the stairs. The man was still dressed in his wrinkled muslin night shirt, the hair on his chest visible—tight red-gold curls. "What's happened?"

The colonel was in good spirits. "It looks like the Missouris are going to miss us!" he said with triumph. "They are headed down the draw to Johnson's Springs." The springs lay about five miles to the west.

Jacob stood for a moment on the stairs, waiting to sort through this news.

For some uncanny reason, Colonel Dame seemed to be able to read Jacob's face. "We'll still drill, son," he said. "It was the drills that scared them off. Never forget," he emphasized with a gesture, "the best defense is readiness."

Though he stepped to the side to let the colonel pass, Jacob did not share the colonel's joy. He was not sure why the safety of Parowan had not made him feel any easier. "I guess you don't need those guns here," Jacob said, not sure how he felt about risking his life to bring them, as though it were his mission.

Colonel Dame, holding up his nightshirt slightly, had climbed a few steps and stood above Jacob on the landing. For a moment he stopped and looked down with a solemn stare. "You think there'll ever be a time we don't need guns?"

Jacob did not know. The Mormons had been lucky this morning. Perhaps forever. "The Missouris passed you by," the colonel said. Holding to the rail to steady himself, he gave Jacob a long steely look. "You don't understand, do you?" he said. "Remember what I'm telling you. I won't be telling it to you again. There are no lucky ones. If one is down, we are all down. We stand together, my boy." For a moment he did not move. With a long breath, he paused. Then he began to move to the top of the stairs, and he gave Jacob a wink. "Now are you going to go to Paragonah after that mule, or do you want to do some drills today?"

Because he had slept in his clothes, Jacob was ready as soon as Colonel Dame disappeared behind his bedroom door. He raced into the road, where he saw the men of the town gathering, preparing to drill in Colonel Dame's field. Soon more than thirty men stood about, waiting for the colonel to come. When Dame finally came out of his house wearing his blue coat, carrying three new rifles, they stood at attention. Most of the men held their rifles against their shoulders.

Standing with the others who were not in rows, Jacob observed the men who were about his age, and who, like him, were unarmed. The colonel knew his troops. When he walked down into the field, he spoke to all of them.

"You didn't pick up a gun?" the colonel asked Jacob. He handed him one of the slick new ones. Jacob thought the top of his head would come off. "Thank you, sir," he managed.

When Colonel Dame put the men through their paces, Jacob had never seen anything like it. The sweat poured from beneath the officer's hat as he focused on the commands. As they shifted the positions of the guns, he imitated the others as though he had handled firearms a hundred times, ignoring the fact—even to himself—that he had shot a rifle only once, at Percy's barn. He weighed the barrel in his hands and felt the pieces move against one another, like music.

At target practice, Jacob's mouth felt dry. "Ready, aim, fire," Colonel Dame shouted, and the firearms went off like so many firecrackers into the morning mist. Laban Morrill, who stood next to Jacob, helped him load powder one time into his slick new rifle. After that, Jacob was on his own. He pulled the trigger and aimed toward the target, though he was unable to know which was his mark. He shot again. He felt the jerk of power, the click against his shoulder.

For the entire morning he believed he had not wanted the drills to end, ever. But when the women finally brought barbecued beef into the field and served it with large chunks of dark wheat bread, he was ready to stop. Jacob sat in the grass with Laban Morrill while they watched David Lewis Indian wrestle with Jimmy Crabtree. Of course David Lewis won. Good-naturedly, the men laughed.

Jacob felt alive in the company of these men. Nothing had ever seemed so important to him before. Everything else flew from his mind.

On his return to Paragonah with Flossy, Jacob wanted to ask Colonel Dame if he couldn't take this new rifle with him for protection. He told the colonel that if he could take just one rifle, and enough ammunition to load it, he would feel much safer. Even though he asked calmly in a practiced voice, he expected to be refused.

"You want to take that gun you shot this morning?" Colonel Dame smiled at Jacob. "Well, I don't see why not, Brother Lorry."

Without letting the colonel know of his excitement, Jacob bit his tongue. It was all he could do to keep from shouting. He was in possession of a firearm!

As the men prepared to leave, Laban Morrill sacked up Jacob's powder for him. While Jacob stood to watch, Laban turned to him and said quietly, "You treat a gun like it was your mother—the gate to life." He laughed at his small joke, but grew serious. "Guns are for people who know how to respect life." Then he paused. "Don't you never forget that, boy."

When Jacob mounted Deany's mule Flossy, he waved at the men who were still milling about in Colonel Dame's yard. As he rode out of the yard, he flung the new rifle across his back. Mrs. Dame ran from the door with a package of hot rolls. "Take care," she urged. "You must get there before dark."

Jacob would have been in Paragonah before dark if he had followed her advice. But he had never had a gun on his back before. Nothing could have stopped him from trying it on a rabbit or two in the field. When he put the gun up on his shoulder and shot at the first animal, he said to himself, "This is the first time I have ever shot to kill." He missed.

By the time he reached the fields outside town, a half moon was sailing over the hill. There was no lamplight in the windows of the village. All seemed quiet and deathly still. No one was on the road. Perhaps the residents were still suffering from the shock of the traveling wagon train, the looting of their barns.

Jacob had counted himself lucky that he had not been in Paragonah when the Fancher train had passed through. However, he had celebrated too soon. In the quiet now, from a clump of willows in the field not far away, he could hear a frightening scream. He heard the thud thud thud of a beating, and at each contact a yelp of terror. His scalp crawled with sudden fear.

When he urged Flossy forward, the mule balked. Jacob jumped off of the animal and tied it to Deany's fence near the willows. Awkwardly slipping under the fence with the gun still slung over his shoulder, he followed an irrigation ditch to the noise. Only a hundred yards away two men, their horses nearby, raised heavy clubs over a heap barely visible on the black ground. By now, the whimper of the victim was a sob. And Jacob knew the voice—James Deany, the blacksmith.

Heart pounding, he lowered himself to hide behind the willows. He was not sure how close he could get without being seen. The sound of Deany's sobs tore at him. Without even analyzing his position, or the consequences, he took the gun from his shoulder. He cocked it, cradled it in his arm, and before he could believe what he was doing, he pulled the trigger.

The field cracked with the sound. Neither of the silhouetted figures had guns. Jacob's shot had the desired effect. The perpetrators stopped in mid-air with their hefty sticks. They looked at one another. They lowered the sticks to the ground.

Jacob shot his rifle again. This time, neither of the men looked into the brush where Jacob stayed hunkered down. They made a dash for their horses, mounted, and without a sound, rode away.

Jacob tasted the hot gun powder on his tongue. When the men were gone, he ran to the motionless body, carrying the gun in his hands. "My first," he thought to himself. "I have won this war."

James Deany was barely conscious. Jacob, kneeling on the ground, rolled him over and made a pillow of the man's coat for his head.

"They was angry with me for giving some onions to the Fancher party when they came through," Deany rasped. "I gave a man some onions because he said his wife was sick."

Jacob couldn't believe what he was hearing; his heart sank. "You mean your own neighbors did this because you gave supplies to the train?"

"It's against the rules," Deany said, his voice nearly inaudible. "I knew it was against the rules. Oh, I'm hurting bad." And then he said, "I'm glad you had that gun."

It was almost impossible to get Deany up on the mule, but they managed. Lying stomach down across the saddle, Deany flopped about in a state of semi-consciousness. Jacob walked Flossy down the road as quickly as he could. In the distance he recognized the barn and the house beyond it against a clump of trees.

He had intended to get straight to the house, but when the barn loomed first, he decided to see if Foresight was there. He found the wire on the barn gate easy to remove. While he walked to the barn, he kept one eye open on the lights of the house three hundred yards away. He could hear the lowing of cattle, the mewling of kittens in the hay. No one would have known he was present. When he let go of the gate, however, it swung crazily against a post with a loud "thwack." For a moment he stood not knowing if he should have taken Deany to the house first. But after a while, when he heard nothing, he tugged at Flossy and brought her inside the corral. Then he turned to open the barn door.

There was so much noise as the door drew open, that he did not hear the feet on the path. He was shocked to hear a stringy female voice shout, "Get your hands up, you scrawny chicken thief, you ugly mole-headed snake. Get your hands up, you fool!"

He would have recognized Greta's voice anywhere.

"What the heck are you doing in our barn, you pig! Find yourself some-body else to rob. Get out of here and don't show your face . . ."

"It's me!" Jacob held his hands high. "And I got your mule and your father!" By this time he was uncertain whether to laugh or cry. Greta had been getting ready for bed, and she had her red hair half tied up in rag curlers. She looked like a mop.

"What the . . ." she said, stepping closer with her rifle to see. "Who?" When she came quite close, Jacob was certain she must have been nearsighted. She peered at the body lying across the animal. "No, it can't be!"

"It is," Jacob said. "I'm returning both of them to you."

She put down the lantern and the gun abruptly. The moonlight glowed behind her, and the lantern threw round shadows on her large cheeks. "Father!" she cried out, running to him.

In his stupor, the man made a low moaning sound. She lay her palm on his forehead. "They beat him because he gave onions to the settlers," she said.

Jacob watched her hover over him for a moment. Finally she pulled away and looked him squarely in the eyes. "I told him not to do it," she said. "It's against the rules."

## 24
### Jacob

With mixed feelings, Jacob left the Deany house as quickly as he dared. Though he felt he had not hit anything, he knew he had fired at a human being, and it had not been an immigrant, but an ally. He left Deany and his daughter at the house without going inside. Mrs. Deany came to the door, but at the sight of Deany's battered body limping over the stoop, she was so distraught she turned quickly back into the house. Greta shut the door, and Jacob did not see any of them again.

Since Jacob found Foresight in fairly good condition, he rode through the night to Parowan as fast as he could. By the time he got there, it was morning and the men were drilling in the square. When he saw them he stayed back for a few moments, reviewing the possibility in his mind that one of these men could be the same one who had beaten James Deany for giving away his onions to a needy family. He could not help but look at them now with a warier eye.

Milling about in the square, he caught sight of a familiar face—his father. J.B. Lorry had returned from his journey with the Indians, and he had come as far as Parowan. Chewing on a big piece of straw, J.B. looked as though he were expecting someone. Jacob smiled, believing his father would not know it was his son. His father looked up suddenly and Jacob saw something he had never seen before in his father's eyes. Not only gladness, but respect. As though Colonel Dame had told him, "Your son Jacob did his job well."

Jacob felt a kind of release as he rode toward J.B. He might have been flying—as though his head had broken through a mysterious cloud and was floating in the sun. When J.B. reached for his son's hand to help dismount, Jacob felt the roughness of his father's fingers, but he had the sensation of leaping through the air into his father's embrace.

There was no embrace. But when Jacob jumped to the ground, his father took his hand. The men, milling in the square as they waited to drill, nodded their heads and smiled toward father and son.

However, as his father pulled away, Jacob wondered if J.B. had found out anything about the drill. He must have known. Perhaps he had talked to these men, and they had told him, "Your boy did a fair job with a gun." Of course J.B. could see the gun slung on Jacob's saddle-horn.

J.B. stayed close and put his hand on Jacob's shoulder for what seemed like a long time. "That's all there is to know, boy, that we're back together again."

"Foresight got hurt. I had to go back to Paragonah . . ."

But J.B. silenced him with a slight shake of his head. "We'll just start over again, Jacob," he said.

Though their initial reunion was warm, Jacob still felt uneasy. His father didn't seem interested in learning any details. He didn't want to hear that Jacob had been drilling and shooting guns, because it had gone against his orders. Yet he must have known it was the only thing to be done.

Jacob didn't broach the subject. He tried, instead, to draw his father out on something else. "The Indians smoked the peace pipe? Will they fight for us?"

J.B. hesitated, as though he still did not want to talk about anything at all. "If there's war, the Indians are ready to fight for us. Yes, they smoked the peace pipe with Brigham Young." He turned back to the militia as though the subject was closed.

For the next few days with Colonel Dame and the militia, J.B. and Jacob drilled together as though they had both been soldiers all of their lives. Together they said good-bye to the Indians when they left for their tribal homes. Father and son stood with the others in the hot street at noon, sweating under the weight of their clothing, walking the glistening mules. Jacob felt as though he were falling through a vacuum toward the time when he and his father would return home. Yet, perhaps for the first time, he was beginning to realize that it was not his father who had made him feel at home.

*Home, the color of white against the dark wash of the hills. You may be miles closer to home. Yet if you are not at home, you might as well be on the other side of the world.*

When they talked to Colonel Dame, he seemed to think that none of them would go home until the Arkansas train left the valley entirely. He seemed nervous talking with them. "It's imperative that we support the troops in Cedar. It will be the last post to get supplies." He appointed J.B. and Jacob, with others of the militia, to stay in Cedar City until the immigrants had passed through.

On that last afternoon, they left for Cedar City with three or four of the militia who had promised to help protect them. David Lewis was with them. Jacob felt safe enough, but the men decided not to take chances of any kind. They would not travel on the road, but take another trail up on the eastern hills. When J.B. and Jacob followed the men into the untrammeled fields just at the foot of the mountains, they could see the valley spread out as long and as unbounded as the sky. Ahead of them one of the men stopped and pointed.

"There they are, son. There they are!" His father's voice sounded like a far-away alarm breaking through the hot sun. "They are almost at our door."

Astounded, Jacob saw the immigrant train—a sea moving in a rhythm, a black mass scarring the ground. Jacob sat on Foresight without moving. The mule stopped beside his father's borrowed horse.

"It looks like they'll be in Cedar City by tomorrow afternoon."

## 25
### *Jacob*

Jacob and J.B. with David Lewis and the others from Parowan reached Cedar City around noon as expected. Having advance notice of the Arkansas visitors, the citizens of Cedar City were gathered in the town square. Five or six of the men had cleverly invented an excuse to be waiting. They were digging a "community ditch" in front of the church.

The Lorrys knew the men in Cedar better than those in Parowan. But they had not seen them for a long time. Jacob noticed how serious they looked, as though they operated in self-conscious fear. With the arrival of the Parowan people as backups, they seemed to relax momentarily.

The immigrant train may have skirted Parowan, but they were not about to skirt Cedar City. The first contingent was the group of hired Missouri wildcats, led by a big dark-headed man on a giant gray mare. In his right hand he carried a sharp leather whip, and he wasn't shy about using it. When he could see that the citizens of Cedar were digging a ditch in the direct path of the wagons, he did not say much, but raised his hand in an uneasy greeting. Dismounting, he tied his horse to the railing in front of the store. Behind him, the other forty men in the group stayed mounted on their horses.

The townspeople eyed the man with the whip as he swaggered to the boardwalk and into the market. Those still digging the ditch looked at one another with hesitation. Some of them leaned on their shovels. The other Missourians, still on horseback, stood their distance. For a while the only sound was the buzz of flies in the muggy hot air and the rumble of Missouri wagons still driving down the road.

After a few moments, the man with the whip came back out of McMurdy's store. He stood poised on the boardwalk. The men digging at the ditch tried not to look at him.

When he spoke, his voice did not seem harsh or angry. However, he stood with his feet apart, his eyes set. "Is there any of you young Mormons—or anybody—willing to go in and buy us some whiskey?" As he surveyed the men, his gaze connected with a young man who pointed at himself. "Who, me?" he stammered, looking afraid.

"Yes, you. Anybody," the big man raised his voice now. "You can hear me, can't you? Your storekeeper says he can't sell travelers nothing. And I got money. I'm asking somebody to set foot in that shop just now and buy me a bottle of whiskey."

Jacob froze. The boys and men digging the ditch stopped working. Their hands gripped the shovels until their knuckles were white.

"I don't know what you Mormons think you're doing," the man continued. "We've got money." He spit now. Under his breath he said, "We've had a hell of a time trying to buy anything on this road." He spread his legs a little further apart, solidifying his stance as he continued his speech. "Maybe you'd like to wish us well. We'll be out of Mormon country tomorrow. Does it hurt you to be hospitable in the last town?"

There was a strained quiet in the road, the nervous sound of unsettled horses, and the "chip" of a man's shovel as he struck it into the dirt.

"Just one bottle of whiskey, boy. Just one measly bottle of whiskey. It ain't like I'm asking you to sell me your own shirt, is it now?" He held out some crisp bills.

But the boy would not move. "I can't, sir," he stammered.

Jacob watched them, feeling cold, even though the sun was at its zenith in the sky.

"Come on, you, boy!" the Missourian swore. "I got the money right here in my hand and you won't even take it. Anybody else want a few extra dollars for a simple errand?" He clutched the money hard and shook it.

When the boys remained quiet, the man began to swear heatedly. His face grew red and the sweat poured down his brow. And now the words that came out of his mouth stung them all.

"You don't know what I've got, do you?" he snarled. "I'm the owner of the gun that blew the guts out of old Joe Smith. And it's still good for blowing out the guts of any other Sam Hill Mormon." He swore, spit in the road again, and climbed his horse. The animal began to stomp and paw at the ground.

"I ain't never seen so many fanatic Mormons, and by Joe Smith's name, I'll carry the gun I got with me all the way to California and bring an army back to wipe out every no good one of you!"

The words hurt Jacob's ears. But what happened next startled him. The leader rode back to the row of rabble rousers waiting in the background. When he spun around, they followed him back to McMurdy's market. The men leaped down, tied their horses to the rail, and stormed the store.

The men at the ditch waited. David Lewis had raised his hand as though he were in charge. He walked into the street with his gun on his hip. "If they try anything, I'll . . ." He didn't finish. And no one finished for him. There was dead silence.

In a few moments the party of Missourians burst from the door of Mr. McMurdy's shop. Shouting, dragging sacks of grain, they swung up on their mounts. The large man on his gray mare held a bottle of whiskey over his head. He rode down the street waving it in triumph. "I gave you a chance. You're fools. You should have took the money." He spit for emphasis. "I guess you didn't know I'd get it one way or another."

David Lewis, still seated on his horse, started forward, but stopped when McMurdy ran from his shop into the road screaming. "I been robbed! Arrest them! They robbed me!" He began by following the horsemen on foot, but as they disappeared into the dust, he turned back toward town and confronted Lewis in the street.

By now, Lewis had straddled his horse. "Come on, all of you! Mount!" Very few of the men were mounted. Jacob was on the lame mule, and his father's borrowed horse was not much faster. Though Lewis continued yelling, the brethren moved slowly. Frustrated, Lewis hit his horse with his reins. But it was only moments before the rabble rousers were gone.

Though Lewis and two or three others followed the handful of Missouri men south out of town, they returned without any captives. Believing the robbers had made a circle to meet up with the party behind them, Lewis took the larger posse north to the large group of immigrants still north of town. But the robbers had disappeared. Only a short way down the road Lewis stopped and turned back, angry. Confronting the colonel, he demanded, "Where's your full militia? Where's Isaac Haight? We're going to need all of the Cedar and Parowan troops to get them."

J.B. Lorry was right behind them. "Isaac Haight went on a short visit to the Indians, but he'll be back this evening," J.B. told him. Jacob looked at his father. For the first time he saw J.B. as one of the leaders of the posse. "First I think we ought to meet to discuss the situation," J.B. was saying.

As the sun slipped across the sky, the town virtually held its breath, when the culprits returned. As the afternoon lengthened, the noisy immigrants drove with their wagons into the town square. The townspeople listened to the loud drunken voices, the swearing and yelling in the streets, but not one of them again entertained the idea of making any arrests.

J.B. and Jacob rode on a west road to meet Isaac Haight. When they saw him and told him what was happening in the middle of the town, Major Haight took J.B. and Jacob to his house just off the main street. Haight lived in a large adobe block home flanked by newly planted cottonwood trees. When the heavy door of the house closed, Jacob felt safer within the two-foot thick walls than he had felt all afternoon. Inside the door, a stairwell rose to a large inside balcony which led to several rooms. To Jacob, Isaac Haight's place was a mansion. One of Haight's wives showed them to an upstairs room, where they waited. The women, with the help of the children, went down to the kitchen to prepare a hot meal.

Jacob watched the downstairs activity from the balcony. He had never seen so many children. There was a constant hubbub of small noises and an occasional burst of crying. However, above the normal noise level of a family at home there seemed to be an odd hum of fear. All of the children had been told about the Missouri Wildcats now camped in the middle of town. And about the large number of settlers camped north for the night, ready to flood through the Cedar Streets in the morning. Every child dreaded what might come. And the whispers they shared were spoken with fear.

Major Haight and his officers carried in the guns that David Lewis and the others had brought from Parowan—the same rifles Jacob had brought from Scipio. Jacob thought that time seemed a hundred years ago. When Haight asked Jacob if he wanted to do some cleaning, Jacob bounded down the stairs. He laid the guns on the tiles in the foyer, helping to get them ready. The children milled about, curious.

Eating the bean supper in the evening, Jacob watched the women. He knew there were many wives in the house, most of them belonging to Isaac Haight. But he thought nothing of it. He was busy wondering what would happen in the morning.

## 26
### *Saturday, September 5, 1857, Jacob*

Saturday morning came too soon. Awake all night hearing the antics of the Missouri Wildcats, Jacob felt sluggish when J.B. urged him to get up and prepare for the drill.

In the dawn light, Jacob could see that the square was empty of immigrants. The Missouri Wildcats had gone. The militia stood in ragged lines under the command of someone he thought looked familiar, though he had to ask his father who it was. It was Sergeant Patrick Moore. He also saw Colonel Dame. And the Jensens, though Percy had not come.

Moore was putting the battalion through its paces. J.B. rode to the drill, dismounted, and beckoned Jacob to hurry. They were not long into the exercise when a cloud of dust stirred along the north road. Soon the men in the militia could feel the rumbling in the earth of hundreds of hooves and rolling wagon wheels. The Fancher train, following close behind the Missouri Wildcats, swelled through the draw like a huge flood of unruly waters. The leaders of the Fancher group came on five horses abreast of one another—a phalanx of ready men. They did not slow as they moved into the city. Behind them, the wagon train crawled. The man who seemed to be the leader, a tall gentleman with a yellow leather hat, raised his hand in greeting. He was seated on a pinto pony. Ready for him, Isaac Haight also raised his hand. The militia held its ground.

"You Danites going to prevent us from passing through?" the man from Arkansas asked Brother Haight.

Jacob breathed hard. So the Arkansians knew about the Danite soldiers, the Mormon militia of Nauvoo? He noticed that Colonel Dame's grip tightened on the gun at his side.

Though there seemed to be no visible hostility, the morning seemed to sizzle with an unseen tension. Calmly, the Fancher party dismounted and stood about on the street watching the drill. But the calm did not last for long. Feeling sportive, one of the Fancher men struck out with the stock on his gun. And maybe accidentally and maybe not accidentally, he hit one of the Cedar soldiers in the shins. The Mormon stumbled and fell, missing his drill signal. The strangers hooted with laughter as the entire line stopped and re-grouped to begin again.

Patrick Moore stopped the drill. Isaac Haight stared at the group from Arkansas who surrounded them in good numbers. "What is it you want?" Haight asked.

"You know what we want," the visitor said evenly. "Just cooperation. Just a little cooperation." He still held his horse by the bridle. The restless animal tossed its head. "Open up your warehouses to us and we'll pay you for grain." After he made that statement, his voice flattened. "Or we'll have to help ourselves. It's your choice. We can always help ourselves."

Haight's eyes narrowed before he spoke. "Seems to me some of your people last night already helped themselves." He stood tall. "Generally we arrest someone who's stole anything from anyone in this town. We have laws here like anyplace else."

The man grinned. "I don't know what our friends offered you. But we intend to pay for all we take. A lump sum. Open your storehouse and sell us what we need." The man's voice was level, certain, though his hand quivered on the reins of his horse.

Haight's eyes softened. He was struggling to be civil. "You know last year we were close to famine. And now we're about to face the U.S. Army. And your Missouri friends who helped themselves to our goods are threatening to bring back an army from the settlements in California. We live on the edge of the earth—and with practically no supplies."

"You may be living on the edge of the earth, but we're traveling on the edge of the earth," the man returned. He added with a dark sneer, "And no supplies."

Haight shook his head slowly. His mouth was closed and as thin as a line. He looked across his militia from side to side. "I'm sorry," he said, shaking his head, "We've been instructed by our leaders. I just can't do it." The line of his jaw was firm, but his voice sounded wary.

The spokesman for the Fancher train actually looked sad for Isaac Haight. He turned from side to side to his men. "It's your choice, sir," he told Haight politely. "And it sounds like you chose." The command he gave to his men was not as blatant as the Wildcat command. He nodded very briefly, and his men raised their guns to their shoulders. The women in the street ran away screaming with high-pitched terror. But there were no gunshots. The men rode to the warehouse behind the store as though they had been able to smell the grain. Still mounted on their horses, they leaned over to break down the wooden doors with the butts of their rifles.

For a moment the stupefied Mormon militia watched, dumbfounded, without a command. Taking hold of himself, Haight grit his teeth, mounted his mare, and rode to the man who had been in command. "You're under arrest, sir," he said, "for robbery."

The visitor stared while a smile began to break at the corners of his mouth. He laughed. "Ho!" he cried out to his compatriots. "We're arrested! We'll have a place to sleep and a meal in jail!" He hit the rump of his horse with his reins and laughed as he followed his men through the town. By now the men had dismounted. They were dragging away the few bags of grain still left in McMurdy's store. Stunned, the militia did not move. Perhaps the commanders felt this amount was not worth fighting over. At least they could count themselves fortunate that the Fancher party had not gone to the mill.

From his place on the horse, the Missouri spokesman tossed a few greenbacks into the breeze. "I told you we would pay," he cried out. There would not have been enough there to pay for half a barrel of oats. "Thank you, Mormons. Maybe you ain't half bad after all!"

Another one yelled back, "We know you got more. We'll be back for it. Don't doubt it!"

Major Haight sat frozen to his horse, holding his gun. From behind, Colonel Dame rode forward, his face dark with anger. "Haight, why didn't you take them? Why didn't we take them on? We're supposed to be a military, aren't we?" He looked very much like a red-faced blown-up balloon.

The faces of the men in the militia were ashen. All of them watched the clouds of dust rise after the Fancher train as it rode away.

Haight dismounted and, turning, spit words through tight teeth. "And get ourselves killed?" He dismounted and knelt on the ground to pick up the floating two dollar bills. "There will be a better time, men," he whispered, looking up. "There will be a better time."

## 27
### *Jacob*

That evening, while the Fancher train was enjoying the stolen supplies for supper in their camp just south of town, several leaders of the militia met in Isaac Haight's home. Jacob and J.B. sat quietly on Haight's stairway while below them the men sat in leather chairs and argued heatedly about what should have happened and what should happen now. Half of the militia swore they could have taken the intruders that afternoon if there had been any suggestion of a command. The other half supported Isaac Haight's counsel to wait.

"Wait for what?" the man Laban Morrill sneered.

"I won't risk the lives of our men. We'll take care of it at a time of less risk," Isaac Haight said.

"How do you mean take care of it?" Laban was the big man Jacob had met in Parowan during his first drills. He was so large that his head looked small seated on his gigantic shoulders. When he rose from his seat, his body filled the room.

Isaac Haight was not a man given to many arguments. Jacob thought his sun-weathered face looked tired. The lines around his eyes were drooping. He leaned forward with his elbows on his knees and lowered his head into his hands. His bony fingers dug at his scalp for a long time before he answered.

Finally he lowered his hands and raised his eyes to the men in the circle. "I'm sorry," he said quietly. "It didn't look good today."

J.B. glanced at Jacob. Jacob hung on every word the men were saying.

"I tried," Haight continued. "Where would we have kept them? We don't have a jail."

The men nodded.

"There are some other possibilities."

No one knew what possibilities he meant.

"Possibilities that carry much less risk."

No one dared to ask him what he was suggesting.

Jacob listened to the stir among the men. There were voices murmuring softly all around the large hall. In the background, from the doors of the kitchen and the downstairs rooms, and from the upstairs balcony railing, the women stood and whispered to one another while the little children hung on their skirts or begged to be carried in their arms.

Haight looked in the direction of J.B. and Patrick Moore. "As you know," he continued, "the Indians smoked the peace pipe with Brigham Young. Hamblin returned here just the other day."

The voices remained silent.

"We must be assured the Indians are on our side." Haight cleared his throat. "What we may have to do . . . ," he paused, "is ask them to . . ." He waited; his voice softened. "This is as serious a plan as any we have ever made."

The method of dealing with the Missourians seemed to glimmer like a lantern on a ship far out at sea, a light that grew more visible with every passing mile. Yet no one would have breathed the glaring truth with a word on their tongues.

"We must fetch the Indian agents, Jacob Hamblin or John Lee. And," he took time for this one, "somebody must go to Salt Lake City to get permission from Brigham Young."

When he ended his speech, Haight kept his eyes straight ahead, ignoring those who lifted their hands to ask questions. The men began to whisper to each other, and the room filled with the din of moving chairs and talk that sounded like thunder within the walls.

"Get permission from Brigham Young?" someone said with a sneer. "The settlers will be to California and back with an army by that time."

"It will take a hundred hours to go to and from Salt Lake City," Isaac Haight said.

No one dared to breathe until a quiet voice was heard in the background. "I'll go," one of the men offered, raising his hand. It was James Haslam, a small man who was known for his speed on horseback.

"Thank you, James," Haight said. "Now, someone has to go for Agent Hamblin."

He waited again. This time one of the men spoke up, "Hamblin is on his way to get married . . ." He added, "again."

Some of the men in the room laughed at the last word.

"Then it will have to be John Lee." President Haight seemed to wind down now, as though the burden weighing on his shoulders had finally dragged him to the ground.

"Where is Lee?" someone asked. "He should have been here."

"He was working with me at the mill at noon," Higbee said. "He and I was protectin' it. And when they passed it by he went home."

"Yesterday I heard him say nobody was going to take nothing from the mill. They'd have to kill him first," one of the others said.

Haight ran his fingers through the graying hair at his temples. He leaned back in his chair. "I'll talk to John D. Lee," he said. "Get a boy . . ." and by a strange fluke his eyes rested on Jacob Lorry. "Maybe Jacob Lorry, here. In the morning, Jacob, will you go to fetch John D. Lee?"

## 28

*Sunday, September 6, 1857, Jacob*

Jacob did not even hope for sleep that night. He lay on the narrow cot next to J.B. with his face to the cold adobe wall. With the wall so close to his cheek, he sensed its rough surface to be like the other side of the moon. If he slept, he slept only a few hours. Every muscle in his body was tense, preparing for his journey. President Haight had offered him the use of his strawberry mare. While he lay awake, he flew the distance in his mind over and over again. And though he probably slept more than he knew, he was up before dawn.

Haight's best mare, the beautiful strawberry, stood in the yard fastened to the gate, gazing at him peacefully. When he mounted her, he turned southward, summoning as much strength as he could in his legs.

The horse was superb, her gallop as smooth as water. Jacob headed into the sun now burning up the Sabbath morning. When he began to sweat, he could feel the withers of the horse grow wet. Once out of Cedar City, the classy strawberry lapped up the miles.

On the right, Jacob passed the old Hamilton Fort. Soon, on the left, was his own home against the mountainside in Kanarraville. The Lorry farm lay on the north edge of the outpost. Only briefly did he think about his mother in the house. And Elizabeth. She would be there, and she did not know that he was passing now. He passed the Jensen farm. And then the vast and windswept basin where Harmony lay nestled back in the hills like a small monument of stone.

Harmony was the outpost of John D. Lee. Jacob stared at the fort as the strawberry pumped and wheezed. Most of the people here belonged to the Lee family. Jacob raced through the gate, slowed the horse, and stared in awe. The people in the fort must have dismissed church only a few moments ago. Large groups were gathered in different areas outside the buildings in the square. They stared at Jacob as he arrived. The women wore shawls, even in the heat, and their Sunday dresses scraped the packed dirt underfoot.

Jacob did not have to ask any of them which man was John D. Lee. The man stood in a corner of the fort on a flagstone walkway near the most impressive home of the complex. A group had gathered around him. They turned to look when Jacob directed the big red animal to the stoop, where he stopped and dismounted. He felt the curiosity of a hundred eyes.

"John D. Lee?" Jacob asked, although he knew.

"Yes, Brother?" Lee turned calmly. He was the same well-proportioned man with the hay-colored hair that Jacob had remembered. The square jaw, the firm cheeks, were brightened by a smile as he greeted the visitor with the red horse.

Jacob did not waste time. "Brother Lee, you are wanted at Cedar City," he stammered.

Lee's eyes grew fixed in his face. The more Jacob tried to communicate his urgency to Lee, the more the man seemed to ask him to calm himself.

Lee turned from the group standing about him and faced Jacob fully now. Jacob had never seen such penetrating blue eyes. He trembled slightly, unable to find more words on his tongue. When Lee turned to Jacob again, his voice was drawn and slow. "You say I am wanted back in Cedar City?"

He sounded a little disturbed, as though he had expected the militia to know he had already spent all day Saturday protecting the interests of the town, and he should have been allowed to spend Sunday with his family.

Jacob nodded now, feeling his heart pound in his chest. "President Haight said, sir . . ." Jacob was breathless. "He wants to see you right away. He says, come prepared to spend a few hours, sir."

"President Haight?"

"Yes, sir."

Now Lee's eyes narrowed and he cocked his head. "Can you tell me something . . . a little of what it's about?"

Jacob didn't know what he would say now. His mouth seemed numb.

"The Indians and the Missouri and Arkansas travelers," Lee said then, guessing, his eyes narrow.

Jacob nodded, feeling the muscles in his neck tighten.

Lee's blue eyes did not leave Jacob's face. Nor did he rush anything. He took Jacob's arm. Jacob noticed his grip was firm.

Lee now turned toward the door where a woman with black eyes and sleek blue-dark hair glanced at them. "Won't you come in, young brother, and have some stew?" Lee said, calmly. "That conference can probably wait for a few hours."

Through that meal, through the remainder of that afternoon, Jacob felt like a stranger in a foreign court. And John Lee was the king. During the supper, more than a half a dozen women served John Lee with every slight wish of his heart. More than twenty people sat around the large table. On other small stools and chairs in the room more than twenty younger children sat. The young girls Jacob's age also served. Some of them Jacob remembered. One of them was Lee's pretty oldest daughter, Anna Jane Lee.

A dark consciousness floated to the foreground of all of the rumors he had tried to suppress in his mind. Vaguely he remembered something had been said once—that the Missourians had violated one of the Lees. He pleaded in his heart that it was not Anna Jane. No one knew. There had always been the strictest silence from the Lees, as though a pact had been made and honored among them, never to speak of the horrors. Jacob also made a promise in his heart in that moment never to ask more, but to bury his questions.

There was little exchange of conversation. The major voice that filled the room was that of John Lee. He said the prayer, read the scriptures, and spoke a few words of wisdom to some of the children. Lee seemed to know what was troubling the heart of each child and how to bless every one of them with some message or charm.

"And Sally," he said, "when God gives you the privilege of taking your little brother with you to school, you have received a charge of stewardship." His voice rose above the women's whisperings, the passage of the food, even the clink of spoons against the bowls. Nervous, Jacob sat nearly motionless, crowding out his darkest fears, feeling that time was passing.

## 29

### Elizabeth

*Saturday, September 5, 1857  We saw the sight of the company from Missouri pass through today—a wide moving river of wagons and people and cattle. All day Suky and I stood near the kitchen window praying they would not see our house standing on this hill east of the draw. I cannot say how we held our breath waiting and how grateful we felt when we saw them turn and pass west along the Penter road. John Lee told us that Jacob Hamblin had suggested they make a camp where there was water and grass for the cattle, and he had suggested the Mountain Meadows. So Brother Lee has sent someone to lead them on their way. I cannot say how grateful I feel to John Lee.*

*Sunday, September 6, 1857  No matter how grateful we are for the gifts we receive, we must pay their price. I am happy for the life that begins to grow inside of me. But the price is steep. I am so sick. I did not want to go with Suky to church. So she went with the*

*Jensens. I wanted to stay alone for a while and think through some things. I wonder how soon J.B. will be back from seeing the Indians? What will he say about the new baby?*

When she closed the book, she sat for a moment before she began shelling the peas for supper. While everything was quiet in the house, she could think better. And now she thought that nothing was as difficult as she feared. She had always believed in miracles—and one of those miracles was the miracle of giving birth. When she looked through the open doorway into the valley where the Missouri party had disappeared on the Penter road, she knew she had seen another miracle when the travelers passed without incident.

The hills on the other side of the valley were low, sharp foothills, which rolled into the slightly higher mountains that rose along the sheep country. She knew that in the midst of those rambling hills was the rich grassy plateau of the Mountain Meadows. The Indians lived close by. She had traveled there once with Jacob and J.B. looking for deer. She was fourteen. The spring grass was so green and so lush it had looked like velvet. She remembered standing by the wagon and holding her sunbonnet on her ears when the wind that rippled through the grass caught the edges of the bonnet and pulled it away from her face. She thought the grassy valley the most beautiful ravine she had ever set foot upon, and she had remarked to J.B. that if ever she was rich, she would buy this valley and build a house on the east rim. The house would have large windows so that she could sit and watch the golden setting sun.

As she picked through the peas, she stopped for a moment. Far away under the Sabbath sun, she believed she could see a rider on a horse coming their way. The rider was so small, the movement so minute, that it seemed almost motionless, like a version of a dot drawn with a feather pen. She turned back to her work, but she could not help but watch the growing dot until she was sure the rider was alone. And it looked like J.B.

When she saw that the rider was in fact J.B., she stood and set the pan of peas on the stoop. Her heart pounded, because she had not realized how anxious she was to see him again. She knew he would be happy to hear that the Missouri company had passed and gone on to the meadows at last. And there was another bit of news she could tell him more precious than the last. In that moment she felt a strange surprise. She discovered that she felt glad.

## 30
### *Jacob*

Jacob rode with John Lee into Cedar City as dusk fell. All the Sunday meetings had been over for a few hours, so Lee headed straight for the house belonging to President Haight. A big moon rising over the east began to throw its light on the front door.

Though he had stayed directly beside or behind Lee on the journey, Jacob jumped down from the strawberry horse to open the gate at the fence for him. But the gate was locked. Rattling it, Jacob called out, grateful to see President Haight come into the yard, his scarf around his neck and his greatcoat pulled tight on his shoulders.

Haight nodded toward Lee and unlocked the gate. He slipped out of his yard, shut the gate behind him, and stood in the road. "We mustn't talk here," he said to Lee. "If you have your bedding with you, let's go down by the iron works to talk. We can trust the boy. Bring him to watch and serve as a messenger if we need one."

When he heard the word "trust" applied to himself, Jacob felt his heart begin to pound. Guessing the gravity of the situation, he followed Lee and Haight to the barn. He watched Haight's gestures to John Lee, the serious look on his face. Jacob waited, anxiously watching the shadows climb the trees while Haight and Lee, talking, disappeared into the barn. They finally returned with Haight's horse and bedroll.

Still dressed in his cravat and greatcoat, his wide-brimmed hat darkening his eyes, John Lee mounted his horse beside Haight. Both of them carried large pack rolls on their saddles. They pulled their hats down against the evening chill. Haight threw a small bedroll to Jacob, who barely caught it as the strawberry moved down the road. At a slow, inconspicuous pace, the three black figures set off for the western edge of the valley. Jacob felt an ominous calm. The few words the men spoke to each other were weighty with the challenge of war.

"I told Tickaboo no, do not fight the Mericats," Lee said firmly.

Haight did not answer.

"I told him that Mericats would fight bad. They knew his people killed American Captain Gunnison in Kanosh several months ago. So I told him no."

Haight kept his eyes focused on the road. He urged his horse to move faster. "The Indians are ready for war," he finally said. "We talked it up to them."

Lee gave a strained laugh that resounded against the empty sky. "One word from us and they're a pot boiling over."

Haight still kept his eyes on the road. For a moment he didn't say anything. But he finally spoke in a low voice. "Let them take these people."

Lee rode in silence. Like strange monuments to some dark deity, or the moon, the iron works loomed before them against the orange sky.

"They have raped and robbed us, killed our Prophet, and driven us from our Missouri homes," Haight said. "There is no innocent blood among them. It is a consensus of opinion that we should retrieve our stolen goods. And if the Indians . . ."

"If the Indians help themselves to the goods, you believe we should be able to retrieve at least some of our own?" John Lee asked.

"We have no control over the Indians. Should you desire to . . ."

"Figuratively speaking."

"They promised to help us fight the Mericats."

"They are ready should we give the word," Lee said.

"Can they do it without our help? That is the question."

Haight drew his horse into the shadows of the giant smelter furnaces of the iron works, which etched the sky like runes that chiseled out both the events of the past and events yet to come. He cleared his throat. He stood tall while he took his bedroll from the saddle. He paused. "If we have to help them, we'll help them. We'll send word," he said.

Lee stopped. Jacob could see that he was staring ahead at the iron furnace jutting into the sky. "It has been decided? Just like that?"

Haight moved slowly. "Just like that," he said.

"Then that's what I should tell them?" Lee grew silent now, watching the gigantic furnace, the unmoving chains. His words echoed in the darkness. Lee finally dismounted and carried his bedroll into the leaning tin hut nearby. Haight followed him and beckoned to Jacob. The boy took his bedding inside the stifling walls. He felt the darkness close around him. Silver moonbeams struck the gravel with a gray sheen, falling on the slab floor in patterns of shadow and light.

"Perhaps it is a calling," Haight dared to whisper, "that these men might pay with their blood for their sins against the Kingdom of God."

The large figure of Lee followed him. "Oh, yes. They have sinned against the Kingdom of God."

"Not a man of them is innocent," Haight said, then grew silent. "They are not innocent." He listened for the sound of the coyotes defending the hill. "If there is a battle against them . . . do you believe . . . the Indians are capable of killing all of the men?" he finally said to Lee.

There was silence in the darkness. John Lee's voice was almost inaudible. "The Indians are capable . . . they can kill them all," said John D. Lee. "But to keep peace with them, we must stand ready with them."

The hours that stretched from dusk into dark were longer hours than any Jacob could remember. Since he had taken the journey from home with the Indians, he had learned to wait. But tonight the wait seemed longer than he would be able to bear. Even the cool night winds could not calm him. When the wind hit the smokestacks, it played them in an eerie tune like the pipes of a giant organ. The sound shivered in his limbs. He heard the rumbling voices of Lee and Haight as though they were far-away wheels on the road, or the moan of rafters. The men talked forever in the shed, the reverberations barely audible to Jacob, so that his head grew heavy, and he caught himself several times falling asleep.

It must have been near nine o'clock when Lee and Haight finally came out of the shack and into the silver moonlight.

"Hold them off for as long as we can. Tell them we need time to get the militia ready . . . to stand by." He emphasized the last words.

"And if they can't do it all . . ."

"Then we'll be standing by, and I suppose . . . ready to join in."

Jacob stayed silent on the big strawberry as they returned to Cedar City to Haight's home. At Haight's house, the sisters brought out a small Indian boy. The child, whose name was Clem, was the adopted son of John D. Lee, and Lee was teaching him to read. Though he lived in Harmony, the boy often rode with Lee to visit his own people.

"And as for you," Haight stopped Jacob and narrowed his gaze. "Should Lee need a messenger, Jacob, you must have a good horse." Jacob hesitated, unsure of what would come next. "A good messenger is needed, and you are welcome to use my strawberry if you'll take good care of her."

"Yes, sir. Thank you, sir. I will, sir." Jacob said. He reached for the mare's mane and clung to it.

"I'll make you an assignment. Stay by Lee and Clem." His look was steady.

Jacob's hair raised up on the back of his neck. "Yes, sir."

Lee did not say a word but began riding southward from Cedar City with the little Indian boy seated in back of him on the saddle.

For several miles Jacob stayed a slight distance behind. He was not sure when he knew there was someone on the road. But he felt it. He sat up in the saddle, alert. He could see John Lee slowing down in front of him. And then he could see in the last wave of twilight, silhouettes of men on horses.

The large band of Indians in the dusk looked like a silent forest of trees. White painted marks on their cheeks reflected the moon. Jacob's breath was knocked from his body.

"Halt!" Lee said, holding his arm to the square. The little Indian boy behind him held tight to his waist.

The ghostly mounts of the Indians made no sound with their hooves on the dusty road. Jacob breathed in sharply. The Indians were painted, ready for war.

"Big Bull!" Lee said. "Moquetas! Where do you go?"

"You tell us fight Mericats. We see Haight, Higbee, Klingensmith," Moquetas said. "They say tomorrow sun come up, time to kill."

Jacob's head reeled.

"We find Lee, the Mor-mon-ee. Take him as our leader. Mor-mon-ees help. We find you. Come with us."

Jacob stayed on his mount at a safe distance behind Lee. The moonlight danced over all of them as though dancing on water, illuminating the dark, slick flesh, glancing from the whites of their eyes.

"Your war. Mor-mon-ee war. You leader."

Lee's head raised slightly as he faced them. His face was bleached white by the moon, his speech halting. "Not now. Wait."

"Wait," Big Bill mimicked Lee, raising his right arm. "Wait and die!"

"Wait," Lee said. "Not ready. I have the orders from the big captain, Captain Haight. Go to the hills and wait."

"How we know you will come?"

"I will come. I promise," Lee said in a solemn voice. "You know I keep my promises." Of course they had always known him as a man of his word. "To show my trust, take Clem with you. You know I will come to take him home."

Jacob was unbelieving. Clem was one of Lee's sons. Now what was Lee doing? He reached behind for the eight-year-old boy on the saddle and handed the child to Moquetas. The boy did not protest or make a sound. The Indian chief settled the boy on the front of his saddle. There was a moment when the Indians stared at Lee, and their eyes burned bright even in the darkness.

Jacob shuddered as the Indians, still steady on their horses, stood in the road without moving. Their hands looked frozen to their weapons, and there was no change of expression in their faces.

Finally, without another word, the chief dug his heels into the sides of his horse and turned it around. Jacob did not believe that Lee had yet taken a breath. And he may not have breathed until all of the Indians in the line followed the chief. Finally, in the silence, the entire line of warriors turned their ponies west, dug their heels into their sides, and were gone.

"And now you will be the only one with me." Lee's voice echoed in the emptiness.

As they pulled past the Hamilton Fort and the fork in the road, Jacob felt the road to the Lorry farm pulling him away. But he kept his sights on Lee's horse in the far distance. He glanced toward the Lorry farm and could see the lights of the fire in the kitchen gleaming. He thought about Elizabeth. But he followed Lee.

## 31
### *Jacob*

They reached Lee's home in Harmony at such a late hour that most of the house had already gone to sleep. Only Lee's daughter Anna Jane heard the door open. When they walked into the house, Jacob caught sight of her in her white gown. She stood in the back of the room in the dark hallway for a moment, until her father came in. At once, she leaned into the wood pile and put sticks onto the fire beneath the black kettle of water to make tea. Pulling a robe from a peg above her, she wrapped it around herself and tied the sash. With her hair loose on her shoulders, Jacob could not take his eyes from her. She moved deliberately and softly as though she were gliding.

"Did you have any success, Father?" she whispered.

"We have not been to the meadows yet."

She did not answer.

Though John Lee was tired, he sat in the large chair to wait for the tea. He smiled at Jacob. The boy's expression toward his daughter did not go unnoticed. When she left, Lee sipped the tea and said quietly, "You are J.B. Lorry's boy?"

Jacob was startled. Through the long hot work of the past days, Lee had not asked any personal questions of him. "Yes."

"There is something I have wanted to tell your family for a long time," he almost whispered, his voice low. "And I haven't ever taken the chance to say it. I saw your sister . . ."

"Cousin?" Jacob corrected him. He was not sure why.

Lee was caught off guard for a moment. "Cousin," he repeated, then decided to describe her. "I took notice of the beautiful girl with the long, light hair—the one who lives in your house . . ." He sipped some of the hot tea. "It was on that first day one of the earlier Missouri travelers was killed out your way. I saw something in your cousin's eyes."

Jacob leaned forward from the low stool he occupied in front of the fire.

"There was something there, written like printed words on a page. If I had read it I couldn't have had a clearer message: that somewhere there was a man buried on your ground."

For a moment Jacob could not hear any of the sounds in the room for the pounding in his ears of his own heart. He could not speak.

"But I would never tell. I wanted you to know that. However it happened—I don't even want you to say it did—you will always be able to trust me to keep it a secret."

Jacob drew in his breath quickly, opening his throat, but still, he could make no sound. He knew that Lee was a man who could keep silent. He wanted to speak, but the room grew so quiet he could not seem to break that silence. And suddenly Anna Jane had returned from the back room with a heel of bread and a pat of butter on a plate.

"You must be hungry," she whispered, buttering the bread. "And tired," she added.

Jacob never heard him speak of the matter again.

"Thank you, Anna Jane," Lee said to her. "We are always glad to be home."

### 32
#### Jacob

When Jacob woke from his place by John Lee's fire on the morning of Monday, September 7, 1857, he could hear the stomp of horses in the yard, and quiet voices. When he went to the window he saw perhaps a dozen men standing in small groups. The sky was barely violet; the men were black silhouettes against the faint light of the sky.

Because the fire had gone out in the grate, Jacob climbed back into his bedding, hoping he could go back to sleep. But it was not long before a willowy figure came into the room with a tarp wrapped around a cord of wood, a cup and a wooden spoon. It was Anna Jane.

As though it were a black wind, his mind winnowed images of the suppressed horrors of the past—images buried without light. He could not seem to put away the throbbing fears—that Anna Jane may once have suffered more than she would ever tell.

Before she blew against the ashes, she dipped into the black edges of the hearth with the wooden spoon. She must not have been aware Jacob was awake, for she did not turn to him. She poured a few spoons of ashes into the large wooden cup, swung the black iron pot across the middle of the hearth, took the ladle and tipped out a drop of water. With her hair loose on her shoulders, Jacob thought she looked like an angel. He could not take his eyes from her as she moved deliberately and softly, as though she were walking through water.

"Good morning, Anna Jane," Jacob said.

When she turned, he thought he saw fear in her eyes. But it was only surprise. "Good morning, Jacob. I hope you had a good rest."

The light filtering through the white curtains at the windows was crimson. Except for the murmur of the men gathering in the yard, it was a morning of strange calm.

In the morning light, Jacob put away all of his dark thoughts. He recommitted himself—he would never think them again.

Anna Jane had allowed Jacob to sleep as long as he wished, but now she signaled to the children, and they came into the room with scrub buckets and vegetable knives. One of the young boys had a box of turnips, which all of them began to trim with great concentration. They laid the tops in rows on a piece of burlap to save for soup. The girls began to set in motion their knitting and crochet needles. Jacob scooped up his blankets in an instant and made room for them to sit down on the settee beside the fire.

"Are you going with Father and the militia to see the Indians?" Anna Jane asked warily. Again she was holding the cup of ashes and stirring it with the spoon. She added a teaspoon of lamp oil. She was making black paste. She had very red cheeks; on her hair she wore a blue kerchief with a gold border. When Jacob did not know the answer to her question, she lowered her eyes. "Perhaps I wasn't to say anything," she said.

After a short breakfast at the table, Lee asked Jacob to come into the yard with the others to help load the wagon. For a fleeting moment, Jacob was surprised at his feelings. He found he would rather have stayed in the house with Anna Jane. But he turned to exit with his host, nevertheless. In a moment he saw that Anna Jane had followed him. She was searching for her father. When she found him, she presented him with the cup of paste. John Lee wrapped it in a burlap sack, tied it, and put it upright in his saddle bag.

"Thank you, Anna," John Lee said. "I hope we will never find the need."

Gathering some of the other men around him, Lee fastened both his horse and strawberry roan to the singletree and proceeded to load the wagon with food and blankets. When finished, he stood back for a moment beside Jacob and said quietly, "Perhaps these next few days . . . there will be some justice done."

Still, not knowing what was ahead, Jacob did not speak. Though he did not recognize the other men, he knew they were members of the Mormon militia from the small settlements nearby. There were few or no words exchanged among the men as they traveled single file for ten or more miles. By the time they reached Penter and moved toward the meadows, the sun hung high in the sky. Leading the group, Lee slowed and brought the wagon around a curve near Hamblins' ranch.

The Hamblin ranch, a two-story pine log dwelling, was built at the northeast of the Mountain Meadows against a low bald hill. The porch stood across the entire front of the house, allowing the windows access to its flat roof. A woman stood in one of the windows above the porch, looking out onto the grassy meadows. As the wagons and men passed, she waved. Even Lee did not know which Hamblin wife this would be. There was more than one, he knew. And even now, the Indian Agent was on a honeymoon in Tooele with yet another woman.

The children gathering in the yard also waved. And though Jacob did not know them by name, he knew they were the Hamblin children. Hamblin had been the one who had suggested that the Arkansas Party stay in the Mountain Meadows. He had told Lee and Lee had told President Haight. And they had sent a scout to show the Arkansas party where to go. They were now only a little south and west of them in the giant draw. The immigrants were now camped in the land that looked like a great cradle scooped out of the mountains where the grass blew like a green sea.

Suddenly Jacob and the others came upon the meadows. Jacob saw the immigrants now, settled in a wide wash. At the bottom lay a jagged scar in the earth, the sink hole where the spring lay. The basin itself must have been one hundred feet across, eighty feet wide. Surrounding that spring he could now see the wagons of the Fancher party. The meadow must have been a mile across and two miles long.

"Yes. There they are," Lee said. There was an undercurrent of anxiety in his voice. The wagons stood in a tight circle close to the spring. As he assessed the scene, Lee pointed out to the others that trenches had been dug around the wagons now. Inside the trenches, propped up on the rocks, were rows and rows of guns.

Now Lee closed his eyes. "They did not wait," he whispered.

Jacob could feel the tension in Lee's voice. There was no question that the wagons had retreated into a protective circle because they had come into a hostile situation. And there seemed little to refute the truth that the settlers had been shooting in that position with those guns. Lee thought he saw a gun with smoke rising from its barrel into the noon sun.

His assessment was true. In that moment, several hundred yards ahead of them, on the northwest rim of the meadows, they turned and saw the men of Tutsegabits and Tickaboo standing on the crest of the hill like a string of feathers barely breathing in the wind. When the Indians caught sight of Lee's wagon they waved their standards of feathers and beads. Finally, in a precise succession, they began to move down the ridge toward them. First one man, then another, and another, until the entire line of warriors entered the Penter road.

Lee stopped the horses as he watched the warriors. On the slope they broke into scattered trots and stirred clouds of white dust eight hands high. Tickaboo rode first. When he reached Lee, Jacob and the men of the militia were hushed. The Indian held his hand to the square. His face was not friendly. "We die!" he exclaimed feverishly. "No trust your God." His brows were knit. His cheeks flushed red. "You make promise to us your God protect us! We die!"

Lee's voice was tight in his throat. "Oh no, Tickaboo," he said—but quietly so that only Jacob could hear. His face was drained of color. "I told you to wait . . . What have you done?" he said out loud.

"We ready fight. Where you people?"

Lee did not move. Jacob felt numb. The wagon felt light beneath them as though it were floating on air.

Tickaboo's eyes were narrow—almost shut. "Best time sun up." He pointed to the sun overhead. "We fight sun up."

Jacob's heart raced. They must have misunderstood the words Lee gave in last night's encounter.

"We kill this many." Tickaboo held several fingers to Lee. "This many Indian die." He held up several more fingers. "Now we angry. You help us kill them. You promise us your God protect if we fight Mericats for you. And our men die!"

Lee seemed frozen. Jacob had remembered he had said, "Not now."

"You get white man fight his own war," Tickaboo demanded. He looked over the small number of men who had come to the site. "You fight."

Jacob followed Lee as though in a trance. The Indians surrounded them on the road. His heart beat against his ribs as the Indians closed around them. Some of them gripped their legs on the flanks of their skittish horses who seemed to be dancing.

"Let's go to your camp," Lee said. "We'll talk about it." He signaled to the other members of the militia who were still trailing behind.

The sun blazed fully over the camp in the draw not three miles away. Lee sweated profusely, wiping his neck with his kerchief. He would not talk to Tickaboo on the road. He did not wish to talk until they had climbed the northern hill and had dismounted at the camp. On the other side of the hill the Indian camp lay stretched out. There were several small leather lean-tos tied together hastily on young trees, and leather awnings tied with rough deerskin thongs. Tickaboo called several of the older warriors to dismount and make a tight circle. Most of the men of the militia pulled back, but Jacob stayed close behind Lee.

Jacob noted the faces that surrounded them: dark faces, clamped jaws, angry brows. The scalp under his hair tightened.

"I told you to wait," Lee said.

Jacob looked at Lee, wondering what to expect. He saw a tremor in Lee's lips. He had always thought of Lee as the paragon of absolute control. But for a moment, he realized that Lee was not going to be able to hold back his emotions. Now, as the tension rose, Jacob knew Lee was doing the best he could. But the pressure of the last four days began to break his voice. Jacob blushed as the grown man held his head in his hands and let sobs shake his body. Down his cheeks coursed streams of tears. Jacob stood feeling helpless, cold.

"Oh God," Lee cried. "What have we done?"

Jacob guessed that the Indians had begun to shoot already. But he also knew that Hamblins' party had taken the chiefs to Salt Lake City and had put them up to it. Now he had the impression that Haight was bringing reinforcements who could smear their faces with Anna Jane's charcoal if they had to.

"Please, my friends, have pity, have mercy," John D. Lee sobbed now, leaning his head in his hands. Though the Indians watched him, they did not seem unduly surprised. Jacob felt his breakfast turn cold in the pit of his stomach. He knew the Indians had seen Lee cry before. One of the names they often called him was "nargutts," or "crying man."

"We die," the dark man spoke. "You make promise, Lee!"

Jacob froze as he stood at Lee's elbow. His hands trembled.

Lee's tears subsided into quiet. He looked numb, even afraid. "Yes, of course," he said. "We will be here!"

After the Indians turned away, Lee paused before he called Jacob close to him. As though piecing it all together from his muddled thoughts, he stroked his chin. "I've been holding back as much as I can. Haight said he would send the other men this morning—but I don't see them. I'll send these men to the meadows. Then if he doesn't come soon, I will send you with a message."

But it seemed he did not want to give an order to Jacob just yet. He fastened his eyes on the small party of men in the field, and then on the meadows ahead. From behind them to the north they could see Jacob Hamblin's boy, Oscar, mounted and riding toward them. He waved and beckoned to them.

"First we'll spend the night at Hamblins'," Lee finally said. He signaled to the others.

Jacob seemed puzzled. "Shouldn't I get that message to Haight right away?"

Lee stared through Jacob as though he were not there. He was taking stock of the meadows, the sky, the hills to the west of them. "Not yet," he said. "No. Not yet, Brother Lorry."

The Hamblin home seemed mysteriously quiet. It may have had something to do with the fact that the father was away on another honeymoon, and both the children and the wives were at liberty to behave any way they pleased. Perhaps whatever they were doing they felt like doing in secret. Even the children were whispering.

Rachel Hamblin would be glad to put all of them up in the barn, Lee said. As they came closer to the house, Jacob could see it was made of well-cut stone, and that the windows on the second story over the veranda were of real glass. It was from those windows that he felt dozens of eyes gaping at him. The young children were openly staring, but Jacob was sure he could sense several young girls hiding behind screens, giggling to one another. He never did see them.

At suppertime, after the men were well fed outdoors, Rachel served Lee and Jacob alone in the dining room.

"The Indians are waiting for our help," Lee explained to Rachel. "I don't know how much longer I can hold . . ."

Rachel Hamblin, a tall dark-eyed woman with large features, carried herself regally from the kitchen to the table. Jacob watched her from a corner of his eye, concentrating fully on his food if she glanced toward him. He thought about Elizabeth and Suky, still not sure if Suky knew where he was. But he did not really care if she knew, either. She would not like it.

"When did the Indians ask for your help?" Rachel asked, concerned. She held her head high as she took dishes back and forth from the dining room into the kitchen. Her voice was low. But she did not flinch as she continued speaking. "We are playing with fire." She paused, but continued. "My husband would tell you . . ."

Lee looked at her. "I know what Hamblin would say."

"Of course you know," Rachel said. But she repeated it nonetheless. "We have spent ten difficult years making friends with the Indians . . ." Her words were halting. "You must stay on the side of the Indians. If the Indians come against us . . ."

Lee looked up at her and saw no tears, no weakness, no hesitation.

"That is right, Rachel."

## 33
### *Jacob*

*There seem to be eyes in the air. I am not speaking just of the dead who hover here before they leave. There are eyes of the Hamblin children who follow us, and the eyes of the Indians who watch what we do—whether we carry out our promises or fail to carry out our promises. There are eyes in these hills. And there are eyes in the Hamblin house, behind the doors, and in the upstairs rooms.*

Jacob's scattered thoughts nagged at him while he waited Tuesday morning, September 8, 1857, for what he knew would soon be the journey to the meadows. But as he waited, the sun came up over the eastern hills. Finally, the other men, anxious, pulled out. Lee's deliberate and careful preparations at the Hamblin home seemed to be in slow motion, unhurried, sluggish. Growing restless, Jacob felt his mind wandering.

It was almost noon before Lee finally mounted his horse. Jacob watched Lee gather in the reins without looking at the road, looking down as though the map of the area were engraved on the backs of his hands. When the horse moved forward, Lee tugged almost imperceptibly as though he were unconsciously hoping beyond hope that he would not have to make the journey down this road he now must travel.

Jacob rode a good distance behind, not wishing to speak or to hear Lee's awkward words. He too kept his eyes down, as though he were riding into a phalanx of soldiers, so that when they saw the riders in the distance, they were not surprised. They had expected them: the lean, driven appaloosa ponies mounted by tall war-painted riders, their black braids and feathers flowing. Some of the men were from their own militia, dressed in loin cloths, their cheeks painted black.

When he came close enough, Tickaboo raised his lance decorated with feathers and the shells of ancient sea fossils from the old Bonneville Lake bed. "We die!" Tickaboo cried out. He pointed his lance into the air, jabbing it as though he were on the underbelly of a giant animal he had undertaken to kill. "Some Mor-mon-ees. But not enough. Where your people? Mericats kill one more time!"

Jacob thought: *There has been another battle. All of the blood in my heart wants to shut down. It is as though I am curling over like a spent dog who has run and run and run until it no longer wishes to run anymore. But there will be running aplenty for me now.*

Jacob felt John Lee's eyes resting on him, though he did not turn to acknowledge that look. Lee waited for only a few seconds before he issued the command. "Yes, it's now, boy," he said as though there were no other words in his vocabulary, nor were any necessary. "Now you must go. We need much more help. Get to Colonel Haight and the others as fast as you can. They may believe the deed has been done. So tell them to bring shovels to bury the dead. But tell them there may be more they can do when they get here."

Jacob glanced one last time at the authentic Indians and the counterfeit Indians. Finally he was able to meet Lee's eyes—the brilliant blue of his piercing eyes. Jacob turned the strawberry around.

### 34
#### *Wednesday, September 9, 1857. Elizabeth*

J.B. had assured them that Jacob was still with John D. Lee. But that had been no guarantee to Suky. Elizabeth saw her look out of the window at regular intervals, almost every twenty minutes.

Finally, little Spencer Jensen came up with a message from Isaac Haight that Lee and Jacob had gone to the meadows. Elizabeth waited, chilled, to hear Suky's response. It came after a long pause.

"But that's where . . . they are!" she whispered, and sat heavily on the settee. "That's where the Arkansas people have gone." Little Spencer left as quickly as he had come, leaving a word with J.B. that left his face pale.

"Jacob will be fine," J.B. repeated woodenly. "If we can't trust John Lee and his Indian friends, I don't know who we can trust."

Elizabeth thought she saw some of the fire burn out behind Suky's eyes. But she wasn't sure. Only twenty minutes later Suky was standing at the window again.

"Suky," J.B. said, almost harshly.

She turned, her eyes flaming. "They're out there!" she hissed. "And war is a brewing!"

J.B. looked at her squarely. "What do you want of me? To go find him?"

"It's not a bad idea," Suky's voice was level.

"Foresight's leg is still bad."

"Then borrow Jensen's mule!"

Elizabeth watched J.B. stare at Suky for a long time, her eyes still flashing.

"All right," he said now. "Tomorrow." He paused. "If we haven't seen Jacob by Wednesday and I'm finished helping George with his harvest, I'll ask if I can borrow the Jensen mule. And I'll go."

Suky's open eyes still burned with anger. Elizabeth prayed she would let go—unloose her hands from the chair. She was so tense she was shaking. That night again, Elizabeth heard Suky crying in the dark.

When Elizabeth woke Wednesday morning, September 9, 1857, and looked out on the fields from the loft window, she could see J.B., Percy, and George Jensen gleaning the straw from the Jensen field. She heard Suky in the kitchen below. Adding to the dawn light, there was a faded glow from the cooking fire. Elizabeth hurried, knowing Suky needed her help.

"J.B.'s already gone. And he forgot his food," Suky said when Elizabeth climbed down the ladder. She had packed some bread in a linen napkin and some cheese in a cloth sack. "If you want to walk down there," Suky's eyes widened with a blank stare, "you can walk down there." But when she saw Elizabeth's hesitation, she said, "or we can just walk down together."

"No, you needn't go, Suky. I can go down," Elizabeth said, finally.

It was noon when Suky said good-bye to her at the door. But Elizabeth hadn't gone a hundred yards when she heard the door open behind her. She turned. Suky, holding her shawl above her shoulders, was flying like a ruffled bird from the house.

"I guess I'll go with you, anyway," she said, stepping unevenly across the dry grass. Elizabeth said nothing. They walked in silence down into Jensens' field.

When they reached the edge of the field, they followed the men at a distance for what seemed like hours while the sun seemed unmoving in the pale blue sky. After the men had gleaned the remaining hay and tied it in small bundles to add to the wagon, George and Percy loaded the cart while J.B. slowly drove the mule across the hay to stomp it down. Finally, as the sun began to slant from the west, a cool breeze passed through the grass. The men finally agreed they would eat before they finished the last load, and before it grew dark.

They took time eating. Suky ate very little, but kept looking over the black hills to the west where the sun began sinking. Beyond the knife-edged hills was the road to Penter and beyond that to Hamblins'. And beyond the Hamblins' was the Mountain Meadows. They had heard rumors that there had been fighting there with the Indians. There was not much talk. The calm seemed to be like a heavy pall against their mouths. The men hurried to get back to work before dusk fell.

Elizabeth leaned over to tuck the last bit of bread into the empty basket when she saw three strangers on horses come around the west bend. They looked unmistakably like the immigrants. She froze. Not long ago there had been the dark wind of a rumor that three gun-toting immigrants had come back to town to steal grain that first Saturday afternoon when Lee was alone at the mill. Someone had said that as they waved their guns in John Lee's face, they told him they had been in the line that raped his daughter in Missouri. Elizabeth didn't know what to believe, as John Higbee had said no grain was missing.

Out of the corner of her eye, Elizabeth thought she saw the men in the field stiffen. They were now working in the northwest corner close to the road.

George Jensen stood still for a moment facing them. But soon he backed slowly to hide behind the hay. Percy Jensen raced to the back of the hayrack and fumbled for something. Elizabeth thought it was probably his gun. His eyes were burning with fear. Suky grasped Elizabeth's arm. "Get back here," she whispered. She drew Elizabeth back behind the hayrack and trembled as the men drew near. One of them they recognized as the man who claimed he shot "Joe Smith."

"It's them!" George shouted.

The large man had his hand on his gun.

"So they are fighting the Indians! And now they are after us," J.B. said between his teeth.

Elizabeth felt Suky's hand stiffen on her arm. Instinctively, the two women ducked. J.B. leaped down from the rack and hid beside Jensen. Only the mule in front of the hayrack stood exposed in the field.

"Your mule!" J.B. gasped. "They'll kill your mule!"

There was a shot. Elizabeth's scalp tightened with a chill. She smelled smoke. The shot had come from Percy's gun. He was bent low on the other side of the rack, only his eyes visible. But he was holding the gun. And it had gone off.

"Give me that!" J.B. dived for the rifle. Elizabeth's blood froze. "Give me that rifle," J.B. said again, and he grabbed it. But before he got it, the young red-headed man on the first horse leaned from the saddle, a spot of crimson appearing on his freckled face. One of the strangers aimed his gun at J.B., who gladly shot at the man but missed. The young man with the red hair fell from his saddle. His foot caught in the stirrup of his frightened horse, and he bobbed like a sack of corn against the dust. Seeing their companion hurt, the others shot into the hayrack. But at the repeated shots from Percy's rifle in J.B.'s hands, they turned their horses back toward the meadows and quickly disappeared.

"He's dead," Suky stared.

"That," J.B. said between his teeth, "is the beginning of the end." There was something so ominous about J.B.'s words that Elizabeth felt numb. "The others may have disguised themselves, but these two men seen whites do it," J.B. continued, his voice two notches lower. "They'll tell what happened. They'll come after us. They'll bring the army from the Pacific."

George Jensen grabbed Percy by the shirt and shook him. He glared at him. "You shot too good! You killed one of them!" he cried. The boy looked pale and scrambled up into the hayrack. J.B. boosted the women into it. George wasted no time turning the mule toward home.

Elizabeth clutched the basket and felt her fingers tighten until they hurt. As the hayrack turned around, J.B. climbed into it, the gun still in his hands, smoking. "We're in it now," he murmured.

### 35
#### Jacob

When Lee asked Jacob to return to Harmony to fetch the troops, the first question Jacob asked himself was how he was to get home safely alone. But the responsibility to bring the men back loomed large in his mind. He fled home. Along the road from the meadows through the hills to Jensens' ranch, he felt the familiar mountains lean over him like black clouds. He pressed so rapidly that the lathering horse began to lose its footing.

Near dusk, when he stopped to let the animals drink at the stream, he saw two strangers pass him on horseback, speeding in the direction of the meadows. A third young man with curly red hair lay bouncing like a sack of potatoes across the saddle of the third horse. The man looked dead. Jacob's heart came up in his throat. He urged Haight's strawberry to move quickly the next few miles.

At last, he was at the Lorry farm. When he reached home, he found President Higbee at his father's house, standing with J.B. on the front stoop. When his mother saw him, she screamed with joy. He waved.

"The Indians are taking care of 'em," he breathed heavily as he dismounted. "Now orders is to to bring shovels to bury the dead."

His mother stood beside him, clasping her hands. He saw Elizabeth's white face.

"The dead?" Higbee said in a dull flat tone.

J.B. glared at him. "The Indians are takin' care of them." He paused, "Bad enough they seen the Indians kill." There was no sound from anyone. "Now they've also seen us kill."

*Killed. The man with the red hair lying across the mule. A Missourian.*

Jacob began to speak, but J.B. hushed him with his hand.

"Let's go," J.B. murmured.

Only moments later, with Higbee on his horse and J.B. on Jensens' mule, they struck across the basin so rapidly that the dust smoked beneath the hooves.

J.B. told Jacob in so many clipped words to stay home. He and Higbee would get to Haight and they in turn would get orders from Colonel Dame to call out the militia from Cedar. "Your duty, boy, is to protect your mother and Elizabeth now." Jacob saw J.B. begin to reach out toward Elizabeth, who stood beside him. But J.B. resisted. He turned to Jacob, almost snarling. "No use your getting into more trouble. You've already had your share of it with Lee, near causing the death of your mother and me."

But Jacob's share of trouble on the meadow with Lee had only begun. As J.B. and Higbee rode off toward Cedar, he leveled his gaze toward Suky and Elizabeth. "There was somebody else killed, wasn't there?" he said thinly to his mother, who was already fussing over him to get him into the house to eat.

Only Elizabeth could answer him, her white hands on her apron. "Yes," she whispered. "Percy shot one of those men."

"They were probably on their way here to ask for our help to stand against the Indians," Jacob knew. "They were looking to us for help."

"Yes," Elizabeth said.

## 36

*September 10, 1857, Jacob*

*One of them has been killed and the other two will tell. And Suky whispered Elizabeth is going to have a child. I cannot stay here even if Father commands it.*

Jacob spent Wednesday at home putting up hay. But one day was all he could bear. On Thursday morning, he woke before dawn and decided he too must go. Without making a sound in the kitchen, he took some bread and left the house before Suky knew he was going.

The miles across the basin and through the hills to the meadows looked formidable in the gray light. Along the road he saw patches of travelers ahead of him. Patrick Moore, Higbee, and Adair led one group. Additional members of the militia were on their way. Jacob felt cold sweat across his scalp. He watched the shadows slip back from the sun.

Many of the militia had spent Wednesday going to the site. But it was clear that many more men were on their way. There were units from Cedar, Scipio, and Parowan, and with them the commanders, Klingensmith and Haight—though no one saw Colonel Dame.

By the time Jacob reached Hamblins' on Thursday afternoon, most of the militia had arrived. When dusk fell, a few of the men who had been fighting in the hills came down on horseback, their faces charred, their loincloths filthy and torn.

"There are too many of them," one of the men said. "Potshots from the hills is not going to work."

As J.B. looked across the circle of men toward the members of the militia, he caught sight of Jacob. He looked surprised. But he nodded warily.

At about 7:00 p.m. the group finally saw Lee ride toward them over the hill. Behind him were the Indians on their gleaming ponies, slick with sweat. The native heads were bristling with war feathers, their faces white with paint. Lee raised his hand to quiet them all, his face red and roughened by the sun.

The militia, standing with their shovels, stiffened when Lee came to the circle. Tickaboo and Tutsegabits followed him. Moquetas and Big Bill stood by. Several other chiefs dismounted and stood outside while Lee eased in to the center of the circle of white men.

"You're all here?" he said. The men did not answer him. One or two of them jabbed their shovels into the ground. When they had been asked to bring shovels to bury the dead, they had brought them. But, Lee inferred, there was another job to be done also.

"You know the situation," Lee said, barely opening his mouth, as though his jaw were clamped shut. "The Indians cannot take care of the immigrants alone."

The Indians glared at them. At the militia. At Lee. At nothing in particular.

Tickaboo pulled at his horse, and his horse snorted.

"Isn't there a better way?" An interpreter came into the circle and stood with Lee and the chiefs as they talked.

"Somebody ought to get military orders."

"Didn't we promise to wait for orders from Brigham Young?"

Lee paused at this statement.

One of the men said, "Haslam went up on Monday. But he hasn't returned. In the best of circumstances, it takes a hundred hours."

Lee shrugged, choosing to dismiss the impracticality of waiting for orders from Brigham Young. "We have to go by what happens in the field. There is no time for orders from a long-distance general," he almost whispered. "By the time Haslam gets back, we may all be dead men."

"Promise," one of the Indians repeated over and over again under his breath.

Lee stood taller as he spoke to the group. "We tried war. Tomorrow will be a different day. All anyone wants is the immigrant men—the ones who killed the Saints in Missouri. There is a way."

A hush fell over everyone. Now some of the group of men sat on the ground.

"And those people are our enemies, too. There is no innocent blood among them."

While they spoke in low voices, the sky seemed to darken, covered by clouds.

"They still think it's only Indians," Lee began.

"Except it's not just Indians no more. The settlers know by now we killed their boy on the horse." Higbee did not say who.

"The boy with the red hair?"

Lee had heard of the killing. The Indians were still glaring at him. For a long time he was silent, the wheels turning in his head as he assessed the situation.

"White man's job," Tickaboo said.

"Yes." Lee nodded toward Tickaboo. "We are all in this together." There was another pause, a wave of fear, a wave that washed over them all. "If we separated the men from the others . . ." He faced the group. "We'll just get orders from Colonel Dame."

After much haggling with the Indians, they decided that Haight and Higbee would ride in the night together to get orders in Parowan from Colonel Dame. As the camp settled down under the light moon, Jacob felt a singular terror, like hot breath, pass over all of them.

Some of the men sat in the circle of the camp by a small cooking fire, prepared to wait until dawn when Haight and Higbee would finally arrive with some news. While J.B. slept soundly, Jacob strained to hear the voices of the men as they talked, but he could hear nothing at all. In the earlier tension he had not seen where Lee had gone. Jacob got up quickly and looked around. He saw a dark figure about a hundred yards away, walking up the ravine. When he reached the spot, he found Lee tramping through the bushes. He saw the man fall on his knees.

*I found John Lee saying a prayer. I could hear this man's voice and I thought that the ears of all of heaven must be listening to him. Though I did not go near him, I could hear him say, "Oh God, is it, like Saul, thy will that we must kill? Is it better to obey than to sacrifice? Speak to me, Father. Speak to me Father." He said it over and over again through his tears.*

That night, in the camp near Hamblins', not more than a mile from where the Missourians were camped by the springs, Jacob thought he heard a low, moaning song. It might have been the Indians from their warriors' camp not far away. But it sounded like a hymn. He wasn't sure. He looked up into the black sky and thought he could sense the distance of the icy stars.

## 37
### *September 11, 1857, Jacob*

*After all the talk, after all the prayers, after the trek west, the sorrows, the losses, the burdens, after talking the Indians into expecting a war, after suffering the robberies, indignities, all that has gone unpunished, Lee says we have only one choice. The Missourians say they will go to California and bring an army against us; they know we killed one of them on the trail. Lee says we must help the Indians kill the men. None of the settlers must be allowed to tell the story. The women and children will be so far away from the men that none of them will know.*

"We are bound to avenge the lives of our prophets . . ."

"God told Saul to kill."

"How can we help ourselves?"

"We can't."

"I have evidence of God's approval of our mission. All of those who could talk of it . . ."

"Oh, that this cup might pass from us."

"Not my will, but thine be done."

While the militia met in a grove of trees on the edge of the meadow, Jacob memorized everything around him—the sky, the flickering leaves—as though this were the last moment of his life. The militia divided into groups, some of them staying in their regular dress to go with Lee, and some moving toward the northwest hills to "help the Indians" who were so insistent on help. But he and his father had been assigned to follow Lee and Klingensmith, who carried the white flag.

"Do your part, Jacob," his father said, sending a dark look. Jacob returned his father's gaze, but he could not speak. All of them watched for several hours while the men in the Fancher train responded cautiously to Klingensmith's white flag. Lee's stature was visible from any distance. He was a strong figure, with the shock of yellow hair, the broad shoulders, the hands stretched forward as the men and women came close around him and the children came running to see. Jacob believed he knew what Lee was telling them.

*We will save you from the Indians if you will do exactly as we command. You must lay down your arms. The sick and the wounded will take the first wagon. I will follow that wagon. Behind me, the women and children must walk in single file. Behind the women and children several hundred yards, we will bring the men. We will send an armed man of our militia to accompany each unarmed man.*

From a distance, Jacob could see the immigrants finally prepare to move their wagons out. They did not take everything. Lee had also convinced them to leave some of their booty to the Indians as spoil. The first wagon to climb the draw to Hamblins' was filled with the sick and wounded. Lee walked behind that wagon. Behind Lee moved the women and the children in ragged single file.

About a hundred yards behind the wagon of sick and wounded, followed by the women and children, the men began to move forward unarmed. Lee had said his instructions must be followed to the letter. The immigrants must lay down their arms or the Indians would not trust them. The Mormon militia moved forward, each man to take a stand by one of the unarmed immigrant men.

Jacob fell in line. He recognized the man who stood beside him as one of the cattlemen he had spoken to outside of Scoville. A lump gathered in his throat the size of a large stone. He had his instructions. At the command, shoot, or if you can't shoot, duck, and let someone else finish the job. He did not know if he could shoot someone he had remembered seeing in the Fancher train.

"Do I know you?" the man asked Jacob.

Did he have to speak? He was greeting Jacob as his liberator. The Cedar militia was supposedly saving their lives. Jacob wanted to draw back, to melt into the mountainside. He reminded himself that Lee had given him permission to duck. Perhaps he would not shoot—though he could still see his father's dark eyes. Perhaps he would not shoot straight. Ahead of him he saw his father's bent figure and George Jensen's tousled graying hair. His father turned around to hurry him, glaring. Jacob walked slowly, feeling the weight of the gun.

"Warn't you that kid drove that wagon outside of Scoville?"

"Yes, sir."

"We do appreciate you takin' us out of this. We had no idea the Indians was going to be on the kill."

They walked another few steps in silence. Jacob's blood still beat in his ears.

"You remember . . . my wife . . . well, she just had our child. A baby girl. Funny. I seen those Indians comin' and I thought to myself, just when I had my baby, that little baby on the plains, I wondered if we was going to die before we got to California."

Jacob could not speak.

"She's up there . . . up ahead. You see her, the woman with the blue and white bonnet."

Jacob stared ahead. The woman was hanging back, staying close to the end of the line.

"I have to be grateful to you." The man looked Jacob full in the face. Jacob could feel his eyes. But he dared not meet them.

It was at that moment that the cry "Halt!" sounded. It was Klingensmith who had shouted it, thick and garbled. From that moment on, Jacob did not follow what happened very clearly. But he heard the terrifying noise, the sudden shots and the blood-curdling screams. There was fire on every side—explosions—the cacophony of gunfire—as abrupt as an earthquake. In his dizziness he saw the men of the Fancher train thudding to the ground. Some of the militia ducked, as Lee had instructed them to do. And then all at once, as if from nowhere, the

Indians and those who had been instructed to stand by them began screaming and running down the hill. Though it was hard to discern the difference, Jacob believed he could pick out some of the militia who had dressed to stand by the Indians. Though they were hollering and jumping, some of them seemed to hold back while the natives, brandished their tomahawks and knives as they ran.

The dark-haired man next to Jacob suddenly grabbed for Jacob's gun and attempted to wrest it away. Surprised, Jacob's taut fingers cramped unconsciously just enough to fire it. When it went off, Jacob reeled. He couldn't believe the strength in his own fingers. He felt his own teeth grinding together. His head swam. The man at his side now had the rifle out of Jacob's hands and was swinging it around. In a flash Jacob suddenly saw blood oozing from a gash on the man's cheek. Jacob gazed at the man's face. His heart raced. He, Jacob Lorry, had made that wound. He watched with terror while the blood began to drip from it.

But the bullet had only grazed the man's face. It did not stop the fire in his eyes as he came for Jacob with the rifle in his arms. He pointed it at Jacob, though Jacob ducked and backed away, his body jerking with fear. Another shot sounded from close by. The immigrant, holding the gun to Jacob's heart, crumpled to his knees. After a few seconds, he fell face forward to the dirt, his dark curly hair matted with blood.

"You was damn near killed," said J.B.

Jacob stared as though he were in a dream.

"Get that gun." J.B. kicked the rifle out of the dead man's hands. The immigrant had fallen over the butt of it, and J.B. pushed the body aside with his foot. The man's eyes were still glazed with a foggy light. He stared at Jacob and began to open his mouth.

"How could . . ." but his words had been only a reflex. He had been almost instantly killed.

Jacob's head swam with fear. He knew the intention of the militia was to place the women and children far ahead so that only the men would be killed. But the Indians, seeing that the militia had adequately taken care of the men, ran ahead while some of the disguised stand-by's joined them, and others dragged their feet. The phalanx ran directly to the women and began bludgeoning them, pounding them into the ground. Stunned, John Lee and the other members of the militia tramped about in the carnage, wondering crazily what to do. It was a moment that seemed like forever. Trooping through the littered field, ducking from the strident screams, the rest of the militia ran to the scene. If there had ever been a plan to save the women, it had been abandoned now. There was a frenzy. The blood began to run down the faces of the women. John Lee waved the militia forward. They began sending gunshot through the skulls to put the suffering and the wounded out of their misery. Darting among the dying through the flashing barbs of light, they stumbled in and out amongst the jumbled colors and screams.

Finally, Jacob could see someone—it looked like John Lee—ahead of them, shooting the sick and wounded in the front wagon. Jacob had not remembered that the death of the sick and wounded had been part of the plan. Was it? He cringed. But of course, even the first wagon would have been able to see what had happened.

He watched as a bullet from one of the guns hit the head of the woman in the blue and white bonnet. He saw her fall forward, her face in the grass, her blood coloring the grass with dark red. Jacob fell to the ground suddenly, the nausea choking him behind his nose and his eyes. He crawled toward the woman now lying heaped on the ground. Shaking, he pulled her shoulder away from the child. The woman had cradled the child in her bosom to soften the fall. Now the blood bloomed in her hair.

George Jensen appeared from what seemed to be nowhere, from the red wash of people that surrounded him, and he knelt quickly to the woman's side. "Is this a new baby?" he said. "I'll take the baby home with me. My wife and daughter always wanted another girl child."

George Jensen took the baby while Jacob still knelt by the woman's body. "Come on, boy. Get up. We're nearly done."

It had taken only five minutes to wipe out a hundred and twenty people from the immigrant wagon train.

*You are walking now. You are walking through columns of air that hang like pillars on either side of an avenue of light. Voices seem distant, like wind moving through the trees. There is only the light ahead of you and the earth falling away from you, peeling back from you. You have fired. You have fired a shot into a man's face you might have killed.*

It was as though he had never seen the earth before today. Not as it was, the teeming crust, peeling away from him with dust, rising and falling as it was, the wind stirring, pouring among both the living and the dying, the dying still stirring, the living walking, walking in and out with shovels, filling trenches with bodies not yet cold.

*You are moving through a haze as though the air itself is the only substance that can be real. Nothing else is real. This carnage cannot be real. All that is real is a perception that below you in the dust is quiet. There is a black quiet reeling through a sudden consciousness that all there can be is quiet. That a weight, sudden and powerful, settles from the quiet like stones, like stones stained with blood. Stones you will have to carry.*

*You are not listening to all that is happening around you, to the commands, to J.B., to Lee. You are not seeing what lies below you on the ground, because tomorrow or the next day you will pull the bread out of your satchel and it will taste all right in the hot sun. Maybe the cheese will seem tart, but it will taste good going down. Or it will be dough boys or scones out of Suky's skillet and rolled in sugar. J.B. will walk into the house carrying his shovel . . . that same shovel . . . on his shoulder, shouting one thing and another about the canal or the ditches, while you watch Elizabeth's white hands pushing and pulling the needle through a sampler that says in the white cloth with thread like drops of blood, "God is Love."*

*Now it is a miracle of air. You reach for it trying to breathe, to find your head above water—to rise from under the weight that forms like a cloud and begins to push down on you—press, push, floating, or circling over you, and you want the air and you don't want the weight and you wonder if you can carry it all the rest of your life, and your children and their children after that, and you pray that you may be able to do enough good in this world to tip back the balance on the scales. Enough that is right. To wrest something out of the soil that is alive and vital and will take away the taste of death on your tongue.*

*For the taste is everywhere. The dead are lying in the pools of their own blood. You want to breathe and so you lift your face and you cannot look any more.*

As though in a dream, Jacob dug with the others, hearing the sound of shovels hitting the ground, hearing the clip of metal against stone. The bodies fell into the trenches, already prepared by the Arkansas train. All seemed quiet. Even the Indians made little noise rummaging through the spoil. They murmured softly in their own language while they went carefully through everything, taking pans, spatulas, sugar, and salt. Shoes.

"No man. Let no man allow this to come off his tongue."

What had happened?

"Stand in a circle. Raise your right arm to the square."

As if in a dream, Jacob followed the commands. J.B. stood beside him.

"No one must know. It was an Indian massacre and no one needs to know anything else."

"Keep it quiet. Don't tell anyone, not even our wives."

"We covenant with one another. And our almighty God."

"It was an Indian massacre."

*Of sorts.*

"It was necessary."

*Perhaps.*

"We would have been at war with the Indians."

*That may have happened.*

They camped overnight at Hamblins'. Colonel Dame came in the night, and on the next morning rode with President Haight out to the bloody sea of grass. Jacob was not with him, but it was reported on his return that Dame sat on his horse to view the scene and murmured, "The horror. The horror."

"Then why did you give the command?" President Haight had said.

Colonel Dame's response was, "I did not expect there would be so many."

The militia finished the digging the next day. They divided up the children to take to their homes.

Jacob walked through those hours of burial trying to breathe above the stench of the decaying flesh. He pulled the top out of a clump of goldenrod, crushing it with his hands to overcome the odor of the bloody field. He barely saw J.B. out of the corner of his eye. J.B. offered to take a six-year-old and a three-year-old, sister and brother of the baby girl Jacob had found. Rachel Hamblin had rescued the baby when she began to cry in George's arms.

"She needs to nurse, George," Rachel said. "She is too little to go now. If you insist on having her, then come back and get her in a few weeks. I'll nurse her with my baby until she's healthy."

Reluctant to let the baby go, George Jensen stayed beside Rachel for a long time. Vowing he would come back for the child, he helped J.B. lift the sleepy little boy to Jacob's strawberry horse, and his big sister to J.B.'s mule. Others also took some of the children with them.

As he climbed onto the horse, Jacob pulled more of the wild yellow flowers, as though by plundering them, he could crush the memories of the meadow that stank in his nostrils. As they rode away, Jacob felt the eyes of the Hamblin home riveted on all of them. He thought he could see one of the young girls staring at him from the doorway. It seemed a familiar face. His first thought was that it was Margaret Seymour. But it could not have been. This girl who stared at him was large with child, and he had left Margaret in Parowan with her relatives.

As they clambered into the road, Jacob felt the presence of the little boy on his horse. He felt the black earth of the meadows beat beat like drums behind him. His thoughts swam to the sky. He was not innocent. They had done a terrible thing. He clung to Haight's horse, biting one of the wild flowers in his teeth. He was aware of the bitter taste in the stem.

Ahead of them down the road the warriors Moquetas and Big Bill banged spatulas against pan lids. They chanted victory tunes, yelling mighty cries of relief against the sunshine. Pots and pans and spoons dangled from their saddles, and they waved shovels and tools in the air.

Jacob looked wearily toward home and calculated how long it would be before they arrived at the Lorry place. Then he felt too tired to care.

## 38
### Elizabeth

*Sunday, September 20, 1857. A week ago, when they came from the meadows and told us of the Indian massacre, they were so overcome with grief they could not speak about it. We may never know, they said, how terrible it was. Now all of these children are alone. Oh dear Lord, how could this have happened? Even their mothers were killed.*

Elizabeth bit her pen. She felt the lump of the new child growing in her body and thought, even their mothers were killed. How could it have been?

*They brought us the little boy, Foster, and the girl, Sally, brother and sister. Suky loves mothering. She said she never got as many children as she wanted, so she wants to keep Sally and Foster. They have brought her happiness. I wonder. Will my baby do the same for me? How will it feel to be a mother? What kind of a mother will I be?*

*Suky wants Sally and Foster to be reunited with their little sister, the baby who was so tiny that she is still at Hamblins'. But George Jensen has claimed her. At least he is our neighbor, and the children will be close to each other while they wait for the Arkansas relatives to come for them. George asked Jacob and Rebecca and me if we wouldn't go out to Hamblins' to fetch this little baby girl back to him. The children have told us her name is Hannah.*

On the morning they planned their trip to Penter, it rained. The clouds stood like black trees across the eastern sky blocking out the sun. Elizabeth felt some movement in her body as she woke and faced the streaked hills. The gloom seemed prophetic, somehow. When the rain stopped, it was not too late to make the trip. It did not take long for Jacob to hook Foresight to the wagon.

"If you're goin' today, bundle up warm," Suky fussed. "And keep a watch out for the Indians."

"The rain has stopped and the clouds passed over, but you can't tell," J.B. said to them.

As they rode to fetch Rebecca in the cart, Elizabeth noticed Jacob again as she had noticed him when he had first come home. He was taller, larger. He had filled out. He was solid. In the silence of their brief ride together, Elizabeth was not sure how much she could say to him about how troubled he seemed since his return. But finally she dared to open up to him.

"I feel that J.B. . . . and . . ." she hesitated. "You too, Jacob, have been suffering in some way. I wish you would talk about it to me and we could help."

Jacob was silent as he looked at her out of wounded eyes. There was still some of the old admiration he had felt for her before her marriage to J.B. Somehow in this past week Jacob had seemed suddenly much older than he was, and she could not have explained why.

"It's like the time that man was shot in our yard," Jacob barely whispered. "Suky can't talk about it. We can't talk about it. We can't talk about the Indian massacre."

Elizabeth felt his pain as though it were mysteriously her own. She too agreed silently that they would not talk about it anymore.

Rebecca was glowing with expectation when they picked her up at the Jensen ranch. She climbed into the cart with a carpet bag. "Baby blankets to bring to the little one," she explained. "Rachel Hamblin may not have enough to spare. We also have swaddling rags and used clothes enough to keep a baby dressed for years." She was obviously looking forward to caring for this new child who was coming into the Jensen household.

Elizabeth nodded and Jacob maneuvered Foresight and the cart out of the front drive. For a few moments the ride was silent. In the distance the wet hills reflected pale light and breathed up an aery mist that seemed fragrant, like tea.

They reached Penter by noon and took the short road up to Hamblins'. Rebecca had brought hard-boiled eggs, and Elizabeth had made muffins. They ate in the cart on the road in silence, although Jacob had offered a short prayer over the food, and Rebecca had occasionally attempted to lead them into a conversation about subjects that sounded to Elizabeth a lot like gossip. Yesterday her cousin and friend in Harmony had seen John D. Lee come into town herding his own sheep along with the addition of many new animals. He was also driving with a couple of the loaded Fancher wagons. The Indians with him wore pans on their saddles and spoons in their hair. Lee had told the people, "We have been delivered. Thanks be to God."

Elizabeth listened to Rebecca carefully when she mentioned John D. Lee. It was evident in her voice, that Rebecca still admired him more than any man living. When she mentioned John Lee's name, she looked at Elizabeth as though to say, "He is the man who, above all other men, has delivered us."

Later, she told Jacob and Elizabeth that John D. Lee was going on Sunday to see Brigham Young in Salt Lake City, "to report the results of the Indian massacre in the Mountain Meadows."

Elizabeth gazed at Rebecca with uncertainty. "Your marriage to John Lee," she dared to say. "Are you . . ." she began, but then stopped, because Rebecca understood her question. And the answer was "no."

"Someday I'll go with him, but probably not now," Rebecca said.

When they reached Hamblins' house, they noted the extra children. There had been eighteen left from the immigrant train, counting the last baby girl, Hannah, born on the journey. Some members of the militia had already taken some of the children. Suky and J.B. had taken Sally and Foster. But from the looks of the Hamblin house now, it seemed there had been an addition of at least seven or eight youngsters under eight years old.

Not only children, but increased numbers of chickens crowded the driveway as Foresight plodded into the yard. The girls flapped their aprons. A young boy disappeared into the house.

Soon there were not one or two, but several people at the door. One older woman must have been Rachel Hamblin, Elizabeth thought. There were two young girls at her side. Another girl stood in the background holding a tiny baby in her arms. Elizabeth thought that was probably the little baby girl Hannah. Several small children and toddlers came out into the harsh September light. Their small brown legs blended with the movement of the dust on the stones.

Rebecca climbed down from the cart quickly and walked across to the house. "Sister Hamblin," she said. "My pa is George Jensen. We're neighbors to the Lorrys, where the baby's sister and brother have gone. He wanted me to fetch the baby." She nodded toward the child in the girl's arms.

Rachel's eyes softened. "Of course," she said. "If you can find a wet-nurse, the baby will be all right." She glanced at Elizabeth. "I suppose she'll be safe in the hands of you good women." She laughed now, her eyes twinkling. "I'm reluctant to give her up, but I know how much George Jensen wanted her."

Behind Rachel and the children in the room, Elizabeth suddenly noticed that Jacob had stiffened. She heard him breathe inward—almost in a gasp. Behind Rachel Hamblin, the young girl with the child in her arms was staring at Jacob from bleak dark eyes.

"Margaret," Rachel called, "bring the baby."

The girl she called Margaret knit her brows. Not one of her muscles relaxed its grip on the child.

"Margaret," Rachel smiled apologetically to Rebecca and lowered her voice, "She seems to take a fancy to the baby, but hers is a needy attachment. She is . . . unpredictable. I'm afraid she's not ready for one of her own."

Jacob was staring. Elizabeth did not know why.

"Honey, we can't keep every one of these children," Rachel said to Margaret. "And the Jensens are willing to take her. She was promised to Mr. Jensen."

Margaret ducked back into the dark house with the child in her arms.

Rachel smiled at Rebecca. "I'll fetch her," she said. "She knows the baby must go. She's just a child herself. And very . . . notional. Won't you come in? You're welcome to come in."

Rebecca smiled back.

The house was dark, cool, and quiet. Children were everywhere. Hamblin children, Fancher children. No one would have known the difference. There were only a few chairs in the large front room. Jacob did not sit, but stood uneasily in the doorway while Elizabeth and Rebecca sat on the edge of two small upholstered Queen Anne chairs.

When Rachel returned with Margaret, the baby was still in the girl's arms. "Margaret Seymour is one of my cousin's daughters." Rachel said, introducing the girl formally for the girl's benefit. "She came to have her baby here."

Firmly, without another word, Rachel Hamblin wrested the baby from Margaret's arms. The girl turned her back to them, though from time to time she watched Jacob out of the corner of her eye as though he were vaguely familiar to her.

Rachel walked with the child to a large chest, where she began to unwrap her own blankets from the little girl. From Rebecca's carpet bag, Elizabeth produced a small quilt.

"All that came with the child was this one flannel rag," Rachel explained.

"I have many baby things," Rebecca said happily. She reached for the small black-haired child and held it for the first time in her arms. Elizabeth thought it was smaller than she imagined.

"I would guess it is only a little over two weeks old," Rachel smiled. "I was feeding her with a cloth soaked in cow's milk for a while, 'til Margaret . . ."

Rachel cut her sentence short. The silence in the cool house seemed large and dark. "She was ill for a time with a fever and we have nursed her to health as best we can. Margaret did the best she could do . . ." Careful to be discreet in Margaret's presence, she stopped and smiled.

Elizabeth felt the woman's hesitation. Had Rachel said something she ought not to have said in front of Margaret? The girl did not raise her face to them. Desultorily, she moved away from the table and began to stomp through the kitchen and toward the back door. The mound of her pregnancy was easily visible under her dress as she slipped through into the back yard and slammed the door hard behind her.

Rachel blushed. Rebecca wrapped the baby up and held her very close. "She's beautiful," Rebecca whispered. "Thank you so much. Thank you."

Elizabeth's neck felt cold when she heard the Indian boy's first scream. She could not see into the backyard, but she could hear the thwack of the wooden gate slamming. She saw Rachel's young adopted Indian child rush toward the house, his face visible in the window.

Rachel rushed to the back door and opened it. "Margaret," she called. "No, Maggie!" The girl was running directly toward a lean, high-strung pony tied to a fence. When she caught its rope, it was easy to see that the rope burned her hands. The Indian boy, who must have been about ten, began chasing the pony while Margaret, with her feet still on the ground, foolishly flung her arms around its head. With unbelievable facility, considering what she carried around her middle, she leaped to its back and began leaning forward on its withers to ride it out of the corral.

The Indian boy screamed again, a curdling cry. With the baby in her arms, Rebecca stayed in the kitchen, but Elizabeth followed Rachel into the yard.

"Catch her!" Rachel cried. "Catch her! Maggie, what are you doing? You'll kill yourself on King."

But Maggie was not listening. She kicked the horse in the flanks and rode fast down the drive. Rachel grabbed the gray horse that stood in the yard. She began to fret out loud. "I wish . . . my husband were here. He still hasn't come home. How do you take care of things when your husband's out marrying another bride?" She led the horse into the front and fumbled with its bridle while Elizabeth, feeling helpless, watched the girl race into the road.

At once, Jacob took the reins from Rachel, leaped to the horse, and began to ride after Maggie.

## 39
### *Jacob*

When he first realized he had seen Margaret Seymour standing in the doorway of the Hamblin house that fateful day a week ago, Jacob felt strangely detached. It was as though he had come upon a lost friend whom he had not seen for a long time and that he could only vaguely remember. One of his most looming thoughts was his memory that he had wished never to see her again. Margaret herself had not yet acknowledged that she remembered him. She had been concentrating on the baby in her arms.

As he raced on after Maggie on Hamblin's other horse, he realized there was no way the old gray mare could catch up with the stallion. This horse was larger and more cumbersome than the one carrying Maggie across the field. And the animal did not seem to like Jacob. Halfway down the drive, she lifted her head at the bit with a snort.

"Hang on!" Rachel cried out. "She's afraid."

Jacob kicked her in the rump. She bolted forward with such force that he was thrown back toward her rear. He clung to the reins and tied up her teeth. Finally he managed to lean forward on her neck.

"Talk to her!" Rachel cried.

For a moment he thought he ought to take Foresight off the wagon, but when he looked back, he could see that Elizabeth and Rachel Hamblin were climbing into the cart and urging the mule into a slow trot to follow him. Rebecca ran down from the house with the baby in one arm, the carpet bag in another, crying "Wait for me. Wait for me."

Jacob talked to the mare. He said all of the most soothing words he could imagine as he leaned forward and felt her pulling out into an easy gallop. She was big, and as his bones hit her haunches, it made an unfavorable impression on his spine. Ahead of him the stallion was pulling out of sight toward the meadows and over the small hills. The mare slowed on its way up a small rise. Suddenly Jacob recognized that they were drawing near to the familiar meadow. For a terrible moment he realized where he was. The cart with Rebecca, Elizabeth, and Rachel was not far behind. Jacob slowed the mare and gulped with a cramping pain. Ahead of him lay the death-trampled field.

He would have given anything never to see it again. He spent precious moments looking back to check the progress of the wagon. He wondered if he could somehow turn the women away. But the hack carrying Rebecca, Elizabeth, and Rachel had already reached the draw. They stopped at the top of a rise. Jacob's blood chilled. What they saw was not the meadow with its trenches newly covered, the new earth stamped and raw. What they saw was a field of bloody grass covered with bodies dragged up by the wild animals—human carcasses left twisted and chewed up to rot in the sun and rain.

Jacob swallowed, turned. The faces of the women on the cart stared white, blank, at the scene. Jacob saw Elizabeth's eyes. Her face had changed to a ghastly white. He felt sick and turned the mare around. The cart stopped at the hill.

"I . . . I didn't mean to lead you . . . She came through here," he said.

Rachel stared at the scene. Her voice choked and she held a hand to her throat. "Oh, dear God," she said, closing her eyes, swallowing hard. "Oh dear God."

Rebecca held the baby close to her cheek and buried her eyes in its dark hair.

"Maggie'll come back," Rachel Hamblin said in a small voice. "Let her return when she is ready. I don't think we should go any further." Rachel straightened herself to climb down out of the cart. She appeared to be a woman who knew her limitations, and she had met them here. It was as though she had no respect for Maggie, and nothing more should have been expected of her. When she was on the ground she walked to the mare. Jacob dismounted and handed her the reins.

"Let Maggie go," Rachel said. "Until Jacob returns she will have to bear some of the burden for her own sins."

Jacob watched as Rachel mounted the mare. She talked to it, speaking calmly, though her voice trembled. At last she managed a weak smile. "I'm sorry to trouble you young people." Jacob noticed there were tears in her eyes. "Goodbye." She turned on the horse and was gone.

Jacob was aware that Elizabeth was still staring at the grass. Littered with blood-spattered and stiffened limbs, there must have been more than a hundred bodies torn up out of the shallow graves. He climbed into the cart feeling a deep nausea, as though the bloody scene had risen in a great flood that would drown all of them. "Don't look, Elizabeth," he whispered. "Don't look at it. Don't ever come here again."

She said nothing. Jacob felt empty. As he turned the cart toward home, he could not think of anything to say. But he felt he must fill up the terrible silence. "They really ought to come and bury them again."

## 40

*September 23, 1857, Elizabeth*
*While I am trying to sleep they still come up from the ground.*

For nights afterward, Elizabeth lay awake, never really falling asleep. If sleep did come to her, she sank into a void where she swam through a kind of darkness that seemed like suffocation. When she could not breathe, she woke, sweating. For hours afterward she could not seem to shut off the vision of the bodies in the ground as though they were etched to the backs of her eyes.

It was not immediately after their return home from the meadows, but in the following week that she lost the baby. At first it was a throb of pain, a sharp jab like none she had ever known. And then, in the quiet loft she heard her own breath from deep inside of her—a wail of softness as though she were separate from herself. She tried to stop her cries, but the pain grew. She buried her face in the pillow and stopped breathing for long moments of time.

No. No. It could not be. Not so terrible as all of that. The pain wrenched and tore in her until she winced. She clamped down on the muscles in her body to stop the urgency. But the blood came.

## 41

*Elizabeth*

Winter seemed to arrive early. First, the autumn winds blew like howling birds flapping giant wings against the sheer red cliffs, wiping every leaf from the sky. The bleak wind scoured out a hollow for winter's icy rain.

Though the harshest weather did not last long, it seemed to last forever because there was so much fear. A report came from Salt Lake City that the U.S. Army was camped in the mountains many miles north of Salt Lake City, not far from Fort Bridger.

It often fell to Elizabeth to care for the two immigrant children in the Lorry household. Watching their antics, their laughter, their playing and running, she was reminded of her own winter. She had lost her girlhood. And now her own child. When she could get away, she crossed the field to talk to her friend. She climbed the stairs into Rebecca's bedroom. Rebecca often carried the sleeping baby Hannah in her arms while they sat in the window watching the winter rain.

"I am so sorry," Rebecca said. She placed her free hand on Elizabeth's hands in her lap. "I know you wanted the baby so much. You should never have married without love."

Elizabeth had nothing to say.

Sometimes Elizabeth's eyes seemed fastened on an invisible world—the ghosts of the massacre, perhaps, who flowed like clouds around them, now unable to stay buried. Or the imagined spirits of the U.S. Army that still lived, hovering so close to their future. For months now Elizabeth and Rebecca had been watching a darkness grow between them, a chasm created by their differences. Though she was no longer to be a mother, Elizabeth was a married woman. The difference sometimes stood between them like a wall.

With longing, Elizabeth watched the child sleeping in Rebecca's lap, her little hands relaxed and white. Rebecca seemed to have much to say to Elizabeth. "Now you have lost your baby, and since the Indian massacre, your husband doesn't even come into your room anymore. But you're married. So you can't leave J.B. to marry somebody else, like John Lee."

"Can you marry John Lee?" was Elizabeth's only response.

Rebecca stared at Elizabeth. She tightened her grip on the child. It was as though Elizabeth had driven a barb through her, for it was true, she had not been able to make her marriage happen yet. "Elizabeth," she whispered, taken back. "Of course you know he's been in Salt Lake City to organize the men against the army that's at our door, and report to Brigham Young about the massacre." There was silence, but only for a moment. "It was so terrible for them all to see the Indians kill so many people. He carried so much sadness when he returned."

Elizabeth waited to speak. "And before that happened things were different?"

"Yes. I do not understand what has happened to create the distance between me and John Lee. But I know he wanted me once."

"How do you know?"

"Because I love him. I understand him. And I saw his eyes."

"There is more to love than that."

"Elizabeth," she whispered now. "You have never been in love." Rebecca leaned close to Elizabeth over the sleeping child in her arms. "If ever you had been in love, you would know it. It is not really what happens, but how you feel that gives you life, joy, light in your whole being. If I have never married, at least I have loved. I would rather never marry than to go through life never having felt this way I feel."

"Rebecca, no," Elizabeth whispered. "Can it be that important to feel what you feel?"

Rebecca leaned to her again, still holding the baby close. "Please believe me. There is always that possibility you could love someone, too. Leave J.B."

"No," Elizabeth whispered. "No. I can't do that."

"The women in Salt Lake City do it," Rebecca whispered, still quiet. "Those women who spiritually married the prophet Joseph Smith, they did it. They stayed married to their husbands, but only temporarily. They stayed with their husbands day by day, but they were sacredly sealed forever to the most glorious man on earth. Some of them did it for the opportunity to secretly bear children of Joseph because they loved him."

"No," Elizabeth whispered. "I am not worthy of someone like John Lee."

Rebecca drew back, aware of the longing in Elizabeth's eyes. She sat without speaking for a moment. They listened to the rain outside the window. They heard the children in the rooms below them, stomping on the stairs. She looked down at the sleeping baby, who moved for a moment, stretching her little fist. "If I didn't love her so much, I would give Hannah to you," Rebecca said as she stroked the child's arm. "She would make you happy, Elizabeth."

## 42
### February 11, 1858, Elizabeth

*There is more than just the fear of the coming war. Something is in the air, and it is not just the U.S. Army or the rain. There is something wrong somewhere, yet I cannot put my finger on it. J.B. does not come to my loft anymore. He does not speak to me. Jacob does not speak to me. Suky has brought gloom into the house. I feel so alone.*

In early February they set up a quilt in the Jensen home. Elizabeth took Sally and Foster to the Jensen household, where she worked on the quilt with Rebecca while the brother and sister played with their little sister Hannah. Elizabeth held Hannah when she was colicky, sometimes for hours. This child had been born at nearly the same time hers had been conceived. "Sweetheart," she whispered in the little girl's ear, and folded the blankets back like petals on a new flower. For a moment she held the round face to her face and breathed deeply, wetting the child's cheek with her tears.

By now, Hannah had lost her crop of black hair. In its place was a soft velvet sheen of blond fuzz. "It looks like she's going to be light," Rebecca said.

Elizabeth put the tiny orphan child in its basket for a morning nap. Rebecca gave scissors and scraps of cloth to Sally and the little Jensen girls, and they began to snip and sing.

It was about ten o'clock when a young man they had never seen before rode up to the house, breathless. "We need help. Does anybody know the Indian language? They want to trade."

Barely opening the doorway, Rebecca stared at the youth with suspicion. Behind him—perhaps for a mile north on the road—were several wagons stopped or moving so slowly that their progress was not visible. In front of them were Indians both on foot and on horseback crossing back and forth in the path.

"Where are you from?" Rebecca asked, not with much courtesy.

"Tennessee," the boy said. "We just come through here. Somebody said the Indians were trouble. But the Mormons would help us on the trail."

Rebecca strained to see past the boy into the distance. "No one's here," she said unevenly, and then caught sight of a small skirmish. Elizabeth saw it too. One of the Indians reached into one of the wagons and grabbed at a blanket wrapped around a woman's baby. The men of the party gathered around the Indian at once.

Rebecca flung her shawl over her shoulders and called to Elizabeth. "Elizabeth, come! I'll go north on the road to fetch help quickly if you can hold them off . . . even if it's just for a few moments!"

Rebecca was gone on one of the Jensen ponies almost before Elizabeth came to the door. The breathless boy followed her. Elizabeth watched the party of settlers move down the road. The Indians walked in front of them pointing to various pots and pans hanging from their bodies, and to the young child on the wagon seat in the woman's arms.

Elizabeth rushed back into the house praying Rebecca would come soon. She told the little girls to stay inside, and she gave them material to cut and sew. But they would not listen to her. The weather was unbelievably warm for an early day in February, and it seemed impossible to keep them in. They wanted to follow her, so she let them come.

"Stay back from me. Stay back," Elizabeth insisted as she moved toward the road. Though she waved the children away, they found it an amusing game to follow her as far as they could. Ahead of her, Elizabeth came close enough to hear the settlers talking to the Indians, and to see the woman's eyes widen, her face pale. She continued to tighten her grip on her child.

"They want to trade blankets for the child," the lead man told Elizabeth.

Elizabeth stared. One of the big Indians strutting in the road grunted in broken English, "Want baby." For a moment Elizabeth could not understand what he said. "Buy white baby."

When she understood what it was they wanted, Elizabeth shook her head. "No." She thought she recognized these as Indians from the south, the Piedes. For some reason they were willing to trade many of their pans and spoons for the woman's white child from Arkansas.

The horses pranced as the dark men held them in check. A few of the Indians on horseback moved their horses away from the small train, backing up as though preparing to charge. Elizabeth felt her skin crawl. On foot she walked with the train and began to pray. Hurry, Rebecca. Oh dear God, send Rebecca with help, now.

"Give them some of your goods," she told the settler who seemed to be in charge of the wagons. It appeared to be his child.

"What?" he shrugged his shoulders. "We don't have nothing. And the Mormons don't want to sell us nothing."

"Pots, pans, some extra dishes. They only want to trade."

"Yes, they want one of our children," the man said bitterly.

"Give them our dishes, Edgar," the woman pleaded.

Mumbling, the man jumped from the wagon and marched to the back, clawing through some of the crates until he drew out a few pans and some tongs.

"Trade!" The settler thrust the pan and tongs toward the old Indian.

"Not good," the chief shook his head. "Two pans for the blanket."

"Then take two," the traveler from Tennessee muttered.

Elizabeth summoned her courage. A mile north she saw another wagon drawing people. She was relieved. Accompanying them, she could see Rebecca Jensen on the Jensen horse.

"Now let's go! Get out of our way," the man in the front wagon yelled to the Indians, feeling strength when he saw the white party coming. Though the Indians continued to snarl and shout, they finally began to move away. Trotting their horses around the party of settlers, they continued down the road, moving south past the Jensen place and toward Penter road. As they went, they threw the Tennessee settlers' pans back and forth to each other like toys, shouting at the tops of their voices. There seemed to be Indians everywhere, some unaccounted for in the woods along the river, some in small groups north on the road. Some seemed to surround the Jensen house, move along the Jensen corral.

The confusion made Elizabeth nervous. She felt little relief even when the

Indians began to move southward again; they did not move fast enough for her. She felt more comfortable the closer Rebecca came with the help she had summoned. Only when Elizabeth was close enough to see Rebecca's eyes could she recognize who it was that came to help. It was none other than John D. Lee. Imposing on the tall horse, wearing a big wool coat with a rich beaver collar and a red scarf, he wore a dark hat over his full head of unruly blond hair. Rebecca's eyes were unashamedly filled with excitement, but there was also apprehension. Elizabeth could tell Rebecca was holding back her feelings, and she wondered why. Behind Lee and Rebecca, in one of Lee's big wagons, a pert woman sat on the front seat, her black curls shining like silk in the winter sun.

"Well, we meet again, Mrs. Lorry," Lee said smoothly as they rode to her. "It's good to see you."

Suddenly Elizabeth was conscious of her windblown hair, of the children in the road clinging to her skirts. Ahead of them, the man from Tennessee waved his thanks to Lee. He waved back.

"They're leaving now," Elizabeth said unnecessarily, for Lee and Rebecca both saw the retreat of the Indians as they moved at various speeds still surrounding the train.

Looking at Rebecca, Elizabeth saw that her face seemed drained of color.

"Whatever you told them must have been the right thing," Rebecca said, still mounted on the Jensen mare.

"You must have a way with them," Lee smiled at Elizabeth as he leaned over his horse and smoothly slipped out of the saddle. Elizabeth found him standing directly before her. He had never seemed tall, but today he loomed large and bulky, as though he crowded out all else, including the mountains behind him.

"They left because they saw you come," Elizabeth said.

Rebecca's eyes darted to the wagon and the woman behind them, and Lee caught her glance. "Mrs. Lorry, I'd like you to meet Emma, who is a new member of my family."

Elizabeth turned to acknowledge the woman on the wagon and smiled at her. Emma returned the smile and climbed down out of the wagon, opening her arms to the Jensen children and the Arkansas child whose name the brother and sister had said was Hannah. When she stood beside Lee, the children gathered about her shyly, staring at her jewelry and her shiny hair.

"She's from England," Lee continued, not looking at Rebecca above him, still perched on the Jensen mare. "She will be a wonderful help to us. We're to prepare for the journey of the Saints to the south," he said, lifting his chest, filling his lungs with air. He straightened as though preparing himself for a burden only he could envision. "We shall conquer because of the diligent efforts of good people like her. And you," he added, smiling toward Elizabeth and Rebecca. "If you good sisters will demonstrate even half of the loyalty and integrity of this good woman to your husbands, we cannot fail."

The statement was obviously made for Emma Lee. John Lee turned toward her and gazed proudly. She had all but disappeared standing beside the bulk of his coat. She blushed and smiled.

Elizabeth glanced toward Rebecca, whose face paled. Lee must have sensed something, for there had been some words exchanged among the Jensen men about Rebecca's hopes. Yet so much time had passed, it was as though the words had never been said.

John Lee tried, though it seemed too late, to recover himself. "And I'm not finished with my family either, now, am I?" But there was probably nothing more devastating he might have said to acknowledge Rebecca in that difficult moment. He should never have pursued the subject, but he turned to Emma as if he had dismissed Rebecca's feelings as the whims of a young girl. "Emma, my dear," he said, "You will get to know Rebecca and Elizabeth as neighbors, and I hope as good friends."

It was a statement probably said without entanglement, but Rebecca's eyes registered shock and devastation. Elizabeth thought Lee was not really telling her "no," but rather he was saying "not now." Nevertheless, Rebecca's face grew pale with unshed tears. She tried to smile.

Elizabeth smiled. "I'm happy to meet you, Sister Lee."

"Sister Lorry," Lee said, "who took my advice to enter the covenant inside her righteous family."

Elizabeth felt that Rebecca was holding back tears until they reached the house. While she tied the horse to the porch, she looked after Lee and his new bride Emma one more time as the wagon lumbered down the long muddy road toward Harmony.

"I hate him," Rebecca sobbed to Elizabeth. She drew her friend inside the empty front room of the Jensen house and shut the door. "I hate him now."

"Rebecca," Elizabeth soothed her. "Rebecca, please. It's all right. Let him go. Love someone else."

"I hate him now. I'll never be able to love him." She paused and looked up into Elizabeth's eyes. "He treated me like a child."

"Love someone else who will share your life with you." Elizabeth tried to comfort her friend, though the damage seemed irreparable now.

"He knew how I felt. He has always known how I felt. And I understood him to promise me."

"He did promise. He has said there is still the possibility."

"I hate him!" she screamed, pushing the words against her throat.

It was in that moment, the moment of Rebecca's most terrible anger that they heard the six-year-old Sally scream. Rebecca jumped up quickly to go to the back bedroom; Elizabeth followed her. The six-year-old daughter of the Fancher train was crying and pointing to the baby's empty crib. The bedroom was a total shambles. The baby was gone. Rebecca's tear-streaked face suddenly whitened with fear.

"Where is she?" Elizabeth heard Rebecca cry. "Where is she? She's not here! Oh, Elizabeth, no!"

The next few moments burned in Elizabeth's memory like few she had ever dreamed. For she remembered most definitely the moment she had put the tiny child in the straw bed. She never forgot those moments. And a million times in the next few months she would recall holding the baby's cheek close to her own and feeling the little body in her hands. Nor did she forget the next few moments in the bedroom as Rebecca screamed, frantically searching the disrupted room for the child who was not there.


## 43

### February 20, 1858, Elizabeth

*When Sister Jensen came back to the house from Cedar with George and learned that the Indians had taken the Dunham baby, she fell screaming and crying in Mr. Jensen's arms. And she would not stop. Not even for the love of her own children. Still, she stands at the window and looks out at the valley. What does she see? Something there dark and unexplainable. There are ugly rumors about what happened at the meadows. Too many have gone there to see. Too many say nothing. No one will speak to any of us, and the Indians have taken the little child. After all of these moves, from Kirtland to Far West, to Nauvoo, it may be time to move again.*

Elizabeth bit her pen and looked out toward the road from the Lorry windows. She prayed silently in her heart that nothing—no messenger from Brigham Young, no mandate from the president in Cedar, nothing would send them away. Finally she wrote: *No one wants to go.*

## 44
### April 4, 1858, Elizabeth

*April 4, 1858. The worst has happened. We may be requested to go. Today we were rebaptized. President Haight wants to know who is committed and who is not, so they will know who will follow them to the south. J.B. vows he will always obey.*

Early in April the leaders prepared a scouting party to search out the possibilities for the move south. Brigham Young had ordered more than sixty men to take twenty wagons. But as a vanguard, President Haight was sending only half a dozen. J.B. chose to go with this exploratory group. On Tuesday when they began to head southward in the warming sun, Suky, grim-faced, watched them go.

Suky was obviously not happy when the men in the family declared that they were both leaving—and in different directions. For Jacob had been requested to go with the scouting party called to take wagons northward up to Salt Lake City to help move the settlers out of the way of the incoming U.S. Army. He would help carry Mormon families southward to safety, as far south as they needed to go. Suky was devastated.

"There will be another place for us," J.B. said before he mounted the new mare he had finally purchased from Dame in Parowan.

"I am tired," Suky said. "Of going."

"Suky, hasn't the Lord always watched after His kingdom?"

"Has he?"

Elizabeth felt a particularly chilling April breeze on her shoulders. She said nothing when J.B. came to her and took her in his arms for a brief good-bye. He had not come to her loft since the incident at the meadows. She was not sure why. But she felt she did not know him anymore.

"Good-bye, Elizabeth," J.B. said, looking stern and grim.

"Hurry back," Suky said in monotone.

"They will find a place in the south for us that no one will penetrate. A bastion. A great wall."

"My uncle said there was a huge hole in the earth the likes of which nobody ever saw," one of the boys in the party blurted out.

Elizabeth stared at the speaker, a scrawny boy from Paragonah astride a thin mare. Next to Percy Jensen were Mr. Jensen and two other men and a big burly man in leather pants and a bandanna; his boots came up to his knees.

"They'll just chase us out again and again," Suky said, her voice flat.

"We'll find a refuge. The saints will find a refuge," J.B. offered, staring into the bleak land southward, "where no one will come. No one will bother us again."

Elizabeth hadn't said one word. She continued to stare at J.B.'s motley expedition, feeling a little sick in the heat, as though she were pregnant. But she knew she could not be.

A stiff breeze coming up from the west chilled them, again. Elizabeth wrapped her shawl more tightly about her shoulders and shuddered. As she watched the men leave, she thought little had changed from the beginning—men leaving women to fare alone. She felt a crowding bitterness in her heart that seemed like poison.

"If they find another place for the Saints this time, I'm not going," Suky said. "I'll stay here and face whatever dangers come." Elizabeth heard her words with trepidation. "I'm going to stay here when the army comes up from California or down from the north," Suky continued. "I'm going to stay here and stand in front of this house and invite them to shoot."

"Suky!" Elizabeth spoke as though it were required of her.

"No. I am sick of killing. I am sick of running. I am sick of answering to so much that is required of us. I have become a bitter old woman." She stopped for a moment.

"Suky, we have so much to live for."

"Perhaps you have."

The April air still felt cold on Elizabeth's arm. She seemed to choke and could not speak for a long time.

"I thought I loved the Lord. No one loved him as much as me. But it is hard to feel anything else but angry now. I am angry because there is no rest. Even though we've come this far."

It had been a long time since Elizabeth had heard Suky say so much. The dried-up woman was still staring after the men, her body tense, her hands clenched. "All the adventures are for the men. So they can ride into the sunset and leave us behind."

"It's all right, Suky. I'll have a child for us all. You'll feel glad again. You'll want to go someplace—where we can protect the baby."

Suky grimaced. "Out of the frying pan into the fire. Here we aren't safe from the U.S. soldiers." She looked out over the bleak hills. "Out there we aren't safe from the Indians. Whoever thought they'd take a baby from the Jensens' cradle?"

Elizabeth watched Suky's eyes. There was too much anger there to soften at this moment, too much bitterness.

"We are supposed to rejoice. We are the Lord's people. Then why do I feel so sad?"

## 45
### Wednesday, April 7, 1858, Jacob

Jacob left the next day with the party going north. Their chief worry was that they were going into territory close to the incoming U.S. Army. They faced possible battle with them. No one knew what was going to happen. The risks were great.

On that first night out, they gathered at John Lee's in New Harmony. The talk around the fire was about the successful attacks on the U.S. militia that had been made all winter by the Salt Lake City militiamen. "They burned the wagons, gave them general trouble," one of the men said, rubbing his leather gloves over the campfire. "Weakened them. But we don't know how much or what's going to happen next."

Though the night was dark, tongues of fire threw shadows against Lee's barn and against the wagons lined up beside the hay rakes. Jacob knew these wagons had not been in Lee's yard before the skirmish in the meadows. They were spoil from the Fancher train.

Later, Jacob could see that Lee did not try to hide that fact. In a quiet voice, he told everyone that these were excellent wagons to take northward. They were a gift from God. They would be hardy enough to haul the Mormons safely out of Salt Lake City. Though the city may burn, the inhabitants could come southward to save their lives.

Jacob did not join the conversation. He was quiet when he followed the men into the large dining room for the bean soup the women offered them. The first woman he noticed was Lee's new wife Emma. He had known months before, when she came with the blacksmith's daughter Greta to make the bed, that she would marry John Lee. Nevertheless, he watched her movements as she served the food because there was an intensity about her that fascinated him. And she was beautiful. By the fireplace in the kitchen he could also see Lee's daughter Anna Jane, who smiled once at him from her post beside a large cauldron that she carefully continued stirring. He knew he had successfully forgotten the dark rumors still lodged in his mind. What he tried to remember was the light brown hair falling close to the smooth brow—how pretty she was.

More than twenty children surrounded them in the dining room. And at least seven women. He felt crowded but strangely intrigued. As they laid out the food and spoke quietly to the children, the women said little to the men. Above the tension of the impending war, the evacuation, and the hubbub of the normal routine, an almost visible softness like diffused candlelight pervaded the room.

"Do you remember me?" From behind, Emma Lee bent beside his ear. He could feel her warm breath on his neck.

Jacob turned, not sure he had heard right. "Oh yes, Ma'am. I met you at Mr. Deany's, the blacksmith."

Emma Lee smiled. "Yes, you do remember. It's nice to see you again."

Jacob watched her closely. Not once did she speak to John D. Lee. Yet there was an aura that surrounded her and the others as they moved gracefully in and out of the dining room. As Lee talked with some of the men who were also staying to take wagons north in the morning, the women poured his water— brushing against his arm just to be near him. All of the daughters served him in the same way.

Finally Anna Jane came out with a large bowl of bean soup. She blushed when she smiled. Jacob saw that she was smiling at him, though she was serving her father as if he were an honored king. The quiet, the warmth in the room began to feel like sunlight. Jacob melted into it.

The peace remained with him through the first few hours of the night as they slept in the barn. He knew Percy but was not fully acquainted with the others who had come to Lees' to drive the wagons and cattle to Salt Lake City. And there would be others to join them in the morning. Though he felt the warmth of his experience in the Lee home lingering, he could not sleep. The night began to stretch into hours of restlessness. Perhaps it was the discomfort in the barn that kept him awake. Or Percy turning on the straw. But he began to feel something strong gripping him, a frustration, a longing. He thought it might have had something to do with Emma Lee and her smile, or Elizabeth and her eyes that had followed him for several miles. But he thought it had most to do with that smile of adoration in Anna Jane. After preparing for war, his mind and body wanted peace. He had been eager for action before. Now he had seen enough to last for more than his lifetime. Now he wanted something else.

He shook his head to avoid the dreams. He tried to forget Anna Jane's hands. He concentrated on the morning, on driving the Arkansas wagon to Salt Lake City. But the vision of the Arkansas wagon kindled thoughts of the trouble that could come. He saw in his mind the U.S. Army marching down out of

Emigration Pass to drive the people from their homes. Then he imagined war. He saw blood on the meadow field and he heard the scream of bullets grazing his ears.

Once in the night Jacob found himself awake in a cold sweat. When he closed his eyes, it was Elizabeth who came to him and held out her white hands. "You'll find a place for us," she said. "All that we suffer will do us good." When she reached toward his face to touch him, he smelled the sweetness of her apron, the sweetness of bread, flour, and cinnamon. He leaned toward her to bury his head in her skirts. He felt his eyes sting with tears. But the white cloth smelling of bread and cinnamon suddenly overcame him, choked him, and he fell suddenly away into a dark void where he no longer saw Elizabeth or felt her hands. He whirled downward and woke again. Next to him Percy was turning restlessly on the straw.

If Salt Lake City was their first destination, they must take advantage of all the daylight hours. The time for departure came long before dawn. Jacob woke cramped and sore. The men hurried him. He could hear the noise of wagon wheels outside the barn. He stared in disbelief at the size of the procession that had gathered in the darkness. Lee had summoned eighteen head of oxen and more than seventy-five head of cattle for the journey as well as the two large wagons. Filling the road, the cattle mewed, bleated, and bellowed.

"The Fanchers," Percy said, his lips still thick from sleep. He looked disheveled, a hundred years old. "All them cattle once belonged to the Fanchers."

Jacob said nothing. He turned to Thales Haskell, who was telling the party they would be picking up more empty wagons in Cedar, Paragonah, and Parowan. He turned to Jacob. "You and Percy drive this one together until we get another and need you both."

As they left Lees', Jacob looked back. Lee, flanked by the beautiful Emma and two of his other wives, stood at his doorstep as the party began to move. Jacob waved good-bye to Anna Jane.

Jacob rode Foresight while Percy drove the wagon. The train, consisting of three older men and four younger drivers, pulled out long before the sun came up over the hill. They passed Jensens' ranch and then Lorrys' at about six fifteen. The windows of the house were dark. Jacob was sure Elizabeth and Suky would still be sleeping. Unexpectedly, he felt the gnawing hunger of the night returning to him as he passed the Lorry house without the possibility of saying another good-bye.

Elizabeth. Lately he saw the pallor in her cheeks—even something that looked like loss, the terrible emptiness in her eyes. Since her marriage to J.B., Jacob had drawn himself away from her. Yet he had always watched her, though it was from a distance. He saw her occasionally glance toward him with a frightened longing in her eyes before she turned away. Elizabeth. He had never said anything meaningful to her. Yet when he thought of her, his heart still beat hard against his ribs. He wanted to call her then, "I have always loved you, but it is too late now. I can never do anything about it now. Too much has happened." If he let himself entertain these thoughts for long, they aroused an anger that frightened him.

As the rescue party moved northward, they picked up not only several more wagons, but other young drivers from Cedar City and other ports along the way. Jacob found himself in the company of many young militiamen whom he recognized from the drills of the previous autumn. When the seasoned scouts were asleep, young ones told tall tales around the campfire at night. Some told dark secrets about their own experiences in the massacre. Percy was the only one Jacob knew very well. He vaguely remembered Eugene Smith, and John Lee's son John Alma Lee, and Paul Farley from Penter.

"My Uncle Lee Farley said he saw the body of the beautiful woman that was never touched by a beast," Paul Farley told them. "When he went there even a few weeks ago, her skin had been preserved as fresh as though she had breathed yesterday."

"They said perhaps she did not die but lay in a coma for a long time," Eugene echoed.

"Or she could have lived. She could have lived in that carnage for a long time," someone else said, their voice low and thin.

"I saw them still unburied, scattered on the ground."

"They was buried."

"They was buried twice."

"And them bones are still scattered on the ground."

"They walk on this ground. They walk all over everybody's dreams."

"It was an oath. We was never to breathe a word."

"We ain't broke no oath."

"Never speak of it again."

Jacob listened to the talk, but he himself stayed silent until he dropped off to sleep.

## 46

### *Monday, May 18, 1858, Jacob*

The rescue train reached the point of the mountain just about the time the first group of Salt Lake City Saints had left their homes. From his perch on the large wagon confiscated from the Fanchers, Jacob gasped when he saw the exodus from Salt Lake City stretching before him in a queue three miles long. Cattle by the thousands were flowing about the wagons, mooing and milling, grazing, cropping the new blades of April's roots to the barren ground. The scene stretched across the valley and over the rise of the next hill.

"Looks like they need us, all right," one of the men called out when he saw the train. The drivers in the rescue party advanced as rapidly as they could toward the mass moving like a river down the draw. The wagons of the exodus were piled high with goods. Children straggled on foot pushing handcarts. Little ones were crying. The mothers looked drawn and haggard under the growing heat of the noon sun.

"We're happy to see you. There are hundreds of others waiting for available wagons," one of the leaders said. He greeted Haskell at the front of the train.

Jacob, still stunned, awoke from his reverie enough to give his oxen a sting with the whip. The beasts lumbered forward off to the side of the road to give passage to the train.

"So this is our answer to war," one of the old men said from his wagon.

"They're coming down fast!" another voice cried out. "If you'll hurry, you can pick some of them Saints up at the Murray place just a few miles away."

Jacob's wagon seemed to lurch so slowly it was as though he were trying to pass through water instead of the smoky mist of the April dew. The dark brown mountains loomed tall on every side. The hills should have offered a feeling of protection, but nothing felt safe now.

"The Salt Lakers are coming down fast, and the U.S. Army right behind them," the same voice repeated, and above the hubbub he could hear the creaking of his own wheels.

Young children waved to him. Boys cried out encouraging phrases to mules and oxen. The women shaded their eyes from the sun. The pilgrimage seemed endless. Where one group of wagons stopped, another emerged from a side road or from around the next bend. Once he found himself in the midst of it, Jacob felt it suck him into its vortex, as though he were fighting a whirlpool. There was no way now to avoid the traffic, the cattle in the road, the hundreds of people on foot milling by. If his own wagon had stopped, he could imagine himself still moving as though floating on a sea, for the crowds of cattle and people were still bobbing like gentle waves down the draw.

By late afternoon Mr. Haskell had easily found families to borrow all of the wagons. Jacob drove to a large home on the left-hand side of the road and down a long lane. The wife of the house came out first, wiping her hands on her apron. "Bless you!" she cried. "The Lord sent you! We'll be out soon!" Children and other wives began carrying crates out into the yard. The husband came into view from the barn wheeling barrows of straw. The younger children, all dressed warmly in sweaters and knitted hats, began to carry armloads of straw into the house.

"My hired boy James will be staying to set the whole thing to flame," the husband said in a pensive tone as he stood beside the oxen with Jacob. "You see that there glass window?" He pointed to a piece of stained glass on the porch over the door. "My old mother—may her bones rest in peace—brought that there piece of glass from her father's old church in Suffolk. We got it this far and put it in there believing we would stay." Jacob did not know what to say to ease the man's disappointment and fear, so he said nothing. The man continued, "If they are coming down as fast as they say they are, we ain't even got time to take it out of there."

The loading took only an hour. Everything had been ready, the man said, for several days. Now the house was littered with dry straw. James, the hired man, waved to the family and Jacob good-bye. When the father climbed up into the wagon, Jacob untied and mounted Foresight to follow the wagon for a short time. After a while, he passed them up and the family waved good-bye. Up and down the road each house was as dark as an empty cave when evening came. Lights in the city did not flicker. There were few carriages on the streets. Only the torch-bearers remained. At only a word they were prepared to set fire to every barn, church, and home.

Finding Percy and a few others, Jacob began to make his way back south-ward riding Foresight along the route of encampments scattered before him for dusky miles. When night came, they drew beside some of the others and camped out under the same stars. He felt the emotion of the hundreds of refugees scattered like orphans across the empty plains. He felt small, seeing the hills rise against the sky.

"Do you think the army will follow us all the way to Harmony?" Percy whispered to him from his bed on the ground.

"I don't know." Jacob could not guess.

"Brigham Young says he'll make his headquarters in Parowan."

"Then maybe only to Parowan."

"Why does the United States Government want to destroy us?" Percy asked.

Jacob could see Percy's face only faintly outlined in the starlight. "I don't know," he said, feeling the cold, hard ground under his bones.

"We never meant no harm. We only want to follow God our own way. The Puritans did the same."

"Nobody," Jacob began sluggishly, feeling sleep come. "Nobody can stand to see people break away or be different, I guess."

"Are we so different?"

"We believe different."

"We believe in the same God as theirs maybe."

"We say we know more. And we vote in a block."

"Maybe we do."

"But nobody likes somebody else to tell 'em they know more."

"It wasn't bragging. We was willing to share."

"It doesn't matter. They thought we were bragging. They think we bragged and then committed treason against the United States by making up our own government."

"We was still U.S. citizens. We sent the Mormon Battalion, supported the union. Ain't there something about freedom of religion in the U.S. Constitution? So didn't they commit treason against us?"

Jacob was quiet for a long moment. He remembered hearing talk about it among the men. "I think they got mad because Brigham Young took over the mail route. That McGraw fellow wrote nasty letters to the president of the United States saying we were trying to dominate the government, to combine state and religion. So they canceled Brigham Young's contract for the mail route. But McGraw kept writing more nasty letters, so they decided to send the army. They just don't like us. That's all. They look down on us and call us a cult or crazy Mormons." Jacob's eyes were growing heavy and he wanted to sleep. Percy didn't say anything for a very long time.

"What does it mean to be crazy?" he asked finally. "Who makes up the meaning of crazy?"

Though Jacob heard his question, it was on the outside of his consciousness, and he was slow to answer it, even in his own mind. Finally, he never answered it at all.

## 47
### *June 5, 1858, Jacob*

Jacob would have returned to Cedar City as soon as possible had he been alone. But an old aunt of Percy's, a Mrs. Harvey, asked the boys to stay over in Provo for a couple of days. She needed help to nail new siding on an old shed. She said she had been standing in the kitchen while her husband was pounding nails on this shed in their backyard. When he didn't come in for lunch, she went out and found him lying on the grass, dead. Both Jacob and Percy felt they could not refuse Mrs. Harvey's request.

So the boys slept on the back porch of the widow Harvey's Provo house, pounded siding during the mornings, and stomped about the city in the afternoons. Finding that the widow's food was good and the porch fairly comfortable, they stayed long enough to watch the influx of the Mormons from Salt Lake City into Provo—and they came by the thousands. Soon, hundreds of wagons lumbered into the city and formed numerous camps in the streets and surrounding fields.

It was on a clear day in early May of 1858 that the community received their most important news. Percy was still putting up the last of the siding while Jacob went to the lumber company to buy more nails. While he was in the lumber store, he saw a messenger ride swiftly through the road to the Center Street camps. Though he could hear the man shouting, he could not understand the words. Without hesitation, he gathered his purchases and raced into the street.

"We're as far as we go! We're as far as we go!" The messenger was yelling at the top of his lungs, waving his arms. Evidently, Brigham Young had sent news that it was no longer necessary for the people of Salt Lake City to go any further south than Provo. The army had passed through Salt Lake City peacefully and then marched out onto an open plain about twenty-five miles west of town.

Jacob looked at the messenger and then at the crowd. Women covered their faces with their hands and cried for joy. Others screamed, waving their arms in the air. The men nodded to one another, shaking their hands, though some of them still looked skeptical. The children danced, joined hands, skipped in circles, or broke into cartwheels or song.

Jacob stepped lightly out of the lumber store, feeling the warm sun on his face and thanking God for the unexpected blessing. He skirted some new wagons parked in the street, deciding to take another road to the widow's to avoid walking through the crowded conditions in town. Wagons were parked in every available spot. Cattle and horses stomped and sneezed. The stench was unbearable. He crossed over to First East and walked southward to avoid Main.

But soon he found himself dodging other wagons. He paused, seeing he would have to walk by people no matter which way he turned. He heard shouting, an occasional child crying, a man's voice loud and strident nearby, the sharp crash of a door as it slammed. A young girl with a large bundle in her arms suddenly appeared in the street, running. She was lurching forward, her disheveled hair flying in the wind.

"Oh, Jacob!" she cried out, and Jacob's heart stood still. "Oh, Jacob Lorry! Oh my lucky day!"

In the door that had slammed in the house to his right, Jacob saw the eyes of an older man peering darkly from the glass in the window. Hearing his name, he felt suddenly chilled. He recognized the girl rushing toward him now, her face flushed, her curls awry. It was Margaret Seymour, holding a bundled child in her arms!

"Jacob Lorry!" Margaret gasped as she reached him. He held out his hands to protect himself, though she fell against him, nevertheless, letting the child rest for a moment between them. As she leaned against his hands, she trembled. "Jacob! Oh, God help me," she cried. "God help me!"

"Margaret!" Jacob said, helping her to stand. The child in her arms looked up at him with a blank stare, then began to cry.

"Hush," Margaret whispered. "Hush. I brought her out because . . ." She was breathless. "Because I thought the grandfather would accept me if he could see his son's child." When she stopped, she glared into Jacob's face with a stricken gaze. "Jacob, I lied to you." Now she began to cry. The child hushed when she lay its head against her shoulder. She lowered her cheek into the baby's hair. She was standing so close to Jacob that he could smell the strong odor of sour milk.

"There was no Missourian," she confessed. "All this time there was no Missourian. Even Wesley's father knew it." She inclined her head toward the house where the dark eyes behind the glass stared menacingly as though the windows had become a thousand eyes. "That man's the grandfather. It was his son Wesley who is the father." Surprising Jacob, she looked toward the man's eyes in the windows and hissed like an angry cat. "I hate you," she said between her teeth. When she turned back to Jacob, she was full of explanations. "My parents sent me to Fillmore, and then to Hamblins' to have the baby. And no one wanted me. I didn't want to go back to Wesley. I would never go to his parents. Until now. To show them their own granddaughter, my baby girl."

Though so many other memories had been crowded into his mind since that time, Jacob could remember everything. He would never forget that afternoon in the cart in the dark rain, Margaret's hands on his arm, her threatening words, "Jacob, don't leave me."

"He won't even let me in. But he remembers me. I know he remembers me." Margaret's mouth hardened.

Unconsciously, Jacob placed his hand on her arm.

"Jacob!" Her eyes were dark holes. "Jacob, take me with you. Oh, God, please have mercy. Take me with you. If only you knew what I have suffered."

Margaret's eyes were ringed with weariness. Fear crawled up Jacob's spine into the back of his neck.

"Take me with you," she said again, almost whispering now. She stood close to him and he felt her hand on his arm. The baby between them smiled, seeming alert for her age.

"Where are you staying?"

"Shhh, hush, Margaret." They were the first words Jacob had spoken. He put his hand on the child.

"I can't run forever. Take me with you, please. Only promise not to leave me in Scipio."

Questions crowded Jacob's mind. He wondered how she had come here and where she was staying. But he decided that now was not the time to ask questions. He felt overwhelmed by a sudden burden beyond his capacity to bear. But he knew he would help.

"Walk. Just walk with me," he said in a clipped voice. He knew he sounded curt. He was very much aware they were causing a scene. He began walking forward. But where would he go? Mrs. Harvey was the only one he knew in Provo.

Margaret turned and fell in beside him, breathing hard, still holding the child's head against her cheek. Unwrapping the child, she juggled another small bundle of her belongings in her arms. They passed the dark eyes of windows in the house. If there were a reluctant grandfather of this child, would he have been satisfied to see the girl walk away? Jacob felt cramped by an awesome responsibility, somewhat of the same weight he had felt when he drove Margaret Seymour to Fillmore through the rain. Had a Missouri Wildcat never touched her then? He felt incapable of processing her lies. There were always so many and so varied. Finally, he thought he would ask questions to discover her responses, even if those responses were not true.

"Where have you been staying?" he asked first.

"I was in Salt Lake City working like a slave for a family. They're here now. And they'll never see me again."

"How did you get . . ."

"I left Rachel Hamblin long ago. That day . . ." She looked toward him as though pleading for an appeal. "And I lived with some . . . Indians . . . south . . ."

Jacob remembered the day she had taken off on the horse through the meadows. Evidently Rachel had never been able to find her again.

"Take me with you," she whispered, walking so close to him that he felt her stumble against his feet. "Please, I beg of you. If God is merciful, you will let me come."

Jacob felt torn between his inclination to protect her and his fear. "Don't keep stumbling," he said, and held her up by her arm.

"If you—only knew everything," Margaret said. But she cut her words off as though they were poison in her mouth. Her lips hardened into a thin line.

"Walk right. Try to keep calm. Maybe I should . . ." he hesitated, feeling clumsier than a bull. "Try to carry the baby."

"She'll cry," Margaret said.

No one knew them here. Yet he felt the eyes of every Saint from Salt Lake City to Provo on him as he walked with this girl and the child in her arms. Take her? What was she asking? He couldn't take her anywhere any more than he could take the man in the moon.

"Why did you leave me in Fillmore? And you must have known Proctor died in the night. He died from skinning the animal at the spring the Missouris poisoned. They poisoned that spring."

"Walk straighter," Jacob said uneasily. "Just walk straighter."

"Nobody wanted me. Not even Rachel. I found somebody in Santa Clara."

The street was filled with restless people now, making preparations to return to their Salt Lake City homes. Men were shoveling the manure into the ox-carts. Women began mixing their flat bread for the noon meal. Jacob thought he would have been lost in this crowd if he had been walking alone. Now he felt himself a spectacle—a walking show.

"Why did they kill those people?"

Her question passed almost unnoticed. But Jacob heard it as it echoed in his head.

She continued. "The people in Santa Clara who took care of me also took care of some Indians. The Indians said they didn't do it. They said the Mormons did it. Did you do it?"

Jacob's throat tightened. He knew too well what she meant by *it*. Margaret Seymour. "Walk faster," he said to her.

"Did you?"

"No. I didn't kill nobody."

"But you was there. I knew it," Margaret whispered. "Why did they kill them all? Do you know why they did it?"

At that moment Jacob wanted to push her away. He wanted to break free and run through the crowds surrounding the wagons, the children, the cattle steaming in the morning sun. There was more than fear in him now. There was anger.

"I got so sick having the baby I never remembered nothing for a couple of months. I never remembered even seeing any baby. When I started remembering again, the people from Santa Clara was gone, and I was staying alone in an old wood house with some old Indians." Still she held the baby's head against her shoulder.

The crowds were the greatest at Center Street. Jacob maneuvered Margaret through the wagons at the crosswalk, still holding her arm. He was conscious of her hair, and of her skirts against his leg. He remembered the strange feeling of attraction. Suddenly his anger and hatred began to nag his body into a furious desire.

"The Indians said they delivered my baby. The old man said he loved me and wanted to marry me. I ran away."

Why are you running? Jacob wanted to ask her now. Why are you running? The crowds closed around them; cattle crowded the street. There was a group of children in the church yard playing ball. Jacob quickened his step and guided Margaret by her elbow over the bridge on the canal.

"The lady we live with is my friend Percy's widowed aunt," Jacob explained as he hurried toward the house.

Margaret hesitated before she stepped on the lawn. "What are you going to say?" she asked.

When Margaret stopped, Jacob also stopped on the front lawn, still feeling wracked by the pressure of the noisy crowds in the street, his own desire to return home, the need of the Widow Harvey for his help, and now Margaret's presence with the baby and her nagging request to take her with him. He thought he could hear Percy's hammer in the background. He was suddenly conscious that he still held in his hand the package of nails.

"I don't know."

"Don't tell the lady the truth, please," Margaret whispered. "I'm afraid. Tell her my young husband was killed."

Jacob stared at Margaret, really seeing her face for the first time. Her eyes were wide with a terror he could only guess, not fully understand. He wasn't used to hiding shame with lies.

"Let me tell anything that needs telling," Margaret said again.

Now Jacob felt tired. He could have guessed that Margaret Seymour would operate by deception, but he didn't know how else to handle it. He nodded, "All right." He glanced behind to check out the crowded streets. Not waiting to knock or receive an answer, he opened the door and the two stumbled into the dark cool house away from the noise.

# 48
## *Jacob*

For his first few moments in the widow's house, Jacob could not see. He could feel Margaret and the child near his arm. He blinked hard and leaned forward, leaning on the door knob.

"Mrs. Harvey!" he called. But she did not seem to be there. "Bring the baby upstairs," Jacob steered Margaret toward the stairwell. "There's a place to lie down."

"She's wet. Does the lady have . . ." Margaret hesitated.

"I can get some towels," Jacob said while Margaret went into the upstairs hallway. Finally, when he mounted the stairs he thought he could smell the faint odor of powder, or flowers. Margaret was dusting the child with powder she had found on the dressing table. The baby was whimpering, its legs and arms beating the air. Margaret took the cloths and began to wrap the little girl, though she jumped out of Margaret's arms and began to crawl awkwardly on the floor. Margaret picked her up again. Jacob turned toward the window and watched Percy pound the newly purchased nails into the shed. It was almost done.

"Do you think she'll mind if I stay?" Maggie asked.

"Percy and I aren't staying here much longer," Jacob said.

Margaret came to the window now, patting the baby to quiet her. "She needs something to eat," Margaret whispered. "But I think she's tired and will sleep for a while." In a few minutes the child's eyes closed and Margaret lay her on the bed. She walked to Jacob who still stood watching Percy at the window. "Jacob, you never said for sure. Will you please take me with you when you go?"

They were alone. The room still smelled slightly of powder. Jacob turned from the window and looked at her again as though he saw her for the first time.

"I can't take you. Me and Percy are alone on the trail. What would you do? Where would you and the baby sleep?"

"I can sleep on the ground, or in the wagon."

"What would a baby do on such a trip?"

"She's used to it."

Jacob breathed hard. "Margaret, please don't ask me to take you."

Margaret stood uncomfortably close to him now. He stood against the window with his arms fastened to his side. She began to lean against him and lay her head on his shoulder. "Oh, Jacob. If you knew what I had suffered you would not mind taking me with you."

At that moment Jacob heard footsteps at the bedroom door. The door was open. Mrs. Harvey peered in. Jacob had taken Margaret's elbows in his hands to restrain her. But now her head lay on his breast.

"Oh, pardon me!" the old aunt said. "I didn't mean to intrude. My goodness, Jacob, I didn't know. Have I met . . . ?"

"Mrs. Harvey!" Jacob's neck grew red. His head swam with dizziness. "Mrs. Harvey I'd like you to meet a friend of mine, Margaret Seymour. She needs a place right now and I was wondering . . ."

"Oh, my goodness! A baby!" Mrs. Harvey exclaimed, entering the room. A darling child!"

Margaret blushed and looked coyly down. "Thank you," she said. "An orphan child I saved from the Indians. She had no one. I am taking her south with Jacob and Percy when they go."

Jacob stared at Margaret. She didn't even blink. Though dark, her eyes were level, without a trace of shame. That's a lie, he wanted to say. But he didn't.

"An orphan child!" Mrs. Harvey touched the sleeping baby's cheek. "About a year old?" She looked at Margaret's thick waist. Her eyes registered some doubt, but it would go unexpressed.

Margaret stared at Jacob. Don't say anything, her eyes told him.

"What a lovely child. Of course, darling. I haven't much. My husband died three months ago. But what I have you are welcome to share. I'll get you some towels. Jacob, we'll let her have this bedroom."

Margaret's eyes continued to send daggers toward Jacob, though her face was blank and calm.

"Why didn't you . . ." Jacob began.

"It's better this way," whispered Margaret. "She'll feel sorry for an orphan child. Please don't tell her."

Jacob began to protest again. Margaret placed her fingers on his lips. Then she leaned up to him and kissed him. Though he drew back, she would not give in. "Please, Jacob. Don't be so afraid. Help me." As she clung to him, he placed his hands on her back. She moved near to him and he felt the pressure of her body. He wanted to thrust her away when he heard Mrs. Harvey's footsteps again. But she leaned back on her own when the old woman brought more towels into the room.

Jacob stammered, still blushing. "I appreciate your help in this matter," he said uneasily. "I met Margaret, well, I've known Margaret . . . for a while . . ."

The old woman wrinkled her forehead knowingly. "I see, she said. "So I see."

What did she see? Jacob felt betrayed. Whatever she "saw" was wrong. He controlled his tongue. The old aunt was still in the room putting doilies in the drawers, folding towels.

"When I met Margaret, her folks were sending her to Scipio because . . ." He tried to communicate without speaking. But he seemed to be doing badly— falling deeper into confusion. Mrs. Harvey's eyes were wary now. Blank with the same confusion. "She's been captured by the Indians. I found her here in Provo. She needs help. She should be going home to Scipio."

"Not home . . ." Margaret's voice was small now. "Not home. My parents hate me." She began to speak further, but Mrs. Harvey's brows knit. Her eyes were fastened to the baby girl in Margaret's arms. "Please have mercy on me."

"Yes, of course," said Mrs. Harvey, but without smiling or returning Margaret's pleading gaze. "For whatever reason she is here . . ." she said in a flat tone of voice. She gazed half-heartedly toward Jacob. "She is welcome to stay."

Jacob could not sleep that night. He cursed an ever-repeating insomnia. Why couldn't he forget about Margaret? But it seemed he couldn't forget. He knew why. He was terrified of her. He knew she was capable of . . . anything.

He knew why he was afraid when Percy came into the bedroom that night after conversing downstairs with his aunt for a few moments. Percy looked at him with very heavy eyes, a dark, puzzled, unbelieving look. "You . . . you. I can't believe it, Lorry." He was quiet for a moment, and in the background was the cry of the child. "Your child . . . ?"

Jacob stared. "That's what she told you?"

"No, my aunt guessed."

He felt as though he couldn't breathe. The baby was still crying. He listened to the baby and heard Maggie's small song against the baby's hair. It put him to sleep.

Waking early on the day of their departure, Jacob heard the tick of the clock as though it were an ax hitting wood. For a moment he imagined that he could get up before anyone else, get the wagon ready in an instant, get Percy up in a split second, and leave before Margaret knew anything. But it didn't happen that way.

As he climbed out of the boys' bedroom on the second floor, he heard the door of Margaret's room crack open. In a few moments, Margaret was up, with the baby wrapped and ready to go. Watching her fumble with the small bundle of her belongings, Jacob remembered when he had tried to say no to her kiss in Beaver. He would never forget it. And he could not tell her "no" this morning as he and Percy prepared to return to Kanarraville.

She followed them so closely that no person or beast could have slipped between them. The baby, like a little doll, lay nestled quietly in the blankets, staring as though she knew exactly what was happening at every moment.

When Percy got into the wagon, Margaret followed him. Without thinking, Jacob took her hand to help her climb to the wagon board. She smiled back at him.

"I appreciate what you have done for me, Jacob Lorry. You will never know how your kindness has saved my life and the life of my baby. I will never forget you."

Jacob was still afraid.

Through her entreaties, she managed a voice as solicitous as Jacob had ever heard. As he cracked the whip against the oxen on the cart, he shook his head to himself, thinking he still did not know why or how he could have felt so angry and yet at the same time so incredibly willing to give in.

## 49
### Elizabeth

*May 26, 1858  Patrick Moore is back at our place again. He brought news that Brigham Young told everyone it was safe to go back to Salt Lake City. The danger of the U.S. Army has passed. The United States has sent a U.S. Governor by the name of Mr. Cummings. And Brigham Young has convinced everyone to think of that man as our governor. We have made peace with the United States. We are not rebels.*

*June 17, 1858  This morning Jacob and Percy drove in. They brought with them a young mother and her beautiful baby girl.*

With the return of Patrick Moore, Elizabeth had not questioned Suky's motive for asking him to stay. Both men slept on their guns, J.B. still silent and uncommunicative. When J.B. did not seem interested in entering her loft, she felt relieved. At mealtime it was Patrick Moore who brought some life into the conversation. He teased the children, calling them his little goats. Sally and Foster loved him. When they didn't eat their greens, he teased them into it. "Didn't you know little goats eat everything? You can't be withering away now, can you? When those relatives of yours come to take you home to Arkansas, do you want to look like monkeys?"

When Patrick mentioned Arkansas, Suky rose from the table angrily, banging pots and pans.

Patrick still goaded her with this kind of talk. But he teased the children. "Well, I guess Miss Suky don't want you to go. So if your relatives come and take you a few miles away, you'll have to wait until they all fall asleep that first night and sneak out of their tent and run all the way back here."

The little girl Sally Dunham screwed up her nose and laughed. Foster didn't understand. Suky knit her brows and glared. "Hush, Patrick Moore. Oh my stars. Hush it, now. Nobody is coming for these children in the first place. Let that subject alone."

"Oh, but somebody truly is coming for these children," Patrick responded. "I'm just trying to help you get used to the idea."

Nevertheless, Suky liked Patrick, so when she stood behind his chair with a pan of biscuits in her hands, she hit him with her elbow. "You can talk about something else," she said with a grimace. "Talk about staying. Talk about a picnic in Kolob Canyon. Talk about the biscuits." She set them on the table with a flourish. "But don't talk about these children going away from us."

Elizabeth watched Patrick's wariness. Sometimes he seemed to be watching her from a distance. Often she wondered why he continued staying with them, although he said it was to take charge of the Kanarraville and Harmony militias. But as soon as Brigham Young bowed to the U.S. government, there should have been no reason for war. To that turn of events Patrick had said that as long as there was a U.S. Army only twenty-five miles from Provo, there should be a well-turned-out army along the Wasatch front. Both he and J.B. continued to sleep on their guns.

As time passed, and J.B. still did not come to her loft, Elizabeth could not understand it, though she did not complain. Something dark seemed to have come between them. She thought it might be the presence of Patrick Moore. It was true that the officer had begun watching her with eyes she feared. She found him waiting for her outside the house one evening. He was standing by the back door in the dark. She heard his footsteps when she began forward with the butter crock in her arms. The sky seemed darker than usual, the stars dim.

"Where you goin' in such a hurry?"

She swung around to him, her heart pounding. "To the cellar. To put back the butter."

"Mind if I come along?"

"It's all right, I guess."

"Can you answer me a personal question?"

"I . . . I guess."

"Is the old man J.B. Lorry any kind of a lover for a young girl like you?"

For a moment she feared him, this young soldier. Yet she found herself wanting to tell him everything. She wanted to tell him the truth, that no, he wasn't a lover. That she felt it unjust that J.B. was so much a part of her life now—it rankled in her. And since she had lost her baby, it hurt more than ever before.

He began laughing, a low unguarded laughter. "You can't tell me he's enough of a lover for you. I been watching you. I know you better'n you know yourself. You're hungrier 'n a tiger. You're just waitin' for somebody really good to come along."

His words hurt her ears, her heart lurched. The cellar seemed to be leagues away. Finally, at the door of the cellar, she leaned against the jamb and tried to catch her breath. *Oh, my,* she whispered only in her mind. *It can't be. He couldn't—* She set the crock down, and felt him close the distance between them. As she rose to her feet she bumped into him. His hand shot quickly around her waist.

He drew her around to face him. She jerked from his grasp. "No . . . Mr. Moore."

He laughed from his eyes. "Ah ha! Every breath of you is asking for something you don't get. Whatever he is giving you, it ain't enough, I can tell you that, Elizabeth."

"It's enough." She wanted to scream different words: *Perhaps it is not enough. Sometimes I hate him.* But those words wouldn't come. "Please, Patrick. Or I'll scream."

When he released his hands from her waist, he lowered his eyes. He shook his head. "You have no idea. You just don't know, girl. He's so old he wouldn't even hear you. He's so old he's almost dead."

"That's not true," she spit between her clamped teeth.

"Could be true," Patrick said, wisely backing away.

What did he mean by narrowing his eyes, by looking askance? She watched and listened, still breathing hard, trying to turn from the cellar to the house.

"If he wasn't used to usin' his gun . . . if he wasn't a murderer, I'd take a chance."

*A murderer! How dare you accuse* . . . but she said nothing. She gasped, instead. Her eyes blazed. She understood the accusation which had followed some ugly incredible rumors. Rumors that . . . but it was too horrible to conceive. It cut her to the heart.

"A murderer," he repeated coldly. "The same as John Lee."

Her head swam. The massacre. J.B. or Patrick? Patrick had been there. He would have known. But it was a subject about which none of them ever spoke. She pressed her back against the door even more tightly, and then sidled away from him, finally coming into the open. She walked toward him, gathering her confidence and then walked away.

It was only because of the unexpected, fortunate arrival of Maggie and her baby that Patrick did not touch her again.

## 50
### June 23, 1859, Elizabeth

*When Jacob finally took time to remind me, I recalled that I had seen this red-headed girl once before—at Hamblins', running away on the stallion with her hair flying behind her in the wind. Jacob says the Indians took care of her while she had her baby. Then she rode all the way up to Salt Lake City. The little girl Missy is a miracle baby—a little doll with cheeks as white as porcelain, and dark brown curls. She reminds me of the little Arkansas baby, Hannah, the Indians kidnapped last year. Suky loves the baby. I haven't seen her so happy since the Indians took Hannah away. Jacob seems embarrassed. The woman Maggie opens her mouth about anything. She says what she feels like saying even though it is embarrassing and often not true.*

Maggie came like a wave of heat into the Lorry home. She came with the ten-month-old baby, who was just beginning to toddle. She forced milk into the child's mouth with a cup, but seemed detached. She misplaced things, hid large chunks of bread and cheese in strange places. She gave the child to Suky's care most of the day, wandering about as though she were lost in another world, refusing to eat with the others for several days until they pleaded with her to join them like a civilized human being. When she finally decided to come, it was a notable event, something like a celebration.

It was easy to see at once, from the very beginning, what might happen. Elizabeth, sensitive to J.B.'s morose rejection and Jacob's anxious eyes, saw the white fire in Patrick's eyes when Maggie came in to that first meal. Everyone, even the baby that nestled in Suky's arms, hushed to a dead quiet. J.B., his dark look focused on the stew pot, raised his head only slightly.

"This here is Maggie Seymour, Jacob's friend . . ."

Patrick Moore took a long glance before he said a word—as though he were processing this information. "Hello, Maggie," he finally said.

It would probably have happened no matter who in the military had stayed with J.B. But because it was Patrick Moore, it seemed that it happened with unprecedented speed.

No one said anything. They just watched. taking in Patrick and Maggie at the table. Patrick smiled at Maggie, who looked down at the baby she held in her arms. And then she looked up with tentative eyes. Maggie and Patrick did not talk very much. But it was not necessary to talk. The language they spoke between them was so thick Elizabeth thought she would choke.

Suky tried to speak. "We have a bit of oatcake in the cellar, Elizabeth. Would you get it, please?"

"I'll get it, Mrs. Lorry," Patrick said, rising from his chair, but not moving his eyes from Maggie's face. She stared at him. Stumbling over his boots, he slipped out the back door.

"If you don't mind, Mrs. Lorry, I need to get the baby's other blanket. I left it on the stoop this afternoon," Maggie said, almost whispering.

"Then I'll take the baby, Miz Maggie," Suky said, the eyes in her gaunt face darker than Elizabeth had ever seen them. "Just give her to me."

They knew, watching, where Maggie was going, and they knew she would not return soon. Maggie thrust the baby into Suky's arms.

After that, there were many other evenings like this one, with the beautiful baby on Suky's lap, and finally in Suky's bed for the night, wrapped in Suky's arms. They were quiet evenings, passing with no alarm. Everyone in the house watched Patrick and Maggie come in the early mornings from the fields. Or from the hills in the east. Maggie spent less and less time with the baby.

One afternoon Patrick Moore packed his saddle bags and left them sitting by the door. He took a cloth bag and packed it generously with Suky's bread and cheese. When it grew dark that evening, he and Maggie left the baby with Suky and told her they were taking a ride into town. In the morning, the saddle bags beside the door—and Maggie and Patrick—were gone.

**51**

*Elizabeth*

The heat came down early now. By midmorning, by nine o'clock, the waves of air that scoured the basin fell heavily to the slopes, dancing and shimmering with steam. When she first woke, Elizabeth could see it: the tangible heat shimmering on the baked dirt. It crawled into the house under the lintel and filled the loft. Then it hung so heavy it fell into the house along the floor until there was no place to crawl away from it.

Now they lived with their hair wet against their necks. Suky brought a bucket from the canal just for rag dipping. She constantly kept a wet towel plastered across her forehead to keep her cool. She tied a large dry table cloth around her neck and crossed it about her waist, where she put the baby. With her head wet and her body weighed down with the little girl in front, she tended the fire, the chickens, the garden, singing in a dry, scratchy voice at every possible moment to the child.

When J.B. came in from the fields on Wednesday, he asked, "Hasn't Miss Seymour returned for her baby?" He asked it as though nothing greatly unusual had happened on Monday. He did not think it notable that Patrick was also gone. Or he knew and just didn't care. Or he was hoping for Suky's sake that Maggie Seymour did not come back for the child.

He was more interested in the upcoming fourth of July celebration John Lee was putting together at Harmony. He had taken enough wheat to the ranch, he said, to aid in the production of several hundred gallons of beer for a large fourth of July celebration. "He's made nigh onto three hundred gallons, I dare say And all of it the best. It's gonna be a big celebration with lots of beef. They're cooking the meat and the potatoes in a ground oven dug out ten feet in diameter, lined with hot stones."

Elizabeth stared at Suky. The woman did not look up at her husband. Her eyes were fastened on the child who lay kicking in her lap, her small hands reaching for fingers.

"I would really like to take the baby to the celebration," Suky said. "Do you think the mother will be there?" Suky's voice was so small it was almost lost in the heat of the room.

"I don't think the mother will be back for a while," Jacob said.

Suky held the baby's hands. "Are you sure, Jacob?"

"She's not . . . she's not . . ."

"Jacob believes he knows her well enough," Elizabeth said softly, clutching the chair until her fingers were white. "He knows her enough to know she's a very irresponsible girl."

Suky looked pale. "But Patrick Moore. He's bound to be back. He's not one to let go of the last ounce of his military pay . . ."

J.B. stopped long enough to look at the baby thoughtfully. "They'll be back sometime. But maybe not soon."

"If they don't come back soon, I'm claiming her to be my own," Suky whispered, almost inaudibly. But though her voice was quiet, her eyes were bright with passion.

Elizabeth feared that Suky was nearly insane.

When the fourth of July finally came, there was still no sign of Maggie Seymour and Patrick Moore. And Suky would not hear of anything else but that she would take the child to the celebration at Harmony. She was not afraid, she said. She dressed the little girl in a clean dress to ward off the sun.

The Lees put on the feast of the year, as bounteous as any Thanksgiving banquet: two fat beeves, two goats, some pork and chicken, all the meats and breads faultlessly prepared by his latest wife, the wonderful Emma who had become known for her culinary talents since her entry into the Lee household.

As soon as the Lorry wagon entered the compound, Elizabeth spotted Rebecca stuffing sausages into a cook pot and boiling them over the outside fire.

Standing beside her was a young man who was fanning the flames with a bellows. When Rebecca saw Elizabeth, she handed the potholders to the young man and ran to Elizabeth, waving.

There was news, Rebecca whispered, although she had turned away from the young man beside her because she had not wanted him to know that she was gossiping about him.

"What is it?" Elizabeth asked. She followed Rebecca toward the back of the house across the tamped-down dirt where dozens of children were jumping rope and playing games with stones.

"I've found someone else," Rebecca whispered.

Elizabeth pulled back, searching her friend's face for some sign that this was true.

Rebecca nodded toward the fire and the young man with the bellows who was dishing sticks to the flames now. "It's a wise decision," she nodded.

"It's him?" Elizabeth asked.

"Yes. His name is Brady Lewis."

"You've given up on Lee?" Elizabeth whispered.

Rebecca took Elizabeth by the hand and pulled her into a corner by the gate of the Harmony wall that stood around the compound. "You have not heard of it . . . ? Surely you must know . . . If you have not heard of it, I must tell you." She gasped. "It is something you must know," she continued. "They have found out that he is a murderer." She said it under her breath. "Remember that first day the wagon train came and he was alone at the mill? He killed three men and hid their bodies. Then he wanted to kill all the people in the massacre.'

Elizabeth felt off-center—as though the earth were turning and she was not turning with it. She had thought Rebecca's complaint might have been the rumor about the two young girls he took to Salt Lake City and refused to marry because they giggled in the wagon. She did not speak. She waited for Rebecca for what seemed like a very long time—then discovered the rumor of the two young girls had escalated into something larger than any of them could handle.

"They found the bodies of two young girls at the massacre he shot to death. And he marries women to make slaves of them. But he hates women and kills them."

Elizabeth stared at Rebecca, not understanding how she could have come to this kind of talk.

"They say it was his idea to get the Indians to kill the Fancher party, and he did more than his share."

Elizabeth forced her voice to speak. "Who says?" Her breath felt like a hot fire in her lungs. She had heard some rumors. But never like this, so indisputably reported from the mouth of a friend.

"Brady says. And his Uncle David was at the site. It was terrible, Elizabeth."

"What you are saying?" Elizabeth breathed hard. "What you are saying could not have happened."

"What could not have happened?"

"Those are terrible rumors about John Lee."

"It happened," Rebecca whispered. "Cross my heart and hope to die."

From their position at the gate, the girls could see the people—at least a hundred—as they milled about at the barbecue pits inside the stone walls. Elizabeth searched for John D. Lee. As always, he was surrounded by doting women and children who were looking to his every need. Though his back was turned to her, there was no mistaking who he was. One of his wives offered him a plate of chicken just then, and he raised a protesting hand. Elizabeth thought it was Emma Lee who stood with him. He was not talking with her. He had turned his rugged blond head to a group of men who were discussing something serious with him, gesturing, pointing toward the south. They were probably pointing toward the new cotton fields they had been commanded to plant in the south by the Virgin River, in Washington County, where Lee had begun building a new mansion that winter. While he listened to the men, he turned his head as though he were drinking in the scene of the celebration. Elizabeth caught his direct gaze before she lowered her head. The memory of those eyes stung her heart. Why do I still feel as I do about him? she wondered. She kept her eyes down, afraid he had noticed her stare. She took Rebecca's hands between her own and pressed them.

"Rebecca, if you have a mind to love Brady Lewis, I am very happy for you."

"May God's blessings be yours, my dear Elizabeth. Take them when they come."

## 52

*Monday, July 28, 1858, Elizabeth*

*Fear is not easy to live with. Suky's afraid that Patrick Moore and Maggie will return and take the baby Missy away. We are all afraid that the U.S. Army is on its way through here to California and that something terrible has happened to us all. There are more rumors about the men around here helping with the killings at the massacre. I cannot believe them. But they say people from Arkansas are coming soon to take the orphan children home, and that officers from the U.S. Army are coming down to make a thorough investigation. I know that some of the men who fear the investigation are going up into the hills to hide. Suky is so afraid that she wants me to go up into the hills and hide with Maggie's baby so that if Maggie and Patrick Moore ever return, they will not find her. She doesn't think Missy is Maggie's baby, because she would never have left her like this for so long. I must agree with her. I have my own opinions about whose child this is. But I dare not breathe a word about it because I, too, am afraid. All of us are afraid of so many things. We watch the road every day. But so far no one has come.*

But someone did come—on a hot July day. The canal had dried up into a trickle. The Lorry family spent the afternoon in the shade of their small trees, and in the path of the canyon's only thread of breeze. Suky lay in the hammock with the baby on her stomach, rocking gently. Sally and Foster played in the shade of the barn. Sometimes Sally slept. But she told Suky she didn't want to sleep today. She was making a chain of horse grass, twisting the sections into links while Foster broke up sticks and lined them up into rows of soldiers. Elizabeth was crocheting a hat for the baby Missy. Every day that passed, she was more certain than ever that Missy was not Maggie's baby.

The hills, the mountains still hung heavy with the heat. But in the distance, from the north, there was a sudden puff of dust, a moving cloud that could only mean travelers. They had not seen travelers on the road since the threat of war. Suky said, "That's them. That's the Arkansans after the children." She had made elaborate plans for Sally and Foster to hide. But when they spotted Jacob coming from the north field, they waited instead for more news.

Jacob had grown taller this summer. He was going to be a large man, like his father. His burnished dark brown hair was so thick it stood up in several places on his head. He had grown muscular in the past year, his brow smooth and broad, his face rugged from the abuse of the sun. He carried a rake on his shoulder. His pants were too short for him, and his shirt tail askew. When he came into the yard, his face was cramped with concern. "It's not the people from Arkansas who are coming," he said. He lowered his rake from his shoulder. "It's the investigating committee from Salt Lake City that's here," he said without any particular expression. "They're hunting for John Lee. He didn't go in by himself, so they came to get him."

Suky grunted a sigh of relief. Elizabeth did not say anything. She wanted to know if there were any other messages.

"They're going to take him and others to Cedar about the investigation. J.B. decided to go to Harmony with them. I think we saw Patrick Moore."

Suky sat up in the hammock at once, alert, as though she had never had her eyes closed. She clutched the baby with so startling a movement that the child began to wake.

"No. No, it can't be," Elizabeth whispered, pleading with Jacob, although Jacob was the last person in the world who could have done anything to make any difference.

"I think so," Jacob said, watching fear cloud Elizabeth's face. "Somebody described a man on a big black horse. It sounded like Patrick Moore."

Suky was still sitting on the edge of the hammock, holding the child. Her graying hair stood straight up on her head. She looked like a wild woman from an asylum. "Then it's time, now," she said in a thin voice. "It's time to go into hiding with this child."

Elizabeth's heart pounded. Perhaps it was time, then, for them to implement at least that part of their plan.

"I'm going down there, too, Ma," Jacob said now. He wasn't asking for permission. He merely announced to her that he would be going to Cedar to look in on the meetings about the event that had taken place at the meadows.

Elizabeth did not say anything when Jacob turned to walk to the barn. When he disappeared into the darkness, Suky got down out of the hammock with the child, and looked after him.

"He don't listen to me no more," she said.

Elizabeth turned toward the house and hurried up the stoop to begin packing some of her things.

## 53
### August 10, 1858, Jacob

It was dusk by the time Jacob began to search for J.B. in the town. There were lights in the church. They were proceeding with the meetings. He thought he smelled jasmine or honeysuckle as he swung down from the saddle. The rich dry odor made his nose itch. Bees swarmed in the small hedges at the church door. He wondered where they had found jasmine to plant beside the church? He had not remembered it being there when he was here last. All of his senses seemed sharpened. He saw the silhouettes of the men inside the open door. He dared not go in. President George Albert Smith was examining a document laid on the table in front of him. Jacob recognized Jensen, Lewis, Amasa Lyman,

Charles Hall, Job Hall, Nephi Johnson, John Higbee. From his angle, Jacob could not see everyone in the room, but when he moved to the left, he saw John Lee sitting in a far corner as though he were trying to remain hidden from view.

There were others, their looming heads silhouetted against the candlelight. Though he could not see all of their faces, he recognized the shaggy curls of J.B. He did not see Patrick Moore. Holding his breath, he listened to their words.

"I don't understand why the men and women were separate."

"The women went ahead of the men." There was a pause. "They were isolated. The women were to be kept apart so we could collect the arms."

Every word President Smith spoke stung Jacob's heart. He hurt, wondering why he had wanted so much to come here, to hear talk that seemed to punish him all over again. Yet he continued to bend his ears toward the voices, to listen with every nerve taut. The jasmine crowded his nostrils until he ached to sneeze.

"We will meet again tomorrow."

His heart fell. They were almost done and he had missed most of it. If they had known he was listening they may not have continued. He knew they would not have asked him to meet with them.

"Brethren . . . I feel that something strange . . . something . . ." Smith stared at the candles. He rubbed his temples with his fingers. "There is something strange here which I cannot explain."

It was at this point that David Lewis suddenly rose out of his chair. He was so large, his body seemed to fill the room. Close to the door, he blocked out the others from Jacob's view. When he spoke, his voice was low. Jacob could hear the trepidation in his tone.

"I . . . I . . ." Lewis started. "I've got to go. My wife wasn't feeling good and I told her I'd be back before it got too dark."

The big man turned away from the table. Jacob clung to the door. The shadows Lewis cast in the candlelight moved like clouds across the churchyard as he disappeared. Jacob did not see him leave through the picket gate. Was there a back way? He listened, his heart beating in his ears. Lewis was still somewhere in the yard. He was sure of it. He could barely breathe.

Now the men began to leave. They coughed or cleared their throats. They stomped on the plank floor. The benches in the church croaked as they rose. They had been seated around the sacrament table. They pushed it into place. It scraped against the wood, jarred against the uneven floor.

John Lee stood so close to the small window beside the door that Jacob could have touched him. He was not as large as David Lewis, but he was tall and his arms were thick as fence posts. Jacob caught a glance of uneasiness in his piercing blue eyes. Words had not come from his mouth tonight. His eyes seemed sunken, almost as though the lights had gone out of them.

"Come back tomorrow night, all of you," someone said.

Most of the men emerged without talking. There was an unpleasant silence, an uneasy silence, the kind of silence that is dominated by fear.

Only President Smith was left standing at the sacrament table, still conferring with Amasa Lyman and Erastus Snow. Charles C. Rich still sat near them, leaning back in his chair. He had closed his eyes as though deep in thought, waiting for something. When the others would have been gone to their homes, Jacob turned slowly to go. But the movement of a bulky shadow startled him. He jumped. He could see the big body of David Lewis still in the doorway. Lewis would have seen him, but evidently he did not care. The man's sweat glistened on his brow. He lunged into the church building, interrupting the conversation of those still seated around the table. His voice seemed overloud for the silent darkness.

"Lord have mercy on me," he sobbed to the men in the room, his tongue thick and heavy in his mouth. Jacob could hear his words only partially through the lighted door. "No matter what they tell you brethren, we have done wrong. We knew it. We could not stop it. For some reason we went forward as though something was driving us to do it. We excused ourselves, believing God gave us the command."

President Smith turned to him, his brows knit in thoughtful silence as he listened to the man's loud speech.

"We was ready for war, sir." David held his hat in both hands, clutching it so tightly, his knuckles were white. "Now I cannot bear the guilt no more." He was incoherent, his breath ragged. "We was tired of fightin' and losin' and we saw a way to win. With none of us dead, sir. We won the war, sir. But it wasn't fair. We led them out of the valley. They thought we was saving them from the Indians."

As Jacob listened to Lewis's words, he heard someone push the door open near to him and with heavy steps shuffle away. When he strained his eyes in the darkness, he could barely see. But he knew who it was that left in the midst of the untimely outburst. It was John D. Lee.

From the door he could barely see Smith's face. It grew pale in the lantern's light. Jacob's heart stopped. Each word Lewis spoke seemed to bring him closer to the terror of their deed. It had not seemed so terrible until it was done. He watched Smith's blank eyes. He remembered the rousing challenge to war that Smith himself had delivered to the conference that last spring. Jacob clearly remembered the impassioned determination they had expressed to do God's will because it had been the speech that had motivated him. It was after that speech that he had ached to use a gun. And now . . . he stood. His hands could still feel the sting of the aimless shot he had fired. He could see the blood oozing from the wound he made on the man's cheek. He felt sick. He turned away. He wanted to go home.

*Now you will always remember the whistle of air as that explosion shook your hands. It is not something easily forgotten. Why did you do it? And who was it that met that slug of lead face on? And even if it were no one—but it was someone—you would never forget the sound of your weapon against all the others as they fell one by one. Down. They were mowed down. Like tall grass. Like wheat. Like grain picked off of the earth, unharvested, a crowded field of stalks waving in the wind, bowing for the last time.*

## 54
### *August 11, 1858, Elizabeth*

The increasing rumors of approaching government investigators finally convinced many of them to hide. When it had been decided that some of them should go into hiding, there was a lull of a kind that Elizabeth had seldom experienced. That afternoon Jacob took Elizabeth and the baby to settle in a safe place under the red rocks of the Kolob Canyon. The canyon echoed every sound. Clop clop clop reverberated against the walls of the rocks as though there were a hundred horses following them. Jacob rode in front on the new mare, Shasta, and Elizabeth rode on old Foresight with the baby in her arms.

Elizabeth was not sure how far they would go into the maze of hills. But Jacob did not go many miles before he found an open cove where he stopped and dismounted.

"This will be fine, Elizabeth," he said. "We don't want you so far away that you can't come down." When he saw her face, he hesitated to pull the tent down from the pack on the mule. "Is this all right?" he asked.

She had never been this far into the canyon. She did not know. Near the small creek and the copse of trees was a huge rock looming above them like a ship. "I guess so. Is it safe?" When she looked around at the open hills, the over-whelming glorious colors, she felt very small.

"I think you'll be all right here, Elizabeth. I need you to be close enough that I can bring the food."

Elizabeth watched Jacob put the tent under the stone wall. When she looked up at the tall rocks on the other side of the creek, she felt that the eyes of Indians could easily be watching her from the ridges and crannies under the sky. "If you brought the food here, I would find it," she said. "But I might try to find a cave."

"You want a cave?" Jacob stood up from his work on the tent, not sure he should continue. "I can move the tent."

"No, Jacob," Elizabeth, thinking of him. "Let me have a chance to look around. I won't have anything else to do. But if you don't find me here, just bring the food to this place and put it under these stones."

Jacob only half-heartedly continued to put up the tent. When he glanced at Elizabeth, she was searching the sky and the hills, finding possible trails, possible dark hiding places in the fissures of stone. "There are still animals here," Jacob whispered. "You must do what I told you—use the gun."

"I'll be fine, Jacob," Elizabeth laughed gently. "You're always worried about me."

Jacob, finishing with the tent, rubbed his hands on his trousers. "I'll always worry about you," he said. It was a simple statement weighted with emotion, and Elizabeth hoped he wouldn't feel embarrassed by it. "I'd stay here if you want to me stay," he said quickly.

"No. No, I'll do fine," Elizabeth said, shaking her head. She had a copy of *Ivanhoe* in her knapsack, and the baby on her hip.

When Jacob left her, she noticed that he looked back over and over again until the horse rounded the bend and disappeared. When he was gone, Elizabeth began her own exploration of the surroundings, carrying the baby with her, holding her close.

Only about five hundred yards away, Elizabeth discovered the cave she had hoped she would find. When she came back to the tent, she laid the little girl in the grass, unfastened the canvas tent from the stakes, pulled up the stakes, rolled them up in the canvas, and placed the bundle on the back of the mule. Moving up into the crevasse, she felt the walls close in on her even further, stern high walls, deep and rocky as though the desert were standing on its end. She believed that if Jacob brought the food, she would hear him come, as she was only about five hundred yards further away from the first location. Only a hundred feet from the stream, this spot, seeming safer, lay below a severe overhang. The rocks, jutting under as they reached the ground, formed a partial cave. As well as more security, this place offered a grassy plot for Foresight, and a small charcoal pit, with black smoke scars against the rock above it. Elizabeth guessed someone had probably been here with their fire some time ago. But the tent would be protected from both storm or heat, she knew.

When she unrolled the canvas and took out the stakes, she put the baby on the grass near a large rock. Tired, the little girl went to sleep. Elizabeth crouched down on the grass near the canvas, and began to tap the larger stakes into the ground.

The noise of the spring water covered up any other sounds. Though she began to sing, she could not hear her own voice, let alone the sound of hoofbeats further up the draw. So that when the shadow crossed above her, she jumped, her hands flew up, and the stake leaped out of her hands.

"Do you need some help with that?"

Trembling, she saw only a large silhouette on a horse, his face a shadow in the sun.

"I'm sorry. I startled you," the voice said.

Elizabeth shaded her eyes from the afternoon light that filtered through the canyon.

The man leaped down from his horse quickly. "Let me help you with that, Sister Lorry."

When he knelt beside her, his arms brushed her shoulders. Now she could see his face. It was John D. Lee! She thought she had recognized his voice. She watched his hands. Without any trouble at all he took the stone she had been struggling to grasp and tapped the stakes into the ground.

"You're getting away from the valley, too, are you?" he said good-naturedly. He unrolled the canvas into a taut floor and placed the stakes evenly. Every movement was vigorous and efficient. "What's your story?"

Elizabeth felt numb. She tried to find her voice. "I . . ." she stammered. "I'm hiding the baby."

Finishing the tent, he rose on his knees to look at the sleeping child lying on the ground. Elizabeth couldn't help wondering—how had he found them here? The afternoon light filtered through his bright hair. "Hiding the baby?"

Elizabeth breathed in. "We don't think her mother is really her mother. She didn't act like it. And then she abandoned her." Nothing she said seemed like enough of an explanation. "We are afraid for the baby's life if the girl should return and want to take her. And she is capable of doing anything."

John Lee was so large beside Elizabeth, he towered over her when he was on his knees. He looked down at her and smiled. "And so?" he said. His voice registered half irony, half a coarse anger, as though he were inconvenienced, and choking on his words. But still, he was smiling. "Why you?"

"I love her," Elizabeth said simply.

Mr. Lee sat on the grass Indian-style. So close to her, his legs seemed larger than she had remembered. He had huge strong legs that looked as though they had grasped a hundred horses more than ten thousand times. Leaning back on his arms, he spread his hands in the grass. Then he removed his hat and turned his face to the dipping sun.

"And you?" Elizabeth dared to ask. "Why are you here?"

He did not answer her at first. He batted at an insect that buzzed around his head. "Me?" he looked at her. "I think I'm here to help you set up your tent." He grinned. "That's as good as anything, isn't it?"

At times a wave of heat seemed to block out her vision. She felt that happening now. She felt she could not see John Lee because he was too large to be sitting here—just as the rocks were so huge that she could not imagine how far they towered over her. She felt her heart swelling as though it would grow big enough to hold this moment. But it seemed larger than anything she had ever experienced. It felt unreal.

They sat for a moment in silence until he offered something serious. "There are reasons I'm here." His voice was low. "And they are my reasons and God's reasons."

Elizabeth's heart raced. His statement seemed to be the open door for her own question that just escaped her. "I haven't been hearing lies?"

John Lee sat up straight then. His clear blue eyes shot a look filled with suspicion and concern. "What have you heard?"

Elizabeth knew she was at risk to be so bold. But the words had been said now. She was on a course downhill. For some insane reason she wanted more than anything in that moment to trust that he would tell her the truth, and she wanted to hear it. "That you're a murderer? That you gave the command to murder those people in the Mountain Meadows?" she blurted. "I didn't believe it when I heard it," she added quickly.

He circled his legs with his arms. He leaned forward to see into her face. "Mrs. Lorry . . . Elizabeth," he said. He was trying to find his words. "I hope you can understand this, Elizabeth." He paused until Elizabeth wondered if she should say something in the silence. When his look pierced her eyes, she knew she trembled. "It wasn't murder."

The afternoon sun slanted down toward the river. The light shimmered on the stones.

As he paused, Elizabeth wondered if he had said everything he wanted to say. She wondered whether or not she was sorry she had asked the question.

But John Lee had not finished his speech. When he went on, he cleared his throat. He looked off into the distance as though talking to a multitude of ghosts. "You and I both know people will say anything, don't you?" He grew very quiet for what seemed like a long time. When he finally looked back at Elizabeth, he searched her eyes. "Elizabeth," he said. "Every day of my life I think about those moments. Every day of my life they will be with me—forever. It was something . . . I don't talk about what happened at the meadows. Not with anyone. When they ask me questions, I do not answer them."

Elizabeth nodded. She waited while he spoke as though he carried a weight on his tongue. She did not want to interrupt him now.

"So I am here because they want to arrest me and indict me for the deed. They have chosen to make me the scapegoat. And I am not the only one responsible. But it was not murder, Elizabeth. Do you believe me? It was not murder. Where is the line between murder and war? We believed it was self defense. We believed we were protecting God's people. We felt we had been driven enough. We did not want an army to come back from California. We did not want to fight the Indians. It was obedience, Elizabeth." He turned to her once more. "It was obedience." He was silent. The sound of the stream seemed to grow so large it threatened to fill the silence.

"We may have been wrong. And now that we look back, yes, it's possible we made a terrible mistake. But at the time, while we were doing all we could do, as distasteful as it was, we believed we were saving our people."

He leaned forward slightly and his voice began to choke with emotion. "We believed we were saving a people who may never be saved."

He closed his eyes as though he were listening for his own voice. "The martyrdoms—all of the murders of our people, the extermination order, the running, the escaping, the sermonizing, the praises to God. All of it is just for one purpose . . . to find our lives."

For a long time his voice echoed in the rocks that surrounded them. It was so quiet, Elizabeth could hear the mule tearing at the grass and chewing it in her stained teeth. Though the sound of the stream crowded her ears, she could still feel the beat of her heart.

Again, she thought he had said all he could say. But he began again. This time his voice was so quiet that she pulled closer to him on the grass so she could hear the words.

"The purpose of all of it was to feel life. To feel joy." He waited. But there was more silence. "And so do we have it?" When he looked at her now, it seemed he could see something that even she could not hide. "And so the question is, are you happy, Elizabeth?"

The unreal world tilted a few degrees to another unreal direction. She did not have words to say. So she waited.

He did not speak for what seemed like a long time. "It's your marriage, isn't it? It's not what you had hoped." He looked away from her, as though he would find the answers written in the river, or on the stones.

Elizabeth's blood stirred. She had always dreamed that someone would know her heart. And he was sitting on the stone close to the fire pit with those words in his mouth, as though he knew everything about her heart. As though he could see the deep marks on her soul that her unanswered needs had left bare.

He pulled a kindling stone out of his pocket and began to start a fire in a few sticks that were lying in the bottom of the pit.

She could not help but watch with eyes unreserved. "I don't think about it," she said quietly.

"I know J.B.," he continued, subdued. "And man is a creature who . . ." He did not finish. "Women have generally done better. Motherhood schools them." He paused. "But sometimes God makes a man more glorious than we can imagine. And it is self-discipline that shapes them." He paused. "I personally knew the prophet Joseph Smith. I am a close friend of Brigham Young. Both are giants in their own way."

While he worked with the fire, Elizabeth watched. She watched his face. His love for the men he spoke of was apparent in the expression of his eyes. The muscles in his jaw tightened and then relaxed.

When he waited for her reply, she said in a weak voice, "I thought I was responsible for my own happiness, and that I could make it work with what I was given . . ."

For a brief moment John Lee raised his eyes. "It's true, the responsibility belongs alone to each individual." he said. "But it helps to have genuine feelings of love. The Prophet responded to the unmet needs of many women. He wanted to offer them joy." The rhythm of his words continued to compete with the sound of the spring. "When women begged him for joy, he—being a compassionate man—could not refuse them."

Elizabeth thought she saw a light around his head. It was more than the sunset, she said to herself. She believed she would have chosen this man John Lee. But she was afraid that the look on her face in that moment betrayed it. In that powerful moment, she believed that he too knew it. He must have known many women who cared about him.

"I'm sorry for your marriage," he said softly.

"Oh, I'm all right," Elizabeth tried, her voice thin.

"Elizabeth, I want to ask you something," he said. "Will you listen to me? Will you keep from passing anything of our discussion along to another soul?" Unexpectedly, he reached up and put his fingers on her mouth. Startled, she did not withdraw from his touch. Instead, she felt the roughness of his fingertips. They smelled like charcoal, but the touch pierced her through her heart.

He drew even closer to her. He whispered, "I want you to know, Elizabeth, that I have not discussed these things with anyone. We had made a promise." He slipped his fingers along the curve of her cheek. He smiled, now, trying to lighten the conversation, "I've always felt I could trust you."

Elizabeth did not move. "I will not breathe a word of it to anyone."

"Things change. I remember you at the meetings with Rebecca Jensen. I remarked to myself how beautiful you were. Who was this girl with light in her eyes? I would have felt honored to make you mine."

She gasped, feeling exposed, as though he could see to the center of her heart. There was no way she could have kept the secret of her admiration locked there.

"And now chances are that even if you were to leave J.B., I could not bring you . . . It's strange." He was not speaking full sentences. He halted and looked down the draw. "And impossible . . ."

Elizabeth did not speak.

"But if you will just hear me out, Elizabeth. Will you hear me out?"

She nodded. He put his large hand gently on her face, turned her head toward him. "If something should change. If J.B. should . . . If things should become less difficult in the valley, I would . . ." His staggered words grew less audible. "I would consider . . ."

The image of this man swam before Elizabeth's gaze. A single column of smoke rose wavering from the sticks in the pit as the fire began to bloom.

She never believed she might have said these words, but she found herself saying them. Almost, her voice was the voice of something else inside of her that she had always dreamed existed, but never acknowledged, never knew. "Yes," she whispered. "I would like that to happen."

He did not touch her further. He withdrew his hand and turned toward the draw. Whatever she was feeling stirred the air and the smoke until there was a wavering blur in her vision. She had never felt these feelings before. They were promptings of awe, presentiments of rejoicing. She basked both in the light of his words, and in the color of the sunset glancing off the stones. And after he shared the pheasant from his saddle bag, she shared her bread with him. They talked and talked into the evening. After Elizabeth fed the child and put her down to sleep, they talked far into the night. After the sun went down, they walked together toward the fissures of rock in the hillside where they stood apart, watching the moon.

If this night were to last one evening or forever, she told herself, it must not matter. Now she had the experience she had searched for in her life. She had never before felt this overwhelming light. More than anything in all of God's world, she wanted this man, and though her reasoning, her other commitments, her honor, her knowledge about her other responsibilities nagged at the back of her mind, it did not seem to matter. When John Lee put his hand on her waist and drew her into the circle of his arm, he gently put his lips on her brow and leaned down into her hair and let the tears come.

"All I know is that I have tried to do what God would have me do," he cried softly. She felt his tears wet her hair. "Sometimes I don't know what it is, Elizabeth. Sometimes I don't know what it is. Do you understand?"

She responded when he drew her close. All the time her heart pounded. She was surprised to find herself in his arms, to find him so close. The world did not seem to exist for either of them. Then he pulled away and walked ahead of her into the camp as though, she thought, he was hoping to escape his own presence, his own needs, the weight of his own ponderous desire. Though they did not kiss, it was an embrace she would never in her life forget. Her head spun. She could not see, for the stars that exploded in her mind.

*Forever on the landscape of the heart, there will be a map of the stones in this canyon that lean as though they are crying for what might have been. Crying stones that cut out a life sacrificed for many causes that may be misunderstood. The world may never know of this night that has come so close, so close to abandoning the laws of God, nor will the world ever care.*

## 55
### August 12, 1858, Jacob

On the following night as the men from the investigation committee met at the church, they were noticeably irritated at the absence of John Lee. They had planned to ask him some questions that only he could answer, and he was nowhere to be found.

But John Lee was not the only one they had hoped to question. They had already had one opportunity to approach him at the first meeting, but there was another person they had never seen. And that was Colonel Dame—the colonel who had been responsible for the command of the militia. Where was he?

No one had seen Colonel Dame for several weeks. The Hall brothers said he had gone to his brother's home in Tooele. And they said he would stay there until the meetings were over. He firmly instructed Isaac Higbee and Isaac Haight that he was to be exonerated. He had given them the rough draft of a letter. William Barton and Priddy Meeks had seen it. In the store on a little piece of brown paper, Sam West wrote down what he thought the letter said. He wanted to talk it over with J.B. And he said James Knight, the secretary who wrote it down in the meeting, said Sam got it correct—almost word for word.

Sam's rough draft swore that William H. Dame had written: "We have carefully and patiently . . ." (Sam couldn't remember if it was patiently or particularly) "investigated the complaints made against President W. H. Dame (although this defense was written by Dame himself) and are fully satisfied that his actions as a saint and his administration as a Stake President . . ." (he had forgotten if that was correct) "are of the right spirit and complaints are not founded in truth." He thought he remembered the word "foundation" in there somewhere, but he could not remember where.

J.B. had not seen it. Isaac Haight, Nephi Johnson, Whitney, Elmer, Barton, and a dozen others said they saw it.

"But it was Dame that wrote the orders to the militia," said Sam West.

"What orders?"

"The orders to disarm the wagon train."

"There wasn't any such orders."

Sam West looked very stern. "There was orders. I saw them. The order was not to precipitate a war with the Indians."

"The orders said, 'on no condition are you to precipitate a war with Indians while there is an army marching against our people.'"

"On *no* condition?"

"John Lee says the written orders come to him to disarm and if necessary, to kill the men. Save the lives of the women and children if possible."

"If possible?"

"John Lee wasn't sure he could carry them orders out, knowing with the Indians that 'if necessary' would have to be 'necessary.'"

"William Dame's patriarchal blessing says, 'Thou shalt be called to act at the head of thy brethren and Lamanites to redeem . . . Zion . . . to avenge the blood of the prophets . . .'"

"God knew it would happen," Charles Hall whispered between his teeth.

"Where'd you get them words?"

"Parowan." Elijah Elmer was a wry wrinkle-faced man with a shock of graying hair.

"Don't talk of it no more."

"Well, now he will be made exempt."

"It was Haight who gave the orders for the militia to arrive . . . to bury the dead, but he added that we might find something else to do when we got there."

"Don't talk of it no more."

"We acted for God. In an act of God nobody believes."

"Don't talk of it no more."

"We will be exempt."

"We shall soon rest peaceful in the knowledge of the Lord."

"It is a scar on our faces."

"It is a wound that will heal."

## 56

### *Jacob*

Jacob listened to the talk in the store without breathing. "It's a scar on our faces." The phrase tormented him with the memory of his own deed. He could see the flash of the shot that brought blood to the man's cheek.

Jacob felt some confusion about his father's ability to dilute the memories of that day. Almost without stopping to think, J.B. had made himself busy with other projects now. After sleeping in the Alexander barn for a few nights until the meetings were over, he buried himself in getting estimates for materials to build the new home on his Kanarraville property so that he might bring his other wives down from Salt Lake City. Now that the war was over, there was safety in expansion. He was ready to make a profit. By a series of miracles, the Saints had been saved.

J.B. was not the only one to concentrate on moving forward. Before the investigations had begun, John Lee had also procured building materials. He had plans to expand at Harmony this winter, to purchase more property in the new town of Washington in the southern valley. He had been looking at sites all over the area—even remote ones—and he had decided upon Washington, although he had said it might be a few months before he could begin construction. He had been in the process of beginning his plans when the investigators came. Others were planning far-reaching projects. With the arrival of the investigators, it seemed that all of them changed plans for more distant parcels of land, except for J.B. He would build, too, he said. But he would stay in Kanarraville. This was his home. It would always be good enough for him.

While Jacob was listening to J.B., he wanted to ask another question. "Is Patrick Moore around?"

"I haven't seen him. People swear he left with the girl for California."

"He has gone to California," Sam West told him in the store the next morning. "And good riddance to him and the girl. They were both drunk the last two nights they were here."

So it was true, they had gone. Jacob was relieved. He stayed in the store for as long as he dared, listening. If it was true Patrick and Maggie were gone, would he feel safe about going in the evening to fetch Elizabeth out of the canyon? That would mean she need spend only one night in hiding. Staying with the men, he tired of hearing the same questions over and over again, of suffering the same impact each one had when it was uttered.

"They still don't know why the men was separated from the women."

"We told them we would protect them if they give up their guns."

"They came forward and gave up their guns."

"The women and children was put into a long line up ahead of them."

"Don't speak a word of it to no one."

"We believed we would save them."

"And so we have. Only blood will atone . . ."

The same lump he had always had lately fell like a stone in Jacob's chest. At the sound of the church bell at noon, he said good-bye to J.B. and turned away from the store. He dragged himself into the heat. The sun was hot. The dust was so dry it rose up around his feet like powder. He took the mare Shasta to the trough, leaning against the horse's neck while she drank. He thought about what he had heard. He was glad that Patrick and Maggie were truly in California. He was looking forward to fetching Elizabeth from the canyon tonight.

He took his time getting back to Suky. It was late in the afternoon when he reached home. It did not take long to convince Suky that it was time to bring Elizabeth and Missy home.

By the time he began up the ravine and reached the hiding place, it was dark. The trees bent in the wind. There was a hush in the leaves. He came upon the open place where he had started on the tent. But, as he might have guessed, Elizabeth and the baby were not there. When he began a search of every nook and cranny nearby, about five hundred yards north of the original spot, he saw the tent neatly staked, and the bedding and clothing folded. But still, there was no one there.

He spent only a few moments looking for footprints, which he did not find. When he did not find them, he began to call. The canyon walls echoed. "Elizabeth, Elizabeth!"

Night came through the ravine so quickly, that he felt fortunate to find his way back. When he came back to the bedding, he sat for a moment, realizing he had heard no answer, and he didn't know what to do. The air was still hot, and his throat dry. He reviewed the conversations he had heard in the past forty hours. Reviewing the facts, the painful facts, he thought to himself, *We have all taken a wrong turn. We did not really know we were losing so much. And now what has happened to Elizabeth?*

He listened to the wind in the dark trees, not knowing what to do. Feeling so much darkness, he sank to his knees. Burying his head in the bedding, he used what few words he knew to appeal to the heavens. He covered his head with Elizabeth's quilt and listened to the wind. He clutched the quilt around his ears. He sank slowly, slowly, almost into sleep, when he heard a faint sound in the leaves. Soon there was a bobbing light, a sound of feet, the rustle of skirts.

"Jacob! Oh, Jacob!" Elizabeth's voice. "Were you worried?"

When he saw her, he knew he had recieved a heavenly, fortuitous answer to his plea! "Elizabeth!" He was startled. "Are you all right?"

She ran to him. "I'm so sorry. Yes, we're fine . . . I . . . you didn't find me, did you? I'm so sorry."

When she came to him he wanted to hold her in his arms. But he stopped. There was a change in her face. Following her was a dark figure against the light from the moon, a large stocky figure, moving slowly. It was John D. Lee. He was holding the baby in his arms.

At first Jacob was uncomfortable looking into the calm face of this man. He remembered how they had spoken of him in last night's meeting, wondering where he had gone, accusing him, blaming him if they could. But of course, they knew he had been in hiding.

Jacob stiffened, wondering if he should open his mouth to tell John Lee about the next meeting. But when he stood before the man, woman and child who had come out of the darkness, when he began to open his mouth to speak to John Lee, Elizabeth raised her palm. In the moonlight, he saw more clearly what had startled him so. It was the bright fire, the glow in Elizabeth's eyes.

## 57
### *August 15, 1858, Elizabeth*

Once she was back at home, Elizabeth followed the wind of news that blew quietly through the town. In the next few days, unable to fully corroborate David Lewis's testimony, the investigators left for Salt Lake City. They had decided that Colonel Dame's orders had been made as a military decision and that the incident was an Indian massacre simply aided by white allies in an act of war. They left without pronouncing a verdict, an indictment, or bringing charges. On Sunday the people in the congregation clung to the words of President Smith, hoping he would evoke the world that seemed to have escaped them—their past world of innocence, protection, a world where peace existed without fear.

His lengthy sermon did not contain any words about the inquiries that had occurred during the week. He spoke from Hebrews chapter 1: 9: "Thou hast loved righteousness, and hated iniquity; therefore God, even thy God, hath anointed thee with the oil of gladness above thy fellows." The bowery, drenched in heat and buzzing with flies, was nevertheless unusually silent. It was after the meeting that the buzzing of voices overwhelmed every other sound: the clop of the horses and mules who stood ready at the wagons on the road, the rustle of the women's skirts and the chattering of the children.

John Lee had evidently stayed in hiding, for he was not at the Sunday meetings, Elizabeth noted. But, in trying to be attentive to Missy, greeting the wives and caring for Suky, she was determined to stop imagining something that could not be. When she walked to the Lorry wagon after church, she noticed

Suky was still in the yard of the meetinghouse, talking. But she was impatient to be home. She did not take time to seek out Rebecca, who by now was absorbed with her new beau, the young Lewis man. She did not know where Jacob was, though she thought she saw him talking to Anna Jane Lee. At this point, she did not care. She gravitated to the side of the wagon, pulling her skirts as high as she could so she would not step on them when she put her feet up. She cursed the impracticality of women's styles of dressing while she slowly struggled into the back seat. But once she settled, she slipped into a reverie.

She had not been with J.B. in the loft bed since the massacre, and she was not sure why. She was only sure she was glad that he had stayed away. But now she could not seem to control the powerful yearning that overtook her when she thought about the red hills of Kolob and John Lee.

He had been completely honorable, sleeping in his own bedclothes a good distance from her and the baby. He had never touched her other than to take her in his arms. He had whispered to her softly, "I am a friend of J.B., and aware your marriage has not . . ." He did not finish his sentence. "But I will see what I can do."

For days afterward, she could still feel his arms about her as he had gathered her into his embrace. After returning from the mountains, she began to turn away from J.B. when he came into the house. Her mind was always occupied with the image of the man she loved. Several times in her thoughts she began to write a letter to him. *Dear friend, that moment in the mountains will always be the high point of my life. And if it is not practical to arrange . . . Please, please do not worry about it.* She never actually wrote the letter, but she completed it in her own heart: *Perhaps I have had all that I am going to have for the rest of my life. And perhaps it is enough. I cannot imagine any greater blessing than what I have already shared with you.*

Again and again she caught herself fading in and out of dreams. But when she woke herself she saw the Lee family at the other side of the church waiting for their husband and father. He was not there. She had been looking through a dark blur.

"There's good news, Elizabeth." It was J.B. He had come up from behind her, and Suky and Jacob were following him at a distance. "The investigation committee will not return."

While she listened, she tried to put away the figure of John Lee in her mind and to return to what she knew to be the realities of her life.

"We're going to begin building the new house we've been wanting to build," he said. "You'll have a room of your own!"

She stiffened. The others—Suky carrying Missy, and Jacob holding hands with Sally and Foster—climbed into the wagon. Elizabeth tried to smile. J.B.'s news was not what she had expected. The thoughts about the new house confused her for a moment before she realized that J.B. was expecting her to say something positive. But by the time she had sorted everything out, Suky and Jacob had reached the wagon.

"We've been talkin' and there's a good chance we can build a new house come spring," Suky said. "Isn't that nice, Elizabeth?"

"Elizabeth don't know nothing," J.B. glanced at Elizabeth, nearly sneering at Suky as he snapped the reins. "Cat's got her tongue." He glanced at her sideways.

His sharp rebuke set Elizabeth back. It was as though he could read her thoughts. What was happening? Was her heart an open book, and J.B. had seen that she was not thinking about him? Could he possibly have seen into her heart—that she was in love with another man? She was heartsick that she had not been able to get better control of herself. She was allowing her mind to dwell on untoward thoughts. It was wrong. She should have been focusing on her own marriage. She felt her face grow hot. When Sally climbed into the cart, Elizabeth pulled the baby into her lap and lay her cheek in her hair. "I don't know. I don't need another house." She was stumbling for words.

"Well, you're going to get one, whether you need it or not," J.B. said. There was a trace of anger in his voice. And it was probably justified because it was true: she had not loved him. She had wanted more than he could give, and now he had planned to substitute a new house for whatever was lacking in her heart. "You'll have your own room," he said.

"That will be nice," Suky tried to smooth over the rough spots. "You were planning on teaching a little class of school children at the bowery this fall, weren't you, Elizabeth? It would be nice for you to have a room where you can put your books."

Elizabeth had offered to hold classes for the families in New Harmony. But it would be a while before she had a place to study if the house would not be built until spring. The conversation was not about a house, she knew. She watched J.B. with a guarded look. The conversation was about why she did not love J.B.

Jacob sat in the end of the cart with his back to them. He did not say a word.

## 58

### *December, 1858, Elizabeth*

As soon as the dust of the investigation cleared, John Lee came back to be with his families in the valley, and like magic, something unexpected began to happen—prosperity.

No one asked why. No one put two and two into the hopper, wondering at the miracle of cattle, wagons, goods that the Fancher train had left behind.

Elizabeth saw that the Lees owned more cattle now. She saw that J.B. took on a couple of sheep that arrived from nowhere as though they had been lowered from the fleecy clouds. She knew why J.B. had suddenly announced the news about the new house they were soon to be building.

Never did she breathe a suspicious word—because she had her own secrets to guard. She began the small school class in the bowery at Harmony, and when the prosperity in the valley began to manifest itself in building starts that fall, she held classes in the roomy church and school combination they built on the same spot in the last two weeks of October.

Though she seldom saw John Lee except at an occasional church meeting, she knew by the whispers at the store, the talk among the women, that it was John Lee who led the economic revolution. He not only began several new homes in the Harmony area for his wives and children, he began to make long journeys to Washington County where he was building another home while he founded the "Cotton Mission" there. The leaders of the stakes had decided to move as many people as they could to the hot country in the south to plant their own cotton, to achieve independence from eastern markets, to continue the quest for freedom of every kind. And John Lee was one of the leaders and organizers.

In December, when J.B. purchased a cord of wood for the new home, the most immediate result of his purchase was a contact he made with the lumber mill. They hired him to transport retail lumber and other construction materials from points further north to Kanarraville, Harmony, and all points south, including Washington County. The money began to flow into the Lorry home.

When the money came, Elizabeth was not as interested in it as she thought she might be. She attended to her teaching, tried to get involved with all of the families of young people who attended the school, especially any of the families who had adopted the children from the Arkansas train. Both the

Klingensmiths and the Lees were caring for some of these children. She spent careful time with those children who could not read, and she spent hours with them planning an exciting Christmas pageant in which everyone would have an opportunity to participate.

But in all of her activities, in the moments she stood by the door and watched the Lee children race toward home, while she stood at her desk and looked out toward the western hills, watching the sun fade, she could not root out the thoughts about John Lee and his testimony of Jesus Christ. She had experienced something infinitely more valuable than money, something that had nothing to do with money at all. It could not be purchased. It could not be forgotten. And because it was so powerful and could not be forgotten, she believed it would be with her forever. And because it was still so powerful with her now, she was continually grateful for J.B.'s withdrawal.

By now Rebecca had gone to Salt Lake City with Brady Lewis, who planned to work for an uncle's haberdashery there. The most concern Elizabeth had felt over Rebecca's departure was that she didn't miss her, that she was even glad to see her go. Oh, she was happy for Rebecca. But it was not Rebecca who occupied her thoughts anymore.

The day of the Christmas pageant was the first time she had seen John Lee in a situation other than a busy church setting for all of those long months since that August day in the canyon. The Lorrys came early, and were standing at the side of the school room with Sally and Foster when the John Lee family arrived. Surrounded by his huge family crowded into three wagons, John Lee strode assertively to the school door while his progeny flowed in a human flood behind him. The children, dressed and ready, seemed anxious to show their father how well they could recite their parts. They jumped down from the wagons like so many lambs springing and leaping with expectation.

The wives, polished and gleaming, came decked in clothes made of amazing new fabrics—light wools and silks that had been purchased recently from bolts that had come down from Salt Lake City. Elizabeth admired them all: Martha, Aggatha, Polly, Lavina, Mary, Sarah, and others. She worked with some of them at the school. By now they were her friends—even Emma. With Emma, however, she felt a shade of envy. Younger than any of the others, and more beautiful, she was blessed with a complexion as smooth as the cream silk of her new gown.

Elizabeth noted that all of the Lees had come to the pageant, especially the older girls who herded the little ones, holding their hands. One of those girls was Anna Jane. The young woman had grown tall by now, her neck slim under her gold-brown curls. She wore a narrow chain of silver under her lace collar. Another young girl accompanied Anna Jane; Elizabeth did not recognize her. But she noticed that when she turned her head, the girl's burnished dark brown hair hid a scar on her neck. John Lee had always made a place in his home for young people, saving them from despair or violence. The girl's open heart-shaped face was as clear and white as the snow.

The pageant did not progress without some rocky incidents. The crown on Robert's wise-man head came tumbling down upon the lamb's wool in the manger. The shepherd tripped the angel with his crook, and Sally Dunham caught a cough in the throat just before she was supposed to say "and there were in the same country . . ." But for all the purposes of its inception and completion, the afternoon was a success.

Someone from every family came: the Hanncocks, the other families living in Harmony with the Lees, the Klingensmiths. Even the Hamblins came to the pageant, bringing their flock of children. Rachel Lee stayed as calm and quiet as morning in all of the confusion that raged about her. When the pageant had ended and each participant had shed his or her rags, paper wigs and sandals, Rachel found Suky in a corner behind the cider table and began fussing with little Missy, now fourteen months old.

The first question Rachel asked was, "Are you sure Patrick Moore and Maggie have left for California?"

"It's what they told us," Suky said.

Elizabeth, standing near them, sensed a strange nervousness in Suky, who for a couple of months now had been expecting the people from Arkansas to come and take Sally and Foster away from her. Suky also knew that Maggie's baby was distantly related to Rachel. The fact that Rachel Hamblin was a relative worried Suky because she was afraid that the Hamblins might have the authority to take Missy away. As she talked to Rachel, she could not face her.

"Did Maggie leave any word of her whereabouts at all?" Rachel's strong hands touched the baby's arms, her smooth cheeks. "She's a beautiful child."

"No. She told us nothing."

Rachel had a way of looking into the distance with her gray eyes while she saw everything without really looking. "Maggie was in her eighth month when she was with me."

Suky stared now, gathering the child closer to her breast.

Rachel opened the baby's small mouth to see if she had any teeth. "Did

Maggie tell you she would be coming back here?" she said.

"No," Suky said. "She left the baby and went with Patrick Moore." She stared for a moment at Rachel, and then ventured, "I've been enjoying the baby, and I admit I do not want to give her up." At this moment she glanced at Elizabeth. The two women spoke their mutual fear with their eyes.

Rachel took the baby's hand. "She looks a bit older than Maggie's would have been."

Suky avoided Elizabeth's eyes. So that nothing would pass between them, Elizabeth did not breathe, praying Suky would not make an explicit statement asking Rachel not to take the child. But the statement Rachel did make struck her forcefully.

"Old Hind Food said that Maggie's baby died. They found her another baby." The words hit Elizabeth with a great force. What was Rachel saying? That this was not Maggie's baby? The intimation roused some suspicions she had never dared to voice or even dream.

"You mean . . ." The inevitable flash that had worked itself through her heart now came up into her eyes. Of course. It was the explanation.

Rachel looked up at Elizabeth, her eyes calm. "I don't believe old Hind Foot . . . necessarily." Again she placed her fingers on Missy's lips. The baby smiled, kissing the fingers.

It explained . . . she dared not imagine it. No one knew what had happened during Maggie's disappearance. Maggie! Unbelievable! Elizabeth stared at the brown curls of hair on the little girl's head. At the time of her kidnapping, little Hannah Dunham had been bald with only a light film of blond hair. The darker wisps could have grown . . . The thoughts leaped into Elizabeth's head like butterflies through the window of a room, though she quickly let the butterflies go.

Rachel's gray eyes were as dark as swamp water. "Yes, this might be . . ." she said, seeing the blush in Elizabeth's cheek.

For a time, Suky seemed lost. She was not listening. Or if she was listening, she was dreaming.

"Yes, but there is no way we can know," Elizabeth whispered.

"No," Rachel said.

"It explains how she could leave . . ." Elizabeth said.

"No," Suky said. "No."

Rachel brought her finger to her lips. She shook her head silently, watching as Suky clung to the child.

"There is no way to know."

Elizabeth saw light as though it were refracted by mirrors. Too much of the sun scarred her eyes, burned in her head. They were too close to the table where the women were pouring the cider for the children. The beautiful Emma Lee was passing out her extraordinary pastries. Elizabeth could hear the ripple of her silk. Louisa was cutting the sweetbreads. There were hot cross buns. The men were drinking cider and laughing, and Rachel's children were climbing on her arms and begging to be held.

"Did you get a cherry tart?"

"No, thank you."

"Baked by Miss Emma herself and sweeter than a plum."

"No," Suky said, still stunned.

Elizabeth looked around for a quiet place. She took Suky's arm. Sally found them, laughed, and gave each of them a tart. Suky stared at Sally's smile. The little girl laughed and threw her arms around the child they had called Missy. Now there was a good reason to believe the baby was their little sister Hannah.

"No."

Rachel's gaze was still calm.

"And when they come for the children . . ." Suky circled Sally and Hannah with her arm. "If they come . . ."

Rachel's mouth drew into a thin line.

"There's no way to know," Suky said.

Now Elizabeth felt the knowledge weigh like a stone inside of her because she was so sure. Of course. Maggie Seymour had been presented with little Hannah Dunham by Old Hind Foot. She had not known about the connection with Hind Foot. But she had always felt that this child was Hannah.

She led Suky away from the table to a stoop in front of the meeting house. Sally and Foster followed them to a group of men discussing the lumber business, the cotton mission in Washington, and the general economic upheaval.

Elizabeth had wanted to end the conversation with Rachel about the baby, when she heard an interruption.

"And so now my Washington house . . ." It was John Lee talking. "I have a house in Washington where I wouldn't be ashamed to bring President Young!" John Lee's home in Harmony had also served as a hotel. People were asking him questions. He said, "I'll be taking Polly and Lavina to Washington."

Though Elizabeth watched him closely, she could not seem to get his attention. She was only one of so many.

"Did I introduce to you my most recent wife, Mary Ann?" he said.

No. Elizabeth could feel her heart beat so loud it bumped against her ribs. She had heard there was a rumor about a new wife. But she had dismissed it as untrue. Now she could see that it was true. He reached with his arm for the young girl she had noticed with the heart-shaped white face and the scar on her neck under the beautiful burnished hair. She could not swallow for the hurt in her heart. John Lee had not even glanced her way. "Mary Ann could go to Washington if she wanted to," he said. "Do you want to be queen of the mansion, Mary Ann?"

Surprised, Elizabeth saw the girl's eyes grow dull. Elizabeth could hardly believe what she saw. Almost imperceptibly, yet nevertheless truly, the girl drew back from John Lee. Elizabeth was sure she saw the look the girl sent to one of John Lee's sons in the background, John Alma. Alert, Elizabeth watched the waves of unspoken communication pass between the son and the father's latest wife. It was not the first time such a triangle had complicated things, she knew. And she felt the hurt of the girl and the son John Alma as she felt her own.

## 59
### *Elizabeth*

Spring had a life of its own. Outside on the dark roof there was dew, and then freshness, and then the thin air in the warmth of the sun.

Still climbing into the loft to sleep when it grew dark, Elizabeth read her books by the light of the oil lamp, or crocheted long after everyone else had gone to sleep. Sometimes she lay on her back, staring upward at the rafters, counting the nail marks in the wood and wondering why her feelings persisted so stubbornly for the man John Lee.

Perhaps she should never have accepted his embrace. For he had caused galaxies of stars to explode like fireworks behind her eyes, and she yearned for more. Though she believed that what had happened was probably wrong, she could not help but be grateful for that moment. For perhaps that kind of love would never happen to her again. With a strange sense of revelry, she rejoiced in her memories, still unable to stifle a stubborn hope that there would be an opportunity to join the Lee family someday. As she taught the Lee children at school, she yearned to have children that would be related to these intelligent, beautiful people. And she would like to have been related to Lee's older daughter Anna Jane, who sometimes came with the Lee children to help the Lorrys build their new home. She might have let her imagined life spoil her real life. But when the house-building began, she found herself as excited as the others.

It was a positive time for everyone. J.B. was invigorated, shouting orders, often repeating his plans. For a long time he had wanted to build a large house looking out over the valley, he said. If the Arkansas people were coming after the children any time soon, the Lorrys had better have some more children and build room to house them. And he also mentioned several times that he wanted to bring his Salt Lake City wives down, to collect his family under one roof—that he was in a position to do that now.

"There are enough people in my family to cheer this place up a little," he said. He glanced at Elizabeth under his thick dark brows. "Or we'll get more, easy enough! We ought to have us a kingdom like Lee's, don't you think?"

He noted with particular interest that John Lee had been able to release his sixteenth wife Mary Ann to his son John Alma Lee with just a word of permission from Brigham Young. While the others rejoiced, he seemed to translate the informal making and breaking of bonds into a kind of permission for a promise of increased marital activity at minimal risk.

Elizabeth felt the fever in his voice keenly and heard him with wariness. She noted his eyes when he told them what he intended to do. He rubbed his hands together as though he were ready to renew a contract with himself. And when he continued by telling them that he intended to marry again, Elizabeth winced. He was not going to let the past hold him back, he told them. There would be other children. He was ready to make their world as glorious as possible—right where they were.

And so the house began to rise—a little at a time. When school stopped for the summer, she and Suky could stay on the premises to help. They held the ropes, guided the lumber to the next position while J.B. and Jacob hammered the nails.

Children from all over the neighborhood came to watch the construction, even children from Harmony. Younger ones followed the older ones. And for several days, the responsible sister who brought the children and got them home again was Anna Jane. Elizabeth watched the girl with interest, now. On the afternoon that little three-year-old Sammy stepped on a nail, Anna Jane was the first to go to him. She bent to him quickly and rocked him in her arms. Jacob laid down his hammer, and Elizabeth followed him. J.B. stopped his work for a moment, but took it up again. The children stood in a circle watching the little boy's face grow red, his lips blue.

Jacob knelt beside Anna Jane, and looked carefully at Sammy's face. "Will he be all right?" Jacob said, concerned.

"I think so." Anna Jane did not move when he knelt beside her.

Elizabeth examined the spot of blood on the boy's heel.

"He'll need to be carried. I'll carry him home," Jacob said, taking the boy without hesitation from Anna Jane's arms. As he took him, his hands brushed against Anna Jane's hands.

Elizabeth had never known Anna Jane very well until now. The girl with the fawn-colored hair and the wide eyes was quiet. Sometimes Elizabeth had wanted to speak to her, but she seemed to see something in Anna Jane's eyes that stopped questions.

When Jacob walked away with the boy in his arms. J.B. saw him and called out, "Where do you think you're going? I need you."

Elizabeth glanced at Anna Jane. The girl looked at J.B. as though afraid.

J.B. continued. "I need you, Jacob, to get the back door frame hung up just now. I'll take you home myself, Miss Lee."

Anna Jane nodded, placing an unsteady hand in the small boy's hair. He was stifling sobs.

Elizabeth watched J.B. get down from the ladder, unhitch the mule and cart from the fence, and move with it into the road. She saw Jacob's eyes and thought immediately she saw unexplainable hurt, pain. It was a curious moment. As J.B. and Anna Jane got up into the cart with the other Harmony children and drove away, Anna Jane looked back toward Jacob and waved.

Not even two days passed after the ride in the cart when J.B. announced to the family he was going to marry Anna Jane Lee.

At these words, Suky spilled gruel on Hannah's cheek and the child made faces and began to cry.

"When the government agents come they'll take Sally and Foster. And when Patrick and Maggie come, they'll take Hannah away," J.B. said. "Then all we'll have is you and a barren girl." His glance at Elizabeth was strangely hostile. The words crashed on Elizabeth's ears.

"How dare you!" Suky said.

"I'm just getting ready to fill up the house."

Fill up the house? In that moment a cramp seized Elizabeth. She thought he had wanted the Salt Lake families to come down.

"Vera and Esther will not be moving down," J.B. said as though he knew what she was thinking.

That was news she had not heard.

"There's rumors that the U.S. Government will be cracking down on plural marriages. There's too much at stake," J.B. said. "And those two are not willing. I think it's safe enough to marry someone whose home is close by. I told you I'd marry again, and I want to marry me Anna Jane Lee."

Suky stared dumbfoundedly. "How dare you say such words about Elizabeth?"

"Such words?"

"A barren one."

"Well, what else would you call it? I'm afraid with her attitude . . ." J.B. said. Elizabeth sat up at his words, stunned. It was true she had not been with him since the massacre. "And Elizabeth! She thinks she's got a liking for John D. Lee." But she had never breathed it! And he had known? He hissed his words. "And how do I know? It's plain to me she don't want me. She looks after him. She asks questions about him." He paused. "I tried once or twice. But she's got a fixation. And she don't know I know nothin' about it, or she don't care. And she don't know what a coward, what a black heart he is. Why, there's rumored true things about him nobody half believes."

Elizabeth stood up from her chair, still clinging to Suky's wrist until it was white. She moved swiftly behind Suky's chair and took both of her hands.

"And until she gets over it . . . oh, I ain't givin' her up. But someday they'll come and pick him up, then prosecute, and hang old John Lee."

Elizabeth kept Suky's hand in hers and stood behind the chair. Now Jacob stood, his face flushed with unnatural color. "On your life!" he said, gasping toward J.B. "As if you wasn't guilty yourself of whatever accusation you make against John Lee."

J.B.'s eyes narrowed and his face colored. "Not even half, if what they say is true. And you, Jacob, you wouldn't be alive if it wasn't for me . . ."

Elizabeth's heart beat so fast, she was afraid it was going to beat out of her body or grasp her with its rhythm and knock her across the floor.

"If it wasn't that Lee was a coward, we would have been in war fair and honest. But . . ."

"Hush!" Jacob stood very tall now. He was taller than Elizabeth had remembered him to be. And the anger in his eyes burned. She had never seen him .stand so tall before his dark-browed father, fending off such a volley of fire.

"I can't believe you," Jacob said. "You who cannot hold your tongue. Do you know what trouble you are making for us all?"

"Trouble?" J.B. said slyly, half crazed. "Some trouble! We have already had trouble made for us all!" He was raising his voice. "By John Lee."

Elizabeth had never seen Jacob stand so still.

"Courts. Prosecutions, government agents are coming here!" J.B. spit it out angrily. "Speak of trouble. Do you know what they do? They investigate! They pry. Already Solomon Hanncock has made a list of people who were in the militia that summer." He paused, looked around. "Don't worry, Jacob and I aren't on that list. I checked, made certain. It cost . . ." When he paused, the unsaid words rang out with more volume than the said ones. So J.B. had paid money to stay off that list! He did not continue until a moment later. "They search. They look in dark corners." What dark corners? The Lorrys had a few of them. "Some trouble we are in because of John Lee."

Pale and shaking, Suky drew her hand out of Elizabeth's palm and placed it on Hannah's hair. Elizabeth clutched the rim of Suky's chair.

"You tell me, Jacob Lorry, what trouble it is you think I am making for us all."

Suky's eyes narrowed. "What happened at the meadows, J.B.?"

He was quiet. There was no sound. Even the baby Hannah was hushed. Sally and Foster had finished with their food, and slipped furtively from their chairs.

"What you heard," J.B. snarled. "All you heard—even the songs is true."

For a moment Elizabeth's heart did not beat but hung suspended.

Jacob's eyes darted to hers. He was livid, pale. "Not that!" he breathed between his teeth. "We wasn't never to tell."

Then J.B. broke into a long loud laugh, a ragged guffaw. "Oh, my dear boy! It wasn't as if I told it. Unless these women has wagging tongues!"

Elizabeth felt the lump of anger growing heavier in her throat. She could not believe this moment. She saw the fire in Jacob's eyes. She held more tightly than ever to the chair. How was it possible that J.B. knew so much . . . and how had all of the details of the terrible secrets come to be known?

Suky looked down at the baby. While everyone else spun crazily, she seemed as calm as a feather on a breeze. She touched the child's cheek. "They won't take Hannah, anyways."

"Well, anyways," J.B. mocked her, crossing his legs, snapping his suspenders, leaning back in his chair. "I'm making my announcement. I may not get along splendid with John Lee. But the father is not the daughter. So I think I'll marry me the daughter Anna Jane Lee."

## 60
### Jacob

At his father's announcement Jacob stood very still as if shutting down his need to scream. He clung to the notion that his mother was right: violence was not the solution to problems. It was sometimes the only way to get attention. But to avoid violence, one must be alert. He felt more alert than he had ever been. In the next few days, trying to keep his anger from showing, he realized that the most terrible blow had not been the revelation of his father's warped anger and guilt, for there had been rumors as tangible as black smoke in all the circles of influence, and one had to know that with all of these rumors something must have been true.

It was something more personal that tore at him. He had grown to see J.B. for what he was—a weak and sometimes inadequate man. And Jacob knew he had seen evidence of that weakness in Elizabeth's eyes, for she had never loved J.B., a truth Jacob had suspected from the first. But never in his wildest dreams—even though he had seen them as a couple walking toward him in the canyon—never had he believed Elizabeth could have felt anything at all for John Lee.

Still, he vowed he would not feel despair. There must be no despair, for he still felt the heat of being alive. He felt a new kind of power—more now than he had ever felt. He was stronger than he had been when he brought the ammunition down from Parowan almost two years before. He sensed a strength he had never felt before as he had worked in the hills with Elizabeth hiding from Patrick Moore. And that power was something he felt erupting into the anger that he carried with him for the next few days.

But he could not seem to suppress his feelings for very long. Only two days after J.B.'s announcement, he exploded at Humphrey's store. When Wesley Hanncock's face appeared before his fists on Thursday, he mashed it.

Of course Wesley, whose family was new to the area, had initiated the problem by saying ugly things about John Lee to Anna Jane. Wesley was not welcome in Kanarraville. His father and mother had come down from Provo last year to be in Harmony with John Lee. Wesley's father, Solomon Hanncock, eagerly filling his time with something he thought to be important, had made a list of men who had participated in the massacre. In the last month or so Wesley had bragged that he was going to submit that list to the authorities. He and his father used the list to extract payments from some men. They stole John Lee's water and blackmailed Klingensmith and Dame.

Jacob was in Humphrey's store that Thursday when he saw Wesley harassing Anna Jane, reminding her that her father John Lee was a murderer and he ought to hang. Jacob watched the boy's rude behavior until the anger that boiled inside of him began to spill out. "Watch what you're saying, Hanncock."

"Please don't," Anna Jane said, touching Jacob's arm. "It's all right. He can't understand because he wasn't there." She grasped the hands of the children who had gathered around her and fastened her bonnet. She took the parcel of cloth she had purchased from Mr. Humphreys and—averting her eyes—tried to sidestep out of the store.

Wesley Hanncock sneered at her. "She thinks she's too good for anybody now. She's got black-hearted John Lee for a father, the greatest murderer the world has ever known." But the bully hadn't dared to say those words much louder than a murmur.

Twelve-year-old Charlie Fancher who had been living with Lee since the death of his Arkansas parents, was standing with the children in the circle watching. When he heard Wesley's words, he ran up to him so quickly that no one could have stopped him. He stomped on Wesley Hanncock's toe so hard that the larger boy pulled back and screamed.

Wesley reached out to hit Charlie, but the youngster was too swift for him. "John Lee's not even my father, but he's the best man who ever lived!" Charlie cried out.

"Don't mess with the Lee kids," Jacob warned.

"Who are you? You think you're some Indian chief or something? You wanna be on the list too?"

Suddenly Jacob found himself facing Hanncock in the twilight street. The store owner followed them to the porch wringing his hands and pleading, "It's not the way to solve anything. Stop it, boys!" But his large fleshy hands were ineffective while the two boys tore at each other. Jacob clearly had the advantage from the beginning because of his size. Hanncock's vicious fists had little effect on Jacob's new strength, for he had grown muscles across his back from long hours of work. It was said in town a few times that Wesley's father, Old Man Solomon Hanncock, had always done softer work than anyone in the valley, that he had come so he could leech off the Lees. But those were crude comments not often heard in the Lee home because the mother, Tabby Hanncock, had been such a good friend to Aggatha and all of the Lee wives.

Anna Jane Lee drew back against Humphreys' pump in the yard with the Lee children and watched, terrified. Then she began to cry. When Wesley Hanncock had been conquered by Jacob Lorry in the street, she held her hands to her face to hide the tears.

"I'm sorry about what he said," Jacob came to her then. "Real sorry."

"You didn't need to," she protested his help. "Especially on my account." But her eyes that met his did not hide her gratitude and respect.

Having buried those dark rumors he had heard so long ago, Jacob enjoyed Anna Jane. The thought flashed through his mind in that moment that he ought to rescue her from the intentions of J.B. He believed Anna Jane liked him. She had come with the children to the building site almost every day. He grit his teeth. He thought he ought to discourage J.B. But in the evening, when he was in the house once more, he knew he was not likely to interfere with his father's agenda. Not without hurting more than he hurt now. He watched Elizabeth with particular sorrow. A wisp of hair fell across her cheek and he wanted to touch it. He closed his eyes.

There were times—some days, some periods of perhaps two or three days—in which he could see Elizabeth with the children, accept her help in the house, and never feel the painful emptiness he had felt when he had wanted her. But sometimes she would ask him to help her churn the butter or clean the milk pail, or kill one of the roosters in the barnyard, and as he churned, or cleaned or fetched the rooster for her, he would find her touch burning on his fingers and the thud of his longing coming over him again.

Those moments of his love for Elizabeth flourished on the notion that someday she would leave J.B. and come to him. And now, though it was hard for him to believe she cared at all for John Lee, he hoped that she would forget her feelings for this older man as well. But he never said a word. He never touched her or made a move toward her. But he knew he would always love the fragrance that followed her, the rosewater, the faint cinnamon and fresh dewy moisture on her skin: her eyes, the small wrists, her slender hands. He was waiting.

## 61

### *Wednesday, May 2, 1860, Elizabeth*

The rumors that the government agents from Arkansas were on their way to get the children made Suky nearly crazy. And it didn't take much, as she often seemed crazy, anyway. In quiet moments, she held the little child that was surely

Hannah, saying, "You're not going anywhere, little Missy." Over and over again she said to the other children, "This is Maggie's baby, Missy; this is Maggie's baby, Missy."

Elizabeth watched the last nails of the house being driven into the walls. She watched the porch arise, a low veranda spread across the front of the fresh two-story home. She watched the neighbors raise the roof—the Jensens, Humphreys, Plattes, the Klingensmiths—all except the Lees. Elizabeth had hoped they would come. But only Anna Jane and two of the wives came, bringing food for the workers at noon.

In her soft, thin voice, Anna Jane told them, "Solomon Hanncock had it out with my father and has left us all at last."

Elizabeth was holding Hannah in her arms. She watched Anna Jane's eyes closely, wondering how the courtship had been going with J.B. She suspected not well, as J.B. had not been back to see Anna Jane since the day he had taken little Sammy Lee home. But she thought J.B. might be waiting to finish the house, and that after it was done, he would attempt to court Anna Jane in style.

"Had it out with your father?" Suky repeated.

"They quarreled and Solomon Hanncock left for Salt Lake City. He left Tabby. Tabby will be marrying my father soon." She said the words without fanfare, as though she had said them many times before. Tabby Hanncock was marrying John Lee. An everyday occurrence. But Elizabeth couldn't stop her heart from lurching. Of course that news would have been normal for Anna Jane. But the words pounded in Elizabeth's head.

"Your father is marrying Tabby . . ."

"Yes." Anna Jane's eyes turned quickly to Elizabeth. She must have heard something in Elizabeth's voice, though Elizabeth tried to control it.

Elizabeth remembered Tabby's portliness. She imagined the tall, angular Swedish woman, large, though gentle. On the few occasions Tabby had brought her children to the meetinghouse, the Christmas pageant, church meetings, celebrations, she had always bent over the little ones, keeping them near to her with a scoop of her large hand. All except for Wesley, her oldest boy, for whom it seemed she had given up long ago. It seemed Wesley was prone to follow in his father's footsteps. He spoke in a loud voice, swore, and had bragged about the list of participants he had helped his father put together. He made ridiculous claims; he was going to "do them murderers in."

Elizabeth had seen Tabby's despair as she faced Charles and then looked the other way. She must have cried sleepless nights over the behavior of her boy.

Perhaps she thought John Lee's family would have a calming effect upon him. Now, for some terrible reason, Solomon Hanncock had left his entire family to the care of John Lee.

Elizabeth turned to Anna Jane. "Why . . . ?" she whispered.

"Why what?" Anna Jane questioned Elizabeth with anxious eyes.

"Why . . . ?"

"Why did Solomon treat my father so? And why is my father marrying Tabby?" The girl paused, but when Elizabeth did not answer, she said simply, "She loves him."

The way of love that had been decreed for them in this culture at this time often tested them beyond the capacity to bear. Elizabeth heard Anna Jane's voice as though it were very far away.

In that moment Elizabeth wanted to confide in Anna Jane as she stood before her. She seemed vulnerable, with fading gray eyes, her hair a wisp, like feathers. Elizabeth felt the urge to speak to her, perhaps to say, "I wish I were in Tabby's place." Rebecca had said to her long ago that it was meant for women to marry someone they could truly love. But she herself hadn't had the courage to break away. How could Tabby Hanncock have had that courage, that good fortune, and she, Elizabeth, whose love was so overpowering—how could she still find herself unable to break away? She wanted to cry, to hold Anna Jane. But she bit her tongue.

At first Elizabeth did not want to attend the wedding at which the entire neighborhood would be present. But Suky insisted that everyone, especially the children, must go. There were still rumors that the government agents from Arkansas were somewhere in Fillmore on their way to pick up the eighteen children in Mormon homes. Suky would die rather than leave the children to be kidnapped. And she needed help. So Elizabeth must also go.

Elizabeth could soon see that staying home would only start an argument and rouse J.B.'s suspicions about her feelings. So she felt that if she said little, it would be better, and she dressed to go to the wedding along with everyone else.

Although there was a wedding in the new Harmony meetinghouse, it seemed that rumors about the government agents took precedence over the ceremony. Even Elder Smith, who married the solemn couple, looked up anxiously at one point in his discourse, hearing a sudden noise at the large door.

"He suspects the agents might be at the door," J.B. whispered hoarsely to Suky, and Elizabeth overheard.

That morning on their way to the chapel, J.B. had repeated what he had often said about going to the meetinghouse. "The agents like to surprise us at meetings, weddings, celebrations, because we're all together and they can make an announcement."

But the agents did not come. Not this time.

The wedding passed uninterrupted, followed by a party at the Lees' to commemorate the event. Though the Lorry family attended, Elizabeth, quietly proper at the ceremony, watched the entire event feeling a very real, gnawing pain. The tall Swedish bride, dressed in drab gray with a white collar at her throat, had pinned some lavender crocus and early wild flowers on her dress. Her hair, a shimmering deep brown, was braided in large thick braids and wrapped around the top of her head like a crown. She was large-boned, her eyes set deep. She had whispered "I do" in a throaty voice. Letting large, clear tears fall down her cheeks, she gazed raptly at her new husband as though he were her savior.

Elizabeth could not take her eyes from John Lee's face. He stood very still, his arms poised on the woman's waist. His handsome cravat was clean and pressed, the tie tacked with a smart pin. In one fleeting moment during the ceremony, he looked up at Elizabeth. She could not help but feel a riveting pain.

It was not an endowment ceremony, but would be followed by one at a later time when John could take Tabby into Salt Lake City. He planned to do it soon, he told onlookers.

At the reception in the evening, Elizabeth followed J.B. and Suky into the large front parlor while Jacob stayed in the back room with the children. J.B. spoke with Anna Jane.

Elizabeth stood by the door. The women were busily preparing sweet meats, fruit breads, and a mild cinnamon tea. The guests moved about to congratulate the bride. While Elizabeth hesitated, she felt a hand at her elbow. When the grip intensified, she felt breath against her hair.

"Elizabeth," the voice said. "I'm glad you could come. "You look lovely. Do you know everyone here?"

It was John Lee. Her heart leaped up into her throat. She couldn't seem to open her mouth to say anything, so he continued his speech. When he turned to her, his face was so close she could see the reflection of herself in his eyes.

"You will like Tabby. She is gentle."

What did he mean? In her obsessive hope, she still believed he was saying to her, "When you are ready to come to me, to join my family, you will like Tabby. She is gentle." Her thoughts amassed fleeting images: the glitter of the water in the creek when she had raised her eyes to him, the mountain camp, the journey into the hills.

"I like Tabby already," she whispered softly.

"I'm glad." And that was all. Brother Haight from Cedar interrupted him at that moment, and that was all.

The words, "I'm glad," echoed in her ears. She could still feel the touch on her elbow. She felt the crowded room spin about her in a blur. She forced herself to focus on the others—Suky with Aggatha and Caroline at the table, and J.B. in the corner with Anna Jane. Beyond, in the kitchen doorway, she could see Jacob and the children and some of the other Lee girls.

In the next few nights, as they moved into the new home, Elizabeth felt more aware than ever of the space she inhabited, both in her heart and in her home. She loved the house, the airy emptiness that smelled of fresh pine. She felt alive and whole as though the rivers of her blood were flowing.

After a time, however, as the headiness left her, she saw images she had not invited: the large Swedish woman unbuttoning her gray dress and letting it fall to the floor, the slippers pushed under the bed, John Lee's hands on the white back, the ample bosom close to his breast. As hard as she tried to turn her thoughts away from the couple in their wedding bed, the darkness swam in her mind.

## 62

### Jacob

The government agent came as they promised he would—a Mr. Forney— a gruff man with a hanging belly and very large red hands.

Jacob first saw him in the Kanarraville store guzzling beer on a Saturday, May 5, 1860.

"There is eighteen children from our best reports, and we got this list from Agent Hamblin," the man said. He sat at a round table with three other government people—a couple of privates and a lieutenant from the new Camp Floyd created northeast of Utah Lake for the U.S. Army. "Ought to be able to pick most of them up in one afternoon."

Jacob had run home from the store to tell Suky the agents had arrived. During the next few hours as she dressed the children, she was not able to hold back tears. "There, there. You're going home to Arkansas to see your aunts and uncles," she told them.

Sally seemed radiant with some memories of her home. "Will we see Grampa?"

"I don't know, dear."

Sally evidently remembered her grandfather. He must have been dear to her, for she brightened at the thought of him. She had been five at the time her parents took their last journey. "He is a big fat man with a white mustache and he laughs big. When we come home he'll take us on his knees and give us candy."

If Sally was hopeful, Foster was numb. He did not cry, but he did not ask questions. He did not seem to understand what was to happen to them. Only much later, when he was placed in the Forney wagon, did he let the tears come.

Suky could not bear it. "Oh Foster! Darling child! My darling!" She stood beside the wagon holding her face in her hands. Jacob stood uncomfortably helpless. J.B. stood beside her and put his arm around her.

"Oh, he'll be all right," Forney said. "We had the most trouble with that boy who stayed with Lee. Dropped him off already at the Kanarraville store. Did you know that little Charles Fancher boy? Son of the leader in the train?"

J.B. seemed numb also. "Yes, sir."

The Fancher boy had loved it at John Lee's. He had been part of the family for a year and a half now. He was twelve. He did not want to part with the Lees, and he made it known.

"We had trouble with that boy of Lee's. He run off a couple of times, but we got him at gun point in the Kanarraville store."

Jacob could only imagine how Elizabeth would have reacted had she heard what he was saying now—that the posse had placed the boy at gunpoint in the Kanarraville store.

"There'll be justice here," the rough man murmured. "Nobody wanted to hold anybody at gunpoint. But what we have to do we have to do. Any of you participate in the massacre? Well, it ain't for me to say who, but we got government agents coming in here soon to perpetuate justice for the sake of these little ones whose parents were murdered here."

"Is this it? Is this all?" the first lieutenant asked as they prepared to leave. Jacob held his breath for Hannah, his heart pounding. J.B. nodded.

"You said something about the bill . . ."

"The U.S. government'll be fair with you. More'n I can say your Deseret government is with their judges, just letting them murderers go scott free." He seemed to be on the stump, pounding something home. "Just submit a bill for their care." He added "And expect Judge Cradlebaugh to be here to convict the murderers who took the lives of the parents of these here children, because he will."

Jacob's heartbeat sounded deafening. He looked at Sally and Foster perched on the bench of the wagon. They had been loved here. They knew nothing. In a flash he saw their father's face and his surprise when the shells from Jacob's gun grazed the man's cheek. For a moment he could not seem to help reviewing it in his mind as it passed in images as vivid as a dream. The man had yanked the rifle out of his hands and pointed it straight at him . . . until J.B. had come . . .

"Just submit a bill for their care," Forney said.

When the children had been rounded up, the agents kept them at the store overnight. J.B. submitted his bill for $483.00 for the care of Sally and Foster Dunham, although Suky had tried to shame him from it.

"All the others is doing it," he had growled. "Jacob Hamblin is gettin' nigh fifteen hundred dollars for his part."

It was not until Thursday when Forney and the others were getting ready to go that word went out to the town that they had found every child except one. They were ready to take the children back to Salt Lake City, but there was no way they could leave the area until every last child had been found.

"There was eighteen. Sure as the report says, there was eighteen. Even Hamblin says there was eighteen."

"It was the baby the Indians took from Jensen," the first lieutenant had finally discovered. "There was a kidnapping a couple of years ago this spring. And I've verified it by several different parties, Mr. J.B. Lorry here bein' the most vocal."

When Jacob brought the report to the house, he carefully measured the fear in Elizabeth's eyes. She was in the rocking chair with the baby Hannah asleep in her arms.

"What does George Jensen know?" she asked Jacob.

"Nothing," Jacob said.

She seemed to breathe more easily at his words.

"But he's telling Hamblin the baby is still out there living with the Indians. So now Hamblin's taking it on himself to hunt for it. The government'll pay him for his time if he goes. Nice job for a week or two."

Elizabeth paled. "But Hamblin suspects . . ." She stopped. "Rachel suspects, remember? They believe Missy is . . ."

Jacob knew her thoughts. "Maybe it's a ruse . . ."

Suky was with them in the kitchen snapping beans. "There ain't no ruse. There is no way we can know. This baby is Margaret Seymour's baby. And the only place we can get the truth is from her and Old Hindfoot, and nobody believes either one."

Jacob was not sure. He thought Elizabeth believed Rachel.

"There's no way to be sure," Suky repeated over and over again.

Elizabeth kept her thoughts to herself, although Jacob often wanted to talk to her about it. It was possible that either the Indians or Hamblins might respond to government money. If they could prove Hannah's parentage, it would have been the right thing to do—to give up Hannah Dunham. Jacob was silent, hoping that money would not tempt the Hamblins. He watched Elizabeth smooth Hannah's gold curls. He knew she loved the little two-and-a-half-year-old as much as she would have loved her own child.

"The baby is Maggie Seymour's baby, so get to work, son," Suky snapped. "We got the last plot to plow today." For Suky the question had been solved.

Jacob stood up, still watching Elizabeth. He thought he knew what she held in her mind as clearly as though it were written with a quill pen.

"Maybe . . . just until they leave," Elizabeth said.

"Until they leave what?" Suky said.

"Until Forney and his henchmen leave. Until Cradlebaugh and the army courts leave. Maybe until it all blows over."

"What? What are you saying? Until they leave what?" Suky was frustrated.

"Suky," Elizabeth said. She leaned forward in the rocker, holding to the child. "It might be that I should . . . should go up to the mountains again. You would not need to tell Brother Hamblin where I was, since he suspects . . . things. And it would just blow over. It's Maggie's baby, anyway, remember? You think me to be in Harmony. Then you think I am . . ."

"Tell them she went to California to find the real mother, Margaret," Jacob suggested.

J.B. was solemn as they talked. "You know, there's going to be more people up in them hills than there is in the towns." They listened. Everything seemed silent as they sat in the new kitchen making decisions. Jacob thought he could hear the bees from the garden.

"I ain't afraid," J.B. said. "But I heard those who was in charge are going up to hide. Lee and Klingensmith."

Yes, Jacob thought. It was the sound of the bees, all right. And a little breeze in the grass that came from the bright windows.

"Who is it that's told on everybody?" J.B. continued. "I'll never know. John Lee gave the orders. Those of us who obeyed his orders or didn't obey his orders hasn't anything really to do with it."

The mention of John Lee's name jarred Elizabeth.

"It was war," he sighed. "But after war everybody forgets what war is like. Then they turn around and want to kill everybody who did the killing. It could go on like that forever."

"Hush," Suky whispered. But what she thought she heard was the wind. There was no one in the front yard, no one on the road.

"Then," Elizabeth said hesitantly, "Perhaps we must go . . . before Hamblin and Cradlebaugh come and . . ."

"Make it a bit easier . . ." J.B. began, then trailed off.

Easier to hide. Elizabeth felt a breath of freshness come to her. The thought of hiding—of returning to the red hills—gave her joy. She stared at Jacob. He knew her so well. She knew his thoughts, also. He might have guessed that she had been happier away from all of them. But he had not known it was because of John Lee.

"For a while. Just to be safe."

"It's Maggie's baby . . ." Suky began, her voice harsh.

Elizabeth put her hand in Missy's hair again. "Can we give her enough?"

"Better to be safe," Jacob said softly.

Elizabeth felt suddenly free. Even leaving the new house would not dampen her joy. All she could think about was that she would be in the hills for a while—with the possibility of renewing her hope that she might see John Lee.

"Well, then," Suky said, her voice hard. "Well, all right then. Go up and hide if it's the best way."

## 63

### Elizabeth

Even from the beginning, with only the knowledge that she was going up again into the hills, she felt the spring air brightening. She felt lighter, as though the effect of gravity had no meaning for her. She wanted to go up into the hills. She told herself she was happy for the freedom, for the need to go. And so it was that she and Jacob built a small shelter on a slope of meadow behind the first rise in a field of blue lupine and aspen trees. And she took Hannah with her into hiding for a second time.

*May 15, 1860 Jacob built a beautiful chimney out of stones. I didn't know he could do such a thing. We found a place to put the cabin further up the trail from where we once stopped at the ravine. A place beyond the cliff on a blue hill, blue with lupine. There are trees on the slope of the hill and under the trees mists of goldenrod sprinkled like sunshine. It's beautiful. Near the meadow is a stream. Above me to the east is the place . . . but I must not remember; it will only hurt.*

*May 18, 1860 J.B. gave us the lumber. He won't come up; he doesn't want to make people suspicious. He laughs about those who hide. "What happened was at the orders of John Lee. I don't have nothing to hide," he says. "I did nothing I wasn't ordered to do." In the meantime, I am with Hannah, and no one knows.*

Now she had the summer sky, her books and her pen, and the baby Hannah. Because she had filled her first journal, she wrote on old brown paper J.B. had torn off of a special order of lumber. She wrote about the moments she walked with Hannah on the trail. She wrote about the weather, and the flowers.

*Jacob is more capable than I ever dreamed. He built our small cabin here, and it is tight as a drum. Let the rain try to get to us now! Each time he rides up on the horse, he brings everything we need—food, newspapers, books. And he is so good playing with Hannah. He lifts her in the air and she giggles and screams. And no one is here to know. Jacob comes every day. We are very happy here, away from everything. I have learned so much about the land. I can hear the thunder in the ground. I have watched the insects and birds. I can hear footsteps in the earth. I know when Jacob is coming. When I see a man and horse in the distance, they look like small flowers blooming in the meadow. When I point them out to Hannah, and she knows they are coming, she begins to run, giggling like the little two-and-a-half year old she is. She gets so excited, I pick her up and twirl her around, and then try to calm her down. So far we've built no fires.*

Elizabeth read everything Jacob brought to her, classics that she hadn't finished reading: Shakespeare, John Donne, Homer's *Illiad*, and the *Odyssey*. Jacob said he took them from the Lee library, that Lee had finally gone into hiding also while Judge Cradlebaugh was camped in the area, that he and Klingensmith had headed also for the hills.

One afternoon Jacob brought more than books—a basket she did not recognize.

"It belongs to the Lees," Jacob said. "He's in hiding, too."

"Are they . . ." Elizabeth looked up from the books in her hands. "Are they here?"

"Up there," Jacob pointed toward a sharp red butte where she had walked with John Lee almost a year ago.

"Yes, they're over there. His wives alternate being with him, bringing him meals. The other day it was Rachel getting ready to go. Emma sent a letter with her, as she is confined." He hesitated at the end of his words.

"Yes, Jacob . . . ?" Elizabeth prodded.

"Emma was packing his food when she gave me the books. I brought you some of her rolls in this basket." That was nice of Emma Lee and kind of Jacob, Elizabeth thought as she accepted the gift. It had been since Tabby's wedding that she had seen John Lee. It was good that thoughts of love had no color in someone's face, or they would be painted on her cheeks.

The miracle was that though she had not seen Lee, she had not felt any particular loss. While she had helped Jacob to build the stone fireplace and the cabin, she had enjoyed Jacob's company and the baby. For a week now, the only adult she had seen was Jacob. She had seen him every day. And she had been happy.

But now, when Jacob revealed that John Lee had also gone into hiding, she realized how powerfully her feelings for the man had influenced her desire to come here. She was not sure what she had been expecting. But she dare not breathe a word of it. For several days, she struggled to keep all of her conversations with Jacob about surface things. Yet, as the days passed, Jacob's eyes seemed to register a keen awareness—as though he could see into her mind.

"I won't come tomorrow," Jacob said suddenly on a chill evening in late May. He had brought extra bread to last the day.

Elizabeth questioned him with her eyes.

"We think Cradlebaugh and his soldiers are leaving from their camp outside Cedar. They finished gathering up the bones to take back to Arkansas to bury them. They erected the stone monument."

Elizabeth nodded. Jacob had told her about the monument. "They weren't . . . able to arrest anyone?"

"So J.B. and some of the others believe the posse will disperse now and watch anyone who comes up into the hills. Make one last try. I'd better not make the trek up here at all."

Elizabeth stared, her eyes unfocused.

"The people they have on their list have either gone south to get out of here, or they're in hiding."

"J.B.?"

"I . . ." Jacob hesitated. "I think J.B. paid Hanncock to leave off our names, remember?"

Elizabeth swallowed. She couldn't speak.

Jacob was so silent that the only sound was the whisper of the wind in the chimney, and then the patter of Hannah's feet on the dirt floor.

Out loud, Elizabeth mused, "I wonder if we will ever know what happened at the meadows?"

Jacob did not speak for a long time. "It was war."

Then she said something she was not sure Jacob would grasp, or even hear. "Even if you would have killed someone, I would understand."

He glanced at her. The heat came up his neck and into his face. The silence ebbed around them in great waves.

"I didn't kill anyone," he said simply. And the words flooded into her heart, washed over her mind like balm. He had admitted there had been killing, but he had not killed. "I felt like a coward then, but now I feel only relief."

"Well, they will never arrest anyone from here." With these final words, Elizabeth rose from her place on the cabin floor. She lifted Hannah into her arms and walked out into the coral light of the May evening. She climbed to the lookout above the camp.

Jacob followed her. She knew he was behind her. In the distance and to the northwest lay the ravine and the old Lorry cabin. South of the cabin lay the new home. They could see smoke from Kanarraville, perhaps Suky's cooking smoke rising over the trees. To the east they could see the path rising to the point where Elizabeth suspected she would find John Lee. Beyond that point on the hill were the red bluffs rising like ancient pipes against the sky.

"They won't come here—Cradlebaugh's men," Jacob said. "There isn't enough evidence to arrest anyone. No one says anything. And like I told you, they've either gone to Mexico, or they're hiding."

"Even John Lee?"

As soon as she said it, she realized how much she had revealed. The words crossed the air, joined the currents of sound from the hills, the birds, the water in the stream. The words said all that could have been said to Jacob, who heard them, and whose face immediately changed. He should have known, though he had probably denied it. After J.B.'s words, after all these months, he could not have helped but know of her feelings for John Lee, but he must have hoped that her feelings had changed.

Now his voice was gentle. "Elizabeth," he whispered, caressing the sound of her name on his tongue. "Elizabeth." And she knew by the sound of his voice he was aware of her impossible dreams about John Lee.

Elizabeth saw the hurt in his eyes, but before she could stop herself, she nodded slowly. The nod—slight, hesitant, revealing—unveiled her fears should she open up to him. Slowly she sank into the meadow grass. He knelt beside her. She did not speak for a long time.

"Oh, Jacob," she whispered. "You know I have never been happy with J.B."

Jacob was silent, a silence like a mourning bell tolling the death of his own hopes, for she had always seen his pain. "Jacob, I love you. But in a different way," she pleaded, wanting him to understand.

Jacob nodded, his eyes cast down. He knew that. He had no reason to believe otherwise. "I know," he whispered. "But I always hoped. We built this house. I hoped for you and me . . ." There, the words were released.

There was a moment of silence. Hannah had drifted from them into the meadows.

"I know," Elizabeth whispered. She pressed his hand. "We love each other in a wonderful way."

What was so wonderful about it? Jacob's eyes asked. What could have been more wonderful than possessing her heart?

"You and I have a love that will never die," she continued. "Like a sister for a brother. We are not possessive, like J.B."

"Nor impossible, like John Lee." His words came out with an edge. Elizabeth pressed her slender hand on his arm again. His eyes sparked fire.

"It's not impossible," she whispered. "You'll see."

He waited for her.

"I love you with a sister's love, Jacob, a love that can never die. I will never leave you. We will always be together as friends."

As she sat near to him in the grass, Elizabeth took his hand in both her hands. "Do you love me so much you want me to be happy?"

He looked up now. He drew her hands into his and held them still. Slowly he smiled. "I love you that much, Elizabeth," he said.

She took his head in her hands and leaned toward him to touch her lips to his ear. "I love you that much, Jacob, and I know what is best for both of us."

Now her lips were against his cheek and she held his face very still. "So please. Now that John Lee is here, and now that you understand . . . and you love me, then let me go to him. Leave. Please."

Her lips brushed his hair. She felt the hair against her cheek. He was beautiful to her. All that had passed between them in the meadows—the cabin in the grass, the baby, the water, the blue flowers, the air, the breeze—all stayed with them like the memory of music now.

"You will always have my love, Jacob."

# 64
## *Elizabeth*

Jacob had left her many times. But his departure this time seemed different somehow. A weight had lifted from her, for she could feel something almost tangible that he had given to her. The words of his love for her filled her with warmth. She was not sure what had happened just now to change things. It may have been Jacob's love. Or perhaps it was the realization that she had made a decision to find John Lee.

When she returned to the empty cabin, she gathered handfuls of meadow flowers. She felt a deeper joy than she had ever felt before, and thought it was because she would soon be with John Lee. That evening she waited with Hannah, plotting the next day, watching it unfold in her mind.

The following morning came slowly. There was something so new in it that she felt buoyant about the very air she breathed. Part of the difference she felt was simply in waking to the early traffic of quail, the scrambling of a rabbit in the nearby brush, the fragrance of the dew on the meadow grass. Every sense was sharpened. And her heart pounded. She had questioned several times whether or not she should make her quest. Some of her good sense had told her to leave John Lee alone. But she knew she must try.

She dressed Hannah in her cleanest dress, wrapped her in a lace shawl, and climbed the meadow with the two-year-old in her arms. The sun in the east rose slowly over the red bluffs, slowly brightening the shadowy grass. When she reached the first rise of the hill, she stopped to rest. The morning spun webs of light and shadow in the ravines falling away from her to the right and left. She was remembering her previous walk here several months ago, when suddenly she saw a small figure meandering down from the mountain to the valley below. Clutching the baby, she ducked behind some trees so that she would not be seen.

The figure was not John Lee. It was Rachel, one of Lee's wives. She wore a blue shawl over her hair and carried an empty basket on her arm. She did not see Elizabeth, though Elizabeth feared she might.

After a few moments, Rachel was gone. When the meadow was silent again, Elizabeth raised her eyes to Lees' Point. She saw nothing but trees. It was calm. A quiet that told nothing. Anyone watching from any angle in the valley would see nothing. But she knew Lee was there. She felt some disquiet about climbing that hill. But she knew she would go.

The baby grew restless in her arms as she drew near enough to see the roof of the small home through the trees. She felt the breeze on her hair, the heat of the sun warming her shoulders. Finally she could see the roof of the house. About a hundred yards in front of the rough log house, she saw Lee standing, holding the spectator glasses to his eyes. He was watching from the point—watching Rachel wind down into the valley.

Elizabeth remembered she had seen Harmony from that spot just as the dusk closed over them—Harmony with its small fires, the twinkling of its windows in the distance, the corral, the fields outside the walls. She saw the smoke snaking up into the clear sky. He was totally occupied. She stepped forward into the clearing, hesitant about making herself known. Hannah's voice reached him, and he lowered the glasses to see the two facing him. Elizabeth's lace shawl slipped to the ground.

"Well, well . . ." He smiled as he walked toward her. "Elizabeth . . ." There was a strained energy in the way he said her name. She did not move but waited for him to come. He held out his arms. The baby reached for him and he held her. He lifted her and then rubbed his cheek against her hair. When he lowered her to the ground to let her run about, he lowered his eyes to Elizabeth's face.

"It's good to see you here, Elizabeth."

She smiled, not trying to conceal her joy at seeing him.

"Come." He held his hand for her. She took it. They walked to the point where he climbed the rough stones. He gave the spectator glasses to her. She lifted them to her eyes and stared into the valley below. She could see it as though it were only half the distance away: the fort walls, the windows in the walls. She could see Lee's sons taking the horses around to the corral.

"It's not so far away."

"No." He was silent while she looked. The horses looked like toys, the people like tin dolls.

"Home is never far away. Miles do not make the difference."

While she stared through the amazing lenses, she saw a row of men on horseback stirring the dust in the road.

"That's them," Lee said.

"The men . . ."

"The posse . . ." He paused. "They've been here almost a month. They've been told that nobody knows where I am. Or Klingensmith, or Haight."

She lowered the glasses. He smiled at her.

"They will try for a while. And then they will go away."

She looked at him. How could he be so sure?

"But they are making one last effort tonight. And no one will be coming back through the ravine."

She let her eyes rest with him. "When will they leave us alone?"

The light shimmered on the leaves as though the world were alive with tongues asking the same question.

"I don't need to talk about it again," Lee said finally. He took her hand and led her back through the trees, the baby following them. They walked away from the cabin, where Klingensmith would ordinarily have been. Lee walked directly to a spot where a broken tree lay beside the creek.

"You must be tired."

"I am."

"Rachel brought food." He took bread from his large pocket, a knife and a round pad of cheese. "Whoever made the baby made her beautiful beyond . . . almost beyond being real . . ."

Elizabeth smiled. "She may belong to . . . the Arkansas travelers."

He paused. They were watching the child toddle after butterflies in the rough grass.

"Yes . . ." So he had heard.

"Of all of that memory, she may be all we shall ever keep."

"Yes."

They spent the next few hours walking near the stream, viewing the valley through the lenses, watching Hannah. Elizabeth hoped it would never end. Crossing the stream, she grew unsteady. Lee reached for her and held her so she would not fall. She was so close she could have touched his cheek with her lips.

"I'll see that you don't fall," he said.

For a moment she was quiet, feeling the power in his words.

"I've always trusted you, John."

At this, he reached the opposite bank and brought her safely to solid ground. He stood above her and took her hands. "You are one of the Lord's choicest handmaidens," he said. "I feel I've known you from our life before. Haven't I told you that?"

"Yes," she said.

"And do you want to know a secret which, if you will allow me, I believe I have guessed about you?"

She nodded.

"I saw you with Rebecca—long ago, two years ago. Then I saw you with Emma on the road that day, and again at the wedding—mine and Tabby's. I saw something in your eyes. A hunger to feel something more . . . to feel love."

Yes, that was it. She wanted to feel love. The kind of love that Rebecca spoke of. The singing in her heart. The worship she felt for a towering man.

"And you believe in me," he said quietly. "And I'm honored, Elizabeth. The sweetness in you is very precious to me. Very dear to me."

What did he mean?

He smiled and folded her small hand in his own. "It is in your eyes, Elizabeth. You . . . I believe you would like to leave J.B."

J.B. intruded, coming between them like a dark force. And an empty force. J.B seemed to be emptiness personified, and she felt the emptiness press against her.

"Yes, I would," she whispered, unable to believe her words. But they were true.

"Like Tabby," he repeated, "You are disappointed in love, aren't you? You would like to look up to someone, wouldn't you, Elizabeth?"

The words hung over her head as though they were tangible, and she might have been able to gather them as one gathers apples from a tree—nourishing words from the knight-errant who had rescued Tabby from Solomon's hold.

"Solomon—what an evil man . . ." He was shaking his head as he paused. "But I do not see J.B. in the same . . ."

What was he saying? A blackness gripped her.

"J.B. is a better man. He is not like Solomon Hanncock."

Then what? What was he like? She felt a gnawing pain weigh heavily inside of her.

"You are committed to J.B."

*But love*, she wanted to say. *What about love?* But she could not speak.

"If both people are good people—they can learn to love."

The words swam like fish above her head, catching the light. She stood feeling waves of hurt like shadows across her eyes. She did not move.

"I . . . feel . . ."

"Hush," he said quietly. Still holding her arm, he pushed her gently away from him. "You are lovely, Elizabeth."

She felt weak.

"I always feel close to you. What could our friendship mean, I wonder? I wonder, Elizabeth." He spoke her name as though he were playing a musical instrument.

Yet J.B. loomed between them. Now, at last when they were alone together, this cloud was still between them. She looked toward the valley. She imagined J.B. there now—with Suky and Jacob in the new home that now seemed so far away, yet still close, somehow.

She saw the beginnings of dusk slip down into the chasm below them. It seemed the sky was already growing darker in the distant hills. There was a red cast of light over everything, though it seemed to be more than sunset. The sun filled the distant scene with an unusual light. Briefly, she remembered the men on horseback, the Indian Agent's posse. And she wondered where they were. She walked toward the point with John Lee.

Now, far below them, she could very clearly see smoke. John Lee let go of her hands. She felt the sudden tension in his body.

"What is it?" she whispered.

He looked for another moment to be sure. "Fire."

She felt the blood draining from her face. "Fire," she repeated, feeling the word sting her tongue.

"Fire," he said, raising the glasses to his eyes.

"Where?" she dared to ask.

"Kanarraville," he said slowly.

Her heart beat against her ribs. Kanarraville. Her home was in Kanarraville. If it were her home . . . The sight of the fire seemed to send heat up into her ears. "No," she said and brought her hands to her eyes.

"I'll go down with you," Lee said, and scooped Hannah from the ground into his arms.

## 65

### Jacob

Jacob had stayed close to the house during the morning. But in the afternoon Suky asked him to go into Kanarraville to the store. Jacob knew it was a chance for him to check on the agent and his posse. He thought they had headed toward Harmony. But when he rode up through town, he found the lawmen in the street in front of Mr. Humphrey's store. Not wanting to make himself known, he left his horse on the north side carefully hidden behind the north wall. He stayed out of sight while he listened to the government agent Forney's high talk. The man was waving his arms in wide circles, pointing to the hills, pointing west to the long vacant valley, and pointing east to the red bluffs. While Forney was gesturing to his men, Humphrey still stood in the door with his stalk of wheat between his teeth watching the gathering with intense eyes, as though he were waiting for something.

"I have combed this place," Forney said. "Harmony is empty. But there is people here. There is even others not on this list who belong behind bars. And I'll get every one, too. I know there's perpetrators still in hiding. Somebody told me a man named Lorry would know who's up there."

Jacob cringed at the reference to J.B. who at various times had nearly turned states' evidence—had offered to confess more than just the offhand statements he made in the store.

"The child. He may know about the child," someone spoke up.

"He was in the massacre, too," someone else said. Jacob could not see who the speaker was. They had not seen Jacob, or they might not have spoken about it. "His name ain't on the list some say. But they say his son and him were in the massacre, too."

Jacob broke into a cold sweat. His head felt light. He forced himself to walk nonchalantly around the store onto the porch, through the door. When the big storekeeper saw him he opened his mouth slightly, but he closed it again on the stalk of wheat, glaring at Jacob from under his dark brows.

When Jacob slipped past Humphreys and Forney and the others into the store, Humphreys turned to follow him. Jacob bought the oil Suky had ordered for her lamp, the dill, and a piece of cloth.

"I think your baby is safe. They ain't goin' up into the hills I'll wager you," Humphreys rasped. "They don't know their way around. But you never can tell. And they is settin' on searchin' the homes here tonight. Have you got your home search-proof?"

Jacob wasn't sure what Humphreys meant by search-proof. But he told Suky when he came in to hide the little girl's things and to place Elizabeth's clothing in her own closet. Suky sat in the parlor with her sewing, and her hands shook as she lit the oil lamp on the table beside her. She took up the needle and thread and trembled.

"Are you ready?" Jacob said.

Her eyes looked dark.

"Will they find anything?" he asked her.

Suky didn't speak to him. Her eyes burned like two live pieces of coal. She nervously fingered the hem stitches in J.B.'s new overalls as she settled them over something she was keeping in her lap.

He dared to confront her now. "What do you have under them overalls, Suky?"

But she continued to stare at him without response.

"What is it?" He looked at her again.

She touched the heavy cloth like a naughty child. He suspected her. He tried to put the possibility from his mind. She would not . . . but he was not sure.

"They're searchin' uptown for a while," Jacob said. He was telling her she did not have to be so ready for so long. Because he thought he could see beneath the garment . . . the pistol . . . the same pistol. Her eyes were opaque.

"Come on in and make supper, Mother, and don't worry so hard. They won't find anything here."

But her eyes were glazed. She stared at him as if she couldn't hear him.

When J.B. came in, he let the door slam shut. Jacob stiffened when he heard his father's words: "They're coming, I think. They certainly gave enough warning," he said. "It doesn't matter what they're looking for. They think they can find anything."

Jacob's tongue felt thick between his teeth. "They might find us if we don't hide someplace."

J.B. looked through Jacob's eyes.

"They asked about you. And maybe me," Jacob said.

"We're not on any list."

"Somebody told them you'd know about the child. Then somebody said you were informed on . . . that you were in the massacre too."

J.B. stopped, his face white. He stared at Jacob and then at Suky. She was still glaring out of hard little black eyes. The calm Jacob felt earlier was gone. He stared into Suky's lap. J.B. saw his glance.

"And then what you plannin' on doing, Suky?" J.B. said, his eyes as sharp as ice. "Don't you learn your lesson goin' through it more than once?" He lashed forward and snatched the overalls from her hands. Beneath them lay the pistol, a hard, dull shape in the folds of her dress. It was at that moment they heard the voices in the yard and then the pounding on the door.

"Mr. J.B. Lorry?" a loud voice cried out.

Suky grabbed for the pistol, but it fell to the floor. The door was knocked open by the search posse. They began to swarm into the room.

J.B. reached for the pistol, but Suky knocked it from his hand with her foot as it lay on the wooden floor. Seeing it, Jacob Forney reached for his own gun. Suky screamed and grabbed the oil lamp beside her on the table. She threw it with force toward the agent with the gun. The glass shattered and the oil splashed over the floor and onto the rugs and chairs. The flames, leaping from oil spot to oil spot, burst into bloom.

Suky screamed and rummaged on the floor for the gun. When she found it, she rested the heel of her hand on the floor and began shooting upward—uncontrollably—into the posse. In the growing flames, their faces white with terror, they backed away. Once, twice. Suky stood up and shot again. The fire from Suky's pistol began scattering the crowd. One man screamed, grabbing his arm. Blood spurted onto the floor. Wrestling with Suky, J.B. leaped toward Forney, who had his gun ready and was not shy about using it. Once, twice, Forney shot at nothing. Jacob wrested the gun from Suky's hand and headed for the pump in the kitchen. He drew water to douse the fire, his head swimming with fear.

"Murderers!" Forney was screaming. "Murderers!" He shot again. This time directly at J.B., who fell to the floor, blood oozing from a graze on his ear.

The flames had caught every spot of oil that had been splashed on the carpet, in the embroidery, in the chairs. The flames leaped up a wall on the other side of the room. Now Forney held his gun to J.B., writhing on the floor.

"Don't you come near this door," Forney said to Suky, who had now miraculously found a kitchen knife, which she held in her hand. As she walked toward Forney, Jacob followed her with the water and threw it on the fire.

Feeling the water on her feet, Suky screamed. She turned and threw the knife at the man in the doorway. It missed him. But one of the men behind him shot one last shot. It hit Suky in the side and she shrieked.

Jacob dragged her away from the flames toward the door, but her dress quickly caught on fire. She began screaming again. But now, choking with blood, all she could make was a gurgling sound in her throat. J.B. dragged himself from the floor and beat at Suky's dress, but to no avail. The flames leaped around her legs, and the sound in her lungs began to fade.

J.B. cried out, "Oh God. Oh God." He lunged toward Suky, the fire licking at his arms. He pushed her toward the door while Jacob pulled at her. Once on the steps of the house, the woman was a flaming torch, her hair broken and charred, her weeping eyes glassy through the smoke.

As the fire followed J.B. out the door, he pushed and pulled at Suky, until she lay across the front stoop. With great effort he rose and dragged himself over her, then turned and pulled her away from the house and down the steps onto the ground.

"Suky! Suky!" J.B. screamed. He pulled at her, tore at her still burning clothes, yanking them away. Finally he fell back from weakness and from loss of blood. He looked at Jacob, who was still standing, staring, unsure what to do.

"Idiot!" J.B. screamed. "Put out the fire! Both your parents lie dying and you stand there like an idiot watching the house burn!"

By now the Humphreys and the Jensens had arrived and were beginning to form a line to bring water from the well. Mrs. Humphrey ran to J.B. When Jacob joined them, he felt raw in the pit of his stomach—the same old anger he had always felt for J.B.'s authoritarian commands. At the same time he wanted to excuse his father, who was now bleeding profusely, and he realized he was feeling a strong sense of guilt.

"Suky!" J.B. was screaming. "Suky!" And while the neighbors rolled her in the dirt, he crawled beside her and continued to beat at the flames. He rolled himself in the dirt to put out his own fire. Over and over both of them rolled. His flames went out, but her dress kept burning until it was a charred smoldering rag matted with blood.

"Suky!" he sobbed. "Suky!" And while the neighbors got a cup of water to drink, J.B., from his position on the ground beside her, slapped her face, shook her arms, pulled at her, pounded her as though he could bring life back into her. But her limbs did not move. His voice rasped in his throat, "Suky! Oh God, Suky! Whatever in tarnation got into you! Wake up. Get up. Get out of here!" But her body did not move.

When the flames were out, he crawled up beside her and threw himself over hers. He lay there for a long time draped over her body, sobbing, his voice scratching through his sobs.

Jacob stood in the line of neighbors who had brought the buckets of water up to the house from the well. But the fire was too far out of hand. Jacob could not breathe now. The smoke billowed out of the roof and blew upward in heavy clouds. The grass caught fire and bits of the roof flew into the surrounding field. Some of the neighbors ran screaming toward their own homes to put out the small fires that flared into their dry bushes and trees.

"Get out of here!" someone yelled as the roof of the Lorrys' new wooden house began to cave in. The beams beneath it crumbled like paper and everyone scattered. Only the Jensens stayed to watch. The fire, with its backdrop of white and gold, lit up the sky while the people ran like small black spiders away from the heat and smoke.

Jacob worked at the pump until the sweat poured from his brow. His arms grew hot and tired. His anger kept him going. He saw the townspeople out of the corners of his eye. He saw that the government agent Forney was gone now. Far gone. Probably on his horse very far away. They were probably drawing out of town now, taking their camp with them, letting the murderers burn. He hauled water from the pump, threw the water into the flames, went back for more. It was like putting out a bonfire with a teaspoon. His muscles ached. Everything ached. Everything hurt. He spit, his eyes watered. He wanted to die. He came to J.B. and knelt at his side.

"Are you all right?" he asked his father.

"Put out the fire," J.B. growled. Still bleeding through the gauze bandages the neighbors had helped to apply, he spoke with a voice full of scorn. "Get out the fire!" He lay almost completely still for a long time. Jacob continued to haul water. Throwing it at the pump house and in the kitchen, he saved one wall of the kitchen. Soon all of the rest lay in a heap of smoldering coals. Jacob returned, limping painfully to J.B. who had gravitated again to the body of his mother who lay beneath him. Then, out of the distant gathering darkness, he saw the slight figure in the shawl come running toward the figures on the ground. The shawl and the night framed the white face made luminous from the hot red light from the coals. Elizabeth! And behind her, John Lee, holding Hannah in his arms.

### 66

#### Elizabeth

Elizabeth knelt to J.B. "Oh, no," she whispered. She touched him and he reached for her with his bandaged hands. Then her eyes rose and she saw Jacob shaking with fatigue. John Lee stood wordless behind her. "No. No," she choked. "It's not true!"

Seeing the body of Suky below him, she allowed J.B. to grasp her hands and raise himself away from the lifeless woman. "Suky! Oh, dear God! Suky!"

J.B. gripped her hands, and she felt the heat in them. He began to whimper now.

"Elizabeth," J.B. rasped, his eyes rolling white in his blackened face.

"Yes," Elizabeth whispered.

J.B.'s eyes rolled back to take in Jacob, then John Lee with the frightened Hannah in his arms.

"Elizabeth," J.B. rasped again. "Don't leave me, Elizabeth."

"I am here," she whispered quietly. "I won't leave you."

"I need you." He looked up now at John Lee. "Brother Lee . . ."

"We'll help you," Elizabeth said.

"I need . . . I need you," J.B. choked.

"We are here, Brother Lorry." Giving the child to Sister Jensen who was still standing by, John Lee came to him. He placed his hand on J.B.'s brow. "I'll get you to Harmony now."

"No. No," J.B. croaked. "No. Take me to the cabin. The old house. Over . . . over to the left field."

Elizabeth stared at Lee, her eyes wide and fearful that she would now be responsible for all of this. She felt alone.

"Will he be all right there?" Lee asked her.

She nodded slowly.

"Take me to the old place, J.B. said again."

Elizabeth scooped Hannah away from Mrs. Jensen and into her arms. She held her close while Lee and Jacob prepared to lift the broken man to Lee's horse. He groaned. John Lee touched the wound in J.B.'s head where the blood had grown sticky now. "It's just grazed."

And Suky. The fire was dying and the neighbors gathered around them. Brother Jensen took Suky's head in his hands.

"Bring her too," J.B. rasped. "She'll be all right. Bring her with me."

Elizabeth stared at John Lee. He shook his head.

Elizabeth leaned close to his face. "J.B., let Mrs. Jensen dress her. She's gone."

J.B. turned away from her with a groan—a long slow wretched sound from deep in his lungs, heavy with anguish. "Oh, dear God," he kept repeating.

The men who were still present braced him against their legs and brought him up to a standing position. Then John Lee lifted him in his arms as though he were a child. He braced him against the horse and lifted him on his back. J.B. fell across the horse like a pack of rags.

John Lee led the horse while Elizabeth walked beside him, carrying Hannah, measuring her steps in the charred grass. She did not look at Jacob, though she felt him to be there, confused, dazed, weary from the drain of this impossible hour.

Elizabeth looked back only once. In the stark emptiness of the lot where the house smoldered, a group of neighbors now gathered around Suky's blackened form. They were like reeds of grass silhouetted under the light of the vast black sky, slender shapes of persons who knelt to raise her, who took her in their arms and carried her against the moonlit distance—a funeral procession impromptu under a bleak and faded moon.

Choking now, Elizabeth stared at John Lee. He led the horse toward the old house. It was filthy now. The sheep had left wool and waste in it. The floors were broken, the walls scarred with weather and neglect. But the roof still appeared to be in fairly good condition. It had kept the rain from damaging several pieces of their old furniture they had not taken into the new home. And the loft . . . Elizabeth looked up into the old loft. The ladder, the straw that cushioned her featherbed, the place she had first known J.B.—it was all still there.

Jacob and John lay J.B. on the moth-eaten settee by the hearth.

"Water," he said, choking.

Jacob fetched water for him, and Elizabeth bathed his face, his eyes, his cheeks, his parched tongue. The well had not been destroyed. Jacob pulled at the bucket without stopping, without complaining.

"That's enough," she said finally. "Why don't you rest, Jacob?"

His eyes looked hollow and deep as the space in the star-speckled sky. He did not rest, but instead built a small fire.

"I'll help you," said John Lee. And rolling the large body of J.B. from side to side, he removed some of the man's charred clothing. They worked in silence on the burns until the man was washed and made as comfortable as possible on the saddle blanket. In all the time they worked, Elizabeth never looked up to acknowledge the presence of John Lee. She bound the wounds with sheep tallow and strips of her petticoat. Finally, when the man on the hearth began to sleep, she raised her head and saw that Lee was again holding Hannah in his arms. The child slept now. He set her down beside J.B. Nearby, Jacob stood, silently watching.

"Then you will not need to come up into hiding again," Lee said slowly to Elizabeth.

"If they are gone." She looked to Jacob.

"They will be gone," Jacob nodded.

"Elizabeth." Lee's eyes were very bright. "You are surely needed here."

Her heart swelled with frustration as though it would burst. But she swallowed her anger and nodded. "I know."

"Blessings to you, beautiful woman," he whispered. "You are an angel of mercy to this home."

His words cut her to the core. She felt the cadence of her heart like the tap of a distant drum, from very deep inside of her.

"You are an angel," he repeated.

It doesn't matter, she wanted to say.

"I have to go now."

"Yes," she said. "Yes, I know."

Of course he would go. The air of the hut overwhelmed her, the fetid odor of sheep dung, the dirty clutter of straw.

"Jacob will take care of things while J.B. recuperates." Lee looked up at the boy, the sweat still glistening on his brow. He was almost eighteen. He had grown tall.

"If it's true they are gone, I'll go to Harmony now. I'll be back if you need help."

She did not look at him for a moment.

"I'll help him." Lee looked sidelong at J.B. The man's breathing came unevenly, the air slipping between his lips. "I do not look at his betrayals. He has always been my friend." J.B. was not asleep, but Elizabeth did not know whether he heard John Lee's words or not. He was in too much pain.

"You've done . . . already you've done so much," she managed to say to John Lee. "Please . . . please don't place me any more in your debt . . ." Before she finished the words, she felt the stinging tears come into her throat. "Please. Good-bye."

"Elizabeth . . ." John Lee put his hand on her arm. "The answer to your prayers."

She didn't say it out loud, but the words formed in her mouth. Did it matter that the answer was no? There was silence now, a deadly marvelous silence as heavy as the stone of her heart.

"God be with you now." His gaze burned her—the eyes so blue.

"Good-bye," he whispered, raising his fingers to touch her cheek. "Good-bye."

She stared, not able to speak again. He turned to acknowledge Jacob. Then he rose from the hearth where she knelt and he was gone.

Elizabeth turned to minister to J.B. Then let her tears come.

## 67

*June 15, 1860, Elizabeth*

*Sometimes the days blur together. You do not see the sun in the sky. There is only a passage of light and dark. Light and dark. Something has happened to you to make you disbelieve. You do not believe any longer in sunshine. You do not believe any longer in love. Somehow there is only memory. And the memory of today reminds you of yesterday's emptiness.*

Through the darkest hours she clung to Hannah. She held Hannah and walked with her in the empty hut that reeked with the smell of dung and hay. She paced around J.B., who lay on bedding near the fireplace. Sometimes he rolled on the floor, crying with the pain.

"Shhh." She soothed the little girl into another sleep. "Shhh, little one. Shhh."

She held Hannah when the child was sleeping. She held her while J.B. sent Jacob to Jensens' to take care of Suky's body. She was not surprised to see Jacob's eyes blank with terror.

"And stay there. Stay to Jensens'. Don't come back, boy. This ain't no place for you. Or for any of us for that matter."

"I'll fetch the Jensens," Jacob said.

But J.B. wouldn't hear of it. He spit angry words between the gasps in his throat. "Get out of here and don't you come back, boy. You ain't ready to bear this pain."

She was not ready to bear it either, she knew. Nothing in her nineteen years had prepared her for it. When the house was empty and she couldn't help but hear the phlegm deep in J.B.'s lungs, she wished Jacob had stayed. She still held Hannah tightly in her arms. She had been crying so much now that no more tears would come. She stood in the middle of the room still clutching Hannah, feeling every rasp in J.B.'s throat, feeling his burns, his wounds.

"Suky," he cried out over and over again in his restlessness. "Oh dear heaven! Suky!" Then his voice swelled into a lamentable howl as terrible as the call of any wild animal she had ever heard. It bubbled and rippled over the tears in the deepest hollows of his throat. "Oh, Suky, you've left me. Suky. You are gone! Suky!" It was after a few hours that he began another call: "Elizabeth!"

Walking in the room with Hannah, she heard her own name as though it came from very far away. She jerked awake as though by reflex. And for a moment she stood trembling, but alive in every nerve. After each outbreak he would fall quiet until he broke into new sobs. Still, Elizabeth held the baby, as she continued to stand too frightened to move in the dark room.

"Suky. Elizabeth. Oh Elizabeth." He turned, opening his eyes. "What I need is sleep. Please, God have mercy on me," he groaned.

She clutched Hannah, still rocking her, as though the baby were a lifeline. Only Hannah could save her, as though she were the only one who could carry her upward like an angel, float with her into the dark smoke-filled sky.

"Suky. Suky. Elizabeth."

Elizabeth's scalp chilled. She felt sorrow, compassion, fear. J.B. turned now toward her, the flickering light full in his face, light dancing from the hot coals still in the fire. "Come here, Elizabeth," he finally said. "Please come here." The words were measured, stiff.

The night felt tangible to her, as though woven of a dark cloth, a suffocating furry substance that crowded her breath.

"Come here, Elizabeth. Leave the baby. Come." His last cry was the result of lifting himself up from the settee to reach out toward her, his hand clutching at her like a claw.

Love for someone is something you can learn, John Lee had said. Elizabeth felt waves of nausea fall over her, crowd her, make her tremble.

"Elizabeth! You know I need you!" His hand lifted outward again.

Slowly she moved her feet. She moved toward him over the rough floor. She set Hannah softly in one of the chiffonier drawers.

"You are my wife. Come here, Elizabeth." Now his eyes, like cat's eyes, were filled with yellow pus. "Don't be afraid." His voice was narrow, like a knife. When she reached him, she stood close. He lay back, trying to turn himself.

"That's it," he said. "Come here. It don't hurt you none to love me. You're my wife. And I need you. God knows."

Need her! She knew what he wanted and she froze. It had been so long. "Elizabeth. Lie down." He spread the bedding. "Come here, girl. Lie down beside me. I'm sorry, Elizabeth. I let you go. I didn't look after you. I was jealous. Please, girl. Suky's gone." He gasped again, his breath ragged. "Maybe . . . you can do this one thing for me."

When she lowered herself to the floor, he pulled at her. She felt nausea, but she steadied herself. This was life itself—hanging on.

He warmed to her, held her, still sobbing. Finally his breathing began to lengthen. He clutched her so closely she could not move. Soon the breath grew longer, longer. She couldn't believe that with all of his injuries he had still felt this overwhelming need.

When they had finished, he slept, and she stared numbly at the ashes in the grate.

## 68

### *Jacob*

For Jacob to hold down his anger, he had learned to count. He breathed air into his lungs and began to count to ten, though often he did not count quickly enough, and the anger erupted in surprising ways. He threw the wood on the fire. He stomped about while he was performing the work J.B. had contracted, but could not do. At present Jacob must help the neighbors make adobe bricks to build their new houses, while he still lived in a pig sty. No amount of washing, sweeping, or burning seemed to make it clean.

But there was more than the destruction of the house that oppressed him. As his father began to heal from the burns he had suffered in the fire, old sources of contention continued to fester. In deference to his father's condition, Jacob felt constrained to stand by and watch while the man—as he healed—continued to approach Anna Jane. On some Sundays Anna Jane would throw a look toward Jacob when J.B. came to talk with her. The look might have said, "Save me from your father," but no words ever passed Anna Jane's lips. And so Jacob could not be sure. And he could not act against his father's interests now. All he could do was pray, and he did a lot of that.

J.B. began sharing his plans to build an adobe house with his son. "And it won't burn," J.B. said. He went over the details with Jacob as though the house would be equally his.

In August he was almost glad that something happened to take his mind off his father's courtship, though the message wasn't any too pleasant. A robbery was reported in a Cedar City store. Jacob would never have wished harm to anyone, but he was secretly grateful to contend with something else besides his father's problems. It had been on a Sunday and the rider from the Cedar militia alerted the church in Kanarraville.

"I'm sent to tell you there's been a robbery at the General Store," the messenger yelled. "Get your posse together! Watch for a coach and four. It happened Saturday night, and the whole town is up in arms over it. They were coming this way. Our posse tried to catch 'em. They got away with about a hundred and fifty dollars and some spirits that shouldn't have been in the store in the first place!"

The messenger went as far as the Lee place before he returned to Cedar. The congregation at Kanarraville could talk of nothing else. The Kanarraville store braced itself should any strangers come into town.

And they did come. In the late afternoon on Monday, August 27, the coach drove into town, its window blinds drawn. Jacob, who had been watching for it, saw it in plenty of time. J.B. and Lee, who had been in the fields and drying adobes the past few days, both came into town to hide themselves behind merchandise in the store.

Jacob was standing on the front steps of the market when the enclosed coach drew up. He did not recognize the driver or the occupants. A woman peered from the window, the lower part of her face covered with a veil. Her eyes startled Jacob, who was jolted by the direct glance of those eyes. He watched the woman as she walked into the store, the dark red silk of her dress shimmering in the slanted light of the afternoon. Mr. Humphreys, who had been waiting for something to happen, asked her what he could do to help.

"I'm on my way through to California," the woman said in a clear, level voice. "And I am being pursued by some men who have just robbed the store in Cedar."

That's them, Jacob thought. His heart pounded.

Her voice had a ring of drama to it. "They've just let me out to find your privy. Could I beg you to put me up, or hide me with haste?" Jacob thought he recognized that voice from somewhere. He shook the notion from his mind.

"Hurry. There isn't much time," she pleaded.

Before Mr. Humphreys could take a breath to answer her, there was a sudden clumping of boots on the wooden porch. As though they materialized out of the dust, two hooded men rose up and grabbed her from behind. Jacob's blood raced in his head. Reacting before he could stop himself, he grabbed the woman's arms, pulled her out of the way, and punched one of the men in the belly.

In that instant, he felt a blow to the back of his head. His knees buckled under him and he slumped to the floor. As he swam in and out of consciousness, all he could see were the boots of the men, and the small flashing buttons on the woman's tiny shoes. In the roaring half-consciousness of his brain, he heard the woman's echoing screams. He could see J.B., Lee, and the others standing by, their rifles dangling in their hands.

"Now we got her as hostage," the robber said. He held a gun to her head. "We'll kill her if any of you moves again," the robber said. "Give us your till."

Humphreys did not waste a moment emptying the till. He lost only $15.75, as they had already planned to have very little cash available. Seeing the small amount of money, the men spit on the floor and began filling their bags with bottles of whiskey. After they took all they wanted, they backed away to the coach, dragging the screaming woman with them.

"We'll kill 'er if you raise a hand . . ."

Jacob was just conscious enough to see the crying woman disappear, feathers and satin, into the coach. The hooded men, mounting their horses and holding guns to the driver, hollered for the coach to move. As the vehicle pulled off, he thought, in the hot pain of his head, that he could hear his name in the woman's scream. "Jacob. Jacob Lorry." But he dismissed the thought as an illusion.

J.B. bent over him. "Did that woman know you?" he asked. "She was calling your name." Jacob did not answer.

The robbery left the community stunned. Though the posse chased after them, they returned disappointed. They said the coach must have stopped and hid somewhere. On Sunday morning the Saints met in the Harmony meeting house like children whose toys had been snatched from their hands.

"We weren't surprised," Lee was saying at the pulpit. "And our losses were small. If you will remember, we were once threatened by others who took advantage of us in the same way." Now a hush fell over the meeting—as solemn and cold as ice. Not a sound could be heard. "As when God first used the flood as a tool of his destructive anger, we must now raise the rainbow as a symbol of peace to those who come against us. Never again."

There was pain in the silence now. "Forgive them, for they know not what they do."

Not a soul in the congregation could misread the allusion, as well as the reference to the words, "never again."

Jacob's scalp crawled. They would live in fear now forever rather than retaliate again. It was at that moment that he saw the shadow on the floor, the shadow of a woman with a large round feathered hat. As he listened to John Lee's voice, he sensed the pause. The congregation turned to look toward the door.

She stood in the back door of the church, at first only a silhouette against the light. Slowly she became visible to Jacob's eyes: the woman in the maroon silk, the dress now torn and the feathers hanging in limp ruin over shoulders caked with mud.

Through the congregation there was a ripple of surprise. There was no veil across her lips. Jacob stared. The woman with the dark familiar eyes was Maggie Seymour. His heart leaped in his chest. Torn in front, her dress barely covered her, and she hiked her black petticoats to cross the threshold of the church.

Maggie Seymour. Lee must have recognized her, but he continued his sermon, his voice still warm with compassion.

"Lord forgive them, for they know not what they do," he repeated. "As long as we live in a world where evil dwells we know that any man may choose evil if he so desires. We live in a world where we must battle evil only with good. Should we turn and fight it, then we shall be participants rather than the watching angels. And we shall be judged according to what we do."

Jacob sat very still while Maggie found the narrow space on the bench beside him. As she sat without a word, the dust and grime of her clothing spilled like chalk into the aisle and onto his suit. Nevertheless, he could smell the strong exhilarating scent of her perfume. When he breathed in, it filled his head, and he felt dizzy. Maggie! Who would have guessed she had been the woman in the coach? His nerves tightened every muscle on his bones.

"If we can be strong, we shall stand up against those who perform evil against us. If we truly love them, we shall try to help them turn from their evil ways. But if ever we wield a sword, let it be only the sword of truth."

Jacob sat frozen during the closing hymn, and then through the long closing prayer.

"And dear God, if there are any of us who have done evil, let us repent of it for the sake of our own souls. In the name of Jesus Christ. Amen."

He could feel the effect of the perfume in a space just behind his eyes, as if he were drunk.

"You tried to save my life," she had whispered just before the hymn. "I'll always be indebted to you."

With the last amen, she took his hand in hers and placed a ten-dollar gold piece in it, a five, plus some coins. It was the fifteen dollars and seventy-five cents Humphreys had given to the robbers in the store.

"It isn't mine," Jacob began.

"Please . . . please." Now Maggie lowered her eyes. "If ever I should have a chance . . ." She nodded toward Lee. "As he says . . . love me away from this evil, I pray of you."

By now Maggie was surrounded with Lorrys, Jensens, and Lees.

"My goodness, girl," Aggatha Lee exclaimed. "Where have you been?"

The men who had been in the store at the time of the robbery drew back from her.

"She . . . I believe . . . Maggie Seymour," Jacob heard J.B. say, his voice unconnected, the words garbled.

Jacob stepped back and felt a hand touch his waist. When he looked he could see it was Anna Jane. Her touch sent ripples up his back. Because the others in the crowd could not see him, he reached for her hand while the people gathered about Maggie, asking questions that went largely unanswered. Some were answered only by her tears.

"You . . . you have come back to us, then," Lee said, with a stern look.

But Maggie's eyes rested on Jacob's face. "They used me as a front," she choked. "As long as there is someone on earth who cares . . . enough to risk their own life . . ."

Jacob's hand tightened on Anna Jane's. Among the circles of people, he saw that Elizabeth had withdrawn, gripping Hannah tightly in her arms.

For a moment there was a lull when Jacob caught Maggie's eyes resting on Elizabeth and the child. At first Maggie stared. Then she began to cry.

"That . . . that is the baby . . . my baby . . . " and she lunged forward in the torn dress to reach for the child.

But there was a surprise. J.B. was the one who held her back. He took Maggie's bare shoulders in his rough grasp.

"Wait," he said. His hands tightened on her arm. "You can come with us and we'll talk this all over. But you're not in the best of shape now." Maggie slumped against his arm, breaking into tears. She searched for Jacob's eyes. But Jacob was not looking at her. Finding herself in J.B.'s grasp, she fell against him.

"You want to take her to your house, then?" Lee was saying. His wives surrounded her, trying to dust off her dress, replace the boa in her hair.

"Yes, I'll take her," J.B. said, and he guided her into the sunshine out of the meeting house door.

After J.B. left, Jacob remained behind with Anna Jane, holding her hand.

## 69

### Elizabeth

"My baby, my baby . . ." Maggie's voice wavered as she clung to Hannah.

Elizabeth watched Maggie with mixed emotions, and not a little fear. She watched as Maggie planted kisses on the baby's cheeks, almost suffocating her. Elizabeth looked into Maggie's dark eyes, heard Maggie's tale many times. The girl was animated when she talked. She used her hands to tell the stories, though the one Elizabeth would have been most interested in was still buried somewhere deep. Yes, she had been ill at the time of the baby's birth, Maggie said. And she had fallen into the care of some old Indians. She could not remember much except that her baby girl was taken away from her for a few days because she was too sick, and a few days later the Indians had brought the baby back, healthy and well cared for. Of course she left the Indians as soon as she possibly could, but everyone she had ever asked for help—especially the soldiers—had taken advantage of her. All of them. It had not been her fault that she had fallen in love with Patrick Moore and that he had abandoned her before he left for California. She had taken a job in Camp Floyd, but the men there had done with her as they pleased.

Elizabeth could see in Maggie's dark eyes a look that had asked for it, eyes that had probably even advertised an invitation to every man who passed by. Now, as the days progressed, Elizabeth began to see that same invitation work its magic in their own home. She soon came to see those eyes as a powerful blessing.

Though Jacob had been strangely aloof, Maggie had found something strangely attractive in J.B. Elizabeth, watching the development of this romance, felt nothing but relief. She suddenly realized how Suky had felt, hoping Elizabeth would marry J.B. She felt relief, pure and simple, that Maggie was an emerging candidate to take some of the responsibility of filling J.B.'s needs. Finally someone to share the task Elizabeth had learned—like Suky—to perform: to give to him regularly in the interest of peace.

Her marriage to J.B. was not always unpleasant, Elizabeth admitted to herself. Occasionally something mutual had happened. However, as a general rule, her own needs were only barely considered, and he had been there with his need always—through heartache, sickness, pain. Now suddenly there was Maggie. Elizabeth felt a fresh breath of freedom. And so she watched, not with jealousy, but with the same hope Suky must have felt. She had never understood it until now.

When he came into the house from the adobe fields, Maggie met his eyes with a becoming blush. They seemed right for one another, Elizabeth realized. For Maggie also had an unquenchable appetite. With only the slightest of innuendos, the fire between them would flare. Elizabeth was now content to let it happen, just as Suky must have been.

Now there were fewer nights with J.B., but enough to share the news of the day. And at last Elizabeth had something to tell him. "There is something I must tell you, J.B." After his passion had spent itself in the darkness, his heavy breathing told her that he had begun to drift into a clumsy sleep. "I am going to have a child."

She felt his body stiffen now. Perhaps he needed a moment to awaken fully to those words, unsure of them still.

"Did you hear me, J.B.?" she whispered, "I am . . ."

Now he leaped suddenly from her with this news. At first he frightened her. His words were low with a desperate hope. "Oh, dear God in Heaven." It was a prayer.

There was so much darkness in the old cabin that only the moonlight through the window outlined his burly head as he sprang up beside her. "Oh my dear." Then he pulled at her to sit upright beside him and took her slender shoulders in his hands. "You're not . . . you're not just hoping for my sake, Elizabeth?"

Speechless, she could only shake her head.

"Oh dear heaven." His prayer had changed tone. It was now uttered from the edge of tears. "Oh, oh, Elizabeth." He reached for her and held her head and mass of hair against his breast. "Oh my darling girl. I love you so! I've always loved you and now . . . it's true!" He felt for her body, his hand reaching for the slight roundness of her belly. "It's true." He had not had a child since Jacob's birth. "As I've always hoped. As I've prayed! Oh, thank you, heaven."

It was after those first few days of hushed joy that he seemed most receptive to Elizabeth's whispered requests. Only a few days after her joyous announcement, Elizabeth brought up a similar subject. For a while now she had wanted to discuss Maggie.

"J.B., please. I believe that you . . . I have seen Maggie's eyes bright for you."

"No, no," he said holding her tightly against himself.

"Your feelings for Maggie. I've noticed . . ."

"You needn't worry about Maggie."

"I'm not really worried, but I have some concerns. We are still not really sure, nor is she, that Hannah is not hers . . ." They had reviewed it with Maggie so many times. "Why don't you . . . bring her into the family . . . instead of Anna Jane."

There was a tremor in his body, then. He held her, touched her.

"I think Jacob and Anna Jane . . ." She did not finish.

"Jacob and Anna Jane?" J.B. asked blankly.

She nodded. "Maggie needs you. She wants to change . . . to do well. And of course if we are all together, it will not matter then whose child Hannah was."

He was silent for only a moment. "You think that will solve . . . everything?" he asked.

Elizabeth nodded.

"Then I will. For you," he said, seeming not to mind at all.

### 70
*October 9, 1860, Elizabeth*

*I can't remember so much happiness. It has taken so long for us to find ourselves free. We have had to learn to smile, to laugh. I smile without stopping when I watch Jacob and Anna Jane. I am also strangely happy for Maggie and J.B. Today all four of them were married in the Harmony meeting house by John Lee, accompanied by a lot of pomp and ceremony. Anna Jane looked like a princess in a creamy white satin dress and pink meadow flowers. And we refurbished Tabby's old gray silk for Maggie. We pinned violets on the bodice, and they seemed to match some of the color in Maggie's eyes.*

*Maggie is careful with us. She glances at us out of the corner of those eyes as if fearful that if she says one word out of line, we may ship her back to Scipio. Or to Patrick Moore. Her mother and father—the Seymours—came to the wedding all stuffed into old-fashioned winter wool. This time of the year! Other than appearing to suffocate, they seemed to be happy. Maggie's life has surely not been what they had hoped for, but now, at least, she is a married woman with a respectable position in the house of J.B. Lorry.*

*And J.B. has certainly grown twenty years younger, no doubt about it, drawing up plans for our new adobe house in Kanarraville, to be located in the same spot where our pine one burned to the ground.*

*We are all waiting with somewhat glowing expectations to see what my baby will be. I watch Jacob's solid, patient joy, Anna Jane's radiance, and J.B. and Maggie's hunger for one another, and I feel for the first time—free. I feel at one with this child moving inside of me. I have never felt this way before. The child means everything to me. This child is my future, my touch with eternity. For I shall go on and on and on inside of this child's body. I will be a mother of worlds, for there are worlds locked up inside of me. It is more than I have ever dreamed I would feel—to know the movement inside my body of another human being who will someday laugh and breathe and believe.*

*Some days I remember faintly a whisper as though out of the darkness . . . a whisper of the past and I suddenly feel a chill . . . as though I am slightly afraid. But when I take into consideration all that we have built from our promise to be faithful to one another, it is a miraculous thing. Together we have done so much more than we could ever have done apart. I feel the strength from my commitment to the gospel surge through me like fire. There is something to be said for remaining—unlike Maggie—remaining where you are and working it through. There are rumors that President Young himself will finally honor us with a visit soon, just to see what we have done here.*

## 71
### *Spring, 1861, Jacob*

The rumors that Brigham Young would visit them came at about the same time that Elizabeth's Joshua Lorry was born. The men in the valley were, of course, more interested in the president's visit than in the birth of Elizabeth's boy, or the expected birth of Maggie and J.B.'s child in July, and Jacob and Anna Jane's child in June. Brigham Young had not been to Dixie for three years. No one had ever asked why. But when it was heard that he would now make a visit, there was a hushed excitement and preparation among the members of the church in the valley. There had been enough progress in Harmony and Kanarraville that the president could not help but be pleased. The Lorrys had not only added a child and two expected ones, but by the time President Young would arrive, their new adobe home would be ready.

Jacob, using the materials he had earned from participating in John Lee's adobe business, had created much of the new three-section house on his own. His hands had passed over every inch of the large dwelling. He knew the location of each adobe block, each joist. He had polished the thick wooden baseboards, and the casing on the doors. The house was a masterpiece of craftsmanship. His heart swelled to see the three women occupy their adjoining homes with their new expectations clearly visible, and Elizabeth's child in her arms.

They had held an open house to the new adobe home, and Jacob had stood proudly beside Anna Jane, who was quite far along in her pregnancy. The women opened up all of the doors—both those inside, which stood between the three parlors, and the three front doors outside which led to each of the three houses. Except for a small separate courtyard, which belonged to Anna Jane and Jacob alone, all three homes were just alike, with a main kitchen and parlor situated below two upstairs bedrooms looking out onto a balcony walkway that stretched across the entire front of the structure. It was built like the Hamblins' home, with the same heavy adobe walls and pine plank floors.

Standing in the doorways, J.B. rubbed his hands across the thickness of the sun-dried mud, stroking it, and murmuring to himself that it wouldn't burn. "Just try to burn," he dared it softly. He smiled at Maggie in her condition, and took Elizabeth's small dark-haired newborn Joshua from her to hold in his arms. He had a tendency to draw attention to the progress of the Lorry family, especially to John Lee when he came by.

"We're ready for the president if he comes here tomorrow," J.B. said.

"It won't be tomorrow," John Lee said. "But soon."

Though the rumors were now facts that Brigham Young was on his way, no one knew when. The Lorrys hurried to complete the adobe home, believing he would show up for the dedication. But time passed, and at last they felt they should dedicate it. It was as though Brigham Young would show up during the spring planting, so they had put it off a few weeks. But Brigham Young did not come. Finally, Jacob began to notice a nervous mannerism in his father-in-law, John Lee. Unable to meet inquiring eyes, he glanced aside if anyone should ask what he had heard from President Brigham Young.

Finally, on a warm evening after planting, Jacob looked up and saw his father-in-law's looming figure against the red sun, his face in shadow. The man dismounted and drew near before he answered Jacob's greeting.

"I want you to ride with me to Washington to see Brigham Young," he said without further explanation.

Washington? Jacob watched John Lee's expression carefully. "Wasn't Brigham Young coming here? I thought . . ." He wanted to complete the question, but did not know if he dared. "Does that mean . . ."

"You have probably guessed it. Yes, that means he will not come here," Lee said abruptly.

So, there would be no visit from Brigham Young in this area. Jacob had guessed as much the last few days. He was silent, waiting.

Lee was not finished with his message. "But he'll be in Washington, and he says I am to meet him there. I would like to move faster on building the mill there and may need your help with that. At any rate, we'll throw a feast for him at the Washington house. We'll leave tomorrow."

It was already hot in early May. The heat burned quickly through the dew on the morning grass. John Lee picked up Jacob at about a quarter to nine, bringing a saddled horse hitched to the rear. Jacob could see that John Lee was in a hurry. Even his speech was clipped.

"A few are still against us. Like Solomon Hanncock. And against what we felt we must do at the meadows to stay out of war with the Indians. The same ones who would have turned us in to Judge Cradlebaugh must have filled Brigham Young's ears in Cedar City. There's some criticism of us. They said things . . . to Brigham Young about us. That is why the president has told me to meet him in Washington instead of here."

Jacob, puzzled, did not understand everything. Why would John Lee say these things to him?

The older man turned to him and looked him squarely in the eyes. "Brigham Young believes it is safer for him to see me in Washington."

Jacob thought he understood now. Brigham Young did not dare to associate himself with the rumors or risk negative public opinion. The reputation of the entire Church was at stake. He sensed in Lee's voice and his own heart that from now on Brigham Young might avoid any public visit with Lee.

It was quiet then. Jacob felt almost dizzy as the buckboard drove slowly down the road toward Washington. Lee hurried the horses as though escaping a flood of memories. When he spoke again, there was a peculiar tone of anger combined with nostalgia. "He is my father."

The words came as a surprise but Jacob did not respond immediately. Lee turned to him and asked, "Did you know that? I am one of Brigham Young's adopted sons."

Jacob stared at this man about whom many of his own memories were buried in a clouded reality. He remembered when he first knew John Lee. The man had frightened him. But the father-in-law beside him frightened him no more. Lee was his relative now—his father-in-law. And now Jacob felt some of his pain.

Jacob had expected to ride with John Lee to meet Young's party, but outside of Harmony Lee stopped him. Dismounting, he untied the horse from the buckboard and spoke in a level voice. "I want you to meet Brigham Young for me at the meadows. That is the route he chose to take today. I ask you to lead him to Washington to see me. And please . . . tell me what he says at the meadows . . ."

Lee's last words were forced as though he had given up some of himself to Jacob. As if he had given up his pride out of a gnawing fear.

"You mean . . . you . . . want me . . . to ride to the Mountain Meadows?"

"Yes," Lee said. "I want you to meet him at the meadows. I brought a saddled horse with me." There was a moment, a pause in which the silence might have hurt John Lee.

"Good-bye, son." He shook Jacob's hand. Warmth flowed between them. "Godspeed." But Jacob saw that his father-in-law's eyes registered fear.

Jacob could not believe he was on his way to the meadows again. The heat of the sun drained him. He wished the memories of the meadow were not quite so alive. He could still recall everything as though it had happened yesterday. Consciously, he crowded those memories out of his mind. "It's been four years." The words passed through his mind—almost across his lips. "Then why is it still so real?"

Yes, Brigham Young was on his way to the meadows. He had been in Penter that very afternoon. When Jacob questioned a woman who was walking in the road outside of Penter, she told him, yes, there was a whole retinue there. Soldiers and general authorities. "They are only a few miles out of town now," she said.

When he saw them winding ahead of him a few miles away, Jacob felt butterflies in his head. He was not sure if he should introduce himself as John Lee's son-in-law, or stay incognito. He decided he would speak up if someone saw him, but if he were lost in the crowd, that would be all right, too.

However, when he was only a few hundred yards away, a man on a horse seemed to notice him and came to him with a friendly wave of his hand.

"It's John Lee's son-in-law," the boy on the pony next to him said. Jacob recognized him as one of the Hamblin boys.

Jacob could not get the words out without feeling them to be wrong on his tongue. But he said to the Hamblins, "Brother Lee wanted me to meet Brigham Young and escort him to Washington." They were only a few miles from the meadows now. The brother—a man named Partridge—had ridden with the president for a short time. He said he would take Jacob to the president. Jacob felt a lump in his throat. An awe he had tried not to feel. But the man beside him now was so quiet, so reverent, that a spirit of peace prevailed.

As the sun moved into the hot part of the afternoon, Jacob could see the meadows just ahead. They were nearing them. Why could he remember everything so clearly? And why did he feel so afraid?

The president of the church came into the valley on his horse with a sure step. He rode with so many men beside him, Jacob could not get close. He felt his message might never reach Brigham Young. The party seemed dead quiet as they advanced on the scene of desolation. They stayed seated on their horses on the ridge, miniature silhouettes at the edge of the grassy valley dipping before them for a mile or so like the sloping basin of an empty sea.

As Brigham Young surveyed the valley, there was an almost ringing silence among those who accompanied him. For a very long time the president did not speak. He looked around at the hills, the trees, at the few bleached bones that had been turned up in the dark soil. In the gully there was still a trickle of water from the spring.

So it was here. Jacob heard his own thoughts clamoring. He remembered everything so clearly. He had been only fifteen. Now he was nineteen and would soon be a father. And he had changed. But still his memories were all too real. They had never faded. He watched the portly leader, the president, as he rode up to the monument that had been erected by Judge Cradlebaugh and the U.S. Government dragoons. He read the words in a clear voice while everyone waited to hear what he would say.

"Vengeance is mine, saith the Lord," he read. And then President Brigham Young improvised under his breath so quietly that those who were with him strained to hear, "And I have taken a little of it."

Jacob heard the words. He watched the president turn away on his horse. Behind him, the federal troops took some invisible signal or perhaps they acted in unison as though they had moved as one many times before. The party began to leave the terrible scene.

But as Brigham Young rode away, one of the men threw a lasso over the shoddily painted wooden cross on the pile of stones the dragoons had erected as a monument. As he tugged on the rope, he dragged the cross face down across the grass. With a whoop the man spurred his horse, and the monument toppled and brought down with it the hastily mortared rock. Other men rode into the stones and scooped them away with the butts of their rifles. Some quickly dismounted and tore at them until the pile lay scattered across the valley floor.

An inscription on the flat stone at the bottom of the monument read, "120 men, women and children murdered in cold blood early in September, 1857. From Arkansas." A second slab said, "May 1859. Erected by Company K."

## 72
### Elizabeth

The months before Christmas 1861 moved slowly. At first Maggie had admitted her faults, repented, and begged for mercy. She had cooperated, submitted, obeyed. She bore a fine healthy son whom they named Robert. She seemed to be satisfied and grateful. But slowly her gratitude gave way to confidence. And with her confidence came pettiness.

Elizabeth tried to ignore the beginnings of what she could see happening, because she feared it. But by Christmas time the problems had begun to increase. A young peddlar who had come through town from Salt Lake City, bringing lace and dry goods from the East. The merchandise sorely tempted Maggie. J.B. had said no to all of it, but with some wiles of her own Maggie had wheedled a lace collar out of the young Dutchman Hans Ostler, and on a second trip, she had chosen to purchase some earrings, which looked disgraceful to Elizabeth. She noted that Maggie had forced a hole in her ears in which to hang them.

J.B., whose main source of income still came from working for John Lee's adobe and construction business, questioned Maggie only once and passed it off. It would not have been so devastating to Elizabeth had the girl not traded their precious cheeses for the cheap gems and gotten away with it without so much as a scolding. It rankled her, but with grace she prayed for the ability to forgive, and by Christmas all seemed fairly right again.

But on Christmas morning Elizabeth was disturbed to note that Maggie's baby Robert was wearing a pair of tiny leather shoes. Nothing like those baby shoes had ever been seen in the valley, let alone dreamed of. Elizabeth was piqued that the Lorrys' limited funds might have been spent for those shoes. If they had come from the young peddlar, Elizabeth was curious to know. Aware that she might be simply jealous—perhaps wanting to see the shoes on her own child— she disciplined her feelings when she dared to confront Maggie.

Maggie smiled her disarming smile. "He brought them to me because I asked him to."

When approached, J.B. admitted Maggie had asked for the shoes, and in a weak moment—Elizabeth knew it was to keep peace with the hot-tempered Maggie—J.B. had given her the money for the purchase. "The young man had brought them especially for Maggie, and I could not let him down."

The Christmas dinner, a carefully prepared ham and sauce eaten in silence, seemed tasteless. Elizabeth, torn and gloomy, rebuked herself for her jealousy and tried to smile and hold herself together. Only Hannah's happy antics with the children saved the afternoon from disaster. If it hadn't been for Jacob and Anna Jane and the three babies that belonged to all of them, Elizabeth would have excused herself and closed her parlor door.

After the solemn dinner it began to rain. The cold wind whipped up a gray storm. Even J.B. was morose, taking hot herb tea and retiring to his bed in Maggie's rooms.

On the very next day Hannah came running to Elizabeth with the news that the young peddlar Hans Ostler was on his way to their house through the gray rain. Elizabeth saw him in the distance seated on his cart under his umbrella. He reminded her of a charcoal drawing on an English Christmas card her mother had put in her scrapbook when she was very young. The book had long since been lost on her trip across the plains.

Elizabeth thought it was time she took things into her own hands. She wrapped herself and her baby Joshua inside a couple of shawls and ventured into the rain to meet the peddlar at the gate. Little Hannah, braving the storm in her sunbonnet, stepped out holding on to Elizabeth's skirt. The child looked back periodically to see if Maggie followed. But Elizabeth did not look. She moved firmly toward the buggy, her eyes fastened on the handsome square face beneath the umbrella in the gray mist. When she reached the gate, the rain had stopped. The young man, climbing down from the high seat, sauntered to her with a package in his hands.

"Is there anything you, Miss Maggie, or Anna Jane are looking for that you didn't get for Christmas, ma'am?" He smiled a disarming smile.

"I think not," Elizabeth said, reminding herself to be pleasant.

"Well, I have some yarn Miss Maggie ordered to finish up her needle-point."

"Oh?" Elizabeth knew her voice sounded icy cold. There had been more than enough yarn left from her afghan to finish Maggie's needlepoint—had she been working it at all. Maggie would have argued that this particular thread was the wrong kind, and the colors weren't right, but the family did not have enough money to pay heed to those kinds of whims.

"Shall I just leave it with you, ma'am, and wait until Maggie can pay?"

"I don't think so," Elizabeth said as kindly as she could. "I would appreciate it if you didn't stop here again."

"But ma'am—"

Elizabeth, still clutching Joshua tightly in the curve of her left arm, raised her palm to him. "I'm sorry, Mr. Ostler. We have only limited money and time. And we cannot afford the trinkets that you bring us nor the trouble that they cause."

The smile on the broad Dutch face fell quickly away and the eyes searched the front window of Maggie's rooms. He must have seen her there in the window, for the light of his eyes changed.

"Is it all right if I just tell Miss Maggie I—"

"No," Elizabeth said firmly, more sure now than ever that what had passed between Maggie and the handsome Dutch peddlar was not only goods, money, and cheese. Her heart tightened in her chest, and she drew Joshua close to her, barely breathing. "Please, Mr. Ostler, I beg you to leave us alone."

When he turned away toward the hack and found his seat under the umbrella, the rain began to fall again as though it had waited only for him to find shelter. It came in sheets now—gray sheets pounding the ground into rivulets, spattering and steaming in a mist as high as the wheels. When Elizabeth turned toward the house, she saw the anxious face of Maggie in her window, her hands pressed against the pane. Elizabeth lowered her eyes quickly and moved out of the downpour.

"Mama." Hannah tugged at her skirt. "Maggie wanted to see the man."

Elizabeth's heart crowded up into her throat. She could barely speak. "It's all right," she said to Hannah.

The rain did not stop that day. Elizabeth did not see Maggie at suppertime but thought nothing of it. Then, as time passed, Hannah remarked that she couldn't hear the baby Robert from Maggie's kitchen—even into the evening. There was a hush in the house. Anna Jane and Jacob were quiet as well, their little baby girl Belinda whimpering softly. The families stayed in the house and drew the curtains against the rain. Elizabeth watched Hannah feed the baby Joshua until J.B. was to come in from his work at Lee's adobe yard while Lee was supposedly meeting with Brigham Young in Washington again. But before he came, she put them both to bed.

J.B. did not come until very late, and when he came, he said, "Where is Maggie? She is not here."

"What?" Elizabeth's eyes widened.

"I have searched every corner of all three sections of the house, every cranny. She has taken Robert, and he'll catch his death of cold in this weather. She has gone. And I don't know where."

Elizabeth alerted Anna Jane. Maggie was gone! They scattered to look while J.B. raged.

"One quarrel over a silly pair of shoes and the girl is gone. With my son. And where? No one knows what pain I have had to face within this home—nor what trials may await us. No . . . and in this raging rain yet."

When they could not find her, they knew she had gone with Hans Ostler, but the storm stopped them from taking any action. J.B. was like a caged animal, fuming, sweating, walking back and forth inside the house in a terrible unrest. Elizabeth was surprised at the strength of his fury. She began to suspect there may be more to it. Was there something that angered J.B., something more than Maggie's disappearance? Elizabeth stopped to listen to the unusually forceful timbre of J.B.'s anger, to hear what he was saying. "Is there something else, J.B.?"

He stopped, then, long enough to sink his words home. "The adobe," he said. "It has not cured enough to withstand this rain."

Elizabeth's heart leaped.

"A quake caused a break in John Lee's walls. Now they are sopping up the water. And surely our fate will be the same . . ."

The pounding in her breast made her gasp.

"If I sleep at all, we're homeless," he said. And he plowed into the night in his leather coat, his hat jammed down over his hair. "At least I can make a dam with sandbags."

Out of the mountains to the east there began to pour rivers of rain. Elizabeth stomped into Suky's old boots and followed J.B. into the watery darkness. The water was roaring about them, digging small canyons down the hills.

"Let me help you."

"Grab anything. Old feed sacks. Fill them with dirt. We must build a dam. We didn't put enough straw in the adobe. I tried to tell John Lee . . ."

Jacob and Anna Jane came quickly to their aid. For hours Anna Jane held the light while the others filled the bags. They constructed a small dam against the back of the house. But the water continued to funnel through. It washed against the new adobe, chewed it up and sent it away in rivulets until the foundation looked like curdled cheese scarred by claws.

And it continued to rain. For days and days it rained. They watched helplessly while the new adobe crumbled before their eyes.

In the first few days the foundation had already begun to slip. After the foundation had slipped, the uneven weight in the other walls caused them to shift until a few less sturdy blocks were crushed into mud, oozing out like so much black cream. During the next few days the roof developed cracks and began to leak. And it was then that J.B., distraught over his losses, admitted defeat and began to move the furniture into the old one-room log house lying east of the adobe homes, further against the hills. Humphreys and Lee helped them move on a Saturday afternoon. And just in time. That evening, as they brought the last chiffonier into the hut, it began to snow.

There had never been much snow this far south in Deseret. Elizabeth took Hannah and Joshua into the loft of the old house, and together they huddled in the dry straw. Hannah pressed her nose against the small window pane. The white flakes fell like stars out of the dark sky.

Watching, Elizabeth thought she felt sick again. On Sunday morning she was nauseous. She thought it was the weather and the disrepair of their new home. But after three days of the same morning nausea, she knew she was going to have another baby. And she secretly rejoiced, keeping Hannah and Joshua closer to her in the loft of the old log home.

It was Wednesday before she whispered the secret to Anna Jane. Now in the hut together the two women, making the best of their tight quarters, drew closer to each other. Without Maggie, things seemed to run much more smoothly, although J.B. lamented her absence. There had been no news of her. And although they felt she and her baby had probably gone back to Salt Lake City with the peddlar, no one really knew.

When the weather permitted, Anna Jane and Jacob trudged to the fort in Harmony to help John Lee with his many families. What they found at Lee's compound was a terrible reflection of what the Lorrys had gone through. The entire cluster of buildings was beginning to melt around them like sugar.

On the 15th of January, 1862, the Lee barn fell. To escape the crumbling adobe, John Lee had moved all of his families to the west side of the fort which had been better preserved than the east side. And they had moved none too soon. On that evening Anna Jane came home to Jacob and Elizabeth, her face flushed. She reported that all of her father's families had barely been settled on the west side of the fort when the entire eastern wall had slipped and fallen with a deafening roar. Anna Jane had been asked to bring a message from her father to Jacob and J.B.—that he would like some help to build some temporary shelters on the site above the fort where he had already dug the foundation for Emma's new home. In the next few days the weather let up and they planned to do as much as they could on the 19th.

Elizabeth asked Mrs. Humphreys at the store to care for the children so that she could go with them to help. When she arrived, she could not keep her eyes from Lee as he stood at the helm of the rescue effort. For the first time she saw a strange vacancy in his face. He stood outside his door in several inches of loosely packed snow, his sons and other neighbors gathering around to help. He pointed to the lumber from the fallen barn and they began gathering it up and placing it in the hay wagon. As he worked, he spoke as he had spoken many times before. But Elizabeth noted a new tremor in his voice that she had never heard.

"Klingensmith lost his home in Pocketville," he said. "And his mill, his blacksmith shop, everything he had at that place." Lee stopped for a moment and stared at J.B. "If God is willing, he'll let us stay." It was his loss as well, Elizabeth thought, trying to shut away her memory of the feelings she had once felt for him. And sometimes—though she feared it—like unheralded birds, those feelings soared into her heart and beat their wings. John Lee. John Lee. The only man she had ever fully believed in. And yet so much had changed. And changing, it had all tightened into a web that locked her away from what she believed could have been love.

"There are still some people who believe this is God's retribution for the blood spilt in this valley, going on five years ago now," Lee said.

Hearing this, Elizabeth caught her breath.

"But I will tell you people, God will hold his hand to protect us. I talked to Brigham Young face to face in Washington County. And when he came through not long ago he blessed the work we've done here. He blessed us for it." The words faded as he lifted a load of lumber to the cart.

It was not the first time all of them had heard Lee mention Brigham Young. For a dark moment Elizabeth believed she saw Lee as a man obsessed. For he had mentioned Brigham Young's May visit in church three times. He had told them all what Brigham Young had said at Washington. And of course she and Anna Jane and J.B. had heard it from Jacob who had traveled to Washington with Lee. Lee had made a point of mentioning several times how the president had blessed them all. He had even dared to speak of the past, saying that he did not see how, under the circumstances, they could have done other than what they did . . . especially to stay out of war with the Indians. He was sorry that some people—he did not give names—had wanted to turn the participants over to Judge Cradlebaugh when he and his dragoons came through town. Oh, he had regretted the deaths of women and children, he said, but the men had "merited their fate."

"It's over now. We are ready to prosper, to give this valley our lives, to blossom like a rose." These had all been words Lee had said in church meetings. He had buoyed them with his successes. But now there seemed to be a faded look in his eyes.

"What could God have done for us better than wash us clean in this rain?" Lee looked out toward the meadows with a strange dull gaze. "Perhaps it's the best way he knows to do it."

After they had loaded the lumber on the wagon, they carried out the big black stove. With both the stove and the lumber from the fallen barn on the wagon, the oxen could barely move. As Lee, J.B., and the young men prodded the animals forward, the wheels of the wagon dug into mud as deep as the axle. They debated taking the stove off the wagon and setting it in the mud, but decided instead to use more animals. J.B. brought Foresight and Humphreys' oxen, and Jensen brought a mule and his oxen. With eight animals, the wagon lurched forward and began the slow trek up the rain-washed slope.

Once they were high enough to escape the floods, the men fashioned a shed roof with the lumber and set the stove inside the small shelter, feeding it with the driest wood. Behind the stove they set other large pieces of lumber upright to dry. The women tended the fire and settled the children on small slabs of barn wood close to the stove.

Lee wanted all of his families to move to the makeshift shed on higher ground. But Sarah Caroline had set up her weaving in the lower rooms at the fort, and begged to finish it. She would be safe, she said. And Tabby said she would stay with her.

Lee loaded two more wagons with furniture and goods for his other four families and moved them all to the upper site. It was in the evening after the move that it began to snow.

Elizabeth and Anna Jane took some of the children with them to their own cabins in Kanarraville that night. Elizabeth was not sure exactly who they were. One of them was Aggatha's Ezra Taft. And she believed the other boy to be Polly's James Young. But there were two little girls she was not sure of. The children huddled by both hearths to keep warm. And she and Anna Jane fed them gruel.

For several days J.B., Jacob, and the other men worked as best they could in the falling snow. Some days at noon the ice melted into rain. There were only a few intervals with no rain at all. Finally, on January 31, the clouds drew away from the sun for the first time in 28 days. But just for three hours. By noon the sky was overcast again, and by 1:00 p.m. the sky was a fury of circling flakes. And that evening the front wall of the three-family Lorry home began to slip forward. In only a few hours it became an avalanche of mud and lay in ruins as far as the gate. In the next two days, with the snow piling up around the adobe in drifts several inches deep, the devastation appeared ghostlike—resembling the remains of a huge ship, a shrouded, crumbled hull.

J.B. had come to the cabin covered with snow. "It's gone," he said in tight words between his teeth. "It's gone."

Elizabeth had been startled to hear him come in.

"I have two other families who need me," he said vacantly about the two wives who probably couldn't care less, "So I'm going to Salt Lake City."

Elizabeth was silent, but then whispered, "In this storm?"

"In this storm!" he yelled as she had supposed he would. She tightened her mouth against any more words. By morning he had gone.

Because Anna Jane was feeling ill, Elizabeth went with Jacob to take hot food to the Lees, to help move the furniture, and take care of the children. They found Tabby and Caroline and several children huddled together in the lower floor of the only building still standing in the fort while Caroline continued to labor at the weaving on her loom. All that hung over their heads was the floor of the second story, which now lay open to the snow—a floor strong enough to keep the snow and water from coming through. The roof had long since been destroyed. By now Lee had moved all of his families up the hill except these two women, along with their families—the two older boys and three children: George Albert, six, Margaret Anne, five, and the baby Sarah Ann. Caroline, who sat freezing under the leaning floor with the children, kept assuring them that it would not be long now until her cloth was completed. Elizabeth could see the worry in John Lee's eyes.

"Tomorrow," Caroline said. "We'll go up the hill tomorrow."

Lee filled the fireplace once more with wood before taking Elizabeth and Jacob back with him into the town. Quietly they climbed up on the hack beside him.

"They're not safe there," he said, looking straight ahead.

Elizabeth looked at Jacob. He nodded as though he were not listening.

"Do you need us again tomorrow?" Elizabeth asked. "If Anna Jane can't come, I'll come. She's . . . I think . . ." Elizabeth hesitated, not risking explicit words.

Lee's eyes met hers. Then he smiled.

Jacob was grinning from ear to ear. "It's true," he said.

"And you too?" Lee said to Elizabeth, smiling still. How could he know that she was in a similar condition? "I told you the Lord was blessing us."

Jacob said nothing, but Elizabeth could not help but feel the warmth from Lee's eyes.

"The Lord has been good to us. People of our faith are moving in. We're blessed with children." He paused now. "Do you want to know a secret, you two?" He paused. "Maybe not such a secret, but something that ought to be shouted to the hills. This summer marks the fifteenth year we've been in this valley." His eyes were alive with light. He gestured broadly. "There is a civil war over slavery raging out there. But here? Peace here. Johnston's army is gone. We may be harassed about our polygamy. But no army has come down. No army has come from the west coast. Those that wanted us to disappear from the face of the earth," again he nodded to the east, "they are gone from our lives."

### 73
#### Elizabeth

Elizabeth wasn't there at the Lee house when the floor of the second story caved in. She could only imagine how it must have been from what Caroline and Tabby told her. When the adobe began to crumble about them, it sounded like an avalanche of rocks and sand shifting with the wind.

At first Tabby said she thought it was the ghost of her husband Solomon Hanncock coming back to destroy her. She saw his eyes in the first onslaught of the rain, his large face bleak with his scornful gaze. She saw his smile when the roof of the house fell in on the upstairs bedroom floor and thought she heard his "I told you so."

Four times Caroline emptied the pans which caught the leaks through the upstairs floor. She had been so determined to finish the cloth on the loom that she stayed with it night and day. As the fire had died away, Tabby turned over the coals and pushed some large chunks of hot wood into the foot warmers. She took the warmers into the bedroom and tucked them in with Margaret Ann and George Albert before Caroline kissed them good night.

Only a half an hour later Caroline and the older boys, still beside the fire, heard the rumble above them in the upper rooms. Without stopping to take down the loom, Caroline bolted toward the doorway. In that unsettling moment she truly believed the bedroom under the corner of the heavy ceiling should be safe. Tabby followed her, though she quickly stepped back into the room to drag Harvey by the arm. Harvey and Robert, not wasting time, ducked swiftly out of the door.

For a terrible moment Tabby stood at the door of the old adobe house that was melting before her eyes. Terrified, she believed she could see Solomon Hanncock's eyes in the walls. And at that moment, the walls that were left began to give way. The second story wooden floor, which had been serving as a roof to the room below, suddenly cracked and broke with a staggering din. Any of the walls that still stood above the lower bedroom crashed through the wooden floor into the lower room. The sound was deafening. The roar hurt Tabby's ears and she put her hands to them. But her eyes would not close on the scene. The safe bedroom! No! Margaret and George had been sleeping in the hollow below the debris!

Tabby screamed. Holding the baby Sarah Ann tight against her throat, she reared back into the rooms.

"Oh! The children!" Caroline was crying. But there was no sound from the children. Not even a scream. Harvey Parley and Robert began to run up the hill. The flames in the old stone fireplace flickered and faded away. The dust, still hanging for a moment in the darkness, fell with the rain. Soon all that either woman could hear were the boys' sobbing voices as they bolted up to the sheds. For a moment they stood numb at the door.

*The children. The children.*

Soon the others came: Lavina and Polly and Mary Leah. They came down from the shed high on the hill into the dark ruin, holding oil lamps high in their hands. Caroline was standing at the site like a ghost. Her face was white. There were still no tears. The others lifted the light of their lamps over the rubble quickly, with terrible haste. But there was no movement. And no sound. It took hours of scrambling. Finally, all they could bring from the rubble were the two limp bodies of the children, lacerated, broken, and gray. Sobbing, all of the women ran to them. Caroline held them in her arms, pawing and screaming to heave the life back into them.

It was still raining in the morning when Elizabeth went up to the grave-yard with Jacob and Anna Jane. They took the children with them in the cart, Joshua and Belinda crying from the cold. The rain still fell in sheets and glistened in the flooded fields.

A quiet circle of the wives and children stood in the dark yard of the gray morning. Elizabeth held to Hannah and Joshua as though she would never let go. And she put a hand on the child growing inside of her. *These children are the most precious of all our earthly stewardships*, she thought. She could hear the tap tap tap of John Lee's hammer on the hastily assembled wet pine boxes. She could hear Caroline's sobs. The woman sat holding the dead children like rag dolls in her arms. John Lee took the boy from her and lifted him into the box. She shook with the weight of her groans, clinging to Margaret's small body with a fierce cry.

"Caroline," Lee said softly, standing above her.

"Oh God, did you have to take them? These are mine."

Elizabeth and Anna Jane and the children got down out of the cart and walked over to the group standing in the yard. For a moment there was no rain.

John Lee bent over his sobbing wife and lifted the lifeless little girl from her arms. They had dressed her in a clean white pinafore. And on her feet were tiny leather shoes.

*The shoes.* Elizabeth did not question the shoes. She caught her breath, and then her own tears began to fall.

*They are not ours. They are the Lord's. The Lord giveth and the Lord taketh away. Blessed be the name of the Lord.*

*Come, come ye saints. No toil nor labor fear. But with joy.*

They sang, *And should we die*, while Caroline sobbed in Tabby's arms.

*Oh, dear Father in Heaven. We dedicate this site into thy hand until the time of the resurrection of souls. If it be thy will, thy servant Caroline shall again behold the faces of George Albert and Margaret Ann Lee.*

John Lee had just been appointed to a priesthood leadership capacity. And one of his first official duties was the burial of his children.

Elizabeth listened to his words and continued to hear his voice long afterward. "Let us rest in the peace of the knowledge of the gospel, our dear God. For thou hast made this place the place of our kingdom—a holy place. A place to live and find our lives untroubled by the threat of hatred. And let us be untroubled by thy rebuke. We ask of thee to draw the anger out of thy breath."

Elizabeth tightened her grip on Joshua and Hannah's small hands. Then suddenly, she felt Jacob's arm around her shoulders. He pulled her close to him until she felt his strength.

*And yet, thy will be done.* Now there was a break in Lee's voice and the tears in his throat crowded out the words. The hushed sobs of the women in that clouded moment sounded faint beneath the hum of the soft rain.

When the prayer ended, a few of the men lowered the boxes into the black ground and Elizabeth closed her eyes. She turned into Jacob's shoulder and rested her forehead against him as she heard the dark clay from the shovels hit the boxes with a crack, a crack, and a bitter thud.

As the crowd dispersed, the sky drew down again. And with darkness and with fury, again it began to rain.

## 74
### *Jacob*

As Jacob watched the Lorry's new house slip into mud in those last days, as he heard the sound of the crumbling adobe, the cracking floors, the wrack of the joists, the groans, he heard in the sound the rending of his own dreams, the fury of retribution.

Why had he once so much wanted to go to war? Had it really been because of Percy? Or was it because of his own idea of manhood? It wasn't Percy's fault. So long ago. Perhaps it was no one's fault. He saw in his mind's eye the body of the blacksmith in the orchard under the dark moon. He saw the face of the man in the Fancher train. He had pulled the trigger of the gun with his fingers. He had allowed the gun powder to explode. The terrible blast had cut the man's cheek. And after the unspeakable day at the meadows, he had told J.B. Maggie's dreadful secret which she had finally breathed to him: that she had conceived that first baby not with a Missouri soldier, but with Wesley Hanncock, who had come south with his mother Tabby and his father Solomon to escape from the rumor of his son's illicit love. And when J.B. had threatened to tell the story of Wesley Hanncock, the father of Maggie's first child, Wesley had promised J.B. he would erase J.B.'s name from the list, as well as the name of Jacob Lorry. He had fulfilled his promise.

And now, all of the sins of the Hanncocks were virtually forgotten. It was John Lee who was remembered. Some said that the storm was evidence that God had not forgotten their sins.

Jacob thought it might be true. These had been powerful, more-than-ordinary torrents. And yet he was almost too numb through those last days of the furious snow to comprehend the meaning of that dictum. The others seemed to throw it about as though it were the true natural consequence of all that had befallen them, and it had served as the baptism of pain that would wash their valley clean.

When the ordeal of winter was over, Jacob reviewed it as he moved their furniture into the old shed at the back of the original house. He had removed the furniture of J.B.'s two families, and he remembered moving his father-in-law's children to the hill, carrying babies on his back. Through all of his motions—the coming and going—he felt a jaded shock at the realization that the terror of the floods had truly seemed a judgment. If it was a judgment, it had also been meted to him. For he, too, had participated in the deed.

Finally, after the rains, some of those in the valley walked away. They moved to other locations, away from the destruction, from the reminders, from the scars. They did not whisper anyone's names. Though Wesley Hanncock was still in the valley, and had known many of the more than two dozen names on the dreaded list, he was slow to mention them now. And most of them were gone. Gone were President Haight, John Higbee, Philip Klingensmith, Colonel Dame. Most of them had gone south into Pocketville, Arizona, changing their names.

As though the valley had indeed been washed clean, hundreds of other families began to move in. They lumbered along the drying roads in large wagon trains, some with handcarts, some with coaches. Some were on horseback. Some had only one change of clothing to their names. They were looking for something, Jacob was not certain what. Some said they were looking for warmer weather than the northern mountains offered them. They were looking for more land, saying that the best land around Salt Lake City had been taken. They were also looking for freedom from persecution. Some of those who had wanted the railroads to come in were angry with Brigham Young because he had been trying to stop the coming railroads.

The settlers and immigrants were searching for many different things. But in a strange, dark, almost lonely way, Jacob sensed they were also searching for the true answer to an unreal rumor that by now had been whispered all over the countryside. At least some of them came because they had wanted to find out if what they heard about the Mountain Meadows was true.

Though J.B. had gone to Salt Lake City, he stayed for only a short time. He stayed long enough to lose his job with the Cedar City lumber business, and also let his portion of the adobe business slip through his fingers. He cursed Lee loudly for leading him into the adobe business in the first place, which had created nothing but devastation when the adobe homes slid downstream. He stayed long enough to visit his disaffected wives and to search for Maggie, though he did not find her. He stayed long enough to become more disillusioned, perhaps less alive, less sensible. In some ways, less free.

While J.B. was gone, Jacob held the family together against the dark whispers of the newcomers as they probed the corners of the valley to find the truth. All of the other stories the newcomers could have whispered seemed to die. They could have whispered about the Lee children's death in the storm, Suky's killing, the Lorry fire. But for some strange reason, only the story of the massacre at Mountain Meadows had, like a strange dark breeze, grown into a whirlwind, and continued to blow. And lately it had begun to enlarge in frightening proportions, becoming embellished with every repetition. The children were learning lively songs composed in closed circles and passed by word of mouth like black incantations. Or prayers.

> *This life will soon be over and another coming on*
> *And the perpetrators of the deed must suffer for the wrong.*
> *'Tis true they do deny it, and the crime they will disclaim*
> *To get out of it the best they can, the Indians bear the blame.*
>
> *By order of Old Brigham Young this deed was done, you see,*
> *And the captain of that wicked band was Captain John D. Lee.*

"Where did you learn that?" Jacob asked Hannah, who was saying some of the lines softly to herself over and over again. He knelt to the child and took her by the arm.

"Those big boys at school. Henry Reiter. Peter. It's about Grandpa Lee."

Jacob looked for a long time into the little girl's face, trying to find out how much she knew. "Don't ever sing that song again, Hannah."

"How come?"

His heart beat swiftly. "It's about murder. Not for a young lady to sing."

Ever since the children had been taken back to Arkansas, no soldiers had come. No army had forced their way into the area. But there were new faces—hundreds of new settlers. And the new faces continued to look at the old faces with strangely questioning eyes. Like a cancer in dark places, a poison began to fester, a poison heavy with dark rumors about John D. Lee.

It was true that the songs and stories had begun to bother them all, but especially J.B. When he returned from Salt Lake City, he was an angrier man, more easily out-of-sorts. He had not found Maggie, he said. And he began to talk more openly about the rumors than anyone would have believed of him—to the point of embarrassing his family in front of their new neighbors.

By 1866 the Lorry family had grown right along with everything else in the valley. Elizabeth now had Hannah and two boys of her own, Joshua and Caleb. Anna Jane was ready to have her third. Jacob had been offered work in Washington building Lee's flour mill, but because he wished to stay near Elizabeth, he did not accept. He took a position at Humphreys' store, where J.B. came often to see him and greet visitors or new residents when they arrived in town. Jacob began to fear the way J.B. met them. He was hearty with them, introducing himself and calling them by name. But he seemed to have an obsession about asking any traveler what he knew about the area.

"All I heard about this place was it's the home of John Lee, who led the Indians in the Massacre and killed a whole wagon train of men, women, and children."

J.B. would stand straight up at these words and glare from under his dark brows. "This here is good farmin' country," he would begin. "We recovered good from the 1862 rains. The land is fertile. But we had our troubles in this area. It may be true about John Lee. But he lives in Washington a lot now. We don't want any more troubles. We're peace loving."

Jacob heard his father's words several times as he stocked shelves or added up purchases. Sometimes, as he stood in a circle with the newcomers, welcoming them, he was embarrassed by his father's words.

Since the failure of the lumber business, followed by the failure of the adobe business, J.B. had become irritable and angry. For one thing, he had not been happy to see someone else start up both kinds of businesses in the wake of his failures and become successful. Trying to ignore his defeat, he took up farming again. But he grew as rough as a straw scarecrow. His hair grew unkempt, and he often had a very scraggly unshaven appearance. He had become more nervous as the years passed by—as more newcomers arrived and heard the stories of the massacre. For no reason at all, he began to blame the Lorrys' ill fortune on Maggie's disappearance. He complained about not having heard from her since she had left them, and after all, Robert was his son. He murmured constantly, soon taking it upon himself to warn newcomers to keep their noses out of everybody's business.

"If you talk like that, they'll think you are guilty right along with Lee," Jacob said to him.

"Oh, bosh!" J.B. dismissed Jacob's words. But the next time Jacob heard his father, J.B. had changed his story just a little, bending it to cast a further aspersion upon Lee.

"Lee gets plenty angry with those that bring it up to him," he said.

Jacob mentioned to J.B. that it wasn't good to say this, either. It made Jacob's father-in-law, John Lee, out to look like an ogre.

Finally, J.B. had another story he told. Because Anna Jane's mother Aggatha Lee had died, J.B. added even another twist. "I wouldn't trouble him none, what with his first wife dead."

Jacob took J.B. aside one day and angrily controlled himself from saying harsh words. "You're implicating John Lee. Father Lee has had enough pain. He's suffered enough without you adding to it. Don't make excuses for him. He's staying away in Washington now. Just don't even mention his name."

J.B. had pulled away from Jacob's hand on his arm, looking Jacob steadily in the eyes. His voice was low and straight, as though he were spitting the words between his teeth. "I'm saving your skin too, boy."

Jacob's heart sank at his father's words. Sometimes he thought he could hate J.B. "I'd . . ." he hesitated, "I'd like you to keep John Lee out of it . . . because John Lee is gentleman enough to keep his mouth closed about who went with him into the meadows. He has a sense of family. He's a man of pride." And Jacob was not finished. "And he's the grandfather of my children."

J.B.'s eyes looked opaque, as though he were looking past Jacob seeing ghosts in the air. Perhaps he was seeing apparitions weaving webs of pain. Perhaps there was no way out.

"There isn't anything you can say that won't implicate you or him. So please, say nothing at all."

J.B. thought about this for a moment. For several weeks he did not return to work at the store. Finally, he decided to return to Salt Lake City for a time. But his share in the damage had been done.

## 75
### *Jacob*

The early damage was like a slow rot. About the same time that Lee's first wife Aggatha died, the other children began calling the Lee children names. Perhaps, without their mother, Aggatha's children seemed more vulnerable.

A new family, the Lawsons, who had purchased property adjoining Emma Lee's in Harmony, let their cattle into the Lees' grounds. Though Emma tried on several occasions to shoo them off the premises, they kept coming. None of the other neighbors rallied with the Lees to reprimand the infringement or support a fine. The Hicks, who were also new neighbors, accused Lee of taking too much water for his land, and then they began interfering with Lee's ditches. The Lawsons also disagreed with one of the Lees' fence lines. Though John Lee came up from Washington from time to time to stand firm against these infringements, as soon as he was gone, they happened again.

Shortly after several of these incidents with the neighbors, Apostle Snow came down from Salt Lake City and re-organized the ward. He released John Lee from his church position and appointed Brother Imlay as bishop. There was no particular reason for the new appointments, everyone was assured. It had just been time for some changes.

When J.B. returned, Jacob watched his father's reaction warily. J.B. seemed to eye Lee's fading reputation with the stance of a panther waiting to strike. J.B. had seen Lee's estate increase while his own had suffered. He had become an angry impoverished man while Lee had become wealthy. Although J.B. had rebuilt his house with brick, it was smaller than anything Lee had built. He began to criticize Lee for becoming "stiff-necked."

"You'd think he wouldn't mind letting Lawson's cattle into his fields. He's got more land than he needs." And he added, "He ought to share some of that land with me."

But it was Lee's land. And his water. And Lee and his wives and children held to it.

Most of the winter of 1867-68, it was the wives and children alone who defended it. All during the last months of 1867, Lee was in Salt Lake City helping to launch his boys Joseph and Willard on their missions to England. And after spending a short Christmas in New Harmony, he spent some months catching up on some things in Washington County.

While Lee was gone, his son John Frederick fought off the Lawson boy twice for diverting the water out of the Lee ditches. Finally, Emma Lee received a terrible letter with the return address of "Fort Douglas." A message from the U.S. Government! Jacob first saw the letter on an April afternoon when Anna Jane brought it into the store. She had been crying. Jacob tried to comfort her, but she would not be comforted.

"Emma got this in the mail, Jacob. What can we do?"

The letter was vile, poorly written, filled with hateful epithets that no sane government agent or neighbor would have sent. It accused John Lee and his family of the most heinous of crimes and ugly scandalous behaviors.

"The accusations are not true," Jacob said between his teeth. "It's probably from the Lawsons or the Hicks or the Dodds."

Later it was found that the letter was indeed from the neighboring Hicks family, and when the bishop investigated, and the affair blew over, there was a suggestion that the Hicks be rebaptized, though they felt they hadn't done anything wrong.

Now the feelings against the Lees blew even hotter. Only a few weeks later at the big church dance, one of the Dodds brothers left fifteen-year-old Ellen Lee in the middle of the dance floor when he found out who her father was. When the oldest Lee son, John Frederick, saw the incident, he approached the Dodds boy with eyes flashing. The neighbors stood alert while Ellen flew off the floor in tears.

"What do you think you're doin' with my sister? Don't you have any manners?" John Frederick cried.

"I ain't dancin' with somebody whose father's a murderer," the boy spit out.

John Frederick clenched his fists, watching the brethren out of the corner of his eye. "You could at least show her to a seat."

"I don't spend any manners on a Lee."

At these words John Frederick could not control his hands. He lashed out and hit the big Dodds boy in the face. In return, the fellow ripped into John Frederick's head and slashed his jaw.

The girls screamed until some of the men entered to stop the fighting. There was a lot of tussling until it all got under control. When things finally grew quiet, almost everyone left the dance to go home.

Jacob watched the seventeen-year-old John Frederick tremble when he was called into bishop's court. While Jacob prayed at home for the Lee boy, J.B. sat on the council. He came home mumbling, "Those poison Lees. They're like the last of the poison in this place. A bunch of hot heads doin' nothin' but causin' trouble," J.B. said. "They need to quit it or get out." At J.B.'s words, Jacob looked at Elizabeth with despair.

Elizabeth did not argue about anything with J.B. She heard rumors that the Lees had thought about following their father to Washington permanently, but no one talked about it. She shrugged, lifting a finger to her lips when Anna Jane came back into the room. There was silence then. Silence and nothing more.

There was another bishop's court that autumn. This time Jacob heard that even though Lee was in town at the present time, Lawson and his son-in-law

Dodds began cutting down the trees and willows on the other side of the creek that ran through Emma Lee's back yard. Though Lee was not on the premises, Emma was in the house washing up the breakfast dishes when they started, and she couldn't believe her eyes. Lee's youngest, and last wife Lisanne, was with her.

"Lisanne, look! What in the world do they think they're doing!" Emma ran out the back door with the towel in her hands.

"They're cutting down our shade!"

"This isn't their land. Why . . . what . . . they couldn't possibly . . ." Emma was out in the yard in a flash, Lisanne following her.

"Brother Lawson," Emma called, stumbling toward him. "Please, what are you doing? We need those shade trees for our ducks and geese!"

"The roots is slowin' up the water, ma'am . . ."

"You're on our property! Please! Stop it this minute."

Lisanne stood staring, incredulous. But the men didn't stop. They kept right on hacking. It was then that Emma sent Lisanne to fetch John Lee, who happened to be in the store with Jacob.

Jacob had seen Lisanne many times, but never with such a blank white stare. She stood at the door, her hands against the jamb while she leaned forward. "Please come, John. They have axes. And bring Brother Lorry, too."

John Lee took his toothpick out of his mouth. It was always the neighbors, always the Lawsons, he said. Jacob watched him shake his shaggy blond head with a sad, slow motion that looked like defeat.

As the men followed Lisanne on her horse to New Harmony, Jacob could feel the pistol at his leg. He put his hands on it, praying he would not have to use it. He rode with John Lee hard toward New Harmony. In the half hour it took them to reach the Lee property, three of the willows had already been chopped down. Lisanne greeted them at the door in tears, tears that fed Jacob's rage. He would rather have seen his own trees cut down. Why couldn't they have cut down the Lorry trees instead?

"I can't believe this outrage," Jacob heard Lee say. "Will you please, both of you, take yourselves off my property or I'll gather up the posse."

But the words seemed vain. All of them knew that the posse hadn't come to defend the Lees for some time, now.

Lawson continued to chop at a small willow tree.

"All our shade!" Emma was sobbing. Lisanne put her arm around Emma's shoulders.

"You can't order us off this creek. It's common territory," Lawson leaned on the axe, planted his feet with his legs apart, and sneered.

"Oh, no it isn't!" Lee stood up tall, all the strength in him bristling with the fire of his anger. "Get out of here." He said it between his teeth.

"Make us," Lawson scoffed. "You gonna murder us? Like you murdered them Arkansas people?"

John Lee stepped forward, but Jacob held him back by his arm.

"We ought to settle this peacefully, gentlemen." Jacob walked forward. His size reinforced his words. He had grown not only tall, but strong. "Just let me have the ax and you can go home." He extended his hand.

Lawson glared at Jacob. Jacob steadied his eyes, though his heart was pounding. The other man, Dodds, seemed cowed.

"Just who do you think you are?" Lawson finally said, his voice low. He was not sure but what Jacob would tell him.

"I'm a peace-loving citizen," Jacob said, thinking to himself as he said it that neither of these two men really cared. But their reaction surprised him.

"All right. Seems like you'll do anything for your old father-in-law, John Lee, here." Lawson threw his axe on the ground. Dodds followed him. Cautiously, Lee walked forward to pick up the axe.

Jacob nodded to Lawson and Dodds. "Thank you, gentlemen." Neither of the men said anything else when they turned away.

But that was not the end of it. Emma later described to Jacob how the very next morning Lawson brought four other men to help him cut down the rest of the trees. She was furious. With four men the trees would be down in no time at all. There was no time to get help.

Thinking fast, Lisanne had the first idea. "Boil that wash water and I'll carry it down there and toss it at them," she told Emma. She carried it down to the creek and asked Lawson to stop cutting down the trees. He didn't even acknowledge that she was there. So she threw the water. But she was so far away, that not a drop reached them. Lawson threw his head back and laughed.

Furious, Lisanne bounded toward the house for more water. This time both she and Emma came out into the yard carrying hot pans. Having already set the culprits at ease by missing, the women were now both able to walk closer to the men. Lawson stopped and pointed his axe at them. "You women stand back." His voice was low, a deep growl.

Emma threw her water in his face. Though he held his arms up against the water, it scalded him, all right. He yelped. And as he was distracted, Emma grabbed his axe. Both men, as they backed away from the water, stumbled and fell to the ground. Lisanne jumped on top of one of them, also going for his axe, which in the tussle grazed Lawson's cheek. The blood flowed across his face. He screamed.

Lee had been in the fields not far away. By this time one of the children had reached him. Jacob had come too, from Kanarraville, and later Anna Jane.

Lee had written in his journal:

*When I with several others reached the scene of action, found them both on the ground & Lisanne with one hand in his hair & with the other pounding him in the face. In the mean time Emma returned with a New Supply of hot water & then pitched into him with Lisanne & they bothe handled him rather Ruff. His face was a gore of Blood.*

Jacob raised the man to his feet and sent him on. The bishop's court in Kanarraville rendered a decision in favor of the Lees. They fined the Lawsons for the costs of the court and a twenty-five dollar fine for trespassing and deliberately stirring up trouble.

After the court decision, J.B. maintained a furtive silence. "Maybe the Lawsons are jealous. Nobody ought to tangle with them Lees."

Jacob watched Elizabeth, and saw her reaction to J.B.'s words. Her eyes closed. She seemed to be praying. "Please, let this be the end of it. For a while," she murmured. Hannah, holding Elizabeth's third and latest baby, little Joseph, looked at her mother. "What?" she asked.

Elizabeth had not realized she'd spoken the words out loud. "I said, let this be the end of all the troubles for Grandpa Lee," she said softly.

Hannah, now eleven years old, was in the bloom of young womanhood. She had been blessed with cheeks the color of peaches, and bouncing dark curls that framed her face. She smiled. "I also pray they'll leave Grandpa alone," she said in a soft voice. "I love him too, Mama."

Jacob saw a mist in the child's dark eyes. He understood what Elizabeth understood. He felt his own yearning for peace when he saw Elizabeth reach for Hannah and hold both her and the small child tightly in her arms.

## 76
### *September 11, 1870, Elizabeth*
*I cannot remember when we were not afraid.*

Elizabeth wrote in a blank notebook during the evening while Hannah, now fourteen, often sat in the rocker singing four year old Joseph to sleep. Tonight he was hot with fever from the measles. Hannah leaned her cheek against his burning brow. The lace curtain at the window let in a web of light that danced in her dark hair. The same light played over Joseph's face, casting hollow shadows over his eyes.

*Joseph lies ill with the measles. And I am afraid for him. Now J.B. sends more news from his eight-month stay in Salt Lake City—terrible news that there are rumors of murders and assassinations in which the gentiles and some members of the Church accuse— of all people—Brigham Young.*

Elizabeth knew all of the reasons for the accusations. The townspeople had rehearsed the problems time and time again.

*Brigham Young is only trying to keep out the railroad so the world will not come in. What should happen to the peace of our kingdom if all of the evils of the world come in? The very world we tried to escape is sitting on our doorstep. Why don't the business people, the railroad people, the financiers, understand? Why do they hate Brigham Young?*

Hannah began singing to Joseph. The boy listlessly moved his head on her arm, then moved it back again. "Sleep, my little one. Sleep my little one, sleep."

In a few moments Hannah turned to Elizabeth, her dark eyes wide with fear. "He won't, Mother. He just won't fall off to sleep."

Elizabeth put down her pen and came to the window. The street in Kanarraville was crowded with houses now. But beyond the roofs and through the fenced yards of the small homes across the street she could see the fields that stretched to New Harmony. The Jensens, Fort Hamilton, Penter, and the meadows beyond. "You've done much, my darling Hannah," she said. "Go to bed now. I'll take him. Give him . . . to me."

Joseph fussed when Elizabeth took him from Hannah. But he grew quiet in his mother's arms. He was still her youngest—Joseph, four years old. She held her cheek against his hot forehead under the wet hair. The two older boys had long since been tucked away: Joshua and Caleb, as alike as twins, as much boy as boys could be. It was only today that the two of them had brought a baby rattlesnake in a bottle into the kitchen.

"He was trying to bite my fingernail."

Elizabeth sank, breathlessly, to a chair. "It's a rattler, Joshua! It could have killed you!"

The thirteen-year-old boy's eyes had been bright with questions. Eight-year-old Caleb had beamed with delight. "I told him. I told him not to let it bite."

When Hannah had gone, Elizabeth sank into the rocker with Joseph and held the boy close to her breast. The boy's heart beat as though it were a tiny fish struggling upstream.

"Oh God," she thought, "spare my children." It seemed to her that her children were all she had to defend herself against the odds of life. And then she had heard a soft step come behind her into the room. It was Jacob. He came so softly, she could only feel his presence, like light.

"Did Anna Jane tell you what has happened to her father?" he asked.

No. She had not talked to Anna Jane, though she knew Anna Jane had been excited about going to see her father, who had just come home to Harmony. Not many were aware that he had returned from his long stay in Washington. Now Jacob had news from New Harmony. He leaned forward in his chair, his heavy light brown hair shaggy on his head. "Now listen while I tell you . . . listen carefully. Please help me."

Sensing the seriousness of his words, she did not breathe a sound.

"First, you have known for years that President Brigham doesn't really say much to Father Lee." He paused. "Even when he saw him in Washington, he made his visit brief. In February when he was here for a visit, all he talked about was . . . our safety here . . ."

She felt Jacob's face close to hers now. She could feel his breath against her cheek. She nodded, feeling her heart pounding with anticipation. For she knew—without hearing the ends of his sentences—she felt she knew what he was going to say now, and she could hear the blood beating in her brain.

"Did you know that there were two times that Brigham asked him to move?"

Elizabeth had only guessed that when the whole Church seemed under fire for their part in the massacre, Brigham would want to protect Lee. And he would surely warn Lee to run for his life.

"And you know how happy Father Lee was when President Young asked him to go with him a few weeks ago to explore the area east of Kanab for an approach to the Colorado River?"

These words were like Greek to Elizabeth's impatient ears. But she never liked to hurry Jacob, whose voice was always steady, calm. He spoke without trembling, without moving away from her. But now he lowered his eyes.

She looked down into Joseph's pale cheeks. The little boy was sleeping now. She gently rocked him in the chair.

"Well, perhaps President Brigham invented it all himself, or at least staged the whole thing. For you know how much anger there is from gentiles who are against him in Salt Lake City. Especially concerning John D. Lee."

Elizabeth's heart continued to race, to skip beats. Jacob gently touched the feverish boy who lay prostrate in her arms.

"Well, Brother Brigham must still have a lot of concern for Father Lee."

What concern? Elizabeth needed to know. She was growing impatient. Although she could guess, she needed Jacob to tell her with words—with more than just the hesitation in his eyes.

"Brigham has charged Lee to set up a mill for Levi Stewart in Skatumpah. Lee's to sell out here."

There it was. She knew it. She would have to deal with it. Skatumpah. A place miles east of Washington, deep in the hills, a drop off the face of the earth. There were other times in her life that she had dealt with difficult moments. She had thought of it often: that someday the Lees should have to go. But now it was here. And to Skatumpah. She felt Jacob's strength. Her hands trembled. With the boy still between them in her lap, she reached up and clasped Jacob's hands.

But Jacob was not finished talking.

"And I . . . I have been in Washington with Lee. I feel Anna Jane and I also must go."

The words hit her like rocks. She tried to breathe. She had come to rely on Jacob, to cherish both him and Anna Jane.

"He said he would never ask anybody to go with him as far as Skatumpah—that to go with him would always put us at risk. But perhaps somewhere not too far from them. Perhaps Kanab. At least away from here. I'm sure you can understand."

Suddenly Elizabeth felt the collective memories of this valley spin in her mind and stab at her. She was almost thirty years old—she had lived here for half her life. But there was no question in her heart about what she must do. When she looked through the room, all she could see was Jacob, in a vague hazy light that filled her mind.

"And you . . . and J.B . . . ." Jacob said hesitantly. He had always been her friend, always a gentleman. "J.B. may not want to come. You may do what you wish. But I wish you would also come." He had always loved her.

## 77
### Hannah's Writings, Elizabeth

*What you believe must make a difference in your own life. Even if your beliefs are yours alone and shape only what you alone may do. What you believe makes a difference in the way you say hello.*

One of Hannah's school papers lay open on her bed, so Elizabeth dared to read it. Beyond the multiplication of words, she thought she sensed a depth in the ideas.

*If you believe God loves you and approves of what you do and say you can smile and be friendly to everyone. But if there are secrets in your life and they are dark secrets that you want no one to see by looking into your eyes, you may not say anything at all.*

Elizabeth tucked the paper in Hannah's book, *King Arthur and the Legends of the Round Table.* It was something she herself had read many times when she helped the children with their reading in the school. When she opened the book and leafed through some of the pages, she found a red flower pressed in a worn spot, in *The Book of Sir Launcelot and Queen Guinevere.* She closed the book, feeling guilty for trespassing on Hannah's life. For Hannah was now almost grown. And she suspected that Hannah had a secret now—that she was sweet on John Lee's son, John Frederick Lee.

*What you believe must make a difference in your own life.* And she lives with you and believes with you, and becomes you, Elizabeth whispered softly to herself, watching Hannah on her way home from school. The girl was swinging up the slope in her blue jersey shift, the white ruffled blouse beneath it still crisp and clean. How Hannah had always kept so clean had been a puzzle to Elizabeth. Particularly after she had seen what could happen to the boys. They were following behind Hannah, but she could see them tramping through the ditch about a half a mile away.

When Hannah reached the yard, Elizabeth went downstairs into the kitchen to take out the hot rolls. There was not only her own packing to do, and the packing of the children, but she and Anna Jane had been supplying the busy Lees—who were forced to sell out at a loss—with meals and breads. And Hannah had been taking the meals in the cart to them. She had asked all of the probing questions. Why were the Lees leaving? Could they get money for their farm? If they were also going, would the Lorrys live close to the Lees? She particularly wanted to know the answer to that question, and Elizabeth knew why. The flowering heart would not have wanted distance to crush the bloom. But she could not say, "Close enough," because she didn't know.

"Hello, Mother. Are you ready with the food?"

Elizabeth watched the girl come into the room. She was beautiful now, her oval face framed by the dark auburn curls.

Long ago she had asked other probing questions, especially when some of the children at school had whispered secretly to her that her real mother was Maggie. "And if Aunt Maggie is my real mother, then why didn't she stay?"

"She may not be your real mother. Your real mother may be someone who died long ago," Elizabeth had finally told her, holding both of her hands. "But the children who say bad things . . . those children . . ." She looked up as though pleading. "Those children will never know about your mother's death. It's something no one wants to talk about, Hannah. And you must learn to be silent about it too. Please, honey. Please don't pay attention to anything the children say."

Fortunately, the children hadn't whispered very much to Hannah after that. Now Hannah was fourteen. There were times in her days, weeks, and months of living that she had grown impatient to know. At twelve she had confronted Elizabeth again.

"Is it true that John Lee killed my real mother?"

Startled, Elizabeth had slipped a stitch in her sewing and the needle had pricked her hand. "That's not true!" She led Hannah into the sunny parlor of their new brick home.

Sitting down, Elizabeth asked, "Who told you that?"

"George Lawson." There was anger in her eyes. "I think he's telling lies about John Frederick. About all of the Lees."

"Well, it's not true," Elizabeth said again. But her heart was beating hard against her ribs.

"Well, they're telling me Father Lee killed someone."

That was when Elizabeth told Hannah the story as it really happened, and not as she had heard it from the boys at school. "There was an Indian massacre." Yes, she knew. Everyone knew that. But that was no longer how it was told. "The Indians are our friends. And some of the white men were there." Yes, that is what had been told over and over again. "It is sad . . ." Elizabeth stopped. "It is always sad when there is contention, one person fighting against another. Because there are sides. Instead of helping the white people camped in the meadows, our men helped the Indians so the Indians would not turn on us. They helped the Indians to prevent an Indian war."

"And so Papa J.B. and Uncle Jacob, both . . ."

"They were there," Elizabeth whispered, holding both of Hannah's hands. "But we should not speak of it aloud to them. Or speak of it much at all. Ever again. They felt sad, too, that they participated in the war."

Hannah's eyes had been fastened to Elizabeth's every word. At times when she had watched Elizabeth's mouth, Elizabeth could see the flicker of her eyes dance with questions.

"Why did George Lawson say my mother was killed by John Lee?"

"Because he hates John Lee," Elizabeth said softly. "But Grandpa Lee is a wonderful man and would never have done what he did if he did not believe it was necessary to save our lives."

Yes, that is how Hannah thought of him. "Was my real mother killed in the massacre?"

Now Elizabeth could not open her mouth. She held Hannah tightly in her arms. Then she pushed her slightly away and met her dark gaze with a firm look.

"You were brought here to this home by Maggie, who finally married J.B. some time later. She also had a baby son, Robert. Then she left again and took him. Some don't believe you were Maggie's baby. And you know something?" Elizabeth held tight to Hannah's arms. She was not yet ready to tell the girl all she felt or knew. "I don't think even Maggie knew everything." Now she paused, feeling light-headed, feeling her heart spinning and turning as though all of the blood in her body were alive with a life of its own. "It doesn't really matter at all. You are ours. We love you so much, Hannah." And she held the girl to her for a long time. She whispered, "Please don't let it make any difference at all."

## 78
### Hannah

*Sometimes you have little secrets. Sometimes you have very large secrets. A little secret is that you forgot to brush off your shoes when you came into the house. And a large secret is that you love someone. Perhaps someone will find out about your little secrets one way or another. But it will not make a lot of difference in how you are. But if someone knows your big secrets sometimes it makes you afraid.*

Hannah's heart had reason to fear. Because many of the Kanarraville and Harmony saints whose names had been on Solomon Hanncocks' list were now preparing to leave. And no one knew exactly where they were going. Who would be separated? She wondered if she might never see some of the others again. If there were any way she could have been sure what the future was, she would have moved heaven and earth.

There was not a lot of fanfare about their taking leave of Kanarraville. The plans seemed to progress as though their moving was inevitable. As though it were always going to happen, like the seasons. And now it was happening. It had to happen. But the fears, the uncertainties lay in the foreboding questions about how far all of them would have to go.

The feeling in the Lee household was one of quiet resignation. They would have to sell all of their property at a loss, to a Mr. Redd who, even though he thought much of the Lees and was sorry about their having to go, was nevertheless willing to accept a large reduction in price on almost everything.

The time of their leaving came that autumn of 1870 with the hint of a cold wind from the north. Hannah knew that some of Lee's wives would probably be staying in Washington. She had heard that Lavina, with her son John Frederick Lee, would be one of those. She also discovered that Rachel and her family would depart first with Lee himself to travel to the new mill near Skatumpah—a place far beyond the new lumber camp at Fort Kanab. It was not exactly determined where all of them would be, or if they would live within much distance of one another. All of these details were as yet undecided and foreboding to those who cared. To Hannah, whose feelings for John Frederick were so unyielding, the future uncertainties and the possibility of loss seemed to overwhelm her.

*October 2, 1870. They will be leaving soon now. Perhaps day after tomorrow. If I think of it, my blood wants to grow hot inside of me and I feel like bursting with anger and sorrow and fear. Uncle Jacob says he does not know where we are going, either, and I may never see John Frederick again.*

It was raining when Hannah pulled the cart up to Rachel Lee's gate on Wednesday. Skirting the wagons stockpiled in the road, she held the basket firmly under her arm, the rolls carefully covered.

She was startled to see George Lawson in the yard, frantically chasing a dog. He arrived at the gate just as she did. The dog charged through the gate as she tried to open it. Bouncing against her legs, he knocked the basket out of her arms. The animal tore the cloth away from the basket with his teeth, and some of the rolls dropped onto the ground.

George Lawson, following the dog at its heels, stopped just long enough to nod to Hannah, click his heels and open the gate for her. But when he saw the rolls in the mud, he began to snicker.

"Tucker! Look what you done," he called after the pup. When he turned to Hannah, it was without apology. "I don't think nobody's there. If they're still there, they'll be gone tomorrow." Then he left.

Hannah straightened the rest of the rolls firmly in the basket, but it was too late for the peas, which had tumbled onto the wet ground. When she stooped to pluck them out of the mud, she soiled her skirt, and felt angry tears start.

Emma's twin girls came outside with some of Rachel's boys. Through the blur of tears in her eyes, Hannah didn't really see them. All she saw was John Frederick Lee.

When he came to the gate, he was on fire. "You . . . idiot George Lawson," he yelled after the distant figure. He shook his fist. "The dog's not supposed to be in this yard," John Frederick explained. "Hannah, I'm so sorry. Did you come all this way in the rain?"

Absorbed in brushing off her dress, Hannah had not heard any of his words at all. "Is it true that today is your last day here?"

John Frederick opened his mouth, then closed it. His throat seemed to be stopped up.

"When are you leaving?" Hannah asked the group of boys at large.

"We're leaving tomorrow," one of the other boys called out.

John Frederick was still staring at her. "It's true," he said.

Hannah's heart thudded in her chest.


# 79
## Elizabeth

As Elizabeth watched the Lees' first wagons roll away early in October, fear knotted like lead in her stomach. The first to leave was Rachel, then Lavina, with Hannah's John Frederick Lee. The first exodus seemed to be only the beginning. She thought it might be that all of them would have to walk away one day. All of them. And yet she felt a strange relief. She had always felt it would come to this. Now it was here.

Before the Lorrys could go, however, they would have to lease their new brick home. They could not sell it outright; J.B. would not hear of it.

When Elizabeth and Jacob had first written to J.B. to tell him they were going with the Lees, J.B. had sent an angry letter in return calling Jacob a coward for not being willing to stay in Kanarraville and tough it out. Jacob had always turned away at the last moment, he said, just as he did at fifteen in the meadows. And don't expect him, J.B., to show up to help them go in such a cowardly manner. And don't sell the house. They'd be back when things got tough. J.B. did not bother in the letter to remember anything courageous or responsible Jacob had ever done. And now when J.B. was implying that Jacob was running away, he apparently did not see that he, himself, by spending months and months at a time in Salt Lake City when things got tough, had surely been "running away."

When Jacob had come to Elizabeth with news of the Lees' departure, there had been no question in her mind what she would do. Most of the last few years she had not seen much of J.B. He had been gone so long on different occasions that he had not been able to tell in a line-up of Lees and Lorrys which boys were his own. Nor had he weathered the rumors well. There had been the strained relationships with new neighbors, the failures in the business with John Lee, the disappearance of Maggie and Robert, the darkness of the jealousy and hatred he had learned to feel for John Lee. There had slowly come a pall of bitterness into J.B.'s heart which he could not seem to dissolve. And it grew more unmanageable every day. He found it so uncomfortable in Kanarraville that after a month or two, he usually returned to Salt Lake City where he drove wagons for a delivery service. It wasn't long before he was staying there almost nine months out of every year.

Elizbeth had saved one of J.B.'s letters to Jacob and tucked it under her pillow to read every once in a while. While she made preparations to go, she read some of the sentences over and over again.

*As for Elizabeth, she never wanted to stay with me anyhow. She did it out of duty, and that gets sour after so many years. She's always had a candle burning at both ends for John Lee. No wonder she wants to hie after him. Let her go. A man can stomach an unfaithful woman only so long until he gets sick of the sight of her. You can tell her for me, she was a pretty good woman. You was, Elizabeth. But go to your John Lee if that's what you want. I could never stomach to come back for you after you followed him clumping around the country because you was afraid somebody would say something mean. You don't neither one of you need to go asking me to come with you. You know how I feel about him leading us to do something against our will and hanging these millstones around our necks. And him going off and taking my adobe business when I was gone to Salt Lake City and making it into a brick yard, making so much money and he never even so much as asked me to join in. And you, Jacob, married to his own daughter. You ought to go, too. So go, the lot of you and let the chips fall where they may. J.B.*

It was not the letter she cared about, with the ugliness of the man's bitterness, for he carried a weight so heavy she was sometimes very much afraid of it. It was the release in the letter, which she read over and over again. *So go, the lot of you.* She was not sure of all that the words implied. But she thought about it during the autumn mornings when she sat awake in the rocker with the sick baby Joseph in her arms. Always, she pondered what J.B.'s words might mean. Could J.B. really have meant what he said? Had he, as Solomon Hanncock had left Tabby, left her free at last to marry John Lee?

Through Joseph's illness, through the final days of preparation for the journey, she did not know. The letter might not represent an actual legal release. But she kept it close to her, just the same. And she wondered at the growing feeling of joy that began to flood into her heart, for she began to believe that at last, God in his mercy, was going to set her free. That knowledge alone gave her the strength to pack their things.

For a few weeks Jacob was not able to find anyone to lease their home. Finally one of the older Redd children was married on the first of November and he and his bride gave the Lorrys a first lease payment and promised that within two weeks they would move in. The date coincided nicely with the departure time of the other Lees, though it seemed rather late in the season to travel. The Lorrys were somewhat concerned about waiting so long—for by this time Anna Jane was four months along with her fourth child.

"We'll find a place to live," Jacob promised them when they loaded the wagons. With some of the lease money, Jacob had purchased two large oxen, Babes and Blue. Each of the animals was broad and heavy. All of the Lorry boys adored them. They screamed with delight when their father hoisted them up on the big backs for a ride. The horses and the cows and sheep dawdled behind.

"It may be we'll not get as far as the Lees will be going. But at least we'll make it to Kanab," he told the girls.

Elizabeth was weary. With Joseph in her lap, and every bone sore from packing and more packing, she kept her eyes ahead on the valley as they followed the distant wagons in the train. The weather was good for November and it was a beautiful day. Elizabeth glanced up at the red buttes to the east, then at the rim of hills on the west. Ahead of them she could see the Lee families who had left with the same train, scattered on the road as far as the eye could see. She looked up at the store as they drove past—thinking she would not be able to forget the comfort of it if she lived where there was no store at all. She lifted her hand in good-bye to Brother Humphreys, and to white-capped Sally Humphreys, who stood on the front stoop with a broom in her hands.

Like a hazy dream, Kanarraville was passing away from her and she wondered if she would ever see it again. She had spent nearly twenty years living here. She did not know what was ahead of them, though she believed in her heart there could be joy. What was that joy? She wondered if she had thoughts of John Lee? No, she believed it was more than simply the freedom to go to John Lee. It was the joy of simply being released—if there was indeed truth in the suggestion that she was released. She kept the folded parchment letter inside the blouse of her dress, tucked against her waist. She felt for it now, felt its edge, touched it as the wagon continued to lurch forward along the street in front of the store.

Mr. Humphreys had waved, but had then ducked back into the store quickly, as though he had thought of something he had missed.

"Wait!" Sally Humphreys called out, shaking her broom. "Regi forgot something! He wanted to give William Prince a letter to take to John Lee. Brother Prince is in the wagon ahead. Can you deliver it?"

John Lee. As Elizabeth heard John Lee's name, she felt a hope that surprised her. Perhaps she had been talking herself away from the truth, for the old feelings suddenly stirred inside of her. The letter would be an excuse to see John Lee. She tried to calm the beating of her heart.

Jacob slowed the ox and walked back to the store. There wasn't much time if they wanted to catch up with the other families in the group. And he had already done his farewell visiting with the Humphreys.

"Here it is," Sally Humphreys said nervously. She snapped the letter out of Brother Humphrey's hands and handed it to Jacob. "That letter's from the Quorum of the Twelve to John Lee."

Jacob handed it to Elizabeth for safe keeping. An important letter, Elizabeth thought, the white envelope glaring in her eyes. An important letter from the Quorum of the Twelve to John Lee. But he had always been favored with special messages. John Lee had always received letters from the great men of the Church, from the apostles, from Brigham Young. Without a doubt John Lee was among the most important men in the Church. He had built the mills, begun the cotton mission, served in the early militia as agent to the Indians. He had been one of those disciples who, through his own ability to organize, lead, direct, and work tirelessly, had given more than most. The letter, flashing like a white mark, disappeared into her pocket where she had been keeping J.B.'s letter saying she was free.

"Now you have a successful trip." Mr. Humphreys waved again. "We'll miss you, you know."

If the train were truly on its way, Elizabeth was relieved at last. But Sally Humphreys again had a sudden thought and ran back into the store, lugging out a bag full of hardtack. She was carrying her broom.

"And don't you forget us," she said, her white cap still jaunty while she handed the children the hardtack candy and waved.

## 80

### Elizabeth

*November 20, 1871. Toquerville today. We stopped last night at Kelseys' at Ash Creek. They fed all of us: Aggatha's boys, Sammy and Ezra, the Lees, Lorrys, Daltons, Princes. A big meal. Potato soup and sour dough buns. And we needed it to get the oxen up the terrain today. The big ox Blue still limps from stumbling in a hole, but she's got what it takes. Both animals pulling one wagon usually do a good job of getting it all up over the hills, unless it is too steep. Then it takes a second team. It's time consuming to double them up, but we have the time. There is no hurry to go to the desolate place we will go. Joseph seems a little better today.*

*November 21, 1871. Rockville today. A sparse settlement without a store. This is the seat of a treacherous climb. But there'll be plenty of good grass for the cows and sheep on the plateau. I held Joseph much of the day.*

*November 22, 1871. I have kept little Joseph so close to me it is as though we are one. He has a cough now and a slight fever. We bound him up in sheepskins for the night to ward off the chills. But the fever burned him up so hot he climbed out of them while we were asleep. We found him on his pillow in the morning, his little body blue with cold.*

*November 23, 1871. Oh, my dear God. If there is a purpose for us under heaven, help us have the strength to see it. I cannot lose Joseph or I myself will die. We're making it over the plateau an inch at a time. The boys are a big help yoking and unyoking the oxen to double them up over steep terrain. Several of John Lee's other families are having more trouble than we are. Louisa Evaline Prince is having terrible headaches. And I can only be thankful we have been fortunate in our health, except for little Joseph's illness. Sometimes I am sorry we do not have the help of J.B. But these are only fleeting moments. I have never felt so free.*

*November 24, 1871. From the rim of the plateau there is breath-taking beauty. In the distance rock spires turn red in the sunset. This is a canyon of proportions no man could describe. If this was not over-hot in summer, it could be the Eden of man's dreams. Today little Joseph is somewhat better. But I am still worried.*

*We met Bishop Levi Stewart on his way home today. He said he was supposed to meet John Lee to set up the sawmill. But his own mother in St. George has now died, and he must go home to bury her.*

*November 25. Short Creek. We have been making such slow progress that all of us are irritable and ready to scream. What with doubling up teams and keeping the children from falling over the edge, I am hard put to tell how much more of this journey we can endure. If God should be willing, we shall be in the lumber camp of Kanab in three or four days. Where did Hannah get to be such a philosopher? She said to me, "Little distances are all anybody needs to take to get very far."*

Many times Elizabeth heard these words repeat themselves over and over in her ears: "Oh God, give me my children. It is all I have asked of you." She heard herself say the words as though they were not words but prayers. "If I should lose Joseph I should not be able to go on. There is a rock somewhere here that will shelter me if I should fall."

The plateaus still lay before them for incredible miles, and her young son still lay feverish in her arms. Hannah took her turn holding the child so that Elizabeth could rest. Nancy Dalton gave him an herbal remedy, which supplied him with a few hours of sleep.

Elizabeth reviewed the scenes of Kanarraville in her mind. She saw the old house with the loft, which had served them so well through both times of fire and flood. She imagined that when she closed her eyes she could smell the warm hay in the loft. Or she saw the patterns of moonlight on the wood floor of the parlor in the new brick home.

During the next three days, she did not see trees nor sky nor the spires of rock that stood like knives on the horizon. All of it passed before her in a haze. She held Joseph constantly, feeling his heartbeat become slow. And she often felt for the letter in her pocket, but she tried not to think about it.

On the evening of November 28 they saw horses drawing toward them through the ravine. They were within twenty miles of Kanab, Jacob said, and he urged the oxen forward over the rough trail.

So that she would not hope too much, Elizabeth did not think about being in town on the next day. She forced away thoughts about joining the Lee families, or being with John Lee. She thought about how the sun slanted into the valley as though the earth were turned at an angle. She saw the hills beyond them as an extension of the same hills she had left in Kanarraville. If she closed her eyes . . .

Then suddenly she heard the familiar voice. It startled her. She had been thrown out of a reverie. When she dared to look, she saw that it was John Lee.

He was ahead of them alone on one of two horses, riding toward them on a half-charted trail. His eyes were still piercing blue. For his advanced age, he still rode like a young man.

"Hello!" he was calling to them. "Louisa! Anna Jane!"

Anna Jane, now more than four months pregnant, began running toward him, hurrying through the grass and sparse trees.

"Father!" Sammy and Ezra called. They hurried to him as he lumbered up the hill, the wagons groaning with the weight.

Lee's eyes quickly found every face, counted every child, and at last rested on Elizabeth. "So you have come as well?" His voice was tired, but he seemed genuinely happy to see them.

Elizabeth smiled.

He dismounted and stood close by, studying her. He still held children in his arms and spoke his measured words carefully. "I do not see J.B."

"No. He is not here," William Prince said in a level voice.

Lee raised his brows. "Not here?" He was silent. "In Salt Lake City then?"

Elizabeth nodded. "Perhaps for a long time . . ."

Lee looked into her eyes, then he smiled. "I'll talk to you later, Elizabeth."

Lee stayed with the camp for the night. He would have gone back to Kanab with them, he said, but he was on his way to check the lumber supply at Pipe Springs and procure a part for a broken piece in the mill. Perhaps he would have to go as far as St. George.

William Prince handed John Lee a parcel of letters, which seemed to remind Jacob that he had handed Elizabeth that last letter from the Quorum of the Twelve. He nodded to Elizabeth, and she drew the letter from her pocket where she had been keeping it for several days now. Almost reluctantly, she gave up the letter to John Lee, as though there would likely not be another such contact again.

"Thank you, Brother Lorry, Elizabeth," Lee said politely, taking the letters. When he received the one from Elizabeth, he held it out at arm's length to get a better look at it. "The brethren," he said. That was all.

Jacob went back to their wagons. But Elizabeth slipped away. If she had been a schoolgirl again, she would not have felt her heart beating, pounding, as hard as it had been pounding. What did it mean? She was almost angry with herself for believing she could still feel such feelings—a fire that burned in her with unyielding power. But what would she do with this feeling? First, she would never know if she would be able to talk with him. It might never happen, but she knew there was something he could do for her. He could give a blessing to Joseph. It was something she wanted more than anything else. If she were to ask him, she must walk with calm. She and John Lee had become friends. And she would not allow such an outburst of feeling to spoil that friendship.

She did not want too much time to pass before she spoke to him, or she would lose her nerve. So she left Hannah in charge of the boys while she walked to his tent and horses. But she held back while she noticed him still talking in a circle with the men. He was holding the letter she had given to him. She thought he held it in a puzzled way, loosely, in his hands.

It seemed that forever passed while she watched Lee hold the letter. He did not move. And when he did move, he folded it and unfolded it for a long time before he put it into the envelope. Elizabeth felt her mouth grow dry. The darkness began to swallow the camp. The fires flickered low.

"John . . ." she whispered.

Lee drew back, now, startled to find her here. He searched for her in the haze of the moonlight. "Elizabeth?" he said.

"Yes, it's me."

"Come here. Let me look at you."

She came to him, shivering slightly in the night cold.

Lee stood very tall near to her. "So you have come. You have finally come."

She felt other words in her mouth that pressed her. She had come to him to ask him to bless Joseph. "Joseph is ill."

Lee was quiet. Much too quiet.

"And I first . . . I wanted to ask you if you would—there is no doctor—if you would perhaps . . . give him a blessing. A prayer of faith?"

Lee nodded slowly. "Of course I will help him." Then he paused for a moment. "But that is not the only reason you have come."

"No." The memories of her feelings flooded into her. "No," she breathed again. "That is not the only reason I have come."

The moonlight glanced from his eyes. "You have finally made some kind of decision about J.B." It was a statement, not a question.

Her heart drummed against her breast. "I have."

Lee waited for a moment. There were still noises in the camp. The moon seemed to burn gold. He was lowering his eyes. "And now . . . it is too late for me."

She had not expected these words. They seemed small in his voice. What did he mean, "Too late for me"?

He unfolded the letter in his hand. "The letter from the Quorum of the Twelve."

Yes? She had kept J.B.'s letter in her bodice, feeling the paper against her skin. She stayed quiet now, holding her breath. Consciously she held to her belief that no matter what happened, no matter what his excuse, no matter what opposition pursued them, there would always be a possibility for them. And she knew it would be true for her, because she felt it when he grasped her arms with his large hands. Against her skin, she felt the sharp edge of the white letter, still clasped in his fingers.

"I must admit to you, Elizabeth, that when I saw you just now I knew you had come without J.B. There was a feeling which I have not acknowledged for many years—the feeling that I had at Jensens' that day, that I knew you before I came to this earth. That I might still find myself open to love."

Now he drew back from her and gazed at the letter. His brows drew in a heavy line over his blue eyes. "And I saw that in your eyes when you came. Am I right?" His voice was quiet, deep. It stirred her heart.

She nodded, feeling a cold ripple of uncertainty run through her. She hoped his words would not be more than she could bear.

"I would like to have shared some time with you," he continued, still clutching the letter in his right hand and touching her cheek with his left. "How I would like to have shared that time with you."

"But . . . what . . ." She wanted to ask him why he could not. But she waited, feeling something heavy in him that it seemed he might not be able to explain.

"They have, with this letter . . ." The words would not come easily from his mouth. "Ceased membership . . . They have stricken my name from the records of the Church."

So that was the message of the letter she had carried, the letter from Brigham Young. Excommunication.

The very core of his life was to be ripped from him—his reason to stand on this ground, his future kingdoms, principalities, and powers. A wave of darkness suffocated her heart. "Does anyone else know?"

Lee's eyes were shadowed. Even the moon had not found the contours of his face.

"I read the letter when Jacob gave it to me," he said. "I haven't told anyone."

"It doesn't change anything," she insisted, though both of them knew it was a lie. It changed everything.

"It doesn't change anything with me," she repeated.

"Not tonight," Lee said quietly, his voice tight with pain.

Words flew through her. *You live with terror. It dogs you. You are afraid that someday you will suddenly come into a strange light that will illuminate you. And meeting terror at last face to face, you may discover you have not lived at all.*

When Lee turned to lead her back to her tent, Elizabeth could not see. The lantern in Jacob's hands was a blur. The moonlight lay on everything like faded gray cloth.

In the quiet tent Lee's voice was steady. "And now, Dear God." A sharpness gripped Elizabeth. Faith, she said to herself. At least faith in this moment. "Bless this young boy," John Lee intoned. Jacob had placed the oil in Joseph's roughened hair.

"Bless the life of this young child. The children are all we have. Dear God . . . " Lee made a painful sound clearing his throat, congested by tears. "Our Dear Father. If we ourselves have committed wrongs—perhaps in our mistaken zeal—if we have failed to take the large helping of life as we should always have lived it, let it be different for this child. Let him live to glorify thy name."

When Elizabeth found the boy again in her arms, she still could not see. She buried her face against his hair, almost ashamed. Would there have been any greater love she might have felt for a child by John Lee? She could not imagine it. So in that moment when the darkness crowded down, she berated herself.

What did I want out of life as it came my way? she asked. Was I able to take what I had been given and, though painful, live out a commitment because I felt at the time it was the right thing to do? Which demanded the most courage?

A stab of light flashed across her closed eyes, then darkened, then flashed again.

"We'll be in Kanab tomorrow." A tender voice. Jacob's. "He's going to be all right. You ought to get some sleep, Elizabeth."

She looked across the beds on the grassy floor under the canvas tent. Joshua and Caleb lay huddled under a blanket. She tried to look toward the light to open her eyes.

*Which demanded the most courage? To leave or to stay?* It was a question she did not have to answer now. Or ask. Perhaps ever again.

"He'll be all right," she heard Jacob say. She reached over to touch Joseph's head. The fever had gone.

## 81

### Elizabeth

Kanab rose out of the distance as though it were a thimble-sized lithograph behind a lens. At first in a blur. Then as though through window-glass washed clean, at first small, then large until it became a fabric of green at the foot of vermillion cliffs suspended in blue sky. The farms lay like patches embroidered together by threads of fences and rows of poplar trees. And in the very center of town stood the brown buildings of the fort, the center of the logging community clustered like small orderly boxes packed and waiting to go somewhere on a wagon of fortune or a big-bellied railroad train.

Elizabeth saw the town through a mist of hope she had never cleared from her eyes. She held her improving Joseph in her arms as the ox cart lurched toward the curving main street of the town. The distance to the hills gave her room, let her breathe. She was breathing now. She was suddenly conscious of that phenomenon, as though there had been a time when even breathing had not taken place in her life.

The bishop at the main store gave them directions to some homes where traveling families could get a night's lodging. He was a kindly, older gentleman with large gnarled hands, roughened by wear. Even his face, pinched and reddened, seemed older than a man his age should have worn.

"You with the Lees, by any chance?"

William Prince nodded. Jacob delivered his words with care. "We're the Princes, the Daltons, the Lorrys."

"Fine man, John Lee," the bishop said.

Elizabeth heard an audible intake of breath from Jacob.

"I commend the Lee family for representing everything a man and his family ought to be. Industrious. Compassionate. Helpful in a time of need." The old gray eyes in the deep wrinkles of the sun-reddened face glanced upward toward the ceiling of the store. "The roof leaked several weeks ago. He come through here not knowin' who I was, and him and his boys fixed it for me."

William Prince and the Daltons nodded. Jacob smiled a far-away smile. Roof repair was only one of the kindnesses Father Lee had often performed.

"Tell you what. Bertha and the rest'd be awful glad if one of you families stayed with us. Ours is the big white house north out of town. Can't miss it. On the right." He pointed to the road. "Tell her and the girls I sent you. There's also the Bartletts and the Sykes. Please help yourselves. We all got wind of what Lee was accused of doin', but we knew it wasn't him done it alone. And we have sympathy for his cause."

What was his cause? Elizabeth waited for the man to speak.

"He made a commitment to make sure it was safe here. We all made that same commitment. Funny thing. Since that day in 1857, no Wildcats have come here to chase us away."

The very air seemed to lighten with the bishop's words, clearing the atmosphere as though a warm rain had blown the dust away.

Only a moment later the Lorrys found themselves at the big Christensen house near the river on the southwest edge of town. Small farms spread around them like square handkerchiefs. The farmers were harvesting their third crop of hay that year. The barns in the yards were so new that the wood was still green. The animals behind the fences seemed clean and well fed. Behind the barns on the north a canal siphoned water off the river. And behind the water, on the banks of almost every home, stood handsome rows of young poplar trees.

The lawn that stretched from the road to Bishop Christensen's white house was young and green. A little round-faced woman stood in the doorway watching them dismount, her white apron bright in the morning sunlight. When she saw Elizabeth and Hannah reach to help the children out of the cart, she turned back to the house and called an order: "Willa Free! Will you and Maggie make up the back room? Then fetch Polly and let's help these people put up."

Elizabeth heard the words as she often thought she might hear the voices of angels. Suddenly all of the pain, the weariness of the last few weeks seemed to slip away from her. The woman was a harbor. Her very form and shape reminded Elizabeth of a big cushioned chair she could vaguely remember at her Aunt Millicent's home in Nauvoo. She knew she had sat in that chair for no reason at all but just to sit in it. The cushions and the down had held her like a mother's arms.

When Bertha Christensen opened the new screened door into the green yard, she had also let a cat run out. The big mewling gray Persian sprang toward the children with easy, graceful strides.

"Sunny Tail! You monster!" she exclaimed. "Oh, she thinks she's a cougar. She won't hurt you," she called, while the big cat leaped for Joseph's head. The boy blinked large unfocused eyes. Though he was still in a fog from his fevers, Father Lee's blessing had performed its miracle, for he was walking about now.

He seemed almost well. Behind the cat waddled the little round woman, scolding and making time down the walk with every ounce of energy she could muster.

"She's got used to our children, but this latest boy upset her some," the little woman said, puffing and wheezing, out of breath. "I'm so sorry! Please forgive her. You naughty Sunny Tail. You ought to be ashamed of yourself." When she picked the cat up in her arms, it curled into her bosom, wrapping the gray tail about her arm.

Joshua and Caleb went to pet the cat, but Joseph pulled away and backed up into his mother's skirt, as though he were frightened.

"Joseph's been sick," Elizabeth whispered to the woman. "But he's all right." She put her hand in his curls. "You are ever so gracious to allow us to come."

"Oh pshaw! I'm so happy to have you! No trouble at all! And you're to stay as long as you like."

Through the shade of the cool trees, Elizabeth walked to the porch of the house. Behind the screen door she saw sunny patterns on the wood floor. Suddenly the memories flooded into her.

"You had a long trip. You must be tired," the little woman suggested. "So glad you have come. We had several bunches of you these last few weeks. A couple of them are making up the bed here. You folks can take the back rooms. There's some room on the back porch. It don't get cold yet. Oh, your little girls must be weary." She turned to Anna Jane, who was now holding the large cat in her arms. Mrs. Christensen's head bobbed—her hair, sleek in tied silk, stood in a little bun on the top. "You will be addin' so much to this little community. We are so happy to have anyone come. If it just wasn't for the water here . . . But there's plenty for everyone. Do you want to . . . put your boys with mine in the barn? And we'll have dinner shortly."

Elizabeth stood in the cool entryway of the house for a moment, waiting. For what she did not know. For Jacob and Anna Jane to take in their belongings . . . for the children to get settled in the bedroom? For the pieces like a puzzle that did not fit into the other puzzles of her life?

She did not count all of the faces on her first day. There were two other wives and two daughters close to Hannah's age. There was a new girl, she thought she heard Bertha say, and a boy Robert. Then there were three more boys near the ages of Joshua and Caleb and Jacob's boys. When the boys invited the Lorrys and the Lees to the barn, they formed an informal club. All the time she spent in the Christensens at Kanab she hardly saw hide nor hair of Joshua and Caleb.

There were other little ones of varying ages. She counted eight. And she met the wives, although she could not remember if she had met them all. One had been busy when they arrived, and Elizabeth had not yet met the other girl living with them. "She is not a wife," Sister Christensen explained, "but a young lady for hire who needed a place to stay." And there were two large dogs in the barnyard, forty lovely plump hens—thirty-nine after the evening meal—four soft-eyed jersey milk cows, a fine bull, four hogs, and eighteen woolly sheep. And lots of smiles.

Bertha Christensen took them to their room. "You'll want to rest a bit before lunch. Brother Christensen will be here soon to join us."

On that night the moonlight flooded through the screens of the back stoop onto the narrow straw cot where Hannah lay. Elizabeth slipped into the cot beside her when it was time. "Hannah," she whispered. "Are you awake?"

The girl stirred. "How many wives does Brother Christensen have?" she asked.

"I believe three, dear."

"And there's the other lady who stayed in her room during dinner. She did not come down yet."

"She's not a wife, dear, but a hired girl who needed a place to stay."

"She's Robert Lincoln's mother. He told me so." She changed the subject, then. "Will Papa find us?"

"We wrote and told him we were going, but he said he didn't want to follow the Lees, dear."

"Why doesn't he like Grandpa Lee? He's so nice. I like him so much. Why are there so many people that are so cruel to Grandpa Lee?"

"I don't know, Dear. I really don't know." She paused. "Good night, Hannah. Sleep tight, my darling."

It was only on the very next day that Jacob found a five-acre plot of ground he wanted to lease in Kanab. On that same afternoon, Bishop Christensen offered Jacob a part-time position in the store.

Elizabeth did not count all of the faces again on the second day, there were so many. But she was aware that the "hired woman" remained in her room, watching them out of the window. Elizabeth saw her eyes behind the muslin curtains. When the boy Robert came into the yard with his calf to show to the children, she saw the woman watching him from the window.

"Even though he don't marry my mother, Bishop Christensen give me this calf. Going to be a fine bull someday," Robert said.

He let the children take turns leading it in a circle.

"When we was in Mexico before my pa was killed, he promised me a calf someday. The bishop says I can have this one if I take good care of it. And I'm a goin' to. It ain't easy gettin' an unbroke calf and learnin' it to feed on a bottle, but that's what I done."

Elizabeth stroked the velvet animal and smiled at the boy. She struggled with her memories, because she was so certain she was looking into familiar eyes. J.B.'s eyes? When she stared at the high curtained window behind the tall trees, she continued to see the dark shape that faded quickly into the room. A flash of images rushed toward her when she looked again. Could the woman be . . . and could . . . ? The boy's name was Robert, though his last name was Lincoln. Could the strangely absent hired woman have changed her name? Could she possibly be Maggie? Could Robert be her son?

Elizabeth stared unabashed at the boy. Then at the window. The boy had the high carved brow and the quick black eyes, the woolly head of dark curls and the large jaw. And it seemed he spoke with J.B.'s voice! She thought she saw in Robert the mirror image of J.B.

"Robert's mother don't like the Lees," Bertha whispered to Elizabeth while they peeled potatoes. "And she wouldn't come out when he come through. She believes Lee was a murderer in the Indian massacre. But he was no such a thing. He's the kindest man—helped my husband lay down a new roof on his store. Do you know anything about them rumors they pass around? Sayin' Lee murdered a young girl and she stayed lovely on the meadow floor? And her beauty never died away?"

Elizabeth's heart leaped into her throat. "No," she said, her voice a whisper. She sat close to the woman bent over the potatoes, felt the strength of her ample arms.

"Well, that's the rumor Maggie passed on to us. And she says there's truth in the hogwash about the Lees."

*Maggie?* It was the first time Elizabeth had heard the woman's name.

Elizabeth saw a blur when she looked at the potato peelings. She felt Maggie's presence in the dark upstairs room. She thought, lying on the porch that night, she saw a face at the screen.

"Hannah? Are you still awake?"

"Yes, Mother."

"Did you have a good day?"

"Robert and the boys took us up to the head of the canal. Sally and Mary, the oldest daughters, made the lunch. They have boyfriends. So I told them about John Frederick Lee." She paused for a moment. Elizabeth heard a choke in her voice. "But they told me if he was a Lee he would have a thirst for blood in him—that Bishop Lee's tendencies to kill and thirst for blood would be passed on to the children."

When Elizabeth saw her face, she saw grief. "It's all right to talk about it, to get it out, Hannah. Go on."

Through tears, Hannah continued. "They said that everyone who killed the white men in the Mountain Meadows would deny it, and that on the outside the grownups were kinder than kind. They admitted that John Lee helped Bishop Christensen put on a new roof and that the bishop loved everyone as Jesus loved them. But the children said they knew that John Lee would murder them if he got half the chance."

They both looked up, startled at a sound in the yard.

"Did you hear that?"

Hannah sat up straight in the bed. "It's the children going out to the privy."

Elizabeth strained to see in the heavy darkness. "It's not the children, Hannah."

"It's Robert's mother," Hannah breathed. "Oh, she hates the Lees! And that is why she won't come out, Robert told me. She's hiding while we are here. She says the Lees murdered her baby girl. Robert told me."

Elizabeth's eyes, more accustomed to the dark, made out the soft shape of the woman's cloak in the moonlight.

"Is she listening to us?" Hannah asked.

"No, she can't hear us."

"A long time ago, the Indians gave her another baby," Hannah continued. "And Robert said the Lees had murdered that baby's mother."

Elizabeth lay back down on the pillow and stared at the trees washed with moonlight. She touched Hannah's arm, pulled her softly to lie back down. She found it ironic that Hannah was talking about herself and didn't know it. "Let's go to sleep now, Hannah."

"It can't all be true, Mother?"

"Hush," Elizabeth whispered. "No. It is not at all true, darling."

They heard a sigh in the trees outside the wire screen, heard the whisper of a cloak again as the woman moved to the front of the house and to the front stairs. "Mama, where have they gone now?" Hannah wondered aloud. "Aunt

Lavina Lee and Rachel and their families? Are they still in Washington, or have they gone to Skatumpah? Where is John Frederick?"

"I don't know, Hannah," Elizabeth whispered. "You'll find him, darling. Or he'll find you."

## 82
### Jacob

*December 10, 1871. Why are there so many secrets and rumors? We have come to a place of safety—a haven where there are understanding men and women who love us and protect us. Why must some darkness always lurk on the edges and seep into the light?*

There was always dead quiet whenever anyone mentioned the Lees. With Sammy and Ezra Lee now staying with the Princes next door, and some questions about whether or not Anna Jane, also staying with the Christensens, might be the daughter of John Lee, the rumors seemed to multiply in the dark—many rumors that there were valid reasons to hate the Lees. And there was no news of John Frederick or of the Lee families who were reported to be living now in Skatumpah.

Anna Jane began to ask Jacob if he thought their family should make Kanab their home.

"Oh yes. It is only the children who pass the rumors," Jacob assured her.

"But our children . . ."

"They are Lorrys," Jacob said. None of the families in Kanab had the Lee name except for Anna's brothers, Ezra and Sammy.

"In one way or another we are all Lees," Anna Jane had said quietly, under her breath.

But still, they decided to stay in Kanab. They would rent the five-acre plot on the southwest side and the small log home that went with it. And Bishop Christensen had made Jacob an offer he could not refuse—to go into business with him at the store.

If he were to enter such an enterprise in earnest, Jacob would need the money out of the Kanarraville property. But in order to sell the property, he needed to contact J.B.—perhaps even to go all the way to Salt Lake City to talk to him. When he finally decided he must go, he had a long talk with Elizabeth about Maggie at the Christensen home, and about the trouble brewing against the Lees.

"Watch the boys. I'm afraid Sammy and Ezra Lee are stirring up trouble. Or it's that boy Robert. You say you've seen Maggie? When she nodded, Jacob continued, "Then he may be J.B.'s boy," he said quietly, "Never talk of it. Never whisper a word about it. I fear Maggie is going to bring trouble."

Jacob and Elizabeth discussed the rumors that the Lee boys seemed to be in serious controversy. Robert had evidently said something to them—no one knew what, exactly—but it seemed to be an unforgivable statement.

On the evening of Jacob's departure for Kanarraville—after he told Elizabeth he needed to go to Salt Lake City to see J.B.—Elizabeth lay awake thinking for a long time. She knew she worried too much about the dark rumors circulating about the Lees. She hovered over Anna Jane to protect her from these rumors, but she feared their obscurity could not last forever. She forced herself to think more positive thoughts—to visualize the small log house they were going to lease on the five-acre plot east on the road out of Kanab to Skatumpah, the same road that led to the Lee saw mill, built somewhere very far east and north, where the Lee family now lived. Finally she thought how fortunate Jacob was to have been offered half ownership in Bishop Christensen's store, how happy the children had seemed.

While these thoughts crossed her mind, she saw movement through the open doors and raised her head. A lithe figure was running out to the barn. Soon, carefully leading a calf out into the moonlight, the figure led it to the canal to drink. It was an odd hour to deal with any animal, so she got up from beside the sleeping Hannah, drew on her robe, and felt her way down the porch steps and into the yard. If anyone was trying to steal the calf, she would wake someone. The dark figure led the animal to the edge of the water and urged it to lower its head. The little beast, its large eyes reflecting the moon, gazed slowly upward toward the trees, then dropped its nose into the water.

Elizabeth watched uncomfortably for a moment, until she saw that the boy was Robert, Maggie's boy, the son whose last name was now Lincoln, because Maggie had not wanted to be known as a Lorry anymore. Perhaps he was under the illusion that the calf was his, but felt that his ownership must be exercised only in the dark.

Elizabeth had turned to walk back to the porch when she saw two figures emerge from the trees in the neighbor's field. They moved up to Robert stealthily and began to talk. She could not hear the muffled words. But she thought one of the boys looked like Anna Jane's brother Sammy Lee, who had been staying with Louisa Lee and William Prince at Sykes'. It wasn't long before the boys were exchanging angry epithets and began to threaten each other. She heard Robert say in a loud voice, "You know it's my calf! You let it go! You don't have no claim to it no more. You're murderers!"

Alarmed, Elizabeth froze. For a few moments it looked as though Robert, even without a helpful defensive kick from his sleepy-eyed calf, was going to get the better of the two boys. He threw his fist into Sammy Lee's face. Then he turned and kicked the younger boy—it looked like Ezra Lee—in the groin. Elizabeth wasn't sure it was Ezra, but her heart leaped to see him bend over in pain. Sammy Lee hit Robert's neck, and when Ezra came up for air, he plowed Robert in the stomach. Still smarting from the jab in his own stomach, Ezra raised up a big rock in both of his hands. Even though Elizabeth could see what was about to happen, she stood frozen, unable to call out, to stop Ezra. The large stone fell like a meteor against Robert's head.

"Boys! Boys!" A voice called out. "Shame on you boys!"

Suddenly the two larger figures scrambled across the canal back toward the Sykes' home. Bishop Christensen came out in his large flannel night dress, his slippers flapping against his heels. "Here now, Robert boy . . . you been talking trouble again?"

The boy was out cold on the ground. Elizabeth withdrew quickly into the trees. A woman was following the bishop out into the yard, her hands like claws grasping at the air.

"It was the Lees! I saw them, Harold. I saw them!" It was unmistakably Maggie in a large tent-like gown, her hair troubled and knotted with snarls. "Robert! I begged you to leave them murderers alone," she cried fitfully to her inert son. "What did you do? Make them an engraved invitation? You'll pay for it over and over again." Then she turned to the bishop, who was leaning over the boy, feeling for blood in his hair. "I can't stay, Harold. You've been kind. But it is not possible to stay here with murderers."

Bishop Christensen's voice was low and soothing. "Now there's no need to make any quick decisions about anything, Maggie. It's time to get a good night's sleep." He lifted the half-conscious Robert to his feet and leaned him against his big arm, walking with him to the front door so as not to wake the sleepers in the house. He did not see Elizabeth standing in the trees.

As soon as the man led the woman and the boy around the house, Elizabeth turned quickly to the porch. Against the screen was a white shape. At first she gasped, frightened, but then scolded herself. It was only Hannah, her white skin pale in the low light under the auburn hair.

"Mother."

"You startled me."

"Was it Robert?"

"Yes."

"And Sammy and Ezra."

"I guessed as much."

For a moment Hannah was quiet while her mother slipped through the door.

"I didn't think they would do it."

"Do it?"

"Actually go through with the fight."

Elizabeth stopped in front of the bed and turned to Hannah. In the bleak glow of the night sky Hannah looked ghostlike, her skin very pale.

"Ezra and Sammy wagered money Robert wouldn't meet them out here by the canal."

Elizabeth gazed out through the porch screens toward the meadow. The water in the canal whispered quietly against the roots of the poplars; the sky was still.

"Robert had the nerve to tell Sammy and Ezra their father was just a while ago cut off from the Church."

"Go to sleep now," Elizabeth whispered. "Go to sleep, Hannah darling. Please."

## 83

### Elizabeth

Because Kanab was warm, and the rivers and creeks full, the residents of Kane County managed to get in a couple of hay crops that helped to reestablish the displaced Saints from Cedar City. Fruit trees went in, gardens began to blossom.

For the first few months, most of the settlers kept safe inside the walls of the small fort at night, but by spring they had begun to venture out into their newly cultivated fields. They dared to move into the little houses built by those who had left them and gone on. By the time the Lorrys were able to take possession of the little cabin on the acreage they had purchased, they had already been able to wring beets, carrots, and turnips out of their ground. And of the other crops—blackberry and raspberry bushes, green beans, kale, and chard—there was enough promise to make daily gardening a delight. Every day they gave thanks.

Elizabeth and Anna Jane swept the dirt floor of the cabin. They braided rugs out of what rags they could find. They hung a blanket across the middle of the back room to keep the boys separate from the girls, but it didn't always do the job. There were little skirmishes of anger and a lack of privacy among the children. When Jacob returned from Salt Lake City and the sale of the Lorry property to the Redds, he could take time to enlarge the barn, put an addition onto the back. Then the boys could sleep in the barn.

For the harvest at the end of the summer, the townspeople prepared for a huge celebration at the fort. They used bales of hay for tables, where they set up their vegetables—squashes, tomatoes, cucumbers—for sale. They hung colorful strings of flags above the displays along the eaves of the fort buildings. They hooked up lanterns at intervals under the roof. The growers laid out packs of straw under the slanted roofs of the fort, which the boys of the town found tempting. They climbed the roofs and jumped into the hay. Even Sammy and Ezra Lee managed to come the twenty miles from Skatumpah, and took their turns climbing the ladder to the roof, sliding down, and landing in the bales. There was shouting, tussling, and screaming. A couple of times the Kanab boys pushed Sammy and Ezra, but the Lee boys took it well. One of the town fathers pulled them aside to tell them they must behave themselves. It was a holiday and nothing must go wrong.

The bishop set out his peck barrels of hardtack and a tankard of unfermented wine—simple grape juice. The children were buying the hardtack with their pennies and the adults were exchanging their quarters and dimes for a drink of the grape juice. Some of the outsiders—rough inhabitants of the towns round about who were unwelcome in their shaggy beards and odorous clothes—brought their own whiskey and beer. It was to be a church party and the bishop had hoped there would be no drinking, but he let some loggers in to buy the hardtack, and when the fiddlers began to fiddle, he could not very well send the visitors away.

The women of the church families cooked the food, and there was a good share of it in this harvest: squash, potatoes, tomatoes, and rich juicy cobs of buttered corn.

Elizabeth was absorbed by the beauty of the lights, the music, the dancing. She could not take her eyes off of Hannah as the girl swung out on the hard dirt center of the fort in her dark red dress printed with cream-colored daisies. Hannah invited awe, her skin a peach color, her shiny hair dark with a red sheen. But she seemed unfocused tonight, as if looking for someone.

There were several young men who asked Hannah to dance with them in the square. One of them was the hot-tempered, red-headed Jed Stewart. Elizabeth felt wary when he took Hannah in his grip. But Hannah smiled and accepted him. She seemed to be having a good time. Lately Elizabeth had been hoping—she was not sure particularly why—that Hannah might forget John Frederick Lee. And yet she wasn't much of an example, for she had never forgotten his father. She believed she would always remember John Lee, though her dreams for him were fearful ones—fear for his future, fear for hers. She could see that after discovering he was cut off from his beloved church, he had not wanted to taint her in any way. And so now he would have nothing to do with her. He could plead until he was blue in the face with his friend Brigham Young for reinstatement, for mercies, but she felt deeply there were some unknown elements at work. Though mercy may have been granted, there was a long road ahead—an uncertain, anxious road for both Brigham Young and John Lee.

Elizabeth was worried as she watched Jed Stewart lead Hannah forcefully across the dirt floor. She had always thought that his interest had been in Jacob's beautiful only daughter Belinda. And she knew Jacob had warned her against becoming entangled with him. "He always has to have his way," Jacob had said. Belinda had not known how to handle Jed's aggression, but Hannah seemed to have no problems with him.

As Hannah and Jed finished dancing, Elizabeth could not help but continue to watch Jed as he pulled Hannah to the side where he stood over her, propping himself against the hayrack and gesturing with his free hand. As Elizabeth might have guessed, he was gesturing toward Belinda.

It was not long before Jed strode back in a determined manner to Belinda. So he was still after Belinda, Elizabeth thought. Jed approached her, but she must have told him a short "no" because he left her with an angry scowl. Belinda had not chosen Jed, but was dancing with . . . Elizabeth was not sure. She looked again. It was . . . Belinda's half uncle, Sammy Lee. Watching Jed's expression, Elizabeth felt a foreboding at the anger in the air. She wished Sammy and Ezra Lee had never come.

Belinda was a beauty now, with Jacob's dark eyes and curls, and Anna Jane's fair skin. It was not hard to understand why Jed Stewart tried yet again. He tapped Sammy on the shoulder to break in, and Belinda refused him a second time. She and Sammy stopped dancing and stepped off to the side. But Belinda did not leave Sammy Lee.

Elizabeth kept her eyes on Jed's unpleasant face, rugged with scars. He dragged another girl off the sidelines even as he stared after Sammy and Belinda.

At the punch table, while Hannah was sharing a glass of raspberry juice with another young man, Hob Gibson, Elizabeth asked her quickly what was going on. "Belinda is angry with Ted because of the things he's said about the Lees. And he tried to beat up her little brother John." So Jacob's little son Johnny had begun taking sides, also, Elizabeth thought.

"But perhaps Sammy and Ezra Lee . . ." she started in a whisper.

"Don't worry, Mama," Hannah laughed, holding back for a moment from the young Gibson fellow, who was tugging her forward to the floor. "She asked them. She wanted them to come on purpose because she . . . she was afraid of Jed. Don't worry, Mama. They'll protect her." And Hannah was gone, now in place for the polka with the tall light-haired Gibson, his large hands on her waist.

Sammy and Ezra Lee! So Belinda had sent a message specifically asking them to come! Elizabeth stood for a while feeling the news hit her like cold water. Her fears mounted when it was announced from the stand at the hayrack that the games were beginning.

There was a race for the ladies; they were to see who could run carrying an egg in a spoon. At the same time, at the other end of the fort, the boys were lining up on their horses to advance toward the center. The line-up of horses worried Elizabeth. Jed was the first, seated on his father's big white-footed roan. The horse was a monster of power. At first Jed stayed on the edge of the line. But when the girls found their places at the other end of the fort in front of Christensens' store, he moved his horse to a position exactly opposite of Belinda. It seemed he might have been hoping to do it inconspicuously, but it was much too obvious. Elizabeth caught her breath when she saw that he was directly next to the mount that held Sammy Lee. Elizabeth could see the fear in his eyes. And she felt a chill settle in her spine.

The bishop was to blow the whistle, Levi Stewart to count. "One, two—."

Jed's big mount stepped out of line and pawed the ground. Elizabeth could see the tension in Sammy's face.

"We'll have to start again," Jed's father, Levi shouted. "Keep Socks behind the line, Jed!"

Jed's face was a contorted mass of scars and nerves. Elizabeth held tight to little Joseph's hand.

"One, two, three. Go!"

The horses sped out now, Jed still at the front. But Sammy leaned forward in the saddle, pushing his tiny mare until she met neck and neck with the roan. But there wasn't enough space to gather speed.

At the same whistle the girls began running with the eggs in their spoons. Hannah was laughing and running.

Near the center line now, Jed leaned over in the roan's saddle and sped straight for Belinda's spoon. Sammy, on the same course, kept his eyes level across the small mare's neck. Belinda, seeing the potential trouble, sidestepped quickly. But it was too late. Her egg dropped from her spoon. Jed's roan rammed into Sammy's mare, and the Lee boy leaped for Jed like a cat on fire.

Both were on the big horse now, Jed clinging to the saddle and Sammy clinging to Jed. At once, Ezra lunged toward the large horse, hoping to keep it under control. Several of the men standing around the edge of the fort also ran toward them. But their efforts were in vain. The powerful animal veered into the bundles of straw and against the corner of Christensens' store. The big head of the roan, or Sammy's arms, or Jed's legs as he went over and under, knocked the lanterns out from under the eaves of the roof and into the dry hay.

There was an immediate and terrible blaze. The string of colored flags floated down off the shingles and curled into the fire like dead leaves. The women began to scream, the girls to run, dropping their eggs from their spoons. The men quickly stopped the other horses by grabbing bits and bridles, but some of the animals began to panic and run mad. The boys could not control them now, and when one of the horses jerked away, it dragged a flaming string of flags all the way across the fort through the hay. Several men grabbed buckets from the nearby hotel and began a short line from the horse trough to the blaze. But the front of the Christensen store was now in flames.

Elizabeth, clutching Joseph against her skirts, choked back a scream. Where were Joshua and Caleb? She did not see them. She would have to trust they could get out of the way. She saw Jacob dive for his little son John in the confusion. Then Belinda and Sammy and Ezra were running toward the west gate of the fort. Anna Jane followed. So did everyone else. Elizabeth looked back at the store. A piercing terror gripped her. The store!

"Forget the buckets! It's gone!" a voice behind her cried out. It was Jacob. He swung a large ax from his shoulder, cutting away at the walls to get in to salvage goods. Some of the loggers were running and screaming from the burning door carrying saddles and blankets in their arms and on their backs. Some of the boys had also joined the looting, and Elizabeth thought she saw Jed leap off, up, and over the roof with whiskey kegs in his arms.

"Get out! Get out!" Jacob yelled to the visiting loggers and trappers. A few still stood in the front of the store, clawing at the pans under the counter, scooping up cups full of hardtack. They were drunk, bawling at the top of their lungs.

Jacob waved the ax in the air. The bishop followed him with a pan of water, his eyes red. He tossed some water to wet a space leading to some dishes and tools, but he hung back in the smoke and crackling flames.

"Out!" Jacob yelled. Next, the bishop threw water on the opening and on Jacob. Jacob swung the ax up over the hole he was making near the door. When the ax fell on the door frame, the door cracked, leaned in, and crumbled like burnt matchsticks to the ground. The lumber store front followed it, cracking and splintering behind the white-washed letters, KANAB GENERAL STORE.

Bishop Christensen tossed the last water from his bucket on the blaze. Jacob slashed the door with the ax again, and the last logger, the collar of his shirt on fire, ran screaming from the burning building.

Elizabeth stared at Jacob, his eyes white holes in a face black with grime. "Jacob," she yelled. "Jacob! Get out now!"

The roof was beginning to sag. A moment later, it fell. They heard a scream. One boy had apparently intended to jump off the roof and into the hay when it collapsed. Suddenly, his body, like a large black bag, thudded into the hollow of flames.

"It's Jed!" With a bloodcurdling scream, Levi Stewart bounded toward the door, but was stopped by flames.

"It's gone!" Jacob choked. He stood broken beside the giant tongues of fire licking the sky.

All Elizabeth could see was the burning. She could smell flesh burning. She picked up four-year-old Joseph and held him in her arms while she watched the Stewarts, crazy with grief, stare at the charred ruins. In that moment, unbelieving, she looked up into the sky. The ashes blew about like gnats, while above them in the darkness, over the bonfire of the fort that continued to burn, large soft flakes of snow swirled down around them.

The crowd in front of the gate was thinning now. Elizabeth, Joseph still in her arms, backed away from the heat into the snow.

Yellow flames from the straw were still rolling up along the porch posts and into the windows and doors. The men were carting out valuables as fast as they could—chairs, tables, beds. Some were throwing things out of the back windows of the hotel. They were running, crowding, to get out of the fort gate. Jacob turned to look back once more at the scene. Elizabeth stood by him, still holding Joseph against her shoulder. Neither of them said a word until Jacob looked around swiftly. His tone was urgent. "Did you see Anna Jane?"

# 84
## *Elizabeth*

Anna Jane. At first they did not think much damage had been done. She had fallen, she told them. Sammy and Ezra had told her that their father, John Lee, was on his way from Arizona to see her. Now, in the aftermath of the terrible carnival and its fire, at least he would come to administer to her.

John Lee had gone south for Brigham Young. Though Lee had been excommunicated from the church, the president continued to protect him by warning him, and by sending him further and further away. Now Brigham Young had told him to find a place to establish a ferry on the Colorado River so that the Saints could move southward again. Though he was at the Colorado River, John Lee would have traveled across the world to see his daughter Anna Jane.

When he arrived, John Lee studied Anna Jane with a drained, defeated look. She had been running after Belinda and Sammy Lee, she said. She saw them, and she had reached out for Sammy's shirt. But he had never felt her hand. She had fallen, and there were so many people streaming from the fort gate, that no one could have seen her, and no one really knew she was there. She felt them walking over her, stepping on her. She had cried out to them to stop, but there had been so many people, they could not hear her. All of them had been screaming in the wake of the fire. No one had seen her, she said, and she had immediately felt some terrible inside pain. She'd been holding the baby Christa and had tried to roll her under her body, even as boots pounded her back. One boot stepped on her arm hard and she felt the bone break. And then the baby, who had been safe under that arm, had begun to cry.

"Perhaps it was even someone I know. Because no one knew I was there," Anna Jane said. "No one knew." She was sobbing now, and John Lee bent over her and cradled her head in his arms.

Jacob stood very tall behind the bed, his face a puzzled blank stare. Elizabeth sat with Anna Jane's baby girl Christa bundled close beside her.

"We'll call on the Lord to make you well." John Lee cleared his throat.

They had waited so long for John Lee to come after the terrible fire, that his presence seemed like a balm of blessed rain after a long drought. Though he had brought Caroline and her children with him and they would stay in one of the small empty houses in Kanab, he would not be with them long. He had emphasized that he himself would never be able to stay in one place for very long. Ever again.

He came as soon as he could to the Lorry home. But now that he was here, Elizabeth did not, for some reason, feel the relief she had expected to feel from his presence. His usually piercing blue eyes looked gray. Jacob had whispered to her that he had been in Washington with his families, but he never slept in his homes.

The Washington wives had been uncertain about accepting him when they had learned of his excommunication from the church. Lee's youngest and last wife, Lisanne, had left him. As for the others, he would not enter their homes, but always slept in the barns. So he had slept in barns during Christmas. Elizabeth winced, feeling the slur.

"He is a proud man," Jacob had said.

Lee's large hands now lay over Anna's brow. "The fever seems to be gone," he said.

"Father," she pleaded. "God cannot have taken your priesthood away. Please just give me a blessing."

Jacob's gaze met Elizabeth's. She was feeling empty and sad. The specter of John Lee's grief daunted her.

John Lee looked up to Jacob. "Can God's power have left me? I feel I am the same person." In the course of his journey to Washington and Harmony he had stopped in St. George to see Brigham Young. He had pleaded with him for a new hearing concerning his membership, and set up an appointment with the stake president, Erastus Snow. Only a few days later in Kanab, as he was placing Caroline in the house there, he had received a letter unsigned, but obviously in the handwriting of President Snow.

*To J.D. Lee at Washington:*

*If you will consult your own safety & that [of] others, you will not press yourself nor an investigation on others at this time lest you cause others to become accessory with you & thereby force them to inform upon you or to suffer. Our advice is, Trust no one. Make yourself scarce & keep out of the way.*

So his life must now be spent traveling about like Moses in the wilderness, he told them. But if he found loved ones wherever he went, his sovereignty was heaven's gift. Jacob Lorry stood beside him as the older man lay his heavy hands on Anna Jane's brow.

"Dear God, our Father," he whispered, his voice breaking with hidden tears. "Please heal my daughter, Anna Jane. Please. Whatever injuries she has suffered, make her well. If I am not fit to give this blessing, have compassion. Make her well anyway. Please."

Elizabeth had whispered into Christa's ears while the prayer was being said. She had not whispered words that Christa could have understood, but she prayed the warmth of her breath would quiet the little girl and calm her small cries. Now she tucked the sleeping babe into Anna Jane's arms and passed a soft hand over Anna Jane's tears. "Sleep now, Anna Jane. Everything will be all right. Sleep now," she whispered.

John Lee stood with Jacob beside the door. "The president has assured me his dismissal is to quiet the critics, and I must be patient. As far as he is concerned, I am still in God's hands. Now he has asked me to investigate a good place to cross the Colorado River so he can send Saints further into the territory."

Jacob nodded. He had already known.

Finally Lee turned to Elizabeth. "Take care of Anna Jane," he said softly.

"We will," Elizabeth whispered.

He stopped then and placed a large hand on Elizabeth's shoulder. She trembled, as though she felt a heavy weight from that hand.

"You have already stayed with your commitments, Elizabeth," he said strangely. A light flickered in his eyes. Her commitments? "The Lord will bless you for it," he continued softly. "And you, Jacob, my boy."

Into the calm night, hushed under the downy covering of snow, John Lee took his leave, his dark cloak billowing under the receding moon.

## 85

### Hannah

Hannah did not dare breathe what she now felt was true. Not with anyone she knew. She knew it, not in her mind, but in her heart. Oh, someone may have whispered it at school. "John Frederick Lee is in Skatumpah, for I saw him not so long ago." But it was not something anyone would talk about in the same breath as they mentioned the new street in Kanab, the construction of the new stores, the new lumber mill. They did not talk about the Lees, nor the death of

Jed Stewart in the fire, nor the terrible truth that Anna Jane Lorry had nearly been trampled to death at the gate. No one wanted to talk about those things that had brought them tragedy.

The snow lay as a shroud on the world—a thick blanket that softened the harsh landscape. The people of the town—even the Christensens—stayed in their homes for weeks. For two Sundays they held no meetings—not even church. Bishop Christensen came individually to the people in their homes and told them to repent. He suggested that the Lord was reprimanding them for certain animosities and rumors that the children had been allowed to harbor. "If we want to prosper, we must shed those resentments . . ."

Finally, the next Sunday, they had met together in Harold Christensen's home. There were awkward confessions, and some tears. In the following week the community began to work together again, building the new meeting house, clearing out the debris of the fire and laying logs one after another until a crude temporary church house sat on the wide new street.

When spring came, Harold Christensen, in his diligent manner, gathered friends to raise a new store. Much larger than the first, it faced north on the big new road running east outside the fort. With everyone's help, the store rose quickly and boasted over a hundred new shelves.

Without speaking of his own losses, Jacob helped Harold Christensen rebuild the store. He left the gardening to Elizabeth and the children, and spent from early morning until late at night constructing the building that was to be a new joint venture, the Christensen-Lorry General Mercantile.

Only very seldom did the Lees come from Skatumpah into town. The people of Kanab had tried to forget the Lees were close by. Yet another problem loomed on the horizon that would have kept the Lees in obscurity. The United States Government increased its efforts to illegalize plural families. The giant Lee family would have been guilty of plural marriage a dozen times over. Though no one thought such a law would ever pass, there was talk, and the talk began to worry them.

During this time, Anna Jane lay ill in her room. Through all of the months of spring, Elizabeth and Hannah and Belinda carried the household load, which had not been an easy thing to do after the loss of their goods in the fire. But, with the help of the community, the Lorrys found enough to eat, though not to overeat. All of the women grew lean as winter turned into spring.

Elizabeth, now approaching thirty-five, watched her hair grow gray white at her temples. It softened her face. Her cheek bones were more prominent, the flesh still firm, but a rather sallow color. There was a flush while she looked at herself in the glass. She was still a fairly good looking woman. The small nose looked sharper, lighter, like old porcelain. The eyes were still blue and as wide or wider than they had seemed in the past, still set off by the finely arched brows, the fine lashes, now lighter, almost blond. Or perhaps gray? Her mouth included the same slim upper lip set on its full lower one. There was still something wistful in her face, though for a while she had seen herself as a shadow of someone else—a young girl who fought through a mist of memory to keep her young self alive. Yet she knew she had always been a collaboration, always in a tentative transition from a young person into a fully blown rose of a woman—the same kind of thing that was taking place in Hannah.

Hannah. Elizabeth watched Hannah dance into the house with hands full of wild flowers as spring began in the fields. With clear skin, her hair a dark burnished red with highlights of copper gold, she resembled a sunflower. She was a miracle, Elizabeth marveled.

Sometimes frustrated, Hannah would snap at requests or become irritated with the children. But for the most part, she was even-tempered, calm. She did not walk through life. She sailed. She held her chin high. She did not simply move. She carried herself through each moment. She bounced down into the garden; she gathered flowers. She scooped garden vegetables into her arms like treasures. She was alive. Elizabeth watched her as though she had paid money for a ticket to a stage play. Hannah's presence at Anna Jane's bedside brought light. Elizabeth felt it and wondered at it, because she had never known anyone like this child before.

However, for the last few days, there had been a secret in Hannah's face. Elizabeth had watched the sixteen year old girl for so long that she could see the darkness there, a hesitancy, a flicker in the eyes. She knew that Hannah was aware that Elizabeth could see clearly as though she were looking through water or air. Sometimes their hearts beat as one.

Yes, something rankled in Hannah's life, and Elizabeth guessed it was the absence of her John Frederick Lee. But she didn't want to say anything. All of the talk about John Lee had become suppressed gossip that suffocated those who heard it. It had been only two weeks since somebody had taken what they could of John Lee's cattle and had not returned them. The word had come to Kanab through the dark rumbling of voices over fences. Like smoke, the news found ears, blank stares, nervous shifting feet. Everyone waited. Unsure. Then they learned that the people who took the cattle from the Lees took them because a third party owed them money, and the Lees had not yet paid that third party. The knowledge of this roundabout excuse for attaching the cattle in a transfer of property unsettled everyone, but did not open a single mouth. Finally, when the dispute came into court, and the Lees were defeated, the undercurrents of feeling erupted. Some of that tension came alive in Hannah's dark eyes.

But it was not the decision of the local court in favor of Lee's enemies that beat in Hannah's heart. It was the knowledge that as Lee set a new trial for late July, he had fetched help from Washington. And his help was his son, John Frederick Lee.

Not many in Kanab or the surrounding areas knew John Frederick Lee, that he had been making visits to Washington, and that his father had summoned him. But Hannah knew. So when she heard little Jeremiah Christensen whisper in school to Johnny Lorry that John Lee had come through their home the night before and brought his older son from Washington, she heard the name John Frederick Lee and her heart skipped a beat.

Hearing his name in any context would have given her reason to hope. And if not to hope, to wait for what might happen. It gave her a reason to go out to the general mercantile, to get out on the street, to look up the road to Skatumpah and wonder if it would be possible soon that Father Lee would come into Kanab with his son.

Though they did not speak of it, both Hannah and Elizabeth saw the danger clearly. Hannah did not speak because she suspected Elizabeth wanted her to forget John Frederick Lee. Yet even the name was like music to her—the memories of their love were like forgotten melodies she wanted to recall. Those memories made it easier to hang wash, to weed the corn, to mend the quilts, to scrub the floors, to tend the children, and to sing.

"Something isn't wrong," Hannah said finally to Elizabeth's question. And she caught a twinkle in Elizabeth's eyes.

"Then what is so right, Hannah?" Elizabeth said, alert now and with more than a suggestion of a smile on her lips.

Hannah whispered. "Maybe you will be angry if I say . . ."

Elizabeth never made false promises. "I may be angry, but you know I will try to see things your way."

"It's about John Frederick Lee."

Elizabeth was feeding Anna Jane's little Christa hot gruel with a teaspoon. She stopped and put down the spoon, turned to Hannah. Her voice was a whisper, almost not there. "You couldn't let him go?"

"No."

Elizabeth took Hannah's wrist in her hand. "Then I can see things your way."

<br>

## 86

*Hannah*

It was true that John Frederick Lee came down from Skatumpah to Kanab to go with his father to the second hearing on the stolen cattle. But no one saw him. Someone said he had been slightly ill, that he had been suffering a relapse from his bout with the measles.

Hannah waited, sometimes impatiently. But she waited because she knew she would see him. And she did.

It was in the field on an overcast day in June. She was sweeping water from the canal into rows of corn, her hair tied up in a dark red kerchief, her red skirts tied up above Jacob's old leather boots. She stood astride the canal, moving the small wooden dam into the ditch to turn the trickle of muddy water into the field. Then, with the broom and the big ragged apron tied onto the end of the broom, she swept the water down into the shallow lanes. And as she swept the water down, she pushed the amber curls from her eyes. That was the moment she saw the rider on the large black mare riding forward from the corner of the field. The figure in the saddle moved easily with the ragged rhythm of the big animal's stride. He was dark against the distant brightness of the sun.

At first she did not know who it was. But it was not long before she could see his face—the straight mouth beneath a trim moustache set in a firm strong jaw, his hair blown back against his temples. His brows were thick above his father's piercing blue eyes. She saw his eyes at once. They were hesitant, lean with his look.

He did not even say "hello." He simply drew the horse near her, bent low, and held out his arm. "Jump, Hannah," he said. Climbing up to the horse, she felt the land turn under her, the gray mountains turn at the edge of the treeless plain under the blue sky. As he scooped her up into his arms, she clung to the saddle horn, sitting side saddle in front of him, her muddy boots dangling free. Glancing back toward the house, he spurred the horse forward. The animal sidestepped through the corn and then into the canal and down the path to the slope that fell away to the fields beyond. They rode in silence, both knowing that the time for words would come.

The hills passed from the east and north like waves in a sea. John Frederick Lee brought her to the south ravine beyond their land into the fields of the Campbells, into the clearing beyond a row of feathery juniper trees. The branches moved in the light like silk in the sky.

"Did you think I wouldn't come?"

She admitted she wasn't sure.

"My father is going to sell out in Washington and take some of us to a ferry crossing. Miles away."

"Is that where you are going with him?"

"My mother wants to go back to Panguitch where her mother and father are. I may go with them."

*Then I want to come to Panguitch*, Hannah wanted to say, but they were brazen words, and she bit her tongue.

John Frederick stopped near a copse of juniper, jumped from his horse, and tied the animal to a tree. He reached for Hannah. She hesitated when he raised his arms.

"Jump down," he said.

She placed her hands on his shoulder and leaned forward. His grip tightened on her waist and she fell against him. He leaned into her while she slid to the ground.

The steady softness of his embrace reminded Hannah of the old feelings. Breathless, she felt her mouth on his hair, then his hands in her curls, and he was holding her face against his lips and breathing in her eyes. When she yielded, her heart stopped beating.

"Hannah. Hannah."

"John," she whispered, finding his lips.

"You haven't forgotten."

" John," she whispered again. " John," and she felt the light dizzying her.

"I came as soon as I felt I could."

"I know."

"You haven't forgotten."

"No." She rested against his arm. "And I never will."

"Shhh." He touched her lips. "You cannot promise."

"I won't need to promise."

"We stayed in Washington for as long as we could."

"What will happen?"

"My father will win the judgment in St. George."

"And then . . ."

"We'll go again."

You'll go again? Her first thought was that if John Lee were going, what of Jacob? If what Elizabeth had whispered to her so many years ago—that many more than Father Lee had participated at Mountain Meadows—it wasn't fair. Then Jacob too . . . all of them should go again, she wanted to say. But she had never breathed the assertion before, and could not breathe it now. Instead, she said, "Where?" And the question hung on the clear air.

"Shhh. I don't want to go without you."

"No," Hannah whispered.

"No or yes? Say yes."

"Yes."

"It can't be now."

"It's all right." Her eyes were alive with fire. "When?"

"When my father is established again . . . I . . . he needs me. I am going wherever he goes. Perhaps to the river crossing for those who will go into Arizona . . ."

"I'll be here. I promise."

Again he put his fingers on her lips. "Don't promise anything yet, Hannah. Make a promise when you are sure it will never be broken."

## 87
### Kanab, March 17, 1873, Jacob

As time passed—harvest after harvest—Jacob had a more difficult time remembering all of the reasons they had come to the desert. Why had they? Why had they run from Kanarraville? They had lived in the hot empty land for three years now, but still they were barely hanging on. The fire had taken its toll. Now Anna Jane was ill. And there had been the cruel taunts from the boys who had recognized that his son was a Lee. "Lee, Lee, Johnny Lorry's a Lee!" they'd chanted.

If Jacob had forgotten why they had moved to Kanab, the memory came clearly to him in March after the conference in St. George. Before the closing prayer, the visiting authority, President Lorenzo Snow, who was in line to become the next president of the church after Brigham Young, had read a list of names, and Jacob's was on it. He sat up, alarmed.

"For a year and a half, the Lee family has been building the ferry at Lee's crossing," President Snow said. "We are calling some of you to settle Arizona."

When he read the names, those who had not been called breathed audible sighs of relief. Murmurs sounded through the hall.

At the close of the meeting, President Snow took Jacob Lorry aside. "There is more, Brother Lorry," he said quietly. "I happen to know this," he said, and his eyes pierced Jacob's. His words seemed heavy and sharp and cutting. "Even though your wife is ill, she is a Lee. We don't want anything to happen. Can you see things our way? Too much trouble . . . Search warrants are out. Arrest warrants. Finally the ferry at the Colorado is ready to cross. Henry Day will be leaving in early May. Prepare yourself for this group. This is a new colony, a mission. Lorenzo Roundy found sites for settlement. It would be best. We would like nothing to happen . . . and we hope you will understand."

Jacob, trying to read President Snow's face, heard only a few words. The man knew Anna Jane was a Lee. But did he know about Jacob himself? Did he know he had been at the meadow also? Did President Snow know that he, Jacob Lorry, had shot the dark-headed man in the face until J.B . . . He could not process his thoughts. They still burned in him.

"Do you understand us, Brother Lorry? Can you take on yourself the opportunity of going as an emissary of the Lord to colonize the valley beyond the San Juan—to make the Arizona country blossom as the rose?"

"Yes."

He had taken the bitter pill with him to Anna Jane and tried to keep his own mouth closed around it while she lay on the settee in the main room of the small log house.

"I'll be all right. The Lord will bless us," she said, looking up through pale eyes.

"I didn't want this to happen to us . . ." With his hands in his pockets, he looked out of the window to the fields where the children were running toward the house. Johnny, Hannah and Elizabeth followed them carrying baskets of dry weeds to a smoldering weed pile, where wisps of smoke churned into the air.

Life had not been easy in Kanab. The elevation contributed to harsh winters. At least there were no winters in Arizona. Perhaps that would alleviate some problems, but he wasn't sure.

"Are you going to take Elizabeth?"

"If she wants to go."

As before, Elizabeth was stunned. "But we have just planted the fields here."

"Will you go?" Jacob studied her face. Not long ago, they had received a short note from Robert Lorry to his half brothers revealing that J.B. was in Toquerville, where he had been able to find Maggie. Jacob and Elizabeth had agreed that they'd always guessed J.B. would eventually gravitate to Maggie. Though they had never been in touch with either of them, they agreed that Maggie and J.B. had an unusual bond with each other. And there was some kind of irony in the fact that Maggie had once more stepped in for Elizabeth, drawing away J.B.'s attention. "Will you go?" Jacob asked again.

Elizabeth met Jacob's gaze. "Yes."

They had prepared mostly around the needs of Anna Jane. Hannah, now barely seventeen, seemed to be watching faces, seeing things Jacob believed she could see. Yet his fear seemed to keep him from asking the questions he thought he should ask.

"I sent a message to John Lee. You may see John Frederick before long," he said, betraying that he had been reading her thoughts.

There was a crimson flush along Hannah's white neck. She gazed briefly at Jacob, but continued to pack the cups in the towels and place them in the crates.

They had exercised their option here on the land, so that they owned it. But they could not take time to sell it. Jacob gave the property to Bishop Christensen.

"And the proceeds . . . ? All I have is yours, Bishop. If I need help in Arizona, at House Rock, I will . . . contact you."

The bishop took Jacob under his large arm, and put a finger to his mouth. "There is no need to say. No need to say. We will take care of you. You are like my own son."

When they parted, Jacob tried to memorize the view east down the road from Kanab, past the fork to Johnson's canyon and Skatumpah, a place he might never see again. He was ready, he said. He would follow the other eighteen wagons in the Henry Day party, carefully climbing the small hills west of town under the blue hot May sky of 1873. Elizabeth, tall under a white bonnet, seemed different now, unlike the harried woman of her past—almost relaxed and happy. Jacob hoped she and her three boys would go with them always. He hoped it would be always.

Anna Jane lay under a tarpaulin on the wagon, still unable to walk or stand. "The nerves in the spine may never heal," a traveling doctor had once said. But she could smile. So she held the children, read to them, and gave quiet instructions to Belinda. She also listened to Hannah, who often talked to her about their future.

"You believe John Frederick will be at the ferry?" Hannah asked.

"I believe it," Anna Jane whispered. "He would have stayed with his father as much as possible."

And Hannah, herself believing it was true, could sing.

## 88

### *Elizabeth*

*May 15, 1873. Perhaps there is something for all of us in Arizona: for Hannah the fulfillment of her love, for the rest of us a place to find the peace we have sought away from those who would have us believe we are marked because of a terrible occurrence that we wear like a crown of thorns. Perhaps there is something there for all of us if we are on the Lord's errand.*

Elizabeth had borne up under the ordeal of moving across the desert with the Henry Day party as though it were a small part of her life—so small that it did not deserve much thought. It was a journey. That was enough. She tuned out responses to the sun and wind and sky, the barren waste, the discomforts of every day.

With the eighteen other wagons, they dragged across the hot, dry hills, making slow progress, dodging rattlesnakes, setting up camp at night under a sky washed with stars. In early May it was still cold in the mornings. They woke with the wool sheets in their bedding frosty where their breath had made it moist.

Slowly the land passed from its red sage-scarred washes to a bleak yellow desert crabbed with scrub growth barely larger than patches of foam in the ocean. Beyond the trail stood monolithic runes of gray rock forging giant lengths of table land and black bruises as far as the eye could see.

Elizabeth woke from her lethargy only when the scout in the Henry Day party returned. The camp had just finished breakfast.

"We'll be at Lees' ferry today," he shouted from his horse as he rode in.

Elizabeth thought she saw Hannah's eyes light up at those words. Only then did her heart begin to hope—even if it were only for the fulfillment of Hannah's love.

It was a hot day. May 18, 1873. The sun seemed to be high enough and hot enough to bake the earth into sand. The children without shoes began to complain. Later, as the party followed the Colorado River, they skirted the edges to keep from burning the soles of their feet. The spring stream seemed to swell up around their legs as they walked, rising a little higher and running more swiftly than before. At one point Johnny Lorry fell into the water, and climbed out drenched from head to toe. Hannah was close to him, but she had failed to grab him until he was soaked through to the skin.

"I believe I know what you're thinking about," Elizabeth often smiled at Hannah. "Your dreams are showing."

There was no secret about what Hannah hoped. But when they reached the barren hot edge of rock where the small red rock buildings of Lees' Ferry stood in the sand on the edge of the river, only the father John Lee and his wife Emma came to meet them. Elizabeth noted Emma's children, one by one. But John Frederick wasn't there.

The ferry, christened the "Colorado," was moored to a sturdy wharf at the side of the river, a structure built in April by Brigham's twenty-seven men. By now the spring run-off had glutted the stream with such a high current that crossing looked all but impossible.

Finally they caught sight of John Lee. He was standing still against the red buttes. His throat was bound up as if he were suffering from chills and a fever, and his blue eyes were shot with blood. In the midst of his personal difficulties, he was still giving instructions to help the Day party, just the same.

"We crossed eight wagons here six days ago. There's a flat plane across the river that climbs to the plateau." He pointed southeast. "It's a desert up there." When he said these words, John Lee cleared his throat several times and sniffled into his handkerchief, then coughed and drew his head down into the muff of linsey woolsey on his neck.

Elizabeth watched him as he struggled to talk with Henry Day. She had not seen John Lee for more than a year. But there was no time now to talk with him, no time to reminisce about anything. She looked at the wind-roughened cliffs of red rock jutting up into the blue sky. So he had been called to come here. It was fittingly named: Lonely Dell. For outside of this flat space beside the rushing river—a brown sandy flat with a few sparse trees—there was only the bulk of rising rock and terraces of stone.

Listening to what was happening around her only through a daze, Elizabeth was overcome by the bleakness of the landscape. She was grateful when Emma Lee invited her to come to the ranch house for a few moments. Situated a few hundred yards back into the small canyon, it was a pleasant sight. A garden struggled in irrigation water from a small stream. The small log home with its smithy nearby sat against the green and red slopes. A barnyard with a few animals and a small fenced graveyard could be seen in the distance through the draw.

Emma was gracious as she brought Elizabeth out of the hot sun into the small house where she had lived for two years. Elizabeth marveled at Emma's quilts, her furniture, and the needlework she had done. The twin baby girls and the young Frances Dell had followed them to the house. Frances Dell had been born while Emma was virtually alone here. By herself she had cut the cord and buried the afterbirth. Elizabeth could not imagine how Emma had managed all of this in this vast empty place, which seemed as hollow and as resounding as an echo in a prehistoric gloom.

There was enough bread and honey at the house to make thick sandwiches. The children took their own supply with them, and Elizabeth helped Emma to carry the rest to the ferry for the men. When they returned to the ferry and began to talk with the men, Elizabeth thought of a thousand questions she wanted to ask. But she could not bring herself to ask any of them.

As they neared the Day party again, they began hearing Lee's instructions and Henry Day's questions.

"Build a road in the rock?" Henry Day was questioning John Lee. Henry stood a foot taller than most of the other men in the party. He was dark-eyed, with a rough-shaven gray beard and a head furry with salt and pepper gray-black curls.

Elizabeth, still dazed by the incredible mist of a sense of unreal dreams, heard an edge of anger in Day's words. She began to see John Lee more sharply now, for he had drawn up out of his linsey woolsey at Day's voice.

"This country ain't ready for us, then," Day said with finality.

"Ain't ready?" John Lee looked up from his linsey woolsey. His bloodshot eyes stared at Henry Day with grim determination. "We already crossed more than fifty wagons here. Eight of them last week. River's a little higher, that's all."

"Shouldn't be callin' anybody into this country until a decent ferry and road are built," Day said.

Elizabeth's heartbeat quickened. She watched John Lee. He was exerting control now.

"If you don't like the road or the ferry, you can make your own arrangements." By now Lee's voice was cutting, an edge like a knife.

"I wasn't called to build roads or a boat."

Elizabeth felt numb. There was a silence among the entire group. Day's voice was thick with resentment, and everyone watched John Lee. Elizabeth felt a compassion for him she had never felt before. He stood a little broken, obviously ill. It was very apparent that though he was doing the best he knew how to do, all about him were hostile forces that had been wearing him down. The rocks. The wind. The water and the hot sun. And the past—with all that had happened.

The land seemed to close down on them with the crush of its giant fist. She wanted to scream, "Brother Day! Stop it. Let us go on as we can. Brother Day!" And the words "Brother Day, Brother Day" seemed to echo, unspoken, on her tongue. Brother Day.

"Better men than you have passed over this route without as much whining," John Lee said.

Elizabeth prayed, then, and the others must have prayed. Their irritated leader now stalked back to the ferry to unhitch some oxen. The women followed them with the food, although a meal seemed to be the least of their worries at present.

John Lee. She saw him as she had worshipped him once before. So long ago. He led out as a man of decision, purpose, a man who asked no questions of difficulty. Now if she were to communicate with him, it would be only with her heart. When he looked her way, it was through vacant eyes. A few times his eyes wandered in her direction, but only once did a flicker of recognition suggest that he knew her. He scrambled to tie two yoked animals onto the ferry. Only when he stood at the river, with the men standing waist-deep in the water screaming at the tops of their lungs, did he see her, and she thought there was some kind of shared communion.

Finally he turned to her and acknowledged her with a request. "Elizabeth, could you help us with this rope?" Her heart leaped when she took it from his hands. Another of the men standing by also took it while Lee untied the ferry from its mooring.

"If there is time, I'd like to talk with you." That was all. No other words. And no other time.

*For three days the Day company crossed to the southeast side of the swift Colorado River: 62 animals, 15 oxen and cows, 2 calves, 47 horses and mules and 19 wagons— without accident with the exception of breaking two oars, one Rough lock, & one wagon missing the boat as the wagon was roled in & detained us about one hour, & one cow & one horse jumped off the Boat & swam ashore all right,* Lee wrote later.

On the hot rocks on the other side, the children bound up their feet with old cloth. They set up a temporary camp and rested the last half of the last day.

Elizabeth might have guessed there would be no time for her to talk with John Lee alone. On that last night Emma crossed on the ferry with hot breads and butter. They roasted a large pig on a spit and ate pork and bread until they were all very full. Finally, some of the children begged John Lee to take them down the river on the boat under the big moon. One of Emma's boys played the guitar while they sang hymns and old love songs.

Elizabeth heard Hannah's voice, plaintive above the rest. The girl was sitting on the narrow end of the boat across from her, next to Emma Lee. Emma held the little girl Dellie in her arms. Hannah was whispering to her. Only after Elizabeth clearly heard Emma's answer could she guess what Hannah had asked.

"Rachel's at the pools, twenty-six miles up river. Mary's in Paria. Caroline went back to Skatumpah. The others are in Panguitch." There was a pause. "Except for John Frederick. He sometimes comes to help his father here. He was coming from Panguitch. Actually, he should have been here by now . . ."

Elizabeth saw the concern in Hannah's face. She thought she could feel what the girl was feeling, and it touched her, hurt her, created longing in her heart. She was glad that the moment changed when John Lee led out with one of her favorite hymns.

*Redeemer of Israel, our only delight.*
*On whom for a blessing we call.*

Lee's voice was big. Despite the chill or the fever, or the linsey woolsey, he could well be heard with his strong booming baritone. The muscles of his face were tight across his chiselled bones, the large, hard lines in the set nose and jaw. His face was clearly visible, backed by the yellow-blue light of the fire. He watched the hills as he sang with conviction. She thought she saw tears on his cheeks.

*Our shadow by day and our pillar by night*
*Our king, our deliverer, our all.*

Our deliverer. Elizabeth thought she had come alive on this journey because she was in the presence of John Lee. Seeing him had always stirred her blood, wakened her from a lethargy. Now she sat on the boat with him and the others, hearing the rush of the water as it swept them forward down the Colorado River, lapping against the sides. The children scooped up bright drops of water with their fingers and laughed in the spray.

*How long we have wandered as strangers in sin,*
*And cried in the desert for thee.*
*Our foes have rejoiced when our sorrows they've seen,*
*But Israel will shortly be free.*

Will shortly be free. When is shortly? So many years. She was in her mid-thirties. She watched Joshua and Caleb and Joseph dip into the water, laugh and dip into it again. Israel, who is Israel? One's own deliverance is not necessarily the deliverance of all of them. Perhaps in Arizona there would be peace. She saw Jacob's studied gaze toward the red hills. She felt she had not done all she could have done for him—given more help to his household in Anna Jane's time of need. She watched the attentive Belinda seated next to her mother Anna Jane— John Lee's daughter. Anna Jane had never fully recovered from the accident at the fort celebration. She was pale; the moonlight illuminated her face, the slim nose, the bright brown eyes. She looked so much like her mother, Aggatha. Aggatha's death in Harmony before they left had hurt them all. There had been a long line of people who had come to the house before Aggatha left them. "Good-bye. Good-bye," Aggatha had said. "I am going away and will tell God hello for all of you." Aggatha had held Anna Jane's cheek against her breast for a long time.

Aggatha's spirit might even now be only a hand's breadth away. But the memory of her was immediately near.

"It's quiet," Elizabeth said to herself. "It's peaceful. We are delivered in our strength from our enemies. The Lord has blessed us." They were only thoughts, not words she could have said with conviction yet. She barely heard them. But they rang true to her. She felt the cool spray of the water on her cheek and thought to herself, *No matter what happens, now I will be able to accept it. Journeys can help us come other distances as well.*

### 89

*Elizabeth*

*May 30, 1873. Here is what happened at House Rock in Arizona Territory. There was no water. There was nothing. The spring that some had seen before was completely dry. And so we were forced to turn back. It is the end of our going anywhere. Henry Day has turned us back around. As we returned, it was not long before Hannah found her John Frederick. He had heard we were going to make this journey, and he had decided to come along to help. And we needed him. When he heard of our decision to go back, he was concerned.*

*"My father will believe you are not obedient if you do not go the whole distance. If you give up," John Frederick told us. "He will be grieved to think that a people called by the Lord have not had faith enough to believe that the Lord would help them to stay the course." John Lee. Even at this time I cannot but think of all the men I have ever known, he is the*

*most remarkable one. We knew John Frederick was right, that John Lee would have gone the distance for the Lord no matter what happened. He may have gone the distance, but we did not.*

And John Frederick was right. John Lee did not look respectfully upon their giving up. "It's a trick of the devil," Father John Lee said between his teeth to Henry Day. "If you want to listen to the Devil, then keep listening to the voice you are hearing." He paused only momentarily before he continued. "President Brigham Young prophesied that the blessings of God would follow the hand of industry, that the water should increase an hundredfold and springs of living water should burst forth and rich feed would yet cover those sterile plains and a large city would yet be built on that ground. And domes and steeples and spires would reach two hundred and fifty feet in the air. He also prophesied that a flood would come and wash away a stone fort, along with the mill and trees that stood for one hundred and fifty years. He saw the stream cut thirty feet deep and that it would develop springs of living water, eventually increasing to thrice its size. It came true. It now sustains a population of many thousands and the fine city of St. George is being built with fine orchards and vineyards . . ."

Henry Day stared with steel gray eyes, his jaw set tight. Nobody had ever before put him down. He ground his teeth. Elizabeth thought she could hear the sound of the teeth grating against each other. She stayed close to Anna Jane on the wagon seat. For several days now, Elizabeth had known that Anna Jane was coming down with something. She was shivering, holding a blanket around her shoulders in the heat. She had not been able to breathe in the hot sand, to fight the dry wind.

That afternoon, the travelers left their wagons and crossed on the ferry to the Lees' to spend the evening, although Anna Jane and Belinda stayed with the wagon on the other side, helping to prepare for the return crossing the next day. Later in the evening Jacob and Day and several of the other men returned on the ferry to prepare the wagons. In the evening, while Jacob was gone, Elizabeth went with John Frederick and Hannah to the long red rock buildings at the ferry to see John Lee.

The man sat in a great chair in the main room. Although Emma and the children had come down to be with him, they were out of sight behind a blanket

When John Frederick opened the door, his father beckoned him to come in. The weary older Lee was trying to relax after having supervised the crossing of the first seven of the nearly one hundred wagons that day. He leaned back in the chair and closed his eyes against the light from the oil lamp.

"Father."

"Come in, son."

At first Lee did not see Elizabeth or Hannah. He looked tired sitting in the great chair. Emma was putting the little ones to sleep in the other room behind the partition. She was singing the twins a song.

*Let the angels whisper*
*They are calling you to come.*
*Follow them to dreamland*
*And dream about the sun.*

Everything was hushed in the rock house. The camp down at the river where the men and women would be discussing their plans seemed far away.

John Lee's eyes were heavy and it seemed he could not keep the lids from closing. But he looked up now, and saw Elizabeth and Hannah. A gleam of recognition lit his eye. He nodded a greeting to them. But he stayed silent, still holding the linsey woolsey on his throat.

"John, are you all right?" Elizabeth said.

"Elizabeth . . ." John Lee began. But he held back. "My boy," he said, and then he held his hand out to John Frederick, who grasped it with a forceful grip. "Maybe you've got more strength than I have, Son. But I hold on as much as I can. Even a little strength is the first prerequisite to making miracles happen."

John Frederick drew in his breath quickly at the power still left in his father's grip. John Lee looked at Elizabeth. He didn't say anything specifically to her, though his look had a distant fire in it. He turned to Hannah. "Hannah . . ." he whispered. He looked at her for a while through his weary eyes. "Hannah Lorry. Of course I remember you. You are someone special. Isn't she, Elizabeth?" For a moment there was silence. He had not forgotten anything. The air literally darkened with the power of his memory.

"Can I talk to you, Father?"

"Yes, she is beautiful, son." He smiled at her.

When John Lee took Hannah's hand, she too gasped at the strength there.

But John Lee changed the subject, because something heavier—something more weighty even than John Frederick's requests—lay on his mind. "So they didn't want to stay in Arizona? Was it so hard?" he asked them.

"Anna Jane was ill," Elizabeth whispered.

"Yes, yes. Of course." Then he said listlessly, "A hundred wagons. More than enough for a few days' work. It may take more than a week to cross."

"Yes, Father," John Frederick said. But now he was determined to speak his mind. "While we're here . . . Jacob and Elizabeth, and . . . we . . . wanted to ask you . . . Hannah and I want to be married here . . ."

John Lee stared for much too long. It was a moment Elizabeth could not understand. He raised his eyes, and she thought she saw tears. "You know I can't perform it, son. I have no priesthood . . ."

The words rang against the walls of the small rock house.

John Frederick whispered, "I know, Father. But perhaps the bishop . . . or Lorenzo Roundy. Please, Father." He said the words fast enough to cover up the choking silence.

John Lee turned toward the other room. Emma Lee came through the doorway.

"Emma, my darling," John said. "The children want to get married . . . here."

Emma stopped. As she saw Hannah and John Frederick Lee, a smile began on her lips.

"A wedding?" she whispered.

John Frederick nodded. Elizabeth felt Hannah's grip tighten on her arm.

"Oh, yes! We need a wedding at once! It's what all of us need! A large, great wedding."

"Tomorrow, then."

"Tomorrow or the next day. Or at least soon. As soon as all the wagons cross to the north side of the river! Wonderful! A wedding it will be!"

Elizabeth watched a faded smile on John Lee's lips. "And then?" he asked his son.

"Then I will stay here at the ferry to protect you . . . though I won't force Hannah. She may choose."

John Lee shook his head, still leaning against the back of the chair. "No." He held his chin high.

"Yes. I want to stay here."

John Lee's eyes looked empty. He stared at Elizabeth. It was as though he did not see her at all. "All of you. All of you will go to Panguitch and take care of your mother. It is not safe here."

There was a heavy wind in the trees outside. Emma moved into the room and closed the window and the door.

"If you need me, I will stay," John Frederick began again, although he sensed the resolution in his father's voice.

"There is nothing for you here, John Frederick. It's much too dry to farm.

It is best for you to be in Panguitch. Run the farm for all of us. Grow the wheat. We'll need it."

John Frederick began to protest. "Father—" he began.

"What do we have here for you?" Lee's voice was sharp now. "This is my burden to bear alone!" He gestured with his hand. A strong night wind came up again and hummed through chinks in the stone. Elizabeth felt cold. She drew her shawl about her shoulders and backed away. Hannah turned toward John Frederick and nestled in his arm.

"Of course you will go to Panguitch. Because I say you must," John Lee repeated.

"Yes, Father." But John Frederick sounded reluctant.

Lee was quiet now. "So many years have passed. So much has happened." He paused. "Hasn't it, Elizabeth?" He seemed broken.

"He is tired," John Frederick whispered to them as they stood on the wharf, watching the water under the moon, listening to the waves wash against the boat. "If people will not go to Arizona, will he be useful at the ferry? It was obviously their way of protecting him, taking him from harm's way. Obviously Brigham Young sent him on a wild goose chase because he wanted him somewhere safe and he didn't know what else to do."

Hannah stood very close to John Frederick, and Elizabeth drew away. On this side of the river, the few wagons that had already crossed were drawn in a circle for sleep. Across the river they could see the lights of the remaining camp. In the distant circles of light, Jacob would be there with the Lorry wagon and Anna Jane.

"He is a tired man. And ill. And still running away," John Frederick whispered now to Hannah.

Elizabeth listened to the water, to the quiet of the night, to the lowing of the animals who had come down to the edge of the river to drink. She also listened to John Frederick's words, knowing that his concern for his father equaled her own. She thought she heard tears deep in John Frederick's voice. "And I love him so."

## 90

### Elizabeth

*June, 1873. The winds are moving more swiftly down through the canyon now. Only eight or ten wagons are left on the Arizona side. Jacob is waiting to move our wagon—to make the crossing northwest at the safest time for Anna Jane. And until her pains subside. But now the river is swelling with a storm in the north only miles away. And Anna Jane is anxious to move soon.*

"I am fine," Anna Jane said. "The children wanted to hold their wedding this evening, and I want to be there."

Elizabeth, who had finally come back across on the ferry to help, stood beside her and felt a slight fever on Anna Jane's brow. "Jacob," Elizabeth whispered. She looked up, communicating with him silently, then shook her head. "She isn't well."

But it was true the children had held off the wedding for several days now, and it looked cloudy, as though the storm were on its way south. Hannah had come with Belinda to stay beside the wagon bed where Anna Jane lay. The two girls sat inside the wagon and tended the baby Christa while Anna Jane slept off and on through the noon meal. Belinda held the baby while Hannah took Anna Jane's hands and held them tightly. "Anna Jane. We're waiting for you. It's so important to me that you are there. Emma has been up at the ranch house baking for us. She knows how to make the most wonderful cakes."

Anna Jane smiled, first at the girls, and then at Jacob. "The cakes and pies and cookies can't possibly last more than a few days. And I'll be as fine in the wagon on the ferry as I was in the wagon on the trail."

If they could move the wagon without jarring it, Anna Jane would be all right. There was so much tenderness in the nerves of her back. Someone suggested that they could remove her from the wagon. But Jacob thought it was best to leave her where she was. It was not long before all of them decided they could not wait any longer. In the afternoon it began to rain.

"Please, let's go soon," Anna Jane said, gripping Jacob's hand. "Take me across before the storm."

When large drops began falling on the sand, Jacob yoked up the oxen, drew the wagon to the river, unyoked the oxen, and with the help of three other brethren pushed the wagon onto the lip of the ferry and slowly across the surface, holding it steady.

Suddenly there was lightning in the sky. With a terrible wind, black clouds scudded through the crossing and began to spit rain. The covered wagon tarp over the top had been torn, and the ragged edge of its gaping holes flapped in the wind. Since there were no covers to ward off the water, Elizabeth set some small crates up around the sides of Anna Jane's wagon bed and tacked a tarp onto the boxes, stretching it across the baby Christa and Anna Jane. As the crates settled into the wagon bed, the old canvas came within only a few inches of the woman's face. As soon as the wagon stood on the ferry, the men began to push. Elizabeth walked close by, holding to the wagon and the wagon bed where Anna Jane and Christa lay.

"You'll be all right," Elizabeth said. "Hold my hand, Anna Jane."

The worst of the storm came suddenly. The sky opened up and dumped unbelievably heavy sheets of rain. And only moments later, the roiling river swelled from bank to bank. John Lee said he had never seen anything like this before at the ferry. It reminded him of the storm that had destroyed them once before. The water, like a dangerous animal, rose up in a dark swirling mass of foam, mud, and broken limbs.

First they heard the cracking sound. It was like gunshot, a great scarring crack that sent chills up into Elizabeth's hair. She turned toward it instinctively, gripped with fear. Up the river in the black foam, spun a huge gray gnarled tree. She squeezed Anna Jane's hand beneath the tarp until the water forced her to cling to the edge of the wagon. The two men came quickly. Jacob reached inside the box for Anna Jane, though John Lee cried out to him to stop. Taking action, John Lee tied a rope to the wagon wheel on his side of the river and threw the other end of the rope to the opposite shore, now only a stone's throw away.

"Hold to the wagon!" John Lee shouted. "Cling to the rope!"

But any action they would have taken was too late. The giant gray tree gnawed at the center of the ferry until it chewed a huge raw gaping chunk in its side. And then, swirling and tossing about on the water, it turned and scraped the wagon off as though it were a morsel on a plate. Finally, the tree bounced over the ferry, tearing it in two. And the wagon bobbed in the water while the men, struggling in the powerful stream, held to the rope with all the power they could muster.

"Anna Jane! Anna Jane! Hold on," Jacob and John Lee both screamed.

The ferry, now in splintered fragments of torn and crumpled lumber, washed down the river. The wagon bounced and bobbed unmercifully in the cold. John Lee, inundated and fighting the river, a white-faced buoy on the water with the linsey woolsey unraveling from his neck like yarn, yelled at the others, instructing them to pull the wagon with the rope. Finally the taut rope brought it to the bank, far downriver, far beyond the wharf. The water had washed through the wagon like a sieve, sending pots and pans and articles of clothing spinning down the flume like tiny leaves. On the shore stood seven or eight other men along with Bishop Roundy and John Frederick Lee. They shouted and pulled at the rope until the wagon began to lift out of the current.

"Raise the wagon! They're inside!" Jacob cried. He leaped into the water, and fighting the powerful stream, drew the rope around under the wagon bed until, like a match box bobbing in the current, the men could pull it out.

Elizabeth, soaked through in every part of her body clung with all of her power to the tarp tacked to the boxes. Holding to the box at the far side, she felt the water pouring into the dark space where little Christa and her mother lay.

*Dear God above, save their lives,* Elizabeth repeated over and over again to herself. She willed them in her heart to live, for they meant more to her at this moment than anything had ever meant in her life. She had a fleeting thought that if anything would happen to Anna Jane, she would want to give up, too. She wasn't really thinking that thought, was she? Was it a moment of decision in her own mind? For she felt the canvas beneath her fingers slipping. As the men slowly pulled the wagon box to the ground, she thought how easy it would be to let her fingers relax and let the water dash her away, carry her downstream—like a leaf bobbing into the blackness. A momentary darkness eclipsed her brain, and she saw nothing but stars behind her eyes. Going. She felt she was going until she saw Jacob force himself around the bobbing wagon box and tie the rope while the men pulled it out of the sand and scum.

*Going. Oh dear Lord. If Anna Jane is still alive, let her be well enough to smile.* Suddenly Anna Jane's smile was something she saw in her mind's eye like a hot sun.

"Hold tight, Elizabeth! You're going under!" Jacob screamed. "Hold to the rope!" Bishop Roundy cried from the shore where the others stood praying. "Hold to the rope, Brother Lorry!"

Now Elizabeth saw them reach out to the dark waters to rescue John Lee. When he reached the bank of the river, he paused for a moment while the debris of the storm crashed about his shoulders. When the men pulled him up out of the water, he resembled a drowned cat from his tousled hair to the leather boots. But at last he had been wrenched free. Though looking broken, with his linsey woolsey dragging several feet from his throat, he did not stop for any more formalities. When he was on solid ground, he turned back to pull at the wagon rope until the box reached the shore. As Elizabeth, soaked and bent, climbed out of the water, Lee tugged to lift the precious cargo up.

"Anna Jane!" Lee cried out, knowing the exact spot in which his daughter and granddaughter lay beneath the canvas tarp. Almost before the struggling men had brought the wagon out of the water, John Lee was clawing at the wagon cover. "Anna Jane!" he cried, tearing away the canvas. The bed was filled with water. The bobbing woman and the baby looked like wet paper, their faces flaccid just above the surface, their eyes closed.

Was there breath there? John Lee tore the canvas away and reached inside for his daughter. Jacob tore the baby away and handed her to Emma, who immediately held the child upside down to allow the water to drain from her nose and mouth. The baby began to sputter, to cough. Elizabeth breathed a sigh of relief. Jacob then turned to Anna Jane, as frantic as his father-in-law.

"Don't let her go. God save her." Lee pulled the wet hair back from Anna Jane's brow. She was as pale as white clay. John Lee leaned toward her and put his fingers on the pulse in her neck. "Her blood's still beating," he shouted, waving his arms to push the crowd back. Then he pushed at her breast until the water poured from her mouth. Gathering her into his arms, and with Jacob's help at her feet, John Lee carried her into the rock house. Emma had come down from the ranch house with the children. A few of the women warmed some water and stoked the fire in the ferry office fireplace. The little rock building seemed small, but it was warm.

Elizabeth followed them into the largest room, feeling cold and wet. Hannah gave Elizabeth a down quilt, which she wrapped around her shoulders until such a time as she could get out of her wet clothes. But now was not the time. Lee, Jacob, and John Frederick Lee lay Anna Jane on the cot behind the blanket partition and Lee began rubbing his daughter's cheeks.

"Anna Jane! Anna Jane," he begged. He turned her face toward his, and then away, toward him, and away. "Dear one. Wake up. Cough. Breathe."

Jacob was leaning over her, listening to her heart. Again and again he pumped her chest. Water still dribbled out of her mouth.

John Lee stood and placed his hands on her head. "Dear God. Please," his voice was choked. "Must she always suffer so? If it be thy will . . ."

Jacob stepped close to John Lee. He held Lee's hand. "Shall we get the oil?"

"Emma," Lee said. "The oil."

She found it in a cupboard quickly and passed it to them. Jacob parted Anna Jane's hair and poured a drop of oil on her head. Bishop Roundy came close to them.

"Can I help you?" Bishop Roundy whispered.

John Lee's gaze was stricken. "My priesthood . . ." he began. "My own daughter. Am I deprived of blessing my own daughter?" Then he looked Jacob fully in the face, as though he could remember all too well the reason and the morning all of them had walked into the meadows together. For a brief moment he stared as though all of his life were flooding back into him. He turned politely to Bishop Roundy. "You may participate," he said, "but I will bless my own child." He turned toward Jacob. "And he will bless his own wife. If God is willing."

Jacob anointed her with the oil, and John Lee sealed the blessing. "And Father, if it be thy will, if I should be inadequate, please heal my daughter with thy power . . ." He paused. The quiet in the room hovered above the sounds of their voices—as though there were no echoes in the dead space of air. Elizabeth thought she could hear a thin watery breath in Anna Jane's lungs. Was it her imagination? She held tight to Hannah's hand. "Through all of these years, Oh God, my Father—" Lee's voice broke. Elizabeth heard a stream of tears. "I have done it all . . . for You." Now his voice fell to a whisper, as though he had been completely broken. Even his body seemed to shrink as he stood there over Anna Jane. "For Anna Jane. And You. You and I, Lord. We have had these talks before. So let me speak if only once again. Please heal my precious daughter Anna Jane. She has suffered. Suffered. Spare her this time. In the name of our Lord and Savior Jesus Christ. Amen."

The rain and thunder still raged in the darkened skies outside the windows. The firelight in the stove flickered dimly against the solemn circle of worried faces in the room. Emma quickly fed more wood into the fire, and the flames darted upward, lighting John Lee's gold-gray hair.

The onlookers were still hushed. Anna Jane, with what looked like great effort, opened her eyes.

"She's alive!" Jacob breathed, and he knelt to her and held her face in his hands. The children came to her beside the settee. She held her hands out to them.

"Father," she whispered. "Father." When she saw John Lee, she held up her arms. He took her hands between his palms and rubbed them.

"God has given us all another chance," he said, the words thick in his throat. "He has given us another chance . . . again."

## 91

### Elizabeth

*June 18, 1873. The wedding gives us a reason to live. Everyone has been so good to us. Sister Longecker leant us her wedding dress—a white linen—and her pearls. Hannah looks like a cloud—or an angel. And her face is like a rose framed in that deep auburn hair.*

They held the wedding in the house at Lonely Dell. Elizabeth sat through it in a straight chair beside the settee where they had settled Anna Jane.

" . . . receive kingdoms, principalities and powers. For the building up of the kingdom of God upon the earth . . ."

Elizabeth heard Bishop Roundy's voice as though he were a part of the storm that had passed over them, the last whisper of the storm, the final voice that would part the veil for them. She saw darkness because so much of the time her eyes were closed while the tears spilled down her cheeks.

"Do you, John Frederick Lee, take this young woman, Hannah Lorry . . ."

The storm had left a great calm. They had been surrounded by pain . . . a great hungry pain which had ravished them. Now the wedding seemed to feed them with light.

"To love . . . to honor throughout life. Throughout all eternity. Forever."

Through eternity. Bishop Roundy said "forever" as though the word were a precious tone struck on a bell of gold. This would be the civil ceremony. To seal their love in God's priesthood for eternity, the young couple would go at a later date to the endowment house in Salt Lake City. That time would come soon enough. As she listened, Elizabeth heard the same words of the ceremony she had shared so many years ago with J.B. This is real. This is a commitment. This is binding. Echoing in her heart were the years she had lived that commitment in so much distress. What could all those years have meant? She could hear John Lee's words: "You are an angel. An angel of light to this home. Make a commitment. It is a gift to God. I have made such commitments before."

There was quiet.

"Do you take Hannah Lorry to be your wife?

"I do."

"And do you, Hannah Lorry, take this man . . ."

John Frederick stood tall, his neck stiff, limbs straight. He was a duplicate of his father—the lines of his face, the blond hair, darker than his father's, but the same coloring, the same steel blue eyes, and the careful tongue.

"Yes." The room hushed. All of the families were still. All of the children were seated on the floor. The men and women choked back tears.

Hannah's hand was trembling. It was as though it were Elizabeth's hand. Elizabeth stood there feeling as she had never felt before. Hannah in love. Completely sure. Totally knowing. This was the perfect moment in her life—that moment when the veil should be raised from her eyes and she could see the spirit-like images around her.

"Someday you will make an eternal bond of what you have."

Elizabeth pressed Anna Jane's hand while the bishop continued, "Blessed be the name of our God who has sealed unto you all blessings upon this earth, who shall seal all the blessings of heaven upon your heads. For he is God our Father in heaven."

*John Frederick, the son. And John Lee, the father.* Elizabeth saw the tears in his eyes also.

"Let virtue garnish thy thoughts unceasingly. Let God be thy light. Press forward with a perfect brightness of hope . . ."

After the ceremony, the children rushed to their father and Grandfather Lee. Elizabeth watched his large hands as he touched their curls. They clung to him. She and Jacob and John Frederick and Hannah had at last accepted his decision that they should go to Panguitch. But for several days, they had tried to convince him to come with them also.

But John Lee had simply stared at them as though what he heard was only the last wind under the empty sky. "And die?"

"You won't die. Soon they must see how wrong they have been to dishonor you—you have only done that which was commanded of you. You tried so hard to carry out their orders, keep out of trouble with the Indians. You have done so much for them all, to make it safe here for us all . . ."

He did not speak then.

Someone had gone to the window. It was Belinda Marie. She was looking out into the large hills and down the great ravine where she saw a horse in the distance. "Someone is coming," she whispered.

"Promise me . . ." he said without moving his head, as though the dark figure on the horse were death itself.

"Promise you what?" John Frederick asked.

"That you'll safeguard my name, my life, by prospering in Panguitch. That you'll go there and live good lives in the kingdom. That you will grow, rejoice, and live to make my life mean something after all . . ."

"We'll do the best we can, Father," Anna Jane whispered.

"Promise me," he repeated.

Soon the dark horse, rippling with foam, came into the yard. On its back was another of John's daughters, Nancy, who had come from the cluster of "pools" further northwest in the canyon. And with her was her little brother John Amasa Lee.

Belinda Marie sped to the door with her brothers. And Elizabeth's children, Joshua, Caleb, and Joseph, immediately came behind her. When the horse reached the house, Nancy dropped to the ground quickly, a small dark bird in a black cloak. She was thirteen now. John Amasa followed her. She carried a large white envelope in her hand. It flashed in Elizabeth's memory. She recalled other envelopes and the news they bore. John Lee took it in his hands slowly, slowly.

"Letter from Mother in Panguitch," Nancy whispered. "And an urgent message from Brigham Young. You must go further again—to Arizona—away." She was breathless, the air coming and going in gulps and gasps. "They are bringing six hundred troops here to arrest Papa Lee."

## 92
### *Jacob*

The Lorry family finally decided they could not continue to follow John Lee. They would obey his injunction to all of the families: go to Panguitch, grow, rejoice, and live to dignify his life. On July 18, 1873, the Lorry family moved northward into Panguitch with several other Lee families, while their grandfather and friend followed President Young's dictum to ride away from the ferry. He was to travel southward, through land as barren as rock, as far south as Moencopi—one hundred miles or more into the dead, hot desert.

Driving his teams along roads that began to show greener grasses, Jacob could only guess what his father-in-law faced in the barren wastes of the sun-baked sand.

As the Lorry wagons moved, the only major difficulty was the comfort of Anna Jane. Jacob walked beside the wagon most of the way, often holding her hand. Her back hurt her so much that as the wheels jarred against the rough road, she sometimes could not help but cry out. Finally, when at last they reached the Lee home in Panguitch, Caroline and her family lifted her gently from the wagon, and took her to a bedroom to rest.

In the days that followed, everyone insisted Anna Jane sit quietly in the kitchen without lifting one finger to help. But because she was unhappy doing nothing, she took it upon herself to read stories to the children, mend clothing, peel the potatoes, or snap the beans.

The neighbors of Panguitch—mostly Lee relatives from the Cedar City area—helped Jacob lay a foundation for a small brick home not far away. One of the men, a Hod Chandler, was purported to be the son-in-law of Philip

Klingensmith. His daughter Molly was a pretty dark-eyed sixteen-year-old, eager to help, who followed the men around as they dug for the foundation stones. Along with the other children, she lugged the rocks to them without thinking a moment of her clothes and shoes. At the end of the day she looked like an impoverished urchin. But she did not seem to mind.

While the Lorry children worked with the Lees and the Chandlers, Molly sometimes talked about her grandfather, Philip Klingensmith, lamenting how unfair it was that he had felt the need to leave them and change his name.

Finally her father spoke up. "Molly, please. We are trying to work."

Molly looked at her father with a blank stare. "They don't know anything about Grandfather."

"And the less the better," Hod said.

After that, Hod Chandler talked about his sheep. It was Hod who convinced Jacob he ought to go into the sheep business. Jacob, who still had a small savings from the sale of the Lorry property to the Redds, was even more convinced it was the right thing to do when Mr. Chandler offered to sell him his big ewe at a knocked-down price.

Their arrival in Panguitch marked the beginning of the Lorrys' adventures in the sheep business. When their brick house was built on the east side of town next door to Caroline's large place, the backyard faced up to the green fields where the lambs dotted the meadows that slowly rose into the hills. From their back window, Jacob could see lambs gamboling from day to day. Belinda Marie and the boys helped nurse them so that by the following spring of 1874, the sheep business was paying Jacob handsomely, and he was supporting not only his own family, but Elizabeth's family and Caroline Lee and her family, too. The joy in their success, however, could never replace their anxiety about their grandfather John Lee who was exiled in Moencopi so far away.

It was in the summer, on June 10, 1874, that a news photographer, James Fennimore, who had been at the Lonely Dell ferry last year, came through Panguitch and took many pictures of the Lee family on their land. But the pictures he took were not his only interest. It was soon evident that he had a soft spot in his heart for Belinda Marie Lorry. And it was plain that she had feelings for him, as well. Still young, Belinda was soon caught up and carried away by her feelings. She could only wonder if everyone felt as alive as she felt—as amazed at the fascination of love. As she became good friends with Molly Chandler, both girls shared talk about love, and Molly confessed that she was as alive with it as her friend Belinda Marie.

It was not long before Molly Chandler's energetic approach to life began to manifest itself in the Lorry family in an unusual way. She began to hover about Jacob, talking to him about her grandfather. Jacob felt uncomfortable with her talk, because he could not respond to it other than to show interest in the subject for her own sake, wondering why the subject of her Grandfather Klingensmith was something that Molly could not seem to abandon.

Both Belinda and Molly, in their excitement for life in general, went to a lot of trouble to plan a picnic that Belinda and James Fennimore could take together alone into the mountains on a Saturday. Jacob had not generally let Belinda go like this without an adult along. So, Belinda agreed that Molly should go. But Molly was not an adult and certainly not what Jacob had in mind as an escort. Since he had not been at all satisfied with her choice, Belinda reported that Molly would bring Sammy Lee. She had asked Sammy Lee if he would go, and he had said yes. Jacob and Anna Jane had given in at last, thinking that the four of them could have a good time.

Not feeling quite right about the arrangement, Jacob felt the need to warn Belinda. "You may go and have a good time. Just don't let romantic notions enter your heads."

"Molly doesn't even like Sammy," Belinda Marie whispered to her father.

She looked about the room to make sure Aunt Elizabeth or Anna Jane were neither one present, knowing that the secret she was about to reveal was one that her father could well find difficult to acknowledge.

"Then who does she like?" Jacob asked.

They were standing in the vestibule as Jacob prepared to leave. He drew on his coat. He was going into the town to a meeting with the town fathers about the Panguitch mercantile.

"Who is it?" Jacob asked again.

"Don't you know?" Belinda looked surprised.

"Don't I know what?" Jacob asked again.

Belinda sprang upwards toward him as though to surprise him with the wonderful news. "She loves you," she whispered, almost afraid to speak for fear of what Jacob would say, but determined that he should know.

Jacob hadn't been completely blind. He had wondered. He had seen Molly's laughter behind the blue eyes and wondered if there was more in that look than what was visible on the surface. He remembered how he had witnessed too many moments between Molly and Belinda Marie that had been filled with meaningful glances toward him.

Now that the news had been told, Jacob could not help feeling honored that a young girl should think of him in such a manner. Klingensmith's granddaughter was pretty, her bright sandy-colored hair heavy on her shoulders. She was tall and healthy with large bones, and her skin was fresh and clear.

He felt flattered. But still, she seemed a child to him. He was thirty-two and she was fifteen. What did she want of him? He was afraid to think of it. It was out of the question that he should take another wife. His resources were drained with the illness of Anna Jane. There had been rumors that soon the United States government would no longer allow polygamy, for the rumors were that the congress was planning to pass the Edmunds Act, which would make plural marriage illegal—a felony. Yet the Saints were still practicing it. And perhaps at an unprecedented rate. For Chandler himself had taken another young bride just recently, and the Arringtons, the Hatches, and the Farrells.

"Me?" Jacob said, feigning surprise. "She loves me?"

Belinda Marie was heart-wise. "You know that, Papa," she teased. "There's no way you could not have known it. Yes, she loves you. Can't you bring her into the family?"

Jacob could only feel amused.

"You mustn't tell Mama, please," Belinda Marie whispered. She put trembling fingers on his mouth. "She is so ill. Or Aunt Elizabeth. She would not like it."

Her last words struck Jacob as strange. Why did Belinda say that Elizabeth wouldn't like it? he asked himself. She had no claim on him. Perhaps if he did marry someone else, it would jar her awake. For she had never seemed willing to leave her marriage to J.B., even though J.B. seemed totally absent from their lives. If it had not been for that short letter that had come to Kanab from Robert to his Lorry brothers, they would never have known that J.B. had actually found his way to Toquerville and was once again living with Maggie. So Maggie had kept her commitment to J.B. after all. At the time the letter came, Elizabeth had been relieved to hear the news, almost certain that J.B. would never be back. Yet why had Elizabeth continued to live out her commitment all these years to J.B.? Though J.B. was Jacob's own father, since his marriage to Maggie, he had treated all of them with anger and disdain. The only tie that seemed to hold Elizabeth was that he was the father of her children.

No, these were angry thoughts, selfish thoughts. Jacob tried to put them away. He knew Elizabeth's heart had always belonged to John D. Lee.

John Lee. The most recent news was that the man who had been driven into the desert as far as Moencopi, was now very ill, and might possibly return soon. One morning in Panguitch, Jacob had been with the sheep in the sheep pen behind the house when a post came for Rachel. When she received the letter, she said she was not surprised. She told them that only a few days ago a little bird had come to her in the garden. His head bobbing up and down, he had told her the same news—that she should go quickly to Moencopi because John D. Lee was ill. She left immediately. It was true. She had found him in such sickly condition that he could not walk. Only one man—a Brother Williams—had been living with him in the wasteland, and their existence had been so minimal that neither of them was doing well. The family was notified by pony express that though he was stubbornly insisting on staying, as many as possible should come to take him to Panguitch, for no one wanted to risk his death in the hot sand.

A change had come over the Panguitch households at this news. It effected the Lorry household as well. Anna Jane had wept. "I, too, want Father here no matter what the risk," she had said, holding fast to Jacob's hand. Please, darling, urge him to come home."

All of them had insisted that their father and grandfather be brought to Panguitch. Caroline would keep him in her house, she said. He had been gone long enough. The world had forgotten him. There would be no questions asked anymore. How could the government be so cruel as to hunt down a sickly man, an elderly man, their grandfather, a man forced into exile these many years? He had done so much for his church—he had always done what he had been commanded to do, and yet in his time of need and sorrow, he could not even live with his family.

Jacob thought of all of this as he heard Belinda's whispers that day in the vestibule. She had taken his hand and then reached up to kiss his cheek. "Please, Papa, think about Molly."

He had not planned the words to come out because he hadn't wanted to honor the idea with any statement at all, but before he knew it, he openly spoke the question, "Why me?"

"Why does anyone fall in love?" Belinda whispered. "She just loves you. Can't you listen to her heart?"

But he was amused rather than impressed. She was a child! However, if it should come to the point that he would be called upon to obey a commandment . . .

Jacob looked at Hod Chandler and the daughter Molly with different eyes after that day. He saw the marriage as a way of connecting himself, his family, and their growing estate to the Chandler holdings. Though he felt mercenary thinking about it, at moments he allowed himself to ponder it. Chandler was an industrious man who owned a lot of land. Why not be concerned about the future of his children? And perhaps there would be more children if he were to wed Molly Chandler.

For the next few days—or for the days after the meeting at the mercantile where he had watched Hod Chandler with unusually perceptive eyes, he had felt light-headed, as though he saw the green hills spotted with the white lambs for the very first time—and as though he saw Molly for the first time. He brooded sometimes at home, feeling ill at ease, watching Anna Jane and Elizabeth when they were unaware he was watching them with his dark eyes. He felt some guilt, not understanding why this sudden prospect should so disturb him.

He watched Elizabeth bent over her needlework, unaware of what was happening in his heart. The work in the fields, the lambing, the building, haying, graining, all passed outside his consciousness as though it were something he watched another person doing. From an endless distance, from a long way away, above his consciousness he was thinking "Perhaps I should participate in obeying the commandment to enter plural marriage. Perhaps Molly . . ." At night in the dark room with Anna Jane curled like an animal in the hot sheet, her tortured nerves fluttering in her pain, he felt her against his body, loved her, then wanted her, and through the dark terror of his need, refrained.

Often he began to think that someone like Molly would have possibility. But in the deep recesses of his mind, the other woman in his arms was always— Elizabeth. Often he saw Elizabeth bent over her needlework, the stiffness in her neck telling him something of her need—something of a desire that she still felt to remain a part of all that was happening around her. He was reminded of the weight she carried from all that had happened in her past. Perhaps she was used to carrying all of it, and she would not have known what to do without it.

He loved her as a sister. But there was more that he had always kept unac-knowledged—a passion he had tempered with true concern for all of them. But it was still there. He knew it. It remained with him, that hunger he was feeling. Elizabeth. Elizabeth.

## 93
### Elizabeth

It was October before John Lee arrived in Panguitch. Elizabeth had followed the boys out of the house when Jed Stewart ran breathlessly into the yard. "He's here! He's here!" he screamed.

The whole town swarmed out into the road. They flanked the family buckboard while the children laughed and cried. The mothers began weeping with joy. And everyone laughed at John Lee's words. "I wonder if I'm alive? I see so many angels here, I think I'm come to heaven!"

So weak he could hardly bear himself up when he walked to the porch of the house, he sat with his grandchildren on his lap and held them for hours. He answered questions, raising his hands to demand quiet, telling in soft words that while he was ill a little bird in his yard had carried a message home. Rachel had seen the bird before the news had come that he was ill. She had already known that she must go to fetch him back. But the little bird became a legend.

Elizabeth did not speak to him alone, though she felt tears come several times. It was only soon after his arrival, in November, that the government posse came.

It was on a Saturday, November 7, 1874. At breakfast one of the Simon boys raced toward the Lee home. "They're here!" the out-of-breath Simon boy gasped. "There's a sheriff and a posse who slept all night hidden in the hills. They just rode to the middle of the town after John Lee."

"No!" Caroline reacted.

Rachel held her head in her hands. "No."

The two women roused Father John Lee out of his chair at the table. Caroline gave him an extra handful of bread and cheese and sent him with the children behind the log pen out to the corral. The family members watched anxiously while he crouched down into a corner behind some bales of hay. One of the children pulled open one of the bales and covered him with straw.

The Lorrys heard the Simon boy shouting. Jacob took his rifle down from the hook.

"No," Elizabeth said, putting her hand on his arm. Jacob caught the fierce warmth in her eyes. "Please. Please, Jacob." He saw fear there, and he knew she was right. He should keep guns out of it. What happened before would never happen again. He lay the rifle on the table.

They did not take the time for Anna Jane to walk. Lately she had been shuffling slowly with lots of help. But now they carried her in a chair into the November sun. From the yard they could see the people in town. Jacob let the women in the yard go into the street to meet the posse as it rode through.

"We're lookin' for John Lee," Sheriff Stokes said. The Lees had heard of Stokes. He was one of the deputies from St. George. It looked as though he had gathered the posse from the entire countryside. Six armed men on horseback loomed behind him. They had ridden hard; foam still lay against the necks of the animals.

Jacob stopped as he came near the men. Some of the children who were following him passed him up. His hands grew clammy. He thought he recognized—J.B. The man was at first turned away from him. But then Jacob saw the unmistakable profile of his father, the dark overhanging brow, the large sharp nose. It was no other than J.B.

While the posse was asking questions of the men and women in the street, J.B. turned briefly from his horse and saw Jacob. His face suddenly bleached white.

The father and son saw each other across a gulf where no words were heard. There was so much distance, neither of them attempted any speech. The large man Stokes rode up to Jacob at that moment.

"Your name, sir?" he asked.

"Jacob Lorry."

The man misspelled it when he wrote it. But Jacob let it go. Stokes announced, "We're asking all of the citizens to bring their rifles, come back here in five minutes, and lay them down."

Jacob saw J.B.'s eyes narrow. The look behind those eyes was one of anger and withdrawal. And pain.

The citizens of Panguitch hurried to their homes, but not one returned. Jacob and the boys carried Anna Jane on her chair into the house quickly. He brought the children to the table and he bent low over Anna Jane.

"Please," he whispered. "Please try not to worry. I'm going out to protect Father Lee. We must act as if nothing unusual has happened. Nothing at all. When they can't find him at Caroline's, they're likely to search every house. Just . . . just get out your sewing, Elizabeth. The quilt. If they should come through our place, act as if nothing is wrong . . ."

Jacob left them quietly seated around the table. Every face was ashen, terrified. It did not look like a quilting bee. As he left the house, he leaned back into the room and said, "Please. Smile, Anna Jane, Elizabeth."

As he closed the door Elizabeth rose to her feet and began to clear off the table.

Jacob stayed in the yard, processing his thoughts. What could he do? Finally, unable to think of anything else, he pulled the shovel down from the nails on the side of the house and began digging fencepost holes. For several months now, he had wanted to put a fence along the front to protect the grass. Now he saw the men in the posse exit Caroline's place, mount their horses and ride around in the yard. He saw Rachel move to the back by the corral where he had seen the children cover Lee with hay. He wanted to scream, "Rachel! Leave him alone! They'll see you there." But he was silent.

Almost like a bolt of lightning, he thought he could see the clarifying moment that knowledge of Lee's whereabouts entered the sheriff's imagination. Stokes' eyes were suddenly fixed at the back corral where Rachel was standing, leaning over the fence. Finally, he backed his horse into the road. Now he approached Sammy, who was nonchalantly walking to the mill.

"Young man! I'm going to ask you once, and I don't want to ask you again. I want you to help me find John D. Lee."

Sammy Lee looked at the sheriff, unbelieving. "Sir, he's my father, sir."

"I don't care if he's your grandmother. I have a warrant to arrest him, and by the name of the law I need your help."

Sammy's eyes looked unbelieving into the rough man's dark face. Jacob clutched the shovel. He watched while Sammy skirted the horse and began walking away.

"I'm going for my brother Alma," Sammy said as he went. "He's working at the mill."

Jacob leaned over to dig up another shovelful of dirt from his post hole. He expected to hear the leader of the posse speak again. He heard a sudden sharp "click." The man, holding a pistol in his hand, had pointed it at Sammy Lee. "Stop in the name of the law. Or I'll shoot! Stop, you ignorant kid."

Sammy stopped and wheeled around on his heel. He looked up at the sheriff, saying with his stance, "All right, I'm not going to argue with you then." He met Stokes with a submissive look. "What would you like me to do?" he asked. His eyes, like his father's, were bright blue.

Jacob did not hear the next few words. Stokes leaned down slightly from his horse to talk to Sammy. But Sammy was nodding his head.

"Yes. Yes. I'll do it, then," he was saying.

When Sammy began walking toward the Lorry house, Jacob watched him, feeling some confusion. He gripped the shovel with tense hands while Sammy gestured widely to point out Jacob's house. Sammy was playing the game. "He wants to search your house," he said to Jacob.

There was nothing Jacob could say but, "Go ahead."

As he dismounted, Stokes grimaced at the boy. Jacob's heart pounded against his ribs as the sheriff walked slowly up to the door.

"There's nothing in here," Jacob said. "Except my family." As he walked in, he prayed, "Let them be calm, as though there is nothing . . . nothing wrong." There they sat at the table, even the little ones, still like wooden dolls, their faces pasty white, their hands frozen to the quilt. Elizabeth had laid the quilt on the table like a tablecloth. But it was not something they could have been working on. The table was covered by the part of the quilt that had already been worked. He appraised the look in Elizabeth's eyes—pools of terror. Elizabeth. He wanted to hold her. He knew she was more frightened than he'd ever seen her. But there was nothing he could do.

"Come in," she said in an uneven voice.

The children sat staring, their hands on the quilt. Nobody had a needle. Or scissors. Or thread. The quilting party was a farce.

"Come in. We have nothing to hide," Anna Jane said. She alone was coherent. "Come in." She didn't say, "Please."

The sheriff paused briefly at the door and looked back. Two of the men in the posse were following him now although they were still a good distance away in the street. Jacob's heart leaped up into his throat. One of them was J.B. No, he said silently to himself. Please. No. It makes everything too difficult. But J.B. was still too far away, and Elizabeth had not yet seen him.

Sammy and Alma began showing Stokes into the home. The man looked in corners, checked for trap doors. Soon, J.B. and his partner were also at the stoop. Jacob stood with his back to the door. The man with J.B. whose name was Winn said, "May I please come in?" Jacob watched Elizabeth's eyes. He wanted to protect her from this. As Winn came into the house, she could not have helped but see J.B.

J.B. stopped when he saw Elizabeth. He was immediately pale. And then defensive. "You hiding John Lee?"

There was nothing in his voice to indicate that he knew her, that he had fathered her children. Did the children recognize him? He was rough shaven. Joshua and Caleb were out helping little seven-year-old Joseph Lorry with the sheep. Joseph had not seen him for nearly three years. He stared. He did not move from the table. Of the other children, only Belinda seemed to know.

"You know if he were here we would do everything in our power to save him," Elizabeth said.

Jacob was surprised at the control in Elizabeth's voice.

"He done nothing but cause us all hell," Winn said. "If he ain't guilty he can face trial like anybody else accused, with a free conscience."

Hearing Winn's words, J.B. was silent. His dark stare pierced Elizabeth to the core.

"Well, if you ain't gonna help us out, we'll conduct the search, then," J.B. said finally. His expression toward this woman he had once loved now appeared to be one of deep hatred. Or perhaps it was pain. For if there were ever a choice, she had always chosen John Lee. He walked past the quilt-covered table in the room while the quiet children and mothers stared. Even Anna Jane could say nothing kind when she saw J.B. There was too much to remember. So she said nothing at all.

While they searched the house, Jacob stood with the women in the room, waiting. They waited while Sammy and Alma took the men through every inch of every corner.

When the search party had finally finished, they came through to the front door without a word. J.B. looked back only once. There was loss in his face, and hatred for John Lee on whom he had placed the responsibility for his life's failure. And there was still the anger he felt against his own son, Jacob, for interfering with his marriage to Anna Jane, and now Jacob had practically become a Lee. As the posse left, their boots clattered on the wooden floor nearby. They didn't say a word. Only J.B. had turned back one more time to look at the family.

Hurt pressed down on Jacob's chest. Hurt and fear. Sheriff Stokes had the power to arrest Jacob for his part at the Mountain Meadows. And J.B. also. He knew that. He looked at J.B. through a blur. Father, he wanted to say. You are the one who took our names off the list, aren't you? Please forget the hurt and let go of your pride. But Elizabeth stood silently beside him, and he wanted his father to leave and never return.

"Good-bye." One word. Then J.B. turned to walk out. Sammy and Alma went behind him. Jacob, feeling weight he had never felt before, turned quickly and followed the boys and the posse a hundred feet back to Caroline's. As though there were dark shadows overhead, as though he were in a black hole and could not see, he followed them blindly into the sunlight. The sun hurt his eyes. He knew only that Sammy and Alma were ahead of him. For moments while they searched Caroline's house, he stood in the yard, feeling numb. The November frost still sparkled in the grass. Even the sun felt cold. He watched Stokes lumbering down out of the house, and Sammy, saying, "So you see . . ."

But, wait a minute. They were not leaving.

"I'll have a look in your corral."

This was the moment Jacob realized that Stokes knew! He knew! Jacob had guessed it earlier when he saw Stokes notice Rachel at the fence. The search through the houses was almost a courtesy call.

"You've seen this house already!" Sammy said emphatically. "You've seen the house. We don't have nobody here. Oh . . ." They were indeed on their way to the back buildings. "I wouldn't go back there if'n I was you." Sammy's revealing voice. The high pitch. The broken tone.

They were not good liars. That was something they were not. They were not practiced deceivers. Jacob ground his teeth. They had not learned comfortably to deceive, to protect by deceit. Sammy's hands began pumping; his mouth opened and shut several times.

Stokes walked back to the corral and the others followed him. Alma bolted for the house.

"Come out, Mr. Lee. I know you're there! Surrender yourself," Stokes called.

There was no movement in the straw.

"In the name of the law!" Stoke's voice was level with authority.

Nothing—the bright cold November air and a silence like death.

"Lorry, go in there and disarm that man under the straw.

"Don't shoot! Don't shoot!" Sammy shouted and Jacob came quickly. Finally, sounding far away, Lee's voice came from his craggy nest.

"Hold on, boys. I'll come out." It was a muffled voice, a distant, defeated voice.

Stokes moved the hand that held his pistol slowly to the holster at his side as J.B. brushed the straw away.

Suddenly, the face of John D. Lee appeared. He stared, startled, into J.B.'s eyes. "I . . ." Lee was almost speechless. When he found his tongue, he said, "Well, boys. What do you want of me?"

But his tone held an entirely different question, as if he were telling his captors: *Even though you and I both know why you want me, I must hear it, because only in your mouth is it made real. For I do not believe mankind could perform this inhumanity.*

Jacob stood, the blood beating in his body with the rumble of giant wheels. Stokes read the warrant in a sharply pitched tone. Loud enough that Caroline and Rachel and the children could hear it. By now all of them had gathered in the yard, Caroline and Rachel fraught with visible grief.

At last Elizabeth came. Jacob watched her move down the steps. She had swept her hair into a loose knob at the nape of her neck. Like silver webs, the free curls that touched her cheeks blew in the dazzling sun. Her face was still a shadow. Jacob noticed how she moved—with grace. She was beautiful. The dark face, the pain, the deep lines. Still, she was someone who had made a difference. In all of the breathing, the beating of hearts, in all of the terror in the yard, she made a difference just being there.

"Charged with murder," Stokes finally read.

"Why don't you say wholesale murder? That's what you mean," John Lee said.

Jacob felt pain and wanted to reach out. I am guilty too, he might have said. But his hands, his voice—all were frozen.

"May I see your pistol?" Lee asked Stokes. It was a strange request.

The sheriff, surrounded by J.B. and the other members of the posse, paused, then gave Lee his gun. Lee took the gun in his hands. He said to them without words, *You see, I can be trusted. I will not try anything. I am not a murderer. I am not afraid.*

"That's the strangest pistol I ever saw," Lee said simply. And he handed it quietly back to Stokes. He raised his eyes to the man and looked into his face without trembling, but with visible agony.

He turned and walked with Stokes back to the house. Caroline reached for Lee's arm. She was crying. Rachel held her face in her hands.

"Please, Caroline," Lee said, gently removing his arm from her grasp. "It's all right. It's time I faced up to a fair trial. Then I can be a free man again. Hush." He placed his hand on Rachel's cheek and stroked her hair.

*He is not the only one,* Jacob said to himself. It was a harrowing thought.

In the tension of the moment Jacob now saw both Sammy and Alma Lee come quickly to their father and try to tear him away from the members of the posse who backed Stokes. Jacob felt alarmed. "Please don't," he said silently to himself. "We don't want trouble."

Lee looked at his sons with haggard eyes. Then he turned to Stokes. The sheriff paused, hesitating, then finally nodded. Sammy spoke in a low voice to his father so no one could hear, "You don't have to go, Father. We'll fight for you."

"No, boys," Lee said.

"Please. We don't need to let them take you."

By now almost all of Panguitch had gathered in the yard. People were talking, crying. Too many people. If guns were to be used, there was too much chance someone would be killed.

"No, boys. We won't use guns. I'll go."

Sammy pleaded as Jacob would have wanted to plead. "Father. Father. Please don't go. We need you." The boy pulled on Lee's arm.

"No. It's all right. It's time I was given a chance to be exonerated, cleared. So that I might live out the rest of my life as a free man."

Jacob thought he had never seen a man with so much dignity. Even the posse must have felt the same, for they stood in their places hushed and stunned—even J.B.

In the quiet where only the sobs of the women could be heard, Stokes scanned the empty hills and then looked at his prisoner. He removed his hat and scratched behind his ear. When he dared to open his mouth, he said, "Say, do you know where there's a place me and my men can get breakfast in this town?"

For a moment Lee's eyes clouded. Then he looked up toward the house. "I'm so sorry," he said. "I haven't been very hospitable. Caroline," he called. "Rachel. Please feed the men." Jacob wanted to laugh angrily at the irony—the prisoner host offering his hospitality. John Lee then added, "Do we have a way back to Beaver?"

Stokes glanced about again. "Ah, no . . ."

"Jacob," he called. Jacob felt himself shaking. "Would you please see my team and wagon is got up to take us back to Beaver?"

Jacob nodded and sped quickly back to the barn to prepare the horses and the tack. He seethed. They had come unprepared with any form of transport to return John Lee, his father-in-law, to prison. Oh, they could ride like hell-bent fancy boys through the town, wielding guns, searching houses, frightening innocent women and children, but as for the practical necessities to carry out their assignment, they would have to rely upon their hard-working well-prepared prisoner and his dutiful families. They didn't have their own food, they had no wagon to take him to his jail. So they would take Lee's food, Lee's wagon. He had no idea how much of their resources would be used up by the unprepared posse. But when Jacob came out of the barn, some of the posse—including J.B.—had disappeared.

"They preferred to ride back to Beaver quickly on their own," Elizabeth told him.

When she met Jacob in the yard, she was carrying food wrapped in cloths for both the breakfast and lunches of Lee and his imprisoners. "Please take care. And Rachel will be going, too."

The sun was striking the yard with what looked like a column of light. It hit Elizabeth fully in the face as Jacob came toward the house. The light illuminated her eyes, burnished her hair. For a moment they were alone.

Jacob whispered to himself, "J.B." He did not say the name aloud. He had not said, "Father." But now he saw Elizabeth as though she were totally alone. She stood still holding the food in the cloth.

There was no time to share comfort now. Jacob knew he could not even begin. But he put his hand out to hers and held it, feeling the softness. She tucked the food under her arm and brought up her other hand quickly and placed it over his. They stood for a moment.

"Elizabeth," he said.

She was solemn. "Everything will be for the best good." The words made sense. "It will be all right. Wait and see."

## 94

### Elizabeth

*November 7, 1874. It is almost midnight and finally quiet. But the hush is filled with hurt. Today they came and got John Lee. Jacob drove him with the sheriff and a couple of others in the posse to Beaver. It has taken nearly two hours to calm the children into sleep. Perhaps because it still seems to be daylight—the large moon outside the window seems ominous. I am still shaking and afraid. I did not expect to see J.B. The sight of him took me by surprise—he was one of the men from Fort Cameron who came to make the arrest.*

Elizabeth put down her pen. She stared out through the open window at the moon. It looked like a coin behind a skiff of gray clouds. She was thinking about J.B., but she would rather have thought about Jacob. She shifted her thoughts to imagine where Jacob would be by now as he accompanied John Lee to Beaver. She thought the posse would probably be close to Cove Fort. Or at least as far as the creek. It would be cold, and all of them would be sleeping under that large, silver moon.

She put her journal on the table beside her bed, then leaned over to blow out the candle. As the light flickered and snuffed out, she thought she heard shuffling feet in the yard. She froze with fear. Sammy and Alma were next door at Caroline's. But until this moment she hadn't realized how Jacob's absence would make her fearful. But it was real, the presence of someone else. There was a muffled knock at the door.

Quickly, Elizabeth relit the candle, held her hand close around the flame as though finding safety there. In a moment of harrowing decision, she grappled in the table drawer for the pistol and slipped it into the pocket of her robe. The stairs stretched down before her like a dark mouth. There was a knock again.

I'm coming, she thought. The visitor must have seen the motion of her candle through the window, for he did not knock again. She thought she saw a great shadow against the window. Her heart was so loud she could almost hear its pounding.

"Who's there?" she called before she opened the door.

"Please, Elizabeth."

She stood a moment, her hand frozen to the knob before she could be certain of the voice again.

"Please let me in."

It was J.B. And too late, she had turned the knob slightly. J.B. pressed against the door and shouldered his way in. She gasped. "I thought you had gone . . ."

His face in the candlelight was a map of wrinkles, the embodiment of distress. "I rode off and it didn't take me long to realize I had ought to come back and claim what's mine."

A terror stripped her nerves of fear. She heard the ice of her own voice as though it were not hers. "There is nothing here of yours."

"You're here," J.B. said, now standing heavily inside the door. The small flickering flame of the candle revealed him to be dressed in bulky clothes that smelled fearfully of sheep dung.

She was silent, holding the candle up to better see his glassy eyes.

"And the children are here."

"The children no longer know who you are."

"Please, Elizabeth." He spoke heavily. "I couldn't believe what you done—choose the Lee family over me. I could not believe it when you left Kanarraville. I couldn't believe that of Jacob, either. And to marry Anna Jane. Yes, she was a Lee. She suffered unspeakable trials." By now all of them knew of Anna Jane's unspeakable trials, though none of them ever breathed of it or said the terrible words. "Nobody knows what pain I suffered when he took her away from me. And then all those years you never loved me, but him—a murderer—John Lee."

The words echoed against the dark rafters, drifting up the narrow dark stairs.

"Shhh," Elizabeth pleaded. "Quiet. It has been such a day." She felt the cold of the pistol where she had slipped it into the pocket of her robe, heavy and solid against her leg.

"Yes. It has been such a day."

"It's time to forget, J.B.," she said, her voice cold, as if she were remembering another time, another period of her life in which J.B. had dominated her. Now she could look at this fearful image of a man and choose to restrain the compassion of her heart. "I don't want you to come here."

"Please, Elizabeth. You know damned well you loved me. And you hurt me going with the Lees. And I kept saying to myself, someday she'll realize what she lost. But today you never so much as looked my way. Oh, Elizabeth . . ." He reached toward her now to pull her head to him.

But she stopped his hand. Between her teeth she said, "You wanted me back. So you came to make sure the militia caught John Lee."

"It wasn't my idea."

"No. But you were right there."

"He ruined my life," J.B. blustered. "He has caused me nothing but hell. Telling us what to do, then telling what we done. You don't know what happened on that day."

Elizabeth's nerves were on fire. "No, I don't know what happened on that day," she said evenly.

"Well, he—damned, I don't care if he was following orders from whoever in the military—Haight, or Dame, or whatever. Hate or Damn." His voice was hard. "He was the one that decoyed those people out and made us all to kill them. He did it and he can't deny it. And I can't sit around and watch injustice done when I know what he done on that day, and that as long as this thing is open like a sore—like a wound that's bleeding and bleeding and still they're pouring salt, pouring salt in it. As long as this thing is open like a sore, then O God, let justice be done to end it, to close it up. To end it once and for all. And let him be gone and take his punishment. And then you can come back to me." Suddenly his eyes narrowed and his voice rasped, "What you done, girl? Slept with John Lee?"

Elizabeth's heart raced. "Get out of here, J.B. I asked you nice once. I don't want to see you again."

"My God. My own children. My own wife. You must have slept with John Lee."

Now Elizabeth released words slowly and deliberately, as though if she did not exert control, they would rush out in a frenzy. Yet they were quiet words. "Don't talk like that. I never slept with John Lee. Yes, I loved him. I love him still. He's a gentleman. A great man who never let anybody down. Even those who entrusted him with a terrible destiny. He believed that he did what was ordered by God and the president of the church or he never would have done it. If he faces a trial, they will see they must let him go free."

"Damn, you are a bitch. You lie. You lie. You say you never slept with John Lee. He stole you from me. Him and his black heart and his blacker deeds."

"You were there, Jeremiah Butler Lorry. Heaven above! You were there and held the gun on your own and shot it on your own. Nobody but you made you pull the trigger."

He leaped forward toward her and knocked the candle out of her hand to the floor. As she fought him, he grabbed her wrists and pressed her back against the stairwell and the banister on the stair.

"You are a liar." He bit the words off his tongue. "And all the time you lie to me—still—I love you. I don't understand why. We had good times. Don't you remember? You would put up fights. But you always gave in. And you liked it, too."

He moved closer to her now and pressed his body against her. She struggled, trying not to cry out.

"Give in, you little feisty scrap of a woman. I remember you too well. Give me your . . . mouth." And he reached for her mouth with his foul filthy bearded lips, bringing her up close to him. In the lonely darkness—the only light was the moon—she struggled against him, finally kissing him with fury—with the anger and hatred of deceit until she freed her hand and placed it in the pocket of her robe to retrieve the pistol.

"I won't let you," she gasped. "Oh yes, I have allowed you your way. So many times. I have given so much to you . . . and you have only taken advantage of me."

"And you loved it, every minute of it," he said. "You no good . . ."

Shrinking away from him, she recoiled, struggling to curl her fingers around the pistol—to point the weapon toward him. But when he would not let go, she tightened her fingers on the gun. In the crush of the stair rail pressing into her back, the terror of her mind whirling, screaming as though her brain were on fire, she felt the cold metal in the crotch of her hand and she pulled against it.

"Hell! What are you doing with that?" He finally saw the gun.

And she pulled. She grit her teeth and closed her eyes and felt for the far edge of his ribs. She thought to herself, *Just wound him. Incapacitate him so that he cannot force me.* The cold metal snapped in the grasp of her hand. Almost without knowing it, she pulled the trigger. There was an explosion in the pistol, and a sickening thud against flesh. As her hand backed away, his arm came up to knock the pistol out of her grasp. Too late. As his wrist lashed at her, his hand tore down over her face, scratching at her eyes. He slowly came to the realization that there was pain in his side.

"Oh, I am a dead man." His uplifted hand flopped forward over her neck and tore down at her clothes like a claw while she pulled away. By a sliver of moonlight through the door, she saw the contorted face and the wild look in the glassy eyes.

"Oh, how could you?" He coughed and held his side. When the blood appeared in his mouth, Elizabeth could no longer hold back the scream building up in her. She turned and ran to Caroline's to find Sammy Lee since Jacob had gone with Lee to Beaver. She knocked on Sammy's window and whispered hoarsely, "Help me, Sammy, someone has got to help me!"

She had deliberately shot toward the outside edge of J.B., his ribs. But— had she accidentally shot through his lung? Praying, praying, that she had not killed him, that he would live, she stood panting, waiting for Sammy.

"What is it?" Sammy looked out of the window, dressed in his night shirt, his hair tousled by sleep.

"Hush," Elizabeth said quietly. "It's J.B. He came back to force me. And I shot him. Oh, please." She said the words softly, but her voice was strained. "Someone has got to help me."

"Oh, laws!" Sammy closed the window, and she heard his footsteps as he shuffled against the floor. She waited at the window for a moment, leaning her forehead against the sill.

After a moment, Elizabeth went to wait by the door. By the time Sammy came, she was shaking with the cold. Together they moved quickly over the grass to her house where she expected to find J.B. lying in blood on the stairs. But, seeing J.B. in the shadows, she halted Sammy with an unsteady hand. He had dragged himself across the stoop and was standing now near the horse tied to the front rail. Inwardly she gasped, felt the cold air crowd into her lungs. A small light went on in Anna Jane's room.

J.B. must have seen the light in the window; perhaps he even saw Sammy in the moonlight. He climbed to his horse, doubling over with pain. Once in the saddle, bent and broken, he turned the animal around in the yard. Then, holding his side, he dug his boots into his horse and sped out of the yard and into the road. Then he was gone.

"I wounded him," Elizabeth whispered.

"Oh jiggers!" Sammy said, watching after the figure as he disappeared into the darkness beyond the broad light of the moon.

"What has happened?" It was Anna Jane.

"Anna Jane. Oh, Anna Jane." Elizabeth took her in her arms.

"A man tried to hurt Elizabeth," Sammy said to her.

"And I shot at him," Elizabeth whispered. "I hurt him, Anna Jane."

Anna Jane was still in Elizabeth's tightened grip. "Elizabeth. Why, Elizabeth? Who was it?"

Elizabeth's voice was small, her head still on fire. "Oh Anna Jane. Hold me. It was J.B."

## 95
### *John D. Lee*

*Dear Anna Jane, Elizabeth:*

*Jacob is about to return. I have asked him to bear this to you along with a request from the county commissioner, which he shall read to you, saying that he will defend me at the trial.*

*I did not believe it would have come to this, but it has. Can you imagine someone like me (for I enjoy the open spaces) locked in a small dark cell in back of the courthouse here in Beaver? It is all I believed prison to be: uncomfortable, inconvenient.*

*But I am not lonely, though I may be more so now that Jacob and some of the others have gone. I have my Bible and my Book of Mormon, which I have been able to read continuously by candlelight. I have written letters to Rachel, Caroline, and Amorah, and now I am reflecting upon the possibility of making a record of my life showing some of the things that have happened to those who have suffered for the establishment of God's kingdom here in this land.*

*I must confess that I am not treated like the other prisoners, for I have been allowed to go out of doors almost every day, and to cut wood for the stove, run errands, and stoke the fire. I have made good companions of the plenary and officers who talk at times like soldiers of the devil. But they have a human side to them, as has everyone. On her visit Emma heard them say she was one of John Lee's whores. As you know, Emma is full of the fire and spirit of righteous indignation and I have not seen so surprised a group of men as those knaves who suddenly found her buggy whip in their faces. She was fortunate they did not arrest her, although they did not allow her to visit with me until the next day.*

*Anna Jane, my heart is most weighed with soreness for the welfare of yourself, always the victim, my dear child. I'm glad you have begun some walking with a little help. But if there were some way we could determine what kind of disease that is which has sucked the strength out of your body, I should give my life for that and for any of the pains those who are dear to me have suffered, if it should do any good at all. Perhaps it would be better if I had died in Moencopi, for I see ahead a delayed trial and a long incarceration. However, I am light-hearted, believing in our God, for he will see that the truth is made known to all, and then my name and the names of all my loved ones shall be set free.*

*Yours forever in the kingdom,*

*John D. Lee*

## 96

### *Jacob*

Jacob, glad to return, now focused on putting things back together again. But there were times he could give Anna Jane no relief. In the dark nights, as the moon struck the window, blooming low over the dark wood floor, he held her in his arms while she sobbed. He felt the energy of her body ebbing as she suffered with something no one could explain. He knew he was still seeing her as the young, powerful woman she once was—limbs like wings that beat the breeze as she whipped the carpets on the clothesline. That was in the early days, before the fire, before she was trampled at the fort.

"Anna Jane, a final decision will make your father free."

"You cannot promise that."

"I can promise you God's will to be done."

"Is God's will always done?"

"I believe so," Jacob said, unsure himself. But the fervor of his heart demanded that he believe.

"Is it God's will that I should die?"

"No. No, Anna Jane. Don't talk of it."

"You are not listening. I believe God wants . . ." She held back tears. "I believe God has been trying to tell me through my pain that it is time for you to . . . take another wife."

There were nights in the darkness they talked of this. "Perhaps you should take another wife before it is too late, before the government will not let you marry . . ." The talk always ended when Jacob held her more closely in his arms. "No. No. There is no need to talk of this." Until Molly Chandler had come along, he had always resisted thoughts of taking another wife, though there had been incidents of question. At Christmas time when Hod Chandler brought his family to pay a call, Molly Chandler had asked Anna Jane to sing.

"I have heard you sing, Anna Jane," Molly said charmingly.

Anna Jane was reticent. "Why, I haven't . . . unless . . ."

Elizabeth's eyes had smiled. She had heard Anna Jane sing in private only once.

"She does sing," Elizabeth said. "Only a few of us know it. Don't we, Belinda Marie?"

Belinda's eyes brightened.

"Well, sing, then, Sister Lorry. Please sing," Molly insisted, indicating to her father and mother, seated primly starched in the corner of the parlor, that they had missed a great treat if they had never heard Anna Jane Lee Lorry sing.

Anna Jane smiled but shook her head. "Molly dear, I had no idea you had ever heard me sing. That is quite a compliment. But it is something I cannot do in public. You're a darling to bring it up." The girl's face registered disappointment. And Anna Jane had pressed Molly's hand. Molly had then taken both of Anna Jane's hands between her palms and rubbed them.

Jacob had seen in that moment a warmth in Anna Jane's eyes. And he had seen the intent of Molly's heart as though it were made of glass. He admired the girl in that moment for her cleverness, though he could not feel anything for her. However, he felt it might perhaps be his duty to remarry, to merge estates, and so that night in the darkness under the patches of light on the quilt under the moon, he had whispered, "What about Molly?"

"Molly?" Anna Jane had answered. They had been talking about a possible merger with the Chandler estate. Hod Chandler had begun building a beautiful home in Panguitch on second south—a tall brick home in the latest Queen Victoria mode.

"Molly?" Anna Jane whispered.

"You've said before I should take another wife. If we were to merge with the Chandlers . . ."

"Molly? Oh, darling. Jacob," Anna Jane was pensive, quiet for a time. "Not Molly." Then she spoke the words softly as though they had been lodged very deep for many years and buried in anxiety. "I thought you knew. Elizabeth. I was hoping you would want to marry her. Isn't there something we can do about Elizabeth? I know you have loved her. I love her, too."

Jacob's heart pounded in his chest with such force that the blood seemed to beat in his ears. *What about Elizabeth?*

"Isn't there something we can do about Elizabeth? J.B. is not . . . He is not for her. Oh, ever since . . ."

Since the beginning, Jacob thought. He knew that. But he had not expected the same knowledge to grow in Anna Jane. "Yes, Anna Jane," he had whispered as she drifted off to sleep. "Perhaps there is something we can do . . ."

## 97

### Elizabeth

*December 15, 1874. It is strange how one man can make a difference in so many lives. And he is not even here. He is in prison. And yet all of us are waiting for an event that will set us free.*

Snow fell before Christmas—almost seven inches—which meant they would not be able to travel to Beaver before the holiday. Anna Jane grew despondent and made Jacob promise her that he would take her to the prison in the spring. All winter the wives sent knit mufflers, socks, neckerchiefs, and gloves to the prison by mail.

In mid-March they received the message that John Lee was ill. At the same time they also heard from Toquerville that J.B. was suffering from blood poisoning. However, he apparently thought himself well enough to testify in a trial against John Lee.

More than ever, Anna Jane was anxious to go. But by spring she was much too ill to travel anywhere. It would have been foolishness. So Jacob went to Beaver alone. When he returned, he brought recent news from Father Lee, and a summons that he—Jacob Lorry—had been called to appear as defense in the trial.

When Elizabeth saw the summons request, she felt disquiet. They were in the yard with the children all about them clamoring to see Jacob. When Jacob began to show her the notice, she folded it back up in his hand.

"Later, Jacob. Please. I had hoped . . ."

"Someone needs to defend him."

"But is it safe for you?"

He looked off, as though seeing a mirage. "John Lee will never say a word about me. They have tried to get him to implicate others. Even Brigham Young. But he keeps his oath. His mouth is sealed."

"But the others . . . ?"

"There is a silent agreement not to bring in all the others—only John Lee."

"I am afraid," she said in a low voice.

He had stood firm, placing his hand on her arm. "We must exonerate him. Let the world know why he should be free. A just trial will bring out the truth— that he alone is not responsible. It was an act of war."

She stared at Jacob. Why couldn't the father have been more like the son? There was nothing in common between Jacob and J.B. It was as though they belonged to two totally different worlds.

"What about J.B.?"

"I have heard he is ill, but that he will testify."

"They must know he was also there."

"He has gained their favor."

"By lies."

"I'm afraid so. He may have his own reasons to see the death of John Lee."

The death of John Lee. It was unreal to Elizabeth that such a possibility could exist. Through all of that spring, while the sheep were sheared, the wool carded and spun, she thought about Father Lee. All of them did, in their prayers, in their talk—even Molly Chandler, who continued to come to the family when Jacob was present—always with searching questions. "Do you believe that if they find John Lee guilty they will arrest my grandfather and the others?"

Most of the others had gone into hiding. Some had changed their names.

"I don't know," Jacob had said more than a dozen times.

"Would you believe my grandfather if he was to say he only followed the orders of John D. Lee?"

"I don't know."

At these times, Elizabeth was aware that she saw more than curiosity in Molly's eyes.

Finally Jacob approached Elizabeth about the question of Molly in May, 1875, because some of the general authorities were coming to the conference in the town.

"Molly Chandler wants a place in this family, Elizabeth," he said.

Elizabeth stared at him. She had been right. There was more than curiosity in Molly Chandler's eyes. Elizabeth had never faced it, the possibility of

Molly as part of the family, although the suggestion had haunted her many times.

"The authorities frown on single women in families as you must know. Even Bishop Harper has asked me about your circumstances several times."

A light went out in Elizabeth. "Jacob, please," she whispered.

"I talked to Anna Jane about it. She wants you. You must know that. She wants you to come into this family before we suddenly find someone like Molly in it. You know you belong."

It was true. They had thought about it many times. Elizabeth did not speak. She found no words on her tongue. But she had nodded enough to give Jacob hope, and he was determined to speak to the authorities at April conference to learn about what would have to be done.

It was a problem, as Elizabeth had guessed it would be. "Only if you get a release from J.B.," the bishop had said from his large black chair behind a desk with a mirror-mahogany shine. Sitting before the bishop, Elizabeth had looked into Jacob's eyes then, and he had taken her hand.

"I am willing to perform a ceremony if you can get a signed release from J.B."

"If it's sanctioned by the church, will it be civilly accepted?"

"The U.S. Government don't accept plural marriages at the present time. We believe we will win our rights through just court decisions."

Jacob had left the office puzzled, unwilling to say much. Elizabeth was quiet.

"It seems so senseless you should be with me in my house and that we should be unable to be one," Jacob had said.

Elizabeth did not feel pressured to hurry. As they walked along the greening road, she stopped and turned to him. "I can wait, Jacob. I have been happy with the way things are now. Let's leave things as they are for a while. Don't let Molly press you."

Jacob gave her a searching, wistful look. He had almost not spoken, but the words seemed to fall from his lips. "Are you . . . I almost believe you are still hoping for John Lee."

She felt his hurt. But he must know that the words he spoke were true. "I have loved him," she admitted.

"Would you marry him if he were set free?"

Elizabeth stopped walking and looked at him. "He's an old man."

"Would you? If he wanted it."

She shook her head. "I don't know."

"Then let's wait until he's free," Jacob said painfully.

The trial was scheduled for May, and then put off until June. Jacob kept returning from Beaver with reports that they had, once again, put off the trial. They were trying to find witnesses and an impartial jury, but it was almost impossible. Each time Jacob traveled to Panguitch from Beaver, he returned with more bad news than good.

In June, when he rode down, he found Elizabeth hanging shirts on the clothesline. Troubled by the terrible truth he did not want to speak, he found himself answering the questions he knew she would ask—even before he said hello. "They put Josephus Wade and John Brewer on the jury," he said so quietly that his words were barely audible.

Elizabeth stopped at the line, clothespins still in her mouth. She took them out slowly, squinting slightly to focus on Jacob's face in the bright sun.

"Can I talk with you in the barn for a moment?" he said then.

Elizabeth put the last pin into a shirt to secure it on the line, then left the others in the basket. Slowly Jacob led his horse to the barn, and Elizabeth followed. It was dark there, the light pure and golden through the chinks. The corners were deep with the musty smell of hay, and the webs and the dust of the insects mixed with the filtered debris of the wind. The barn was large and dank. But it smelled good. It had trapped the June warmth and it hummed of animal sounds, and now a cropping noise as Jacob's horse found the hay.

"You know how Josephus Wade feels about John Lee."

"He's anti-Mormon all the way," Elizabeth said as Jacob lifted the saddle from the mare.

"And so is John Brewer. And there's a chance they'll put on J.C. Hester and Paul Price."

"How many sit on the jury?"

"Twelve."

"Who will the others be?"

"They've said Erastus Snow will be choosing some impartial citizens from St. George."

Elizabeth looked up. The sun played in the rafters far above their heads. Impartial in this territory meant fence-sitting. And Mormons did not generally sit on any fences. The sun played in the rafters far above their heads. She and Jacob stood motionless in the empty barn like two wayfarers in a cave.

"I don't really want to appear as witness now," Jacob said.

"Jacob . . ."

He did not seem to hear her. "There is no way Josephus Wade will stand for the freedom of John Lee."

"I thought it was the policy to choose impartial jury members." Her voice was stubbornly hopeful.

"It is."

"He's not impartial."

"He must have lied to get on the jury."

"It was a long time ago," Elizabeth nodded, remembering. "We saw Josephus briefly at the ferry once, remember, with Belinda's friend, the young photographer Fennimore, who was taking pictures of the ferry. He told us that he knew why Brigham Young kept sending Lee further and further away."

"Can you imagine what could happen—the conviction of John Lee? And then, progressively, the conviction of every other man?"

"Jacob . . . please . . ."

But Jacob couldn't let it go. "He must have lied to get on the jury."

"No. It's all right." Elizabeth held her hand on Jacob's arm. "They will surely see that Lee does not deserve to take the full responsibility for the deed, and if they should see how many are responsible, that it was an act of war, they will forget it and let him go free. Surely Wade will see the truth. He was good to John Lee. He just didn't like the Mormons. He was so interested in the young photographer's pictures of the ferry. Belinda Marie's young friend, who comes often to town to visit her, young James Fennimore . . ."

She was making talk to soothe Jacob. He stayed quiet, standing with his hands in his pockets, his mouth a narrow line. A wren chattered in the rafters, then flew up. Its wings struck the wood, rapping with a wild din. Elizabeth looked up suddenly.

"There's a nest under the roof," Jacob said, not moving his eyes from Elizabeth's face.

"Oh," she said, and looked back to him.

"I feel torn," he said quietly.

"It's all right," she said softly, reaching out to touch his hand.

He stood, stiff, not leaning to her touch. He was used to standing firm to the love he had felt for her all of these years.

"You and I, Jacob. We've always been such good friends."

"I love you," he whispered. "I love you so much. I want your happiness more than anything else on earth. Your happiness as much as the happiness of Anna Jane."

Elizabeth looked around the barn, thinking. "Love is a funny thing," she mused. "You can feel it for those you love so much that there is room for others. Room for me. You and Anna Jane."

"Yes. There is room for you." Still, he did not remove his hands from his pockets.

She tried to hold him. She put her arms gently around his shoulders. "Don't worry about it, Jacob. How long have we been friends, Jacob?"

"Forever. And I want it always to be that way."

"Come on, Jacob. Don't worry. Take my hands."

He drew his hands out of his pockets and held her without passion. He drew his hands to her back and held her. Then he began to tremble.

"Jacob?" she whispered. "You're crying."

He was not afraid to cry. He held her now and brought his hand to her head, and in the balmy luxury of her hair, he let the tears fall.

"Shhhh. Why are you crying?" she whispered.

"For us," Jacob said, his voice choked with tears. "And for Father Lee."

## 98

### *Elizabeth*

The Lorry family did not attend the trial when it was finally held in late July. They heard about it third hand from Molly Chandler, who tearfully came to them and told them what her grandfather had said in the courtroom.

"He told them it was all military orders." Molly was more round-faced than she had ever been. She had been eating to drown her frustration and her unhappiness in love. She didn't control her tears. She had come at suppertime, wringing her hands because her own father had been to the trial and had come home in a dither. Phillip Klingensmith had turned state's evidence—had even written out a confession.

"But so did John Lee," Molly said.

They were on the last side of a ham, and Elizabeth cut off a piece for Molly. Molly said she had already eaten supper, but she sat down on a chair and took it anyway. While she ate the ham, she glanced sideways at Jacob and related everything she knew about the trial. It didn't seem to bother her that her mouth was full while she told what her father had said.

"There was other men they let go. They didn't vote the same on John Lee. The whole jury's supposed to agree. All the Mormons wanted him free and the four others wanted him dead."

Choosing to do dishes at that moment, Elizabeth listened rather than looked. The girl's mouth was busy on the meat. Jacob had asked the children to leave. Anna Jane, in all politeness and patience, kept her eyes on the girl.

"So what is the outcome?" Anna Jane asked.

"They are taking him to Salt Lake City to the penitentiary there. And they have to make up another trial."

Elizabeth's heart stopped. She glanced up at Jacob. His eyes were riveted to Molly's chin, which was quivering as the girl talked and ate at the same time.

"They told all about the bodies dragged up by wolves out on the ground. There were arms and legs, and pieces of sunbonnet. And one woman still fresh as the day she died. They said she was so beautiful they could not take their eyes away from her. She had long flowing light hair." The mustard on the ham gave Molly tears, which began to crowd up in her nose. She sniffled and then coughed. Anna Jane gave her a napkin. Molly wheezed into it and swallowed the last bite of ham.

"And one of the men in the courtroon—was old. He had a stroke in the middle of the trial, my pa said. That was after the part about the woman's bones, and he fell over in his chair—backwards like he was dead. And everybody came runnin' to him while he was gaspin' and turning' purple. They got him up and shook him and splashed water in his eyes. And there was a wild-looking lady. Her name was Maggie, my pa said. And she was flutterin' round and round askin' everyone to help her. My pa says he never saw such a fixed-up woman with such black hair and red lips and red dress. He said the neckline came down to here." Molly was very expressive describing the style. Getting up from her chair, she outlined the neckline. Her finger came down on her bosom so far that Elizabeth found herself checking to see if Joseph had left the room as he had been asked to do.

"It come nearly to here, Pa said. And he said she smelled bad, too. She filled up the whole room with bein' so strong that the men and the women in the audience climbed out of their chairs and went to the edge of the room while two or three of 'em were shaking this man who had a stroke, pouring water in his eyes. My grandfather and father both stopped and wanted to help, but the sheriff wouldn't let them. He made all the witnesses stay in their seats. The old man didn't come back the next day even if he was supposed to be a witness, Pa said.

That was the day they said John Lee wasn't even at the meeting when they decided to kill everybody. Mr. Lee got orders to do just what he done. They blamed the whole church and then they voted. And the Mormons voted one way and the others voted another way. And that's why they need a new trial."

Molly's words skimmed over Elizabeth's ears like distant noise. She knew the old man Molly talked about was J.B. She heard the story as though she could see him before her eyes, lying inert and breathless on the floor. She saw Maggie, too, and thought Molly had told the story just to have the opportunity to draw her finger across her bosom as she did. Plump and breathless with desire, she did not hide her affection for Jacob. At the door, as he led her away, she turned her face to him once more and broke into tears.

"Pa wouldn't come here to tell what he knew because he was so discouraged. I didn't want to tell you." She looked up with watery eyes to Jacob's compassionate gaze. "Pa wanted me to tell you all this. I am so sorry for your family. Oh, I am sorry. Please don't be angry with the news." And as she looked at Jacob, she broke into fresh tears. He drew her head against his chest and comforted her with a gentle embrace. She held onto him for as long as she could.

Elizabeth, still numbed by the girl's report, dawdled with the dishes. She wanted to ask if Molly knew anything about the old man who had suffered the stroke. Was he still alive? But she didn't dare.

"Another trial will set Brother Lee free." Molly was trying hard to smile. Another trial. And in the meantime, all of those months in another prison.

Elizabeth, confused by the results of the trial, hurt in her heart for John Lee. Though she was interested to know more about J.B., she did not ask but looked grimly at Jacob. Jacob returned her look while he held the sobbing seventeen-year-old girl in his arms. His eyes were sympathetic, though they held something there of slight amusement, a twinkling at the corners.

"There, there, Molly," he was saying.

Finally the girl withdrew.

"We appreciate what you have told us." He took both her hands in his as though he were pressing shut the leaves of a book. "And I will be over to see your father when time permits. I am sorry I did not go to see him myself."

"I wanted to come here," Molly said, sniffling. "I told Pa I wanted to come."

There were a few long moments in which Elizabeth wondered whether or not Molly was going to leave. Walking into the yard behind Jacob and Molly, she waited for him to comfort the girl away. He was patient with her, even though he seemed to tire of her talk—of her multiplication of words, words and more words.

"Good-bye, Molly. Tell your father thank you," he said several times.

"They can't take a man's life for obeying military orders, no matter who gave them. They won't take my grandfather's life. He killed someone too. We don't even know why they did it. It was all so long ago. And we are not afraid now like the pioneers were then. They were afraid of Indians. They were afraid of travelers. They were afraid they would have to move on again."

"Molly. Your father should not have told you so much. You are still young."

"I'm not a child, Mr. Lorry," she snapped at him. "I have as much right to know my grandfather's affairs and the affairs of your father-in-law as any citizen touched by these happenings."

As he moved toward her, she backed toward the front gate and into the road beyond. "What is sad," Jacob said, "is that you and all of your cousins, brothers, and sisters and the other children have a right to know, if you must call it a right. But it is also a necessity to suffer the pain of knowledge that comes with that right. And you must carry it with you when it is not even yours."

"It is mine," Molly said, feisty still. For the first time, Elizabeth admired her. She was not pretty, or mannerly, or lovely in many ways. But she was willing to share responsibility.

"I am the one who most comforts my old grandfather."

Her honesty and spunk took Jacob back for a moment. He remembered Maggie of so many years ago. "Just what else are you willing to do to pay for it?"

"Bring messages," she said intensely.

Jacob stared at her. His voice, when he answered, was subdued. "Then good-bye, Molly. Tell your father and your grandfather thank you. And . . . thanks to you too."

When she walked out of the gate, she turned back to smile bravely, and then she waved.

When Jacob turned to Elizabeth, his bright eyes were shaded by some concern. "She loves me."

Elizabeth smiled. "I can see that."

"But what she wants, I have only for Anna Jane," he said. Then added, "and you . . ." He took her elbow as they walked to the door. "If we are to make this love real," he said, "then we must do it soon. If the federal officers have their way, there are not many years left in which these marriages may be made."

## 99
### *Elizabeth*

Notice of J.B.'s death three months later came by way of Maggie's telegram to the mercantile. It was not a surprise. Jacob left, then, for Toquerville. He was gone for two days before he sent for Elizabeth and her three sons.

Elizabeth dreaded going to Toquerville. As she readied herself, she looked into the mirror. She was still thin—with large eyes and only a slight blush like autumn color on her high cheeks. Those eyes were still fraught with fear. She had tried to explain away her feeling of guilt. She would probably never know just how much the wound she had given J.B. had influenced his illness and his final death. She would not know how many negative statements about her he had made to the people of Toquerville. Jacob had told her that J.B. had kept the shooting a secret, that everyone there believed he had been shot by a renegade Indian. Even Maggie believed this tale. In his last days, J.B. had only expressed sorrow for the way in which he had abused Elizabeth. He had begun to write a confession in the pages of the old Bible. It was a sad note, saying he did not believe he had ever been needed by anyone. Though he had seemed able to hide it successfully, he must always have been an unhappy man. He had asked Elizabeth to make one last pilgrimage to his funeral to bring the children to honor their own father in one of his more honorable hours.

Joshua and Caleb drove the buggy down the solemn morning streets. It was late in the season now, and cold. Jacob wanted his father's boys to think well of their father. He had mixed feelings of loss, anger, guilt. And he wanted Elizabeth to find relief somehow in her last efforts to please a man whom she could never really please.

It took one and a half days to drive the horse and buggy from Panguitch to Toquerville. Though they left the grandchildren with Belinda and the young marrieds—Hannah and John Frederick Lee—by the time Elizabeth and Jacob and the boys had arrived after enduring the cold nights, the rugged travel, they were quite weary. But they felt well prepared to support Maggie and honor the memory of J.B.

The house was on Main Street, a small log house with a big chimney and stove. They hardly recognized Maggie. Her eyes were ringed with red, the eyelids loose and flaccid as though having been stretched until they were raw.

So, Maggie, Elizabeth thought, you finally settled for J.B. The boy Robert was a lean, gangly sort of young man who only partially remembered anything. Tall, he was topped by a thatch of slick dark hair. His profile, his brows, were surely J.B.'s.

Elizabeth climbed out of the rig, trembling. She remembered too well when Maggie had lived in the house in Kanarraville, and in Kanab. Elizabeth had no use for the memory of those experiences.

But Maggie was much subdued. In the black dress and shawl, she looked sallow and bleached. She seemed ill. And Elizabeth's heart went out to her. As she walked into the small log room and saw the broken Maggie in an old horse-hair chair, fumbling with a black kerchief in her hand, she realized suddenly that both she and Maggie had something more in common now. They had both been widowed at the same time.

"Well, sit down," Maggie said, snuffling into the kerchief. "Robert, fetch the bedroom chair." She did not look up at Elizabeth, but by her glances showed she was aware of Jacob's presence in the room.

The room was dark, with a dark wood floor, heavy rag rugs and lace curtains, old dark green plush chairs. A large stone chimney protruded above a blackened pot-bellied stove. On the chimney hung a few pictures. One was a photograph of a thin-faced J.B.

"I made some tea."

"No, thank you," Elizabeth said with as much kindness as she could. "Maggie, I am sorry." She had meant to bridge a distance that had separated them. But she was not heard.

"Never mind. Robert, fetch the tea."

As she poured the tea into the cup, Maggie's hand trembled. The steam clouded her face, hiding her eyes. "We haven't much time if we're to be to the church by four o'clock." Still, the woman had not really looked up. Her voice was heavy.

On their way out of the house to the buggy, Jacob came up behind Elizabeth. "This is our last opportunity to make things right for J.B."

Elizabeth looked sharply into his eyes. "What do you mean?" she paused. "Make it right how? Are we going to bring Maggie home with us?" As she said the words, she wanted to swallow them again. She had met the end of her compassion. She was facing a dark wall in herself, and she was angry with her closed heart.

"No," he whispered. "She wants to stay here. Just love her, that's all. She is a lost and broken woman. He was everything to her."

Elizabeth stared at the woman who now climbed into the open carriage, hoisting her black skirts almost to her knees. Wasn't it wonderful, the miracle of life, she thought, that two people, no matter how difficult they may be for others to love, might find solace with each other—make their own world for themselves.

There were not many who attended the service in the church. But the bishop was there. He smiled and shook their hands, holding Elizabeth's gloved palm for a long time. "And you are one of the other widows, my dear?" he said with compassion. "I am so sorry. He spoke often of you to me. He had felt as though he had never been able to do right by you, or by the others. Of course, I know he had not seen any of you for a very long time."

Elizabeth gathered her solemn-faced boys around her. Her two oldest, Joshua and Caleb, looked less than starched and snappy after such a long ride and only a cursory soap and shine. Joseph, now ten, stood close to her. She held his shoulder with her free hand.

"And Maggie, my dear," the bishop said, moving to Maggie who stood to the side. He put his arms around her. "Please don't fret, my dear sister. We'll take good care of you, I promise you that. And Robert will be with you, too."

Maybe. Maggie seemed stiff and kept her eyes lowered while the bishop spoke—as though it were a duty to listen to every phrase of his routine statements. "There are no words which can explain the loss of a loved one. It is a time of pain. But only for a moment is there a time of being cut off—a time until resurrection day." The bishop's words were drawn out—solemn. They were words all of them expected to hear.

"He was a well-meaning man who did what he could do for his several families. And that his life did not permit him to do all he had hoped to do—that is the tragedy. There was the failure of his adobe and construction business, the increasing disaffection of his wives in Salt Lake City, which broke his heart more than most of you know. As I talked with him during the periods of his illness, I came to know a man who sorrowed that he could not make things work better, that he could not do more. But through it all he kept the faith. He was a man who attended church until the last. He was a faithful servant who loved justice and hoped to see justice done."

At these last words, Elizabeth felt her face burn. She wondered if he were now referring to J.B.'s attempt to be a witness at the trial of John Lee. At this moment John Lee seemed to be a thousand years away. And yet the burning continued in her cheeks. Should the bishop be talking about J.B.'s "hope" for that kind of justice? She made a note of his name. Bishop Peterson. But she quieted her heart and prayed, "Please do not say justice again. There is no justice. There is very little justice. There is fear, there is pain. There is striking out at that pain and then there is the cut at the strike."

She watched Maggie at the coffin, where the body of J.B. lay as cold as stone. His hair had been neatly combed back away from his face, leaving the white expanse of his forehead, a large bony skull roughened by the scars in his skin. His nose, the large straight nose, his lips tightened, as though he would eternally remember the injustices of his life. His body looked unfamiliar to Elizabeth. He was Maggie's without question. Maggie leaned over and lay her cheek on his face, letting the tears flow—although Elizabeth could not help but feel they were theatrical tears.

Performing their duty, the boys walked past the casket, staring at the man their mother and Uncle Jacob had said was their father. Joseph tightened his grip on Elizabeth's hand. The two older boys remembered him better. Caleb shed a few tears, impressed, it seemed, by death itself. Joshua seemed to bear it without interest, though with some terror. But no expression. He was numb.

"And now we shall take the casket to the grave site. If we may have the pall bearers step forward?"

When the high priests moved to the casket, Jacob looked into his father's face with an expression Elizabeth had seen before in his eyes. It was the same look of compassion he had given her often. He reached up and slowly pulled the lid of the casket down.

They walked to the grave site in a chill autumn wind. The yard lay on a hill, from which they could see the west valley for miles. Toquerville lay on the eastern side of a great basin, up against the mountain range close to the vast red stony country that lay between them and Kanab and Panguitch. It was a long thin town on a road moving south and north. It looked something like Kanarraville, except for the graveyard, which lay on a steep incline. As J.B.'s family walked with the coffin, the wind tore at them, chilling their faces and hands while old Bishop Peterson uttered the last prayer.

"And let justice be done, oh God. Let thy mercy put this man's soul to rest. He was a well-meaning man who tried in so many ways. If he had hurt anyone, he was sorry in his last breath. If he had failed anyone, he was repentant in his dying days."

Elizabeth felt Joseph's fingers tighten against hers in the cold. As the bishop prayed, she scolded her own heart. He is dead. And the father of my children. Is there any reason I should not care about him now? Even love him? I allowed him to marry me, to encumber my life—if it truly was an encumbrance. And he is Jacob's father as well.

At the bishop's last words, she looked up to watch Jacob, who stood a head taller than the others in the circle at the coffin. He turned. His large eyes caught her watching him, and he quickly turned away from her eyes. He helped the men unleash the ropes that let the coffin fall slowly into the ground.

Maggie began to cry. "Oh no! Jeremiah Butler Lorry! How could you have left me so alone?"

Feeling she should comfort Maggie, Elizabeth put her arm around her, pressed her close. "Maggie, we are so sorry. We know how you loved him. You will see him again someday."

Maggie, distraught, turned into Elizabeth's shoulder and shook against her, the tears rolling over the hands pressed to her face.

"There, there, Maggie."

"I'm sorry . . . for whatever it was I did to be so wronged . . . Oh what did I do to be punished so?"

The old Maggie—the helpless Maggie who had loved Jacob and told the woman in Provo that the baby she carried had been his—this Maggie fell against Elizabeth's breast and sobbed and sobbed. Elizabeth saw Jacob now, with a small but grateful smile. "We won't leave you, Maggie," he said. "If you need us, we will stay with you."

She continued to sob, and Jacob and Elizabeth led her away.

After the services, Bishop Peterson took a tearful Maggie to the church office—to talk about property, they said. Jacob, Elizabeth, and the children followed Robert back to the home. Through the tall trees weaving a canopy over the long road, they saw the squat dark house not more than a mile away. Even from this distance, they could see a shaft of gray smoke belching from the chimney. And there were lights blazing. Someone was in the house. Jacob slowed the horses.

"Who could it be? Do you know, Robert?"

But Maggie's boy was concentrating on showing an old Colt pistol to Joshua and Caleb. He stopped and looked far up the road. "I don't know," he said. And he continued to cock the rusty empty pistol, fire it, and cock it again. It bothered Jacob, who several times said, "Guns are not for play." The boy put it away, only to take it out a moment later.

Elizabeth was concerned about who might be in the house. "Just don't go in until we know," she said.

Driving within a hundred yards, they decided to stop the wagon before they came to the door. Jacob tied the rig to a tree and leaped to the ground. Elizabeth climbed down carefully. The boys did not hesitate, but scrambled from the rig, slinking toward the house to see. Robert was the bravest and the first to arrive. He turned from the window when the Lorrys came.

"Two old ladies," he whispered. "The Peterson ladies are settin' the table."

Jacob turned and laughed.

"Of course," Elizabeth said, walking up the walk. "The church ladies are giving us dinner."

The "ladies" were actually Elvina and Laura Peterson, two of the wives of Bishop Peterson, and they had prepared chicken dumplings.

Robert opened the door and walked in.

"Hello, young Robert," one of the ladies said, flipping a cloth to set over the table beside the hearth. "We thought you ought to have yourselves a warm supper. And we hope you like chicken dumplings. These is Elvina's best. And she does make good . . ." She stopped short when she saw the Kanarraville family following Robert into the house.

"Where's your mother . . . and Farrell?" the woman named Elvina spoke over her shoulder as she stoked the fire. She turned fully toward them, a plump old lady with a rough face and fuzzy gray hair.

"Bishop Peterson took my mother to the church office to speak to her about some matters," Robert said politely. He first introduced the Lorry boys to the bishop's two wives. The first woman, a younger version of the other, nodded slightly. She did not seem to mind the presence of the boys, but at the sight of Elizabeth and Jacob, her eyes showed a definite shift in the light. The old gray-haired woman, Elvina, looked very stern as she knit her brows. "Well. Glad to meet you, I'm sure," she said in an unsure voice. "You're the ones who followed John Lee?" Her voice seemed unnaturally low.

"I'm sorry. Did you know we were here?" Elizabeth asked politely. "We don't mean to interrupt."

"Certainly we knew you were here," the more amenable younger woman said brightly. "Bishop Peterson told us some of the family might show up. And you are the ones. We're glad you're here. We hope you like chicken dumplings. Elvina makes the best chicken dumplings you'll ever taste." The woman bustled about at last-minute chores, took the pot of dumplings off the fire, straightened out the tablecloth, and set the dumplings on it.

"I was thinking . . . hoping we'd see Maggie and Farrell," Elvina said, hesitant, a dark look still lurking in her face. "They must be talkin' . . .'"

"Oh, it means not a bit," clucked the other woman whose name they learned was Laura. "She means Farrell, our bishop. It means nothing. Sit down now. We ought to get back to our families."

The cabin was blazing with light. The fire in the hearth, along with several oil lamps, pushed shadows back into the corners of the room.

Jacob said a short prayer. The boys, as hungry as animals, set to the food. But for some reason, perhaps because they did not feel comfortable, the adults did not yet sit down.

Elizabeth said, "This is fine. We can wait to eat until Maggie and Bishop Peterson come. This is so nice of you."

Elvina looked askance at her. She nodded without smiling. Then she surprised Elizabeth by asking. "You the one . . . the daughter of John Lee?"

The air seemed to clear away. Elizabeth was aware of the light dancing in the corners of the room. "Why . . . no," she said, hearing her own voice. "There is no one here who is the daughter of John Lee."

"We heard his son was married to a daughter of John Lee."

Elizabeth shook her head, suddenly feeling deceitful, afraid.

"You know much about Mr. J.B. Lorry and his knowledge about the Mountain Meadows Massacre?" the gray-headed Elvina dared to ask quietly.

Elizabeth was taken back by the woman's brazenness. She could barely mouth the words, she felt so much surprise. "No. Not really."

"Well, Maggie told us they was going to kill John Lee."

Elizabeth, staring at the woman, felt the heavy words come down on her with force.

"We also hear he struck at J.B. with an ax. J.B. barely escaped with his life. It was good fortune Mr. Lorry has lived this long. And him wounded by an injun and fallen upon by John Lee."

Behind Elizabeth the other wife, Laura, spoke softly. "He was trying to make J.B. kill. But Maggie said J.B. didn't kill. He watched all the others who did. J.B. was afraid they was going to accuse him of something he did not do and kill him along with John Lee."

"But he has escaped all of that, bless his heart," Elvina interrupted. "It was Maggie's biggest concern. After his stroke at the trial, she was afraid they would come after him and twist the truth. And Maggie was worried they might come after her too, because she was a witness. She would be one of the few who could tell what really happened."

Elizabeth found she was so tense she had backed up against the sideboard. She put her hand on a lace doily behind her and bumped up against a butter crock. The faces of the two women were bright with the fire behind them. They quietly prepared the food, which they were feeding to the boys first. Elizabeth could hear the boys' spoons against their plates. Jacob was talking with Robert on the settee. The women were upon her too close, she thought. She wanted to back away.

"Come on, Elvina. We ought to go," Laura suddenly said. She turned to look back at the boys at the table, and at Jacob with Robert by the fire. "We just wanted to make sure you was fed."

"It's very kind of you," Elizabeth said, still feeling the lack of breathing room.

"Yes. We need to get back," the older one said. She gathered up a linen towel, folded it and tucked it into the bosom of her dress. "Tell Farrell we just left. We know what he told Maggie. We won't interfere."

Elizabeth did not know what they meant by this last statement. But she felt a sigh of relief escape her when they hurriedly left. She noticed they looked one last time toward the fire, where Jacob and the boys were seated, before they nodded their brief good-bye.

Suddenly, except for the boys' laughter and banter, there was quiet in the room. Elizabeth shook her head, wanting to pinch herself to make sure if she was awake. But she felt Jacob come between her and the light in the room. Though she heard his voice, she could not see his face in the shadows away from the fire.

"What did they say?" he asked.

"What you might expect," Elizabeth said.

Jacob led her to one of the side chairs. He sat on the wood box behind her as she stared into the room.

When the boys had finished their food, they knelt in front of the hearth. Robert again took out the shiny pistol. He also had a small box of treasures, wrapped in newspaper. He began to unwrap each one.

"Maggie . . . is not safe here. She is so very alone," Jacob said.

Abruptly, Elizabeth turned back to look at Jacob, who sat against the rough pine wall on the wood box at an angle slightly behind her. She was not sure what Jacob was going to say. But she believed she knew. She braced herself.

"Alone?" The hideous truth rankled in her. Their involvement with Maggie was now their responsibility—a cross they must bear. Of course they could not leave Maggie alone here, that was true. She, Elizabeth, must quickly find it in her heart to accept the woman and to love her, though it suddenly stuck in her like a knife.

"We must do something for her."

Elizabeth's heart pounded. She looked across the room again. "What should we do?"

"I don't know. There must be some way . . ."

It was up to Elizabeth to speak. She forced the words to come to her mouth. "Are you saying we should take her with us after all?" With the words out, she heard the quiet that followed them. She felt anxious. She wanted to beg Jacob not to speak Maggie's name.

"Oh, Elizabeth. I don't know. Maggie . . ." he sighed. "It would be so difficult for us all. But I don't know what else to do."

"Difficult." Now Elizabeth's throat seemed to shut down. Of course, Jacob would have been concerned about Robert and Maggie. And he would have done what he felt he should do for her out of his sense of care and duty.

"Elizabeth," he said softly. He moved forward. She sat not quite in front of him, but just to his side. If she turned back, she could see his face. She felt his breath in her hair. It was a whisper against her hair, her ear. "Tell me how you feel."

The words would not come easily. *I am selfish. I am closed. I am terrified.* "I wanted our heaven we tried to make for ourselves. You and I and . . . Anna Jane," she said. Her breath did not help the words. When she looked up at him, she saw a thoughtful look in his eyes.

Finally he turned to her and placed his hand over hers. "That's what I want, too . . ."

"But, of course," Elizabeth forced her voice, "of course, we cannot leave her, if she needs us." She saw the light in the room as it spun around her eyes. She smelled the strong salt smell in the food. She heard the boys laugh as they inspected Robert's treasures.

"We must at least find a place for her. Perhaps we can find another place for her."

Elizabeth felt light-headed, giddy. She felt the warmth of Jacob's uncertain hand as he held hers. But when she heard the voices in the hack outside the door, she was afraid. It was Maggie.

In a few moments when Maggie came into the room, everything seemed to change. Bishop Peterson followed her. He unwrapped a long woolen scarf from his throat and began to take off his coat while the boy Robert turned his back and carefully wrapped up the treasures by the light of the fire, one by one.

Jacob rose to greet them, but Elizabeth reached for his arm as though to hold him back. Maggie was not only grinning, her eyes were flashing with excitement. Seeing her so flushed seemed to surprise Jacob. He did not approach her.

The bishop was talking. He drew in a deep breath, as though he were gathering in the odors of the food. "Delicious, delicious," he said.

Elizabeth took the pot of dumplings down from the hook over the fire and set them on the table again. She began clearing the boys' dishes away. Margaret and the bishop sat down at the table while the boys scrambled through the outside door.

When the bishop stood to give the prayer, the room was silent. "And let this household be a household of peace," he said. After he said, "Amen," he bent his head toward Maggie and whispered strangely into her ear. "Do you want to tell them, dear sister?"

Maggie leaned coyly away. She looked like a school girl in spring. "Yes. If you'll help me tell them."

The bishop stood up, a silly grin on his ample face. He was rather plump, and the fold of his chin looked like a rubber beard. He began quaintly. "I am going to add Maggie and Robert to our family," he said. "It was always fine with Elvina and Laura." Now Elizabeth saw more light. She now recalled and understood the last words Elvina spoke, "Tell Farrell we know what he told Maggie. We won't interfere."

The bishop continued his droll speech. "And we know Maggie will be happier if she belongs to somebody. Maggie and Robert will stay here. But we'll be one family. Isn't that right, Maggie?" Farrell Peterson said.

Yes, it was right. She nodded and she gave him her small trembling hand.

How could Maggie have agreed to such an arrangement so soon? Elizabeth wondered. How? So soon?

"We have said so now for your sake," the bishop said to the Lorrys. "For you would have worried about her and wanted to take her with you."

Jacob was speechless. Elizabeth was not sure she could breathe. "We have said so now for your sake." The bishop sat down as suddenly as he had stood up. Raising the pot of dumplings as though it were a kind of sacrament, he set them down in front of his plate, and began to dip up his fill.

## 100

### *Elizabeth*

Trying to sleep in the narrow settee at J.B. and Maggie's house, Elizabeth thought she heard the boys get up from their beds on the floor. She had not slept well, and she was glad they would be going in the morning.

Anxious, she lay awake watching the light from the dying fire flicker along the heavy rafters above her in the room, watching the quiet hump on the floor that was Jacob. If she had been a Maggie, she might have gone to him and held him. But she would never have crossed those lines. She would have died first.

She thought she heard Robert whispering something to Joshua before the two boys rose up against the fading firelight and stole out into the night under the bright moon. She thought she saw them, but in a few moments her mind closed down and again she fell asleep.

It was morning when she opened her eyes. She saw Jacob through the back door, his arms loaded with wood. Turning over and yawning, she held her head in her hands, almost shaking herself awake.

"Good morning, Elizabeth," she heard. "Are you ready to go?" Jacob brought the wood to the hearth, raked the coals, stoked them into flames.

"Yes," she said dimly. "I thought I dreamed the children were walking about during the night."

Jacob was amused. "They have secrets," he said, smiling, shoving large sticks of wood into the fire. "Robert has given them some treasures to take home."

"Oh?"

The family was ready to begin home about noon. Maggie gave them a large box filled with food. Jacob paid her well for her hospitality. Still unusually quiet, Maggie stared after them as they climbed into the rig. Robert hung to the horse and kept leaning in to whisper to the boys.

Elizabeth could not keep her eyes from Maggie. The woman stood outside the house still in her red morning robe, her hair a wild mop, her eyes not alive though it was noon. She did not look up once. She looked as though she were in a daze.

"What was it that Robert gave you?" Elizabeth asked Joseph down the road. He was shaking a small pouch of powder. "Did he show you how to ram powder into a gun?"

Joseph's eyes were large, brown. Saucer eyes. He looked afraid.

"Did he scare you?" Elizabeth said. She happened to glance back into Joshua and Caleb's eyes. Joshua was gazing nonplussed into the distance, though he heard every word. There was terror in Caleb's face. The roof of her mouth felt dry. She saw the mountains loom ahead of her; she felt the jolt of the wagon as it rammed forward over the valley floor.

"What was the game he was playing?" she asked them. She looked at Jacob. He did not know.

"It's poison," Joseph said.

"What?"

"Poison. The poison Aunt Maggie used to put in the tea."

"Poison?" Elizabeth shook the pouch from Joseph's hand. "What is poison? Is this poison? Who put it in the tea?" She looked back and caught Joshua's eyes. What had the boys been doing while they had been busily discussing chicken dumplings and Maggie's marriage to Bishop Peterson? Joshua was still gazing out into the fields, looking bored.

"Joshua. What was it?" Elizabeth felt tight in her throat.

"It's poison. Aunt Maggie used to give it to J.B."

"Poison?" Elizabeth leaned forward with the pouch, opened it and smelled it. It burned in her nose, and she recoiled. She turned the pouch upside down and let the powder fall along the road.

"Who gave it to J.B.?"

Caleb spoke now, his mouth tight. "That's what she used to kill Pa, Mother."

Elizabeth brought her free hand to her throat. She felt she might choke. "What? No. Stop such talk."

"Robert swore us with our blood Maggie wanted Pa dead because she was going to have a baby by Bishop Peterson. He come over often to see her. She wanted him dead because he testified against John Lee."

"It wasn't that way," Joshua added to Caleb's words. "She was afraid when he testified once against John Lee they would keep on usin' him as a witness, and there would be more questions about Pa at another trial. And she hated the massacre and all the stories too. She was afraid to come to the trial herself because she knew things nobody knew. Because Robert told us that Pa really did kill some people at the massacre that day."

Elizabeth still held her gloved hand at her throat. She looked at Jacob. He drove the hack steadily forward, his eyes narrowed in concentration.

"Robert gave us the bullets from the gun that J.B. used to hunt deer."

"He had a dead rabbit in his hiding place, Mama. A big gray rabbit. He gave me one of the foots off the rabbit," Joseph said, excited now. He produced the gray rabbit foot from his pocket. "It's the last animal Pa ever shot. And he gave it to me." Joseph stroked the rabbit paw, rubbed it on his cheek, and snuggled back on the wagon seat close to his mother. He lay his head back, smiling a satisfied smile. "And he gave it to me."

"I think it's all wrong, anyway," Joshua said. "Robert swore to me his mother is already married to Bishop Peterson. She just pretended she was going to get married so we wouldn't take her with us when we left."

"No. Robert told me J.B. was sick and wanted to die."

Elizabeth looked at Jacob, asking questions with her eyes. Jacob returned her glance with a faint smile.

## 101

### Elizabeth

The farther from Toquerville they traveled, the better Elizabeth could see. The blur in her eyes seemed to clear away, and she found the mountains and the sky again. Sometimes when she closed her eyes she thought she could still see J.B.'s grave. Or the body in the coffin. Or the fire in the stone hearth and the penetrating eyes of the women who prepared the food. Or she imagined the boys' games—both the day games and the night games. She saw their bodies as they moved before the imaginary fire.

In Cedar City they stopped to visit Nancy Dalton to ask about John Lee. The Daltons were quiet. "We have heard only that he has been ill in the prison. I have been concerned."

On the night before Jacob and Elizabeth left, they talked with the Daltons around the supper table until long past ten. There was an autumn wind in the chimney. The children in the loft above the room slept restlessly in the wind.

"They wanted to set him free as they did Klingensmith, but Klingensmith offered to turn state's evidence."

"What they really want is to blame Brigham Young," Nancy said.

"If he would give evidence that the incident is the work of Brigham Young, I'm sure they would have what they want, and the whole thing would blow over," Dalton said. "Lee's told me many times about the day he made the report to Brigham Young. The president paced back and forth in the room, crying, 'Most unfortunate, most unfortunate. Why was this done? This should never have been done.'"

Nancy chimed in again. "What he said was to the effect that this incident would cause sorrow and harm to the Mormon Church for years and years to come."

"It is a blot on our history," Dalton said.

Nancy said, "This people had seen enough ills and injustices."

"We overdid our fear."

"And grief."

"It is not justifiable."

"And never will be."

"Is it justifiable to take a good man's life for payment to the past?"

"He would rather die a man who kept his commitment to silence. He made a sacred commitment that he would not tell . . ."

"He says it is lies they want," Nancy said. "And he cannot tell lies."

Finally Elizabeth and Jacob took the children home. They found the house in fairly good order. Belinda had kept things running smoothly and well. And she had taken good care of Anna Jane. While they had been gone, Belinda had become engaged to the young photographer who had taken pictures of the Lee family and ferry at the dell. Mr. Fennimore was a bright, cheerful sort of fellow and had taken a room at Mrs. Marshall's boarding house until such a time as he and Belinda would return to Salt Lake City, where he wanted to set up shop.

"There is a man who will sponsor me in a business of my own. And my mother and father own a large house with a small living space where Belinda and I can live."

Elizabeth and Anna Jane gave Belinda a prenuptial party, and the entire family expressed a desire to travel to Salt Lake City to spend Christmas and perform the wedding in the endowment house.

But only three days before the family planned to make the trip, a deep snow fell. It choked the roads with soggy mud. Lee's first wife, Rachel, would not hear of canceling the trip. Whether the rest came or not, she would go. And Belinda and James would not hear of putting off their wedding. Jacob, putting on his hat as the male authority, said he thought he could take Rachel up. But Anna Jane and Elizabeth and the rest ought to stay.

There was quiet in the house while Elizabeth heard the decision. The children had gone to sleep. Jacob asked her to pull on her boots and come with him to take care of the cattle in the yard. Wrapping his throat in wool, he said, "Help me open the gates to the corral so if they want to they can come in. It might freeze tonight, and I don't want to take a chance."

When he stamped into his boots, pushing his feet hard against the wood floor, Elizabeth followed him to the closet and searched for her own boots. After she managed to pull them on, she wrapped herself in her coat and followed him out the back door. She could not help but catch her breath at the brightness of the moon on the blue white snow. Though the wind still blew through the valley, threatening to chill them, the hot sun had melted the snow into thousands of tiny icicles that clung like burrs to the trees. It looked like a wonderland.

The same little icicles that clustered on the landscape were irritating nuisances on the shaggy manes and hides of the animals, so Jacob scraped some of the heaviest icicles away. The cattle watched Jacob and Elizabeth with soulful eyes as they came into the corral.

"I'm sorry. I don't believe it's practical to bring all of the family with us to Salt Lake City," Jacob said quietly. "It means you and Anna Jane will be spending Christmas alone."

Elizabeth pulled at the ice also while Jacob filled the trough with hay. She did not say anything.

"Would it make it any better to tell you I will take you alone to the temple in the spring?" He looked over the back of the lowing cow to Elizabeth's face. She felt flushed, though she knew her skin probably looked pale in the moonlight. "I would like to marry you in the spring," he said.

She whispered now, resting her gloved hands over the cow's large back, leaning toward Jacob, her breath like a cloud steaming up into the cold air. She did not want to remind him, but the words came slowly. "They have promised us there will be a trial by spring."

### 102

#### Elizabeth

*March 21, 1875. Still they have not announced a trial, and it is spring. Jacob delivered eight lambs today.*

*March 25, 1875. Today we heard some good news from Belinda Marie. She and Mr. Fennimore are going to have a baby in July.*

*March 28, 1875. Hannah is so unhappy, and I cannot seem to calm her. She wants so badly to have a baby, too, and it does not seem to happen for her and her good husband,*

*John Frederick. I believe she is jealous of Belinda Marie.*

*April 16, 1875. The children received marks from their work in school. All but Caleb did exceptionally well, especially Jacob's boys, Richard and Perry. They study even harder than my boys. They say they both want to become doctors of medicine so they can cure their mother Anna Jane.*

*May 15, 1875. We have heard rumors that there has been a riot at the prison. Why don't they hold the trial for John Lee?*

*July 18, 1875. It is so hard for me to write with this, my hand is shaking so. But I must tell what has happened today. We received a letter from Salt Lake City from Belinda Marie. It is good news. She has had a baby boy! Seven and a half pounds! And there is a miracle of all miracles! For I can actually see him! He has dark hair like his photographer father James. I know because sitting on my desk is one of James' prints which he has sent to us. A small daguerrotype. I can stare at it for hours. It is as though at last we can make time stand still!*

*July 19, 1875. Anna Jane loves the pictures, too. But there is harsh news as well. Still there is no plan for a trial for Grandfather Lee. Since Rachel Lee has been living at the prison there have been jealousies and revolts. We heard that in May seven prisoners escaped and the warden was killed.*

*October 11, 1875. There is no word of a trial for John Lee. Anna Jane is so weak she can barely speak. She reads the scriptures. Her favorite is, "Oh God, where art thou? Where is the pavilion that covereth thy hiding place? How long shall we dwell in sorrow and as the victims of sin." She asks constantly about her father, John Lee. Though she cannot walk, she looks out on the meadows while the children shear the sheep. She cries to me, "Where is justice? Why doesn't Brigham do something? Where is the Lord's merciful arm?"*

*March 6, 1876. Father Lee has planted a vegetable garden at the prison and has enlisted the help of Rachel and all of the men to weed and hoe. He also teaches school to the prisoners.*

*April 4, 1876. Will they allow him to languish forever in prison? Will they never set him free? I don't like to talk about it, but it seems that Brigham Young can do nothing for John Lee at this point without saying to the world that he was behind it, and it would hurt the Church more than its young vulnerable organization—already in trouble with the nation—can bear.*

*May 18, 1876. We have heard! Finally they have received a message at the mercantile! They have set a trial so they have let him go free! For the first time in many years he is free. How long we have waited for this day! For some strange reason his freedom at this moment also makes me feel free.*

*July 20, 1876. Finally he is to come back to Panguitch! How long have we waited for this day! Though his summons requires him to appear in court at Beaver in three months, he was released on a fifteen thousand dollar bail. We will have him with us for those three months. Anna Jane and I held each other tight and both of us shed tears.*

<br>

## 103
### Elizabeth

When the McDonald boy from the southernmost farm in Panguitch rode breathlessly into town saying he'd spotted the group traveling with John Lee, several family members—Jacob, Sammy, Ezra, and John Frederick—went out to meet him. Joshua and Caleb were not far behind.

Elizabeth's heartbeat quickened with anticipation and fear. She saw the cart from a distance, and fastened her eyes on the small figure hunched on the center bench, the sun beating on his head. When he arrived in the yard, she stood in the background while the family clamored about, begging for Lee's attention. Elizabeth was stunned at his gaunt look. Now the truth—as though it had sharp teeth— sank hard into her. He was an old man. He was bent. His hair had turned completely gray. His eyes were black holes. But, Elizabeth told herself, it would take time in this place of peace for him to heal. It would take time to heal. He must heal.

For over a week she did not go near to him. She listened to people talk. She learned that he was riding his horse into the hills every day.

On a hot Tuesday morning in July, she finally rode out to meet him. She had thought about the encounter for a long time, passing imaginary scenes through her mind. She had asked Jacob's Johnny Lorry to let her tend the sheep in the morning. She needed to get away. He had looked at her with unasked questions in his eyes, but said nothing. So she ate breakfast quickly and rode one of the mares into the hills. She waited until she knew which road John Lee followed. And once he was in the hills, she took the same road and a short cut so that she would be ahead of him. She waited for him to come. She was amazed that she had the courage to do what she had so much wanted to do.

When he saw her his face brightened. He waved to her as though glad to see her. When he reached her side, he stopped his horse. Her heart beat so hard in her chest that her mouth grew dry.

"Elizabeth," he said. His voice caressed her name. Though the tone seemed lighter, as though worn thin, it was the same rich voice of the John Lee she had known. For a few moments they spoke only pleasantries. "I love it here," he finally said. "I see something more meaningful every day in the land itself— the open emptiness of the land. There is much that touches the spirit here."

"It's a beautiful day," Elizabeth replied, unable to say what was in her heart. Yet all she now wanted so desperately was this moment of talk. This stream of light words between them was the beginning of what she had so much desired—one more time with him, to be alone . . .

"It was suffocating in that prison." He shook his head.

"I can't imagine that kind of confinement," Elizabeth said.

"Can you come with me?" he hesitated. "Could you ride with me, Elizabeth? If it is all right with you, I'd like you to ride up the hill with me."

Her heart seemed as though it were on fire.

They turned up the small canyon into the low eastern hills to find their way to the top of a small rise. They saw Panguitch now like a collection of tiny wooden toys—far off in the distant valley beyond the rolling hills.

"I've been looking at the country with different eyes."

"How so different?" Elizabeth asked.

"Eyes aware of the value of space."

"Because you have not seen space for so long?"

"That, of course, is the major reason. But there is another realization which comes to me.

Elizabeth waited in quiet for his words to follow.

"I see myself in this immense world as very small."

"Yes, she said quietly.

"Remember how Moses was startled by the same realization? 'I am nothing, which thing I had never supposed.'"

"Yes," she said, almost whispering.

"I am nothing here at all. Our lives are very brief. Like a puff of warm breath against the cold. And so I see my life as really very meaningless unless it means something to me." Lee sat in the saddle, shading his eyes from the sun in the west. A haze of gray clouds began moving across the sky.

He had said, "Unless it means something to me." She would not have pressed the question unless he had said that. "Then what must it mean to you?" She wanted him to talk.

"That I can measure it. Not by what others may believe. But by what I and my God know that I am."

There was quiet now. Elizabeth did not disturb it. For a moment they simply watched the far-away fields. Finally they dismounted together, tying the horses to a wind-broken juniper tree. For a moment neither of them spoke until Lee walked to the edge of the cliff.

"What you and Jacob said—about the stories the children created over the death of J.B.—I've been thinking about how stories grow." He was smiling now.

"Yes . . ." Elizabeth froze with some fear. So someone had repeated those rumors to John Lee. "They may not be stories."

"They are stories," he said with finality. "I planted a fig tree at the Washington place. No one will eat the figs because the story is that I murdered a young girl and buried her beneath the tree."

Elizabeth waited while John Lee lifted the reins and spurred his horse up a rise. She had heard a version of that tale from the children.

"No. There are things we will never really know."

Of course that was true. "You mean . . . we will never really know . . . what happened . . . I suppose we'll never know what really happened . . ." Because she was forcing the words, they seemed to break apart on her tongue.

"What happened at the meadows?" John Lee had been willing to help her to sound it out. He gazed into the valley with a studied gaze. "Exactly. We may never really know. Even I can tell it only from what I know, what I saw."

Yes. That was true. Now Elizabeth thought she could have borne any words she would have heard from John Lee. The gray clouds in the sky gathered over the distant sun, but its bright flames still dazzled through.

"And so . . ." He did not wait for her to ask the question. He stared into the valley, seeing what she saw—the matchstick homes of Panguitch, the trappings of people living on the land.

"What do I know? What is my side of the picture . . . ?" He paused, lifted one leg to the stones, leaned over his elbows on his knee. Still he watched the valley below. He was very much aware—as she was—of the endless air. The sun.

"Elizabeth." His voice broke. "I was there to see the deaths of over a hundred men. Women. Children." There was a terrible silence. A silence in which the clouds covered the sun. "I let it happen because I believed other people—and God—wanted our preservation. And I felt this was the only way it could be accomplished." He paused. "I knew that not one soul could escape to tell what we had done. I knew we could all perish. And though we had ten years to settle, it still seemed to be not enough time!" He stopped again. "It was not right. It was not right." He shook his head. "But I believed at the time it was the best thing, the only thing, to do."

Elizabeth stood close to him. She put her hand on his arm. "I know that," she whispered. "I know that." And she pressed his arm. The light in the air seemed to dance. "And I'm sorry."

"But no one seems to understand."

"They will at the Beaver Trial," she said. "Brigham Young will think of something."

"No." He paused. "Not necessarily." A stinging quiet rang in their ears now. "No. The greatest regret of my life is . . . that he . . . yielded to pressure. He let them excommunicate me." He lowered his voice. "That hurt me more than he will ever know."

Still Elizabeth waited for him.

"But Brigham Young must remain the guardian of the entire church," he continued. "God's church, the kingdom, the meaning of struggling to survive as a human being committed to live for Christ. All of this would be placed on trial. It sounds perhaps a bit fanatical, but if we err, it is on the side of struggling to be divine."

She was quiet for a long time. "Then the Mormon Church must not be brought to trial. They will set you, alone . . . you, John Lee, free."

For a long time John Lee stood watching the open spaces that surrounded them. Finally he turned to her. "You really believe that, don't you, Elizabeth?"

"Yes, I do."

He stared at her for a long time. "You and I," he said softly. "We never had our turn."

Elizabeth's heart began to bump again. She felt color come up into her neck. "No, we haven't," she said, short of breath.

"Well, I cannot give you what I do not have to give you: myself, free. I must clear it, without implicating others or breaking my trust to keep the sacred oath."

Elizabeth breathed inwardly, felt a sharp pain.

My sons want me to change my name, to go to Mexico." He shook his head slowly. "Elizabeth." He was again quiet. He faced her, pressed her hands. "I would be admitting guilt to do that. And my guilt is not my own alone."

She felt the silence. They were quiet for a long time. Then he whispered to her. "Do you understand?"

Tears welled in her eyes. "I understand," she whispered. "I understand."

## 104
### Elizabeth

*September 26, 1876. It is hot this month. Something in the water makes the cattle ill. Jacob had to dig out another pond to let in the water from the canal. When the pond was full, he shut it off with a new gate he had built into the dam. Still no news of the trial.*

*September 29. Still no news of the trial.*

Elizabeth dried the apples on the tin roof of the shed, scolding the little boys when they climbed the ladder to reach them. She rescued Christa when the boys tried to feed her pig weed, and she nursed Joseph back to health when he got the runs. She comforted Hannah and John Frederick because Hannah did not seem to be able to get pregnant. And she made sure that Joshua, Caleb, and Joseph, who were building a shepherd's hut out on the hills, didn't take structural pieces of wood out of the barn.

Through all of the day-to-day concerns, Elizabeth still worried about the trial. When she put up pickles in new blue glass jars Jacob purchased for her from the mercantile, she stopped at the coop every day for lids and for news.

"'What are they doin' in the trial?' I know that's what you want to hear, isn't it, Missus Elizabeth," old Mr. Hatch said to her when she passed the telegraph office in the afternoon. "That's what you asked yesterday and that's what you wanted to know today, isn't it? I told you yesterday about that fellow who went by, who said he had a letter to John Lee from Brigham Young. They was going to deliver it to Skatumpah, but they never made it. And now the trial's begun."

Elizabeth nodded, buoyed by the hope she had always had that the results of that trial would exonerate them all.

"Well, they's still gibber-jabbering on in that courtroom and the news don't say nothing is happened yet. But one day soon it will, I tell you. I do know they quit putting the Mormon Church on trial, which is what you was so worried for. They jes' want to find out if they've a case against old John Lee."

There had been a lucky break in the jury selection. Every member was a member of the Mormon Church, or in one way or another connected with the authorities of the Church. And every one of the jurors was aware of the position of John Lee. Elizabeth read the list of participants. Then she saw Farrell Peterson's name. She drew back, startled.

"What is it, ma'am?"

"Nothing, Brother Hatch. Thank you." On her way to the meat market, her eyes began to water.

Each evening Elizabeth knit socks and mittens, large warm woolen pieces she created with their own gray, red and green yarns. She missed Belinda. Anna Jane and Jacob's Christa were the brightest lights in the house. Christa was the dressiest of the family when they prepared for church. All of the boys wore stark creased blue pants or brown coats and straight ties. Little Christa, who looked much older than her ten years, wore pink ribbons in her long brown silk curls, a white collar, pleats, and a wide pink waist band that ended in a bow above the wide skirt.

Anna Jane, proud for the last few months that she could hobble with a deliberately measured step, clung to Christa when they walked into the church.

On this Sunday in September, one of the boys tripped Christa. She fell, bracing herself with her tiny gloved hands. Skidding across the wood floor, her palms gathered enough slivers through the thin gloves to require careful surgical attention. She did not cry. She could not have helped hearing the boys laugh and scatter. But she picked herself up and brushed off her dress.

Anna Jane's eyes filled with tears. "She won't run away. She can't run away. She's a Lee. She's a Lee."

Jacob took Anna Jane to the pew, his arm around her. "It's all right," he whispered. "They're just children." They had been cowards to pick on the only girl. "Leave them be."

But later after church was out, one of the Harrison boys threw little Johnny on the ground and buried him with grass cuttings. "We know what happened to big John Lee. But you don't know," the boy cried out. Caleb and Joshua Lorry took it upon themselves to whip the Harrison boy good. Finally he ran into a crowd of other boys who huddled together to protect him.

The Lorrys gathered at the cart early to take the ride home. Anna Jane kept glancing behind to make sure none of the boys had followed them. Elizabeth looked up at Jacob. "What is the reason for all of this?" she asked suddenly.

Jacob, looking defeated said, "I believe some of the boys got some news from a Mr. Lawson who just came into town. He's telling everyone that a federal officer is here to make a survey of plural families." He paused for a moment, his words heavy with meaning. "The government is going to crack down on plural marriage. That's the big news. But there's something else . . . about a court decision. It can't be released until a week from today. But there are rumors . . . I believe it's a fact. They have sentenced John Lee."

Standing beside the wagon, Elizabeth felt her legs shake under her. The boys climbed into the cart, and Joseph reached out to pull Anna Jane up. Christa climbed in to take a seat beside her mother. Elizabeth saw all of this without moving. She held to the side of the cart, trying to feel the security of the ground under her feet, trying to get a grasp on the edge. "How did you know?" The words came out forced, broken, though she had conscientiously tried to speak clearly.

"Same way I heard about the Brigham Young letter. I asked." Hannah had finally found out from certain underground sources that Brigham Young had written a special letter to Lee urging him to jump bail. It was purported that the president said the church would take the responsibility for the money. But the messengers bringing the letter had crossed Lee enroute to Kanab and Lee had never received it. And was Brigham Young's letter a reality? No one really knew.

"It can't be true," Elizabeth whispered, her face ashen.

"I don't believe it for a minute," Anna Jane said gathering up her skirts. Her hands were shaking. Christa began peeling away her white gloves, and Anna Jane bent close to pinch out some of the tiny slivers.

"It's a rumor."

"How else would it be circulated if it were not true?"

"Somebody said they were planning on taking John Lee back to the meadows to die the same kind of death that happened there," Joshua mentioned.

Elizabeth felt the cart swing in her grasp. Blindly, she felt for the step. She wanted to look at Joshua. How had the boys already heard anything about it, while she had known nothing until this moment?

"It's not true. It's lies like most of the other lies we've been hearing," Anna Jane said, pursing her lips. Elizabeth had never seen Anna Jane look so stern.

With her eyesight blurred, Elizabeth saw the people in their Sunday best coming and going as though in a dream. They looked distorted. She felt perhaps she could not breathe. When she reached the house, she ripped off her bonnet and her shawl and raced upstairs into her bedroom. She climbed into the high bed without taking off her shoes, and tearless, lay with her face breathing into the pillow.

Of course Lee would not jump bond. He was a man totally motivated by honor, and he would never have done it. Even for Brigham Young. Lee should receive honors, not blackguard offers. It could not have happened!

For an hour she did not go into the house below or help Anna Jane and the boys with supper. And then the hour stretched into two. She lay in the bed for a long time, feeling nothing was real anymore. Nothing.

She refused two meals. She did not answer when the children knocked on the door. She did not look out from the squared panes in the window, from the lace curtains that shimmered under the light of the slim moon. She still hurt at night when she heard Jacob's voice below, and finally at her door.

"Is there anything we can do to help, Elizabeth?"

"Jacob, please. If you and Anna Jane could take care of things for me tonight, I would appreciate it."

"All right, Elizabeth," he said softly. But she heard no feet on the stairs. He was still standing outside her door, waiting. If Jacob had wanted to know Elizabeth's heart, there was a devastating clarity for him in that moment when he realized that she was unable to let him come in.

## 105

### *Elizabeth*

Elizabeth did not remember much about the next few months of that winter, all of it shadowed with the expectations of spring. It was true. John Lee was to be killed.

There was snow. There was the monotony of their incessant labors. Joshua shot his first deer with a bow and arrow. The boys all took their turns at being ill. Mr. Lawson made surveys of plural families, though there was as yet no firm law passed against the marriages of existing families. Anna Jane became ill again. They nursed her through one crisis after another until she was almost no longer herself.

The execution they so much dreaded was to take place in mid-March, 1877. Anna Jane summoned Elizabeth to her room. "I'm not well, Elizabeth. And it is time for Father to be called home." That was the way she put it. "It is time for Father to be called home. Please go to see him for me. I am too ill to go."

Elizabeth sat with her, holding her hands.

"You know how we always wanted you—Jacob and I have wanted you—in our family." How many times had Anna Jane mentioned the subject to Elizabeth and Elizabeth had said no? "I need you. And Father," she choked slightly, "does not need you now." Her voice trembled.

He had never needed her, Elizabeth thought now. He was a star she could never reach. Perhaps that had been the reason she had loved him so. People often said you sought most that which you could never have.

"Perhaps you will see it's best . . . it's the very best thing for you to belong to us." Anna Jane paused and let her head fall on the pillow. "Elizabeth, please. Marry into our family while I can see it happen, and while I can say that you belong to me forever."

Elizabeth didn't speak. She drew her hand over Anna Jane's fingers and held to them, believing as she always had that her own silence would never betray her fear.

"Please. We'll have a wedding then. Please. You and Jacob go together to my father and tell him how much I love him."

Elizabeth wanted to cry out then, but she held herself still. Anna Jane clung to Elizabeth's hand.

"Will you go to the execution for me, then? With Jacob? Marry him before you go. Be good to him. He's cried for you at times, though I promised him I would not tell."

*March 10, 1877. I tell myself I am doing this for Jacob and Anna Jane, yet I know I am also doing it for me. It is my second wedding day. I remember so well the first—so many years ago. In this one there is not so much fear. Anna Jane begged me to promise I would marry Jacob and go with him to see John Lee. And so Jacob and I went this morning to the bishop with the family. I noticed that the flowers came out for our wedding day. As though ordered by God to bloom, the narcissus and hyacinth around the door of the church were blazing. After the bishop performed the short civil ceremony, he told us that with my sealing to J.B., Jacob's father, there should be nothing standing in the way of our eternal family, and that someday he believed we could be sealed in the new Salt Lake Temple if that is what we wished. I wore my pink dress with violet ribbons. Anna Jane let me borrow her ring.*

## 106

### Jacob

Jacob was quiet through the ceremony. His silence betrayed his concern for Anna Jane. He was determined to give her all she desired before he and Elizabeth prepared for their journey to the Mountain Meadows. While the couple alternated taking turns to sit with Anna Jane in the night, there was no time to consummate their wedding bonds. He did not speak much to anyone as they prepared for their trip together in the next few days. They would wait.

Rachel was already in Beaver. Caroline left with Sammy and Ezra early to help accompany Father Lee to the meadows. James Fennimore and Belinda wanted to take the baby, though such a long trip with such a young baby looked too difficult for them.

Hannah and John Frederick debated whether or not they should go, but with Elizabeth and Jacob gone, Anna Jane needed them very much, and she asked them to stay with her and take care of things at home.

Elizabeth packed food into the wagon, and enough bedding that they could sleep in the wagon bed if no one they knew happened to be home in either Beaver or Kanarraville. Hannah and John Frederick waved after them as the wagon slowly lumbered away.

Through all of it, Jacob had kept his silence. But his gaunt look told Elizabeth his heart. He had suffered his own pain.

They did not reach Beaver in time to see Father Lee in the prison. He had already been removed to take his last journey. They made the long trek to Kanarraville in silence. The sun was very low for spring. The knife-edged hills that surrounded them on the far edges of the basin became sharper as dusk fell, and blackened with the sinking sun.

As they rode past the old Kanarraville brick home, they noticed that some of the log sheds had been scrabbled and used for firewood. A young boy played outside the house while the young father was cutting wood. Jacob watched the members of the Redd family with interest. Having lived for so long with his weakened Anna Jane, Mr. Redd's daunting health engrossed him—the full rosy-colored face, the thick curly hair loose under his torn green felt hat, the bright color of his blue eyes, and the strength in his hands and arms.

"We're looking for John Lee," Jacob said, his excuse for staring at the broken sheds beside the brick home.

Brother Redd pointed south toward Harmony. "Just this morning they took him to Harmony. And then tomorrow they'll take him down to stay at Hamblins' on the road outside of Penter. You going to watch the shooting?"

Jacob's throat hurt and he did not answer him. He nodded a curt thank you as he took in the faces of the shaggy-haired children, then sped the horses on.

In Kanarraville they found some of the Hamblin relatives at home. More of them were staying at the Hamblin house at the meadows, though Rachel Hamblin happened to be here with her daughter in Kanarraville because the girl had just given birth to a new son.

"I hope this will not be an imposition on you," Elizabeth told Rachel. "I believe John wanted us to come."

Rachel looked very tired. The Hamblins had in the last few years turned completely against the Lees. Or was it that the Lees had turned completely against the Hamblins? Rachel had never been quite sure. She had tried to stay friends with the Lees, she said. But the worry and the stress of it had worn her thin. Happy to see Elizabeth and Jacob, she invited them to stay in the house. But the best she could offer was the parlor floor.

"Yes. I do know John wanted his families to come down," she told them. Caroline and Rachel had already come from Panguitch. However, they had left much earlier to accompany John Lee on his journey from the prison. "All of the Lees are staying with the Redd families who bought the old Lee home. And John is with them. He wanted to see all of you. But they are keeping a close watch on him. He has been forced . . ." she paused, "to wear a ball and chain."

Elizabeth did not let anyone know how Rachel's words cut into her flesh like knives. A ball and chain. The image of John sitting at the dinner table with his family, weighted with a ball and chain, struck her as astonishing. Without wanting to, she could see the ball and the chain on his leg and the vision cramped her heart. She knew they had to operate on the premise that they could not trust him. Perhaps with anything less than a ball and chain, the authorities reasoned, he would have disappeared.

Still feeling her heart pound, yet as visibly calm as she could be, Elizabeth turned to Jacob and said quietly that she would like to go to the Redds' to see Lee that night.

Jacob easily understood her anxiety, but he didn't feel the urgency that she did. When he saw Rachel's worn and guarded look, he thought it best to stay with the Hamblins until morning.

That night on the floor of Rachel Hamblin's home, Elizabeth and Jacob slept with reasonable comfort on the straw mattress Rachel had brought down from her own bed. The room was quiet until the crack of dawn when they heard the young people open the doors of the barn to milk the cows. The morning sun from the hills came early, filtering through the lace curtains to the floor, where it flooded the wood slats with almost tangible light. The odors of pork rind and bacon, hotcakes, eggs, hot applesauce and gruel wafted through the door. Rachel had prepared so large a breakfast they could not have eaten it, even in times of peace.

By the time they left Hamblins', the militia was already accompanying Lee down the road to Penter, the horses steaming in the spring sun. When they saw John Lee seated on one of his old mares, Elizabeth felt her heart stop. He was dressed simply in a rough unpressed brown wool coat, a dark vest, light shirt and tie.

Keeping her voice as calm as she could, Elizabeth asked Jacob if they could hurry the wagon. Because of the traffic ahead, however, the horses could not move. So she climbed down from the vehicle and began to wend her way through the other horsemen, the militia, the numberless members of the family traveling by foot to the site. No one stopped her. But if anyone had asked any questions of her, she had already decided to politely refuse to say anything at all.

There were several family members at Lee's side. Rachel Lee stood beside the horse, clinging to the bridle, her face expressionless. And there were Caroline, and Teresa, and even Lisanne, who had left him at one time. Most of the wives had decided to come. The bishop and many of the men in the ward were there. Elizabeth noticed at once Belinda Marie's husband, James Fennimore, walking beside his own horse. In his hands he held his camera. Surprised, she said a quick hello. While he nodded in recognition, he held his camera at a raked angle to get a shot of Lee on the horse with his foot in the stirrup, the ball and chain hanging just below the horse's belly.

The leaders of the small accompanying militia barked orders to move out at that moment, and Lee's horse started forward. Elizabeth had almost reached him in time, but not soon enough. She ran with light feet to try to catch up with Rachel Lee, but she did not make it. Still on foot beside her husband, Rachel was forced to let go of the bridle. Urged by several other heavily armed horsemen, Lee's horse and the entire entourage began to move along.

"Father Lee! Father Lee! John!" Elizabeth called out, trying to attract his attention. He turned slightly to see who was calling. At the sight of his face, Elizabeth's breath stopped. His eyes were dull with a stupor she had never seen. "We came to be with you," she said. He nodded. When Elizabeth could see into his eyes, she knew that he had already left them. "We will always be with you," she called after him, feeling her breath to be insignificant against the cold wind. *We have come to be with you. We will always be with you.* Perhaps he would not have understood the message of the words even if he had heard them.

"Har! Yup!" The U.S. commander of the militia barked orders that those who were making the journey must get underway. The women scrambled into the wagons at the side of the road. The horses strained at the reins. There was a desolation, a military gloom that accompanied the clank of the chains, the sound of the steel on the guns.

Elizabeth sat very still beside Jacob in the wagon. She paid particular attention to the looming hills. Why did they bring him here? They wound down the Penter road into the little town. Soon on their right they saw the old ranch home of the Hamblins. And at about noon they came upon the gravel and the harsh terrain of the vacant hills. And there, down the road, encircled by a few straggling trees, were the meadows. It was no longer a green meadow stained by dark red blood, but a harsh rocky expanse of gray and the flattened monument of broken stones.

Whose idea had it been to bring him here? Elizabeth wondered, watching Belinda's James Fennimore taking photographs of the expansive waste. There was no grass on the rocky soil. It was now barren. Though no pieces of bone could be seen, the ground, salted by decay, had crumbled and heaved. There were vestiges still of the old two-foot deep bastian which had been dug by the Fancher party to secure their wagons in a protective circle.

For a while there was milling and talking. More than a hundred people were here. Beyond the people, Elizabeth saw the hills, the small rise to the northeast, and imagined, along the short length of thin trees, how the wagons might have rolled. In vivid pictures she could see the Indians and their supporting crew as they hid behind those trees to wait. She looked back into the crowd. The men of the militia had laid a coffin on the black March ground.

She drew close to Jacob, who stood nearby. He was looking into the hills, and then he turned toward the coffin. He said nothing, as though he were remembering. He ducked his head into the high collar of his wool shirt to protect his ears from the cold. A sharp wind blew into his hair.

They stood about in the rough terrain, all of them watching Lee, waiting, not speaking until one of the captains rent the air with a test shot. Elizabeth's reflexes jumped at the sound. The hills reverberated with the hollow empty crack.

"We'll let Mr. Lee say his last words," a rough voice rang out. Elizabeth again drew near to Jacob, who stood close behind her and whispered into her ear, "Rachel says he requested we dress his body in his temple robes and take him to Panguitch."

Elizabeth turned to stare at him. When he closed his hand on hers and pressed it, she felt his warmth.

John Lee's speech was short, but every word held an eternity. By his own request his hands were left free while he spoke. "I tried to save these people," he said. "These people whose bones lie buried here." He looked about into the eyes of the group as though he saw through them, as though he could see the ghosts of the past as they walked or stood in their trenches, or marched on the hill. Above him to the left, Jacob told Elizabeth quietly, was the spot where they had taken the oath to be silent. "I am the sacrifice now," Lee said. He had never made the confession that might have set him free. But in those last months, he had begun to write about his life. He had told everything—about his childhood, his years as a Danite. When the story grew too long to finish, he had allowed a secretary to take dictation.

"I feel betrayed by those who should bear as much of the responsibility as I. Yet I am ready to die. I trust in God. I have no fear. Death has no terror. Having said this, I feel resigned. I ask the Lord, my God, if my labors are done, to receive my spirit."

He whispered to the colonel who stood beside him. The colonel motioned for Jacob to stand nearby. When Lee took off his overcoat, his hat, and his muffler, it was Jacob who took them from him, one by one.

While he took the clothing Lee would never be using again, Jacob could not help but scan the crowd before him. He realized he was the only one there—at least the only one he could see—who had been in the meadows with Lee twenty years before. As his father-in-law pressed each item into his hands, Jacob looked straight at him. The older man's gaze burned an unforgettable image of helplessness into Jacob's mind.

After the last item had been placed in Jacob's arms, Lee held out his hand. He held to Jacob's hand for what seemed like a long time.

Elizabeth stood waiting, watching. As Jacob stepped back, Lee shook more hands. Rachel clung to him and held to him until the colonel drew her away. Suddenly Elizabeth saw Hannah and John Frederick Lee. They had come, after all. Unseen in the confusion of the crowd, they had driven into the meadow, and John Frederick raced into his father's arms, sobbing.

"I'm here, Father," he said.

Hannah followed behind, with an almost imperceptible wave to Elizabeth and a look toward the hills. Though Hannah would not have remembered, this was a place she had been before.

Five gunmen stood a short fifty feet away.

"Aim for the heart. No mutilation," the colonel said quietly, repeating Lee's last request. He seated John Lee on the edge of the coffin and tied a blindfold around the man's eyes. Drawing away, he cleared his throat. "Ready. Aim. Fire," he shouted. And the five gunmen pulled their triggers. The explosion of the guns clapped in waves of echoes along the edges of the world. There was confusion, smoke, the sound of several thuds against flesh. John Lee fell back into the coffin. There was a slight twitching in the fingers of his left hand. But no more.

Jacob clung to the coat, the hat, the muffler. Elizabeth held his arm. She felt the impact of the firing as though her own body had been struck. Under her feet she thought she felt a ripple of movement.

When Jacob turned, she was barely able to sense reality. "Are you all right?" he whispered to her.

"Oh, dear God!" she answered. *A part of us has been killed with John Lee. A part of all of us. We are lying in the coffin where the last warmth in the flesh begins to grow cold. Once my dream of the warmth of this body gave me life. Now my dreams will die— must die with this terrible death. Somewhere deep in my heart I must grow new roots to survive.*

Jacob wrapped and tightened the bundle of clothing in his arms, placing the muffler and the hat inside the coat, and rolling it into a small ball. Choking back tears, he pushed the bundle under his arm. Then, curling his fingers, he reached for Elizabeth's hand.

## 107
### Elizabeth

Elizabeth did not move while the colonel shut the lid of the coffin. Jacob drew his horses and wagon into the circle and the men lifted the box into the wagon. The colonel pushed the box back into the wagon bed and brushed his hands on his sleeves.

The sky darkened and it began to rain.

"How terrible," Hannah breathed to Elizabeth. "How terrible."

"Shhhh," Elizabeth said, pulling her close.

Jacob and John Frederick pulled a piece of canvas over the coffin while Elizabeth held Hannah's hands. "You should not have come," she whispered.

Hannah's face was pale. "John wanted to come. He wanted to come. But I am so sick."

"You're trembling," Elizabeth said.

"I feel . . . I feel nauseous," Hannah whispered. "And sore."

Elizabeth pulled away from Hannah to stare at the girl. She gently placed her hand on the girl's abdomen. "Hannah . . . are you . . . ?" she whispered.

Hannah's open face disclosed her deepest hopes, though she was still too insecure to believe. "I believe so. But I don't know for sure . . ."

"Hannah!" Elizabeth whispered. "Oh, my darling. Those are the symptoms. When you're nauseous and sore . . ." Jacob beckoned to them to get up into the wagon, but Elizabeth signaled that she would stay with Hannah.

"No, we'll walk for a ways," she said. They followed the wagon as it pulled away. Many others were also walking. Hundreds, it seemed. Elizabeth was conscious of the soft cries and anguished wails of the women behind her.

As she held Hannah close, she felt they were crossing over sacred ground. "Hannah, Hannah," she whispered near the girl's ear. "Here, no matter how we look at it, was your beginning." And at her words, she again saw the strange passage of time in a wave that seemed to wash over her, a realization of what had happened here like a sea of blood and tears, so overwhelming that it had almost drowned them all. And then she heard Hannah's whisper as she placed her feet on the stark ground under the thin grass.

"Father Lee," Hannah sobbed. "Father Lee."

"Perhaps he is still here," Elizabeth said. "The spirits of those who die often stay to comfort us." Perhaps all of them were still here. Hannah's parents, their friends. She held the girl even more closely than she did before.

"I believe he is here," Hannah whispered. Without thinking she placed her hand on the smooth belly of her thin gingham dress. "And perhaps his little grandchild is here also," she said, "and talking to my parents about this world." She looked upward, as if for the first time seeing the reality of this place through the rain's gray light.

The rain blew on them as they passed some of the people of the village who had come out of curiosity to see the execution of John Lee. Rachel and Caroline, and some of the other wives who had been able to come were now in the Redd wagons on their way to Harmony. They lifted their hands in passing to acknowledge the Lorrys, who would be taking Lee's body all the way to the cemetery in Panguitch.

"If your darling child is hovering about, it may come into a world unable to understand everything." Elizabeth still held to Hannah. She whispered. The two women walked together, putting their arms around each other—almost as one person—so close that no one could come between them.

"I hope it is a boy. And I will name him John Doyle Lee. Just like his grandfather.

"That may be a hardship for him."

"I am not afraid of hardship." Hannah's eyes were free of tears now, her gaze very clear. "I'm afraid of not living up to the best I can be . . . of teaching my baby to become the best he can become. No matter what . . ."

Elizabeth felt a foreboding. But the heavy weight of all of it was such a burden to her now she seemed blinded by the gray rain. It was pouring in sheets across the hills, blurring the edges into a wash of mist. She walked with small steps, her skirt heavy against her legs. Finally they climbed behind Jacob and John Frederick in the cart as it drove into Penter with the new coffin bobbing softly behind them against the wooden floor and the hay. They could hear the creak of the pine boards held together by new nails as the cart rattled on the road.

The wagons of the other Lee boys followed them, leading the train as it snaked over the trail to Harmony. Most of the Lees stayed at the Redds, but Jacob and John Frederick drove further up the hill to Kanarraville and to the old Lorry cabin on the Redd property up above the valley under the eastern ridge of the hills.

The first old Lorry house still stood on the farm north of Kanarraville. It belonged to the Redds now, who used it for a sheep barn. For a strange moment in the reddening twilight under the blowing mist of the moisture that seemed not quite like rain, Elizabeth felt the overpowering memories of that old house sweep through her. It still stood bleakly dark against the spring mountains—an old gray cottage, its roof still thatched with straw. Under the roof was the same old loft window. Elizabeth was crowded by sudden nostalgia. The loft awakened dark years in her mind. She felt the power of those uneasy beginning years in everything that had happened today.

Jacob stopped in Kanarraville and asked the Redds if their party might be able to stay in the hovel. They were told they were welcome to stay in the new house if they liked, but Jacob said no, they preferred to remember their first days here.

When the four of them reached the old house, their wagon and horses startled the sheep, who lumbered slowly away. They found the rooms inside the house dank and moist, and very cold for spring.

Elizabeth and Hannah stayed close to one another while Jacob and John Frederick cleared out the hearth and built a fire. All of them sat in the empty cabin close to the warmth, the large shadows licking the walls.

"Strange how God has brought us back here again and again," Jacob's voice was quiet, a pensive sound in the cool hollow.

Elizabeth prepared to warm their bread over a hot rock. Outside in the cold spring night, the coffin sat high in the wagon, perched like a tombstone against the rose gray bleak descent of the sun.

Elizabeth, shuddering in the cold near the fire, almost instinctively grasped Hannah's hands. The power of the darkness seemed to swallow them or to spread a kind of peace over them. Elizabeth divided the bread into four portions as they talked. John Frederick told them why he and Hannah had decided to come.

"At the last moment I could not feel right about not saying good-bye. We left shortly after you left."

They talked for what seemed like hours into the quiet night, unable to sleep, unable to reconcile themselves to the idea that outside in the darkness, against the light of the moon in the square pine box, lay the body of John Lee. They talked until it grew very late, until they thought they heard some commotion outside.

Elizabeth sat near Jacob, feeling the tension in his body as they heard the hooves of a horse outside the door. Through the years as his sister, she had learned to recognize Jacob's emotions. Now they had been married for several days—though she had not yet been with him as a woman should be with her husband. There had been so much grief in the air. And there had been little time to heal. If it had not been for Anna Jane's request, Elizabeth would not have married Jacob before the journey to the meadows. However, in the chronology of events, it seemed satisfactory now. It looked better that she was married to him as they had left for the meadows together alone. Now that Hannah and John Frederick were here, however, she felt an unexpected safety in their presence. Only occasionally did she think about the wedding vows she had taken not so long ago.

Jacob stiffened as the familiar sounds of a rider dismounting his horse broke through the cottage walls. Soon someone was pounding on the door with urgency.

Jacob walked swiftly to answer it. Without opening it, he called,"Who is it? Speak up. I can't hear you."

"Joshua! Let me in!"

Joshua? Her son had come all this distance in the rain? Elizabeth paled. Hannah and John Frederick got up quickly. Jacob opened the door.

"It's Anna Jane. She's almost gone. I had a hard time finding you. Belinda Marie sent me. She wants you to come now. If it takes more than a couple of days' travel, you might never see Aunt Anna Jane alive again."

Anna Jane! Oh dear God!

"She's so sick we can't do anything. If she isn't dead by now it will be a miracle, although old Brother Hatch, the McDonalds, the Chandlers, and a dozen other families been spelling off with the Lees to watch out for her."

The color in Jacob's face drained until he was almost white.

"Then there's nothing we can do but get in the wagon tonight and go on to Panguitch!" Elizabeth said.

"Yes," Jacob said quickly, and turning into the room, began to gather up their things. Soon Hannah and John Frederick had climbed into the high cart in front of the new pine box. Jacob stood in the door for a moment and looked back briefly at the old house, its doorway crowded with sheep dung and dirt, its roof broken from the ravages of rain.

Elizabeth was on her way out just behind him. "Don't look back," she whispered, surprising even herself. Don't look back. The words held even greater significance than she had intended.

In the next few hours, the five of them—Jacob and Elizabeth and John Frederick Lee, Hannah and Joshua—hurried the wagon so fast that they pulled many miles ahead of the others who remained in Harmony to take a more leisurely return to Panguitch. The men took turns driving the high wagon with the pine box in it while Hannah lay at the front of the wagon bed. Elizabeth wrapped herself in a wool blanket and lay in back close to the wooden coffin while Jacob drove. The wagon rocked unmercifully, the pine box in it braced against one side of the wagon by stubs of cut timber placed on the wagon bed. Yet the heavy box still slipped inside of the slats with a sucking sound from side to side.

Elizabeth couldn't sleep. She lay between the braces, next to the wood, close to the coffin, and could hear the body slip back and forth inside the crate. *I am with him now*, she thought. *And now it's* . . . She could not say "too late," for the words weighed too heavily on her heart. And she must guard against turning to stone when she had so much life to live.

But she could not black out her vision of him lying on the other side of the plank in the coffin: the thick brush of graying hair, the eyelids closed on the leathery cheeks, the large head whose shifting movement sounded so brutal in her ears. *He is sleeping while I am awake*, she whispered to herself. *And no one will wake him again . . . unless when the angel blows the trumpet . . . Oh, God, let us all be there when the angel comes.*

Her mind crowded with images as she watched the stars. Memories of John Lee's life visited her like pictures of light—his spirit so close. It was only after hours had passed that the scenes dissolved, and she found rest.

There was very little time. Finally John Frederick drove and Jacob lay down beside Elizabeth near the coffin. One by one the miles disappeared under the horse's hooves.

In her wakeful moments, Elizabeth reached toward the front of the wagon where Hannah lay. From the constant motion during the night, the pregnant Hannah had begun to vomit profusely. But they could not stop for her. Though she had begun heaving and wretching over the side of the wagon, she did not ask for any special privileges. They moved onward, a bleak colorless terror in Jacob's eyes.

## 108

### *Jacob*

They left the Kanarraville hills. They left the wide valley and the small hills, the small valleys and the red hills. Finally, many hours later, they neared Panguitch, where Jacob unhitched Joshua's horse and rode hard into the town, leaving Joshua and Elizabeth, Hannah and John Frederick with the slow wagon on the road.

Jacob rode without stopping, though the horse lathered and his own limbs ached with the days of travel with little sleep. Even the hills seemed to scream at him, though the sound was only the screaming pain of his head, a tearing, wrenching pain that clawed at his brain. As he flew toward Panguitch, he believed Anna Jane was dying. The town lay like a mirage floating away from him as he drew near. The past few years flooded into him so vividly he could see her face through the panorama of her crippling pain. There had been blessings, one after another, which had not healed her. Richard and Perry swore they would become doctors of medicine to find out what was wrong. Even Joshua was determined to study with them in their quest for medical truth.

Soon the road veered to the left. Jacob took the fork into the southeastern hills where he could reach the Lee and Lorry homes in a moment. It was then that he saw children in the road playing kick ball. Now the horse, as though it knew at last its important mission was over, slipped and fell. Jacob leaped over the horse's neck as its knees buckled. Calling out to Caleb and Joseph to take the spent animal into the barn, he rushed through the fence and toward the house. Seeing him near, the children screamed and clamored to him. Christa ran to catch his coat tail.

"Papa! Papa! Stop, Papa. Mama isn't there anymore!"

He did not hear her words but flung himself against the front door and into the house, beating his feet on the stairs.

"Anna Jane!" he cried.

But when he pushed the bedroom aside, he could see she wasn't there. The room was empty, even of light. The shades were drawn and the cool odor of emptiness, the knowledge that no one had been in this room for some time fairly breathed from the walls. By this time Christa was panting behind him, and Joseph was on the stairs.

"She's at Aunt Caroline's," Christa shouted. "You wouldn't listen to me!"

"Oh, Christa, darling." For a moment he knelt to her, ashamed that he had not paid attention to her. He reached out and held her in his arms. "I'm sorry, little one. I'm so sorry."

Hand in hand, father and daughter raced down the stairs to Caroline's house. The noise in Jacob's head seemed to grow. There had been so much. So much had been expected of them. How much further could they push themselves in the face of their trials?

Caroline and Rachel were not here, of course, but still on their way back from the meadows. But Amorah was in the house with Harriett Josephine and Thurza Jane. Nellie had come with hot breads and was standing in the kitchen washing mustard plasters out of cloths. The babies were on the beds and the settee. For the most part, the other children had been sent out to the road to play ball.

"I'm afraid it's pneumonia," Thurza Jane whispered to Jacob when he came to the door. "You're just in time."

She led him quickly into the front room. Anna Jane's face on the white sheets of the settee looked so pale, he could not see her features for a moment. Briefly her eyes met his without recognition until he came to her, knelt to the bedside, and pulled at her hands.

"Anna Jane! Speak to me!" he demanded, not sure of his own feelings, not sure of the pounding that threatened to undo his blood. Was it the sound of his own life or the beat of another drum?

"Jacob," she whispered. Barely.

"Anna Jane!" He wanted to kiss her, to hold her face, but she raised her small hand. "Listen to me, Jacob," she said, the movement in her lips scarcely allowing her to form words. "Listen to me." She spoke with such effort he wanted to silence her, to reserve her strength.

"Hush," he said.

"No, listen," she whispered. "I believe my mother . . . my father . . . they need me . . ."

"Hush. What nonsense," Jacob said. "I'm here now. You'll be well. The women have everything ready to relieve your congestion. Look at me, Anna Jane."

"No, no," she whispered, turning her face away. "Don't press me, Jacob. Please. I can't stay. I want you and Elizabeth to send Richard to the university with Joshua so that both boys may become physicians. And Perry, too, if that's what he wants. And take care of Christa. Please take good care of Christa."

"Hush. Keep your strength, darling. Please."

"No, Jacob. Please listen to me. I want Elizabeth to have the loom. And anything of mine she wants. The rest can go to Thurza Jane, Harriett, and Nellie. They have been so good to me."

"Don't talk like this!" Jacob said between his teeth. "God . . . don't let her talk like this." The room seemed to spin and reel in the background, as though he were off balance, afloat, suspended. "Don't talk like this, Anna Jane," he begged. He leaned over to her hot cheek. "Oh please. Please, Anna Jane." He began to sob. He lay against her cheek and sobbed, the tears wetting her neck and his hands. "Forgive me, God, but I won't know how to take it all so soon."

"You'll be fine," Anna Jane whispered, barely breathing. "You'll be so fine. You have been such a good man. I had such a father and such a husband." She brought a thin white hand to his hair and rubbed it gently.

He stopped sobbing against her cheek. He listened for the beat of her heart in her breast. There was a small sound, still. He did not move. He listened to the heart beating, beating. He lay against her breast and sobbed.

"Oh Anna Jane. Please stay with me. I love you so, Anna Jane."

## 109
### *Jacob*

At the end of March, they welcomed the April rains. After holding a funeral in the chapel in honor of John Lee, they carted the coffin out into the bleak black countryside above the far hills of the meadows, on the plains of the vast uncompromising land. The men had dug a deep pit in the small empty cemetery for the last resting place of John Lee.

Harriett and Nellie carried the white temple clothing to John Lee's pine box and Jacob pried open the top of it. As soon as the lid came up, Nellie bent to the body and leaned into the hollow, sobbing hysterically. "Father. Father!"

"Hush," Jacob said gently. "He is not there. He would be ashamed . . ."

Harriett came to her and pulled her away. "Please, Nellie, we must let him go."

"We must dress him!" Nellie whispered hoarsely. "Take him out of the box and dress him."

"No. No," Jacob said gently. "Just put the clothes into the box."

"No. Oh, please."

"Yes," Harriett said. Her eyes pleaded with Jacob to lower the coffin as soon as they could.

Jacob lay the clothes on John Lee's body. With the clothes laid over him, his face was barely visible—the shaggy gray hair, the furrowed cheeks, the eyes closed in repose. As soon as he lay down the clothes, Jacob pulled the lid of the pine box down again and nailed it shut. The sound of the hammer against the nail—the tap tap tap—echoed in the bleak rain. They stood in the gray drizzle above the box as Thomas McDonald and Horace Chamberlain prepared to lower it into the grave.

Bishop Chandler spoke the dedicatory prayer. "We dedicate this grave with the power invested in us until the morn of the first resurrection when this thy loyal servant shall come forth in his glory to take his family into thy presence forever and forever . . ." Perhaps the Church authorities would not have buried him with such honors, but his own people, the people who knew him, could not do otherwise.

As they lowered the coffin, it bumped to a stop in the deep hole. Thomas McDonald began to shovel the dirt over it. Clack. Clack. Small rocks hit the box with a shattering sound, and Elizabeth turned away. The ladies had prepared a hot meal in their home, and they were hungry.

Jacob was anxious to return to Anna Jane. When they reached the house, she was sitting up in bed allowing Thurza Jane to feed her gruel.

It was not in that moment, nor in the few days after John Lee's funeral that Anna Jane passed away. It was a quiet passing, without Jacob's permission, without Elizabeth's knowledge. It was in the night while Jacob held her in his arms. He woke on the morning of April 8 in the continuous rain, and he could no longer feel her breathing. Her skin was clammy and cold, as though she were clay in his arms. After he knew she was dead, he still held her for a long time.

"You have gone away from me," he whispered, "and now I will not see you in this life again."

They buried her beside her father on April 11, dressing her in full temple clothing, finding the same deep space in the earth to place her coffin. Surprisingly, it was Elizabeth who now lost control. She sobbed, clinging to the coffin until Jacob gently led her away. There was not much left that could have happened to them now, she had cried out.

For a solemn period of three days after that, Elizabeth kept to her room. There was quiet in the house. The children were cared for by Belinda Marie and Nellie, who still came in to help.

"What are you doing?" Jacob once asked her from outside the door. "We're worried about you. Can't you let me in?"

"Soon," Elizabeth said, her voice barely a dim note above the outside rain.

"When you feel better, we'd like to see you again."

Finally, on the eve of the third day, Elizabeth accepted food from the children. She wrote a small note to Jacob: "Tomorrow morning, will you please take me to see the graves?"

It was still raining. The sun was buried in deep clouds. There was no light in the valley except for the bleak gray cast of the sky and the reflection in the pools along the road. When Jacob knocked at the door she opened it slowly and whispered to him that as soon as she pulled on her boots she was ready to go. They walked haltingly in the mud, the soft dark moist soil oozing under their feet. "This is good land," Jacob tried to say. "Good black soil. No wonder the sheep thrive."

But Elizabeth was not ready to answer him. She did not whisper a word. They walked quickly to the site of the graveyard. Jacob stood near to her and held the umbrella up with both of his hands.

"Remember, you were the one who said 'Don't look back,'" Jacob leaned to her. She did not reply. They stood for a few moments watching the rivulets of water mark the two fresh graves.

Soon the rain seemed to stop. The clouds parted and the sun shimmered through. Then suddenly Elizabeth spoke, her words clear as a bell on the rain-washed air. "Do you think Richard is old enough to be sent to school with Joshua to study medicine?"

Jacob stopped to let the words fall into his consciousness. He had not heard her voice for a long time. "I believe so," he said. "We can see."

"I want Joshua to go soon to the University of Deseret, or perhaps the new Brigham Young Academy."

"As soon as the shearing is finished this spring, we'll have a better idea of how much money we will have."

"We have always had a lot of success with the shearing. I'm sure we'll have enough money to send both of them to school."

"Yes, I believe we will, Elizabeth." Jacob was quiet then.

"Hannah's going to have a baby. Can we help John Frederick build a new home?"

He had seen Hannah when she was ill on the way home from the meadows, but he had not yet been told that she was going to have a baby. And not unusual for a man, he had not guessed. "Good," he said. "Wonderful! I had hoped . . . Yes, of course we'll help build a house for John Frederick Lee. That's a good idea!"

Elizabeth didn't answer for a moment, so that Jacob had a chance to look at her closely, hoping he could find what he was looking for in her eyes. "Is there anything you want for yourself, Elizabeth? Is there anything I can do for you?"

Elizabeth was quiet for a long time. She stared at the graves, but they had not changed. So she turned away. "Yes," she said slowly. "I believe there is."

He waited. She raised her shoulders and began to rub her arms. "I'm a bit cold," she said. "You can keep me warm."

Jacob smiled. He changed the umbrella to his other hand and brought his arm to her shoulder to warm her. He held her close. She leaned toward him as they turned to walk back on the road to the house. Then she raised her hand and covered his hand with her own."I love you, Jacob," she said.

EPILOGUE

*Hannah*

March 21, 1927. It's been a year now since Elizabeth was buried. It's been that long. This is the first day I went through her things. I didn't accept it all that well, her passing. But it's been a year now, so I went through her old things.

First I took out the photographs and found long-ago things—things long before Elizabeth and Jacob were married, things precious to Anna Jane. First there was that little tintype James Fennimore took of Belinda Marie's baby. That tintype never left Anna Jane's hands. I can remember it as if it was yesterday— Anna Jane holding on to the picture of little James Fennimore. She was on her sick bed then. All of us tiptoed away from her so she could look at that picture without interruption. It was a miracle, she said, and she stared at the picture like it was the grandchild itself. It was the first picture of a grandchild she ever saw.

But there were many many more. Richard and Perry and Christa all had so many children you wouldn't have guessed they would be spread from here to California. No one could have guessed that after Anna Jane and her father John Lee died, all those children would gather around us like a buzzing swarm of bees.

I remember how we all wanted Anna Jane to stay. Elizabeth, especially, loved her so and begged her. And she lay clinging to Anna Jane's coffin and wouldn't let go, even though Uncle Jacob was there and wanted to go on with their lives. He was so in love with Aunt Elizabeth that he was never far from her. And here he had lost Anna Jane too, and it seemed even harder for him to hear Elizabeth cry.

"I will be with Father," Anna Jane had said, smiling. "I will be with Father. He began as an orphan boy. But he does not deserve to be alone ever again."

Yes, yes. That was all right, Elizabeth said, taking that white hankie she had made for Belinda Marie's wedding and wadding it up into a little ball.

"Please do as Father says. Preserve everything for him." Anna Jane held tight those last moments to Uncle Jacob's hand. That was enough to give him a lot of strength. He stood up straight. I could see it in his backbone. I was pregnant and pretty sick at the time with my first child, little John Doyle Lee, but when I saw Uncle Jacob standing straight, I felt like standing right up straight myself. So I stood up straight and felt the blood going through me like cool water, and it felt good. I felt washed, clean, then, and I knew God was really in charge of everything and it was up to us to come up with the faith to cope with it. One had to be prepared for what was ahead.

No one knew at that time that—as though it were scheduled—Brigham Young died only a few months after Father Lee. I always felt it was planned, and that now Brigham Young would not be afraid to sit down and discuss how difficult it had been for him to sacrifice his adopted son.

No one knew Joshua, Richard, and Perry would all become doctors because they were inspired by what happened to Aunt Anna Jane. And no one knew that those boys and Belinda and Christa, too, would give Grandpa Lee and Anna Jane all those grandchildren.

I was glad for all the children because they needed each other. There was a lot of persecution heaped on the Lees. Most of the children played with my eight boys. We had whole cities of families—Elizabeth's three boys and the two baby girls she and Uncle Jacob had, though they are all married now and have huge families of their own. And because the family was so big, you had to accept many hard times, like when Caleb cut off his finger in the thresher and Perry's boy Harold got himself hit by one of the tractors with a gasoline engine. And then when Richard's Sally Jane caught pneumonia and her three-year-old lungs froze. Richard was a doctor by then, doing all he could while Uncle Jacob blessed her. But there was nothing more they could do. And Elizabeth cried. She cried for her dead little grandchild Sally like she had cried for Anna Jane. And yes, I remember Uncle Jacob's shoulders straightened up then, too. In a time of a lot of stress he had a way of picking up his back bone and looking up to the sky as though he found God's face. And he would touch Aunt Elizabeth as he had always touched her, with the tender love he felt for her, and she took his hand and silently wiped away her tears with his fingers. It was good to see.

We had a couple of accidents at the mill that summer too, and about four dead lambs when the bobcat came down out of the canyon and ravaged our sheep pen. The lambs was crying out and bleating in the night until Sammy Lee shot the bobcat. Then Christa's husband Jake stuffed it and put it out in the barn. Already the moths have got to it.

But those few things was the worst of it really, as though all the bad things had already happened before that, and God let us be all those years just so we could have all those weddings and children. It was as though Grandpa Lee went up in heaven and said, "Now God, you took me and you took Anna Jane. Isn't that enough? I love my family so much I'm willing to do anything up here: polish the harps, string the violins. I'll even polish the gold pebblestones in the street if you'll let my family live and rejoice in the gospel together without much harm."

He must have added, "Oh, you can send me one of those little grandchildren to play with—I might take Sally Jane. Anyway, Anna Jane would love that, wouldn't you, darling?" And so he and Anna Jane must have rejoiced when Sally Jane came to heaven.

The others all started to die sooner or later: Rachel and Caroline and Nancy and Teresa. The older wives went to join Papa Lee after a few years, and we had as many funerals as weddings after a while. But things were different by then. We were settled down living the gospel as best we could in the valley, putting to practice all the things no one before wanted us to live: love thy neighbor, do good to them which despitefully use you. And there were many of those. The Lees had to stick with one another as the Saints around us persecuted us because we were Lees. I can remember my children walking on the other side of the street to protect themselves from the other students on the way home from school.

We had another kind of persecution too when the Edmunds Tucker Act was passed, making all of us who were living in plural marriage instant felons. Later, with the Manifesto, a terrible cry went up to heaven with the destruction of so many families.

I can barely remember all of the unhappiness, but I know it was there. I wanted that unhappiness to change for my Johnny Doyle Lee. And it made him strong to live a life of goodness as a namesake for his grandfather. We rejoiced in our strength when I got eight boys one after another and John Frederick was so proud! And Elizabeth said, "You're rearing an army, Hannah and John Frederick Lee! An army of righteousness. They will fight for John Lee's name." She said it bravely, never letting on how she thought someday she would see him again and that she had been rehearsing what she would say. By then she and Jacob had given birth to Melissa and Frances Marie, and they were so happy together it shone in their faces.

I remember looking out in the sunset one night in the fall and watching Jacob and Elizabeth walk along the back fence when the boys was out irrigating the fields. They was leaning together near to the fence as though nothing was going to come down between them. They were together and only the sun shining through. I often wondered what she was going to tell John Lee if she saw him again. She was so happy with Uncle Jacob. And, I guess, due to the fact that Grandpa Lee didn't steal her, she has him to thank for that part of her life. To think that now she is there with Grandpa Lee, probably shaking his hand.

Uncle Jacob is getting bent and old but his grandchildren won't let him stop giving them piggy-back rides. He is the dearest one of them all. He will never stop trying to stand up straight that way he stood up straight when Anna Jane and Sally Jane died. And he looks up to heaven as though he sees them all. When Aunt Elizabeth died, he cried. I saw him.

Uncle Jacob said he had loved Elizabeth since he was a boy. And she really belonged to John Lee. I just said, "Pshaw. She belongs to all of us. And we have every reason to be grateful for the life she lived for all of us—a life that showed dedication and strength and commitment." I loved her so much. She was, more than anyone else, a mother to me. I love her still and want to be like her. She told me I was not one of them really, but a daughter of the people who were killed. A daughter of those whose bones still lie in the soil under the sea of grass. But that never mattered to me. I would never know my other mother, and I loved Elizabeth dearly. I knew she would be with us forever, with my family and with Uncle Jacob and Grandfather John Lee. And that now while I'm still here to see Uncle Jacob and his family and all of mine, my eight boys, with all of them married and with families of their own, Aunt Elizabeth is probably setting right down and having a chat with Grandfather John Lee.

"Now that we're in the kingdom, we all belong together anyway," Grandpa Lee would be saying. "Getting married is just something that gets the babies there. Now that we're all in the kingdom we are all together in God's love."

It's like wrapping yourself up in Jesus' arms. I always knew Jesus wrapped up my own Arkansas parents, too, wherever they are. And when I see them someday they will know I was happy, that we were sorry for wrongs and have asked for forgiveness. And we can all be together in God's love.

*Hannah Dunham Lorry Lee*

READERS' NOTES

This story is fiction, with the purpose of bringing many close details of conversations, feelings, and relationships to life as they might have been lived by these people in this period of our history. However, for those who might be interested in certain facts, these brief statements may help point out what is based on truth or only imagined.

1: No one knows how many times such a "mini-massacre" as this took place--perpetrated by one side or the other. This one is not of record. But according to John Higbee, who would have known, the rape of Lee's nine-year-old daughter by six or seven Missouri rabble rousers is true. Of course, for his daughter's sake, Lee would never have spoken of it.

2: It is a fact that the Missourians reported fifty deaths when there was only one. David Patten's death is actual. He was there and his statement is on record.

3: Elizabeth's background is fictional.

4: The mail contract was canceled because the U.S. Government received complaints from self-aggrandizing parties that Mormons were combining state and religion.

5: President George Albert Smith, appointed Commander in Chief, was the General Authority who stirred the people up for war.

6-7: Though usually reluctant, young girls were often unable under the plural marriage system to resist the authoritative pressure to marry older men. Economics played a larger part than romance.

8-9: The Fancher party with its vanguard Missouri Wildcat cattle drivers was in Salt Lake City about this time—late July of 1857.

10-13: The movement of the immigrants is fairly accurate. The story of Serjay's dead calf is true. Serjay's and Proctor's names are actual.

14-17: The story of Proctor's death from handling poisoned cattle at the spring is true. No one knows if the immigrants actually poisoned the springs. The story of the Indian who was shot and killed while trading arrows with the

Missourians is also true.

18: John Lee was historically the Indian Agent responsible for keeping the Indians in check. He was attractive to women. One story reports that two young girls hoping to marry him giggled about their up and coming ceremony while they were in the back of a wagon he was driving. But he didn't marry either one of them.

19: Bishop Anderson was in charge in Beaver when the Missouri party came through. An Indian in the hills was killed. There is no evidence that the immigrants really poisoned the springs. There were some who thought the poison was mugwort. The poison is echoed in the death of J.B.

20: There were indeed a "couple hundred rifles and several hundred pounds of gunpowder" on the way to Southern Utah with the full knowledge of Salt Lake City. The Parowan meeting is factual. David Lewis and Laban Morrill were true characters. Both were big men.

21-22: Deany was in fact beaten up by his neighbors because he shared his onions with the immigrants. This incident shows how forcefully the saints frowned upon anyone who disobeyed the Salt Lake City injunction. Klingensmith's testimony states that the Saints obeyed in fear of their lives.

23-24: Cedar City was the scene of a lot of military activity. They were in fact digging a ditch when the Missourians came and robbed the store. The Missourians did threaten to bring an army from California.

25-26: The Wildcats did carouse in the town until early morning.

27: The Fancher train from Arkansas also came through and stole grain while the Cedar Militia—again—watched. The city did not have a jail, and the militia discussed possibilities for justice. It is believed the idea about participating with the Indians in a massacre was introduced at this time. They did seek permission of Brigham Young. And sent James Haslam to get it. It is on this first Saturday afternoon of the Fancher train's arrival in Cedar City that I have placed Lee to face the gunmen who bragged to him they had raped his daughter.

28: After the meeting, Haight and John Lee went out to the iron works to discuss what should be done.

29-30: John Lee had already had contact with the Indians who had reason of their own to hate the settlers—the imagined poisoning of the springs and Indian deaths. They had been holding back from fighting. When the Indians had killed US Army Captain Gunnison in Kanosh, it had created tension. Clem was in fact an adopted Indian son of John Lee.

31: The meeting of John Lee with Moquetas is historical.

32: Hamblin deliberately planned to be on his honeymoon while the immigrants were camped in the meadows. The Indians had probably jumped the gun and now called upon Lee—who had actually been referred to as "Nargutts," or "crying man." The whites dressed like Indians and participated in the massacre sooner than the Brooks account admits.

33-35: The Mormons did shoot one of the Fancher messengers who came for help. This seemed to me a pivotal event. The red hair is fictional and symbolic.

36: "Bring your shovels" was later attributed to Haight's instructions. Brigham Young's orders did not arrive soon enough. John Lee did pray.

37: The details of the massacre are on record. There is, in fact, a newborn baby girl who is taken to Rachel Hamblin's home. New evidence says she was born in March, a few months older than I have portrayed her for the purposes of this story.

38-39: The militia took an oath to be silent, so the civilian population did not know what really happened—even when they saw the carnage. They still attributed it to the Indians.

40-42: The small girl baby who stayed with the Mormons was actually raised by Klingensmiths. Anna Jean Backus, in *Mountain Meadows Witness,* (Spokane: Arthur Clark Company, 1995), tells the story. The Indians were known to trade in human flesh and often kidnapped children. Emma Lee married Lee at about this time.

44-45: When the spiritual rot began to fester, rebaptism was tried as a solution. They also sent six explorers south to find suitable land. At about the same time, others traveled north to help move the Salt Lake City residents out of town because the U.S. Army was coming through.

46: Those who escaped from Salt Lake City moved as far south as Provo. They stuffed their homes with straw and left people to light torches should the U.S. Army attack.

47/50: They did receive news in Provo that the army had passed through and the citizens could return to their homes.

51: There was indeed a big fourth of July celebration at John Lee's this summer. The measurements of beer and oven are accurate. As is mentioned under Chapter Eighteen, the story of John Lee taking two young women to Salt Lake City and tiring of their silliness is true. Also, if Alva Matheson and John higbee are correct, the accusation that Lee killed three men may also be true. Mr. Matheson says that after the immigrants took the grain on the road to Penter,

Lee took a shortcut and ambushed them. He must have buried them in secret at the mill.

52: Government investigators did come in the late summer of 1858.

53: David Lewis's confession occurred in a manner close to what is written here.

54: John Lee did go into hiding.

55: Although John Lee went to the first meeting, he was in hiding at the second. Colonel Dame never showed up. It was true that Dame gave the military command. The order to "disarm, and, if necessary, kill the men" is supposed to have come late from Salt Lake City, but new evidence suggests questions.

57-58: At first it was treated as an Indian massacre and an act of war. The spoils of the train were an economic boost to the settlers. To this day there are many who say that the real motivation for the massacre was economic. This would certainly have some truth to it if one considers that the immigrants had robbed the Saints of their supplies.

59: The U.S. Government was puzzled as to what to do with the Mormons. They continued investigations and began to stir up legislation against plural marriage.

60: When the authorities came to retrieve the Fancher children, they took seventeen of them back with them. They did not retrieve the baby girl who had been born on the trail and was then with the Klingensmiths. One of the goals of my story was to invent an imaginative way to show how she might have been retained.

61: There were lists made of those who participated in the massacre. And there was plenty of blackmail and intrigue also. John Lee did marry Tabby.

62-63: Judge Cradlebaugh and his dragoons from Camp Floyd were the ones who erected the monument at Mountain Meadows.

64: Records show that Rachel visited John Lee in hiding. The fire is fictional.

65: Forney did come with a posse to find John Lee. Their problem with the Lorrys is fictional.

67-68: Robberies were common, as were adobe homes—which are still found around Utah.

69/71: Brigham Young was going to come to see John Lee, but it seems likely he was persuaded not to. He said he would meet John Lee in Washington, which was even farther away to the south. It is now a little town by St. George, where one of John Lee's homes is designated by a historical marker. I have sent

Jacob to the meadows because the factual scene of Brigham Young and his cohorts tearing down the monument is too good to tell just in passing.

72-73: There was a severe rainstorm that destroyed the uncured adobe. The tragic details of the destruction of John Lee's homes and children is accurate.

74: The settlers coming into Harmony and Cedar, etc., heard so many songs and tales they didn't know what to believe. John Lee traveled between Salt Lake City, New Harmony, and Washington. The letter by a rabble-rousing neighbor, Hicks, and the incident on the dance floor are both actual.

75: Lee lost his church position. Brother Imlay was the bishop. It was true that the Lawsons chopped down the Lee trees. Lee's journal entry is exactly as he wrote it.

76: Criticism was leveled at Brigham Young for discouraging the railroad. It was at about this time that he sent Lee to Skatumpah to get him away from government prosecutors.

77-78: Mr. Redd did purchase property in this area.

79-80: John Lee's important letter did indeed follow his departure for the south and contained the news about his excommunication, which devastated him.

81: Of course there are many fictional characters: Jacob, Elizabeth, and Anna Jane. Also, Hannah is not the real name of the Arkansas girl, nor did she marry the fictional John Frederick Lee—whom I originally named John David Lee. John David was the father of the famous Ettie Lee who contributed so much to society through the boys' ranches, but I have chosen to invent this young man, as his resemblance to John David took too much departure for the story.

82: Controversies were common. Sammy Lee is a true character.

83: The harvest festival is true, and so is the fire.

84: President Snow's note is factual.

85-86: Many of Lee's families moved to Panguitch.

87: The call to colonize Arizona was not welcomed. Henry Day was the leader of the eighteen wagons that left in May of 1873.

88: The ferry is described as it still exists. The note about the crossing is from Lee's diary. He was ill at the time.

89: They did turn back from House Rock, Arizona. The prophecy was actually made. A wedding was held, but not this fictional one.

90: The storm was actual. Trees came down and broke open the wagons.

91: The government sent six hundred men to arrest Lee.

92: John was sent to Moencopi where Williams lived. Rachel's story of the bird is a popular family legend.

93: Saturday, November 7, 1874, Lee was arrested by Stokes as it is written here. He handled the gun and gave it back. And he was hospitable to his captors.

94-95: Some of John's letter is true. He admitted he was treated better than other prisoners.

96-98: Getting a fair jury was a problem. The first trial resulted in a hung jury.

99-100: The government was beginning to crack down in earnest on plural marriages.

101-102: More than a year passed before another trial was held. No one knows what kinds of pressure had been brought to bear on Brigham Young or the authorities, but there is evidence they hoped Lee's execution would put a stop to the continued slander against the entire church because of this tragic episode.

103-106: The execution is accurate. There is a photo of John Lee on the horse wearing the ball and chain.

107-108: John's body was brought to Panguitch in a wagon. Descendants have said that it was laid out on William Prince's table and dressed. But accounts vary. So I have left the one that seemed dramatically most powerful.